NEPTUNE'S RECKONING

ROBERT J. STAVA

SEVERED PRESS
HOBART TASMANIA

NEPTUNE'S RECKONING

WWW.SEVEREDPRESS.COM

This novel is a work of fiction. Names, characters, places and incidents are the product of the author's imagination, or are used fictitiously. Any resemblance to actual events, locales or persons, living or dead, is purely coincidental.

ISBN: 978-1-922323-64-4

Dedicated to my father, Reid Stava,
who inspired in me from an early age
a love of ships and the sea.

I miss you, Dad.

"What would an ocean be without a monster lurking in the dark? It would be like sleep without dreams."

— Werner Herzog

"There is, one knows not what sweet mystery about this sea, whose gently awful stirrings seems to speak of some hidden soul beneath."

— Herman Melville, 'Moby Dick'

INTRODUCTION

It's a picture-perfect morning out here at Montauk; one of those early September ones that you wish could stretch out forever. From the deck of our lodgings where I sit, I have a fine view of the Atlantic. It's one of those tranquil interludes in life where the world—much of it here at least—hasn't quite woken up and the sun has just emerged in a fiery birth from the rim of the ocean. Aside from a few sunrise stragglers, the beach is pristine before an incoming tide, the surf and breeze powerful enough that one can see white mist flying off the tops of the rolling breakers. For those of you who haven't been here, the ocean is that somber grayish-green of the North Atlantic, the sand a sun-bleached shade of tan, the dunes topped by thick clusters of sea-grass and shrubs.

If one has to kick-off a new day, there are far worse ways to do it.

Plenty, in fact. Right now, even as I write this, Hurricane Irma is busy beating the hell out of Florida, having already pummeled Puerto Rico and Cuba. Texas is still recovering from getting hammered by Hurricane Harvey a little over a week ago. And who knows what may come this way, what storm or disaster may lurk just under the horizon.

Or in the murky depths of the Atlantic.

Having survived through more than a few hard left-hooks in life, I know all too well how unpredictably fast—and treacherously–things can go to hell in the proverbial handbasket.

Even here at the place known as 'The End'.

Because the ocean is a vast and mysterious place. A place filled with untold and undiscovered wonders... and nightmares, waiting in its twilight depths. Even now, in the second decade of the 21st century, less than 5 percent of these underwater realms covering 70 percent of our planet has been explored.

That's a heck of a lot of uncovered territory.

Speaking for myself, I'm convinced all manner of surprises may yet await us down there. That may include a terrifying one in particular... one that has been curiously arising–pardon the pun–in my thoughts lately. Somewhere off the coast here of Montauk and Block Island where the continental shelf drops away into the abyss.

So, what do you say? Up for a little exploration to see what may await us? Checking my watch, I see there's a deep-sea trawler due to depart from the crowded fishing docks up at Montauk Harbor, and, if I'm reading the schedule here correctly, ready to take us to certain coordinates where a luxury yacht was discovered floating adrift, with no sign of its crew. Other than the few grisly remains, that is.

Well, then: *chop-chop!* Drink down that coffee. I just caught word that something even stranger has been spotted out there recently. Ready? Good. And don't bother with packing that lifejacket. It won't do you much good where we're going.

-RJS, Montauk, September 2017

WHAT IS FEAR?

As a pathology, it's a straightforward function: the area of the brain known as the amygdala—a pair of almond-shaped clusters of nuclei in the temporal lobe—sends up the emotional alarm bells. If the hippocampus agrees the threat is real, the emergency fight-or-flight services kick in: ACTH hormones flood the bloodstream, cortisol ramps up the heart rate and blood pressure... epinephrine and norepinephrine prepare the muscles for violent action. The pupils dilate, the mouth goes dry, non-critical functions shut down.

In the early days of the human race, these functions were critical to survival—the world was an endlessly dangerous place–predators, disease, natural disasters. Then came civilization and all its trappings: the fears became increasingly less tangible, more anxiety driven—the fear of fear. Now, in the early part of the 'Digital Age', we've become a fear-driven society—death, terror and uncertainty bombard us daily from our smartphones and computers. It comes at us from all angles, ceaseless, all-consuming.

To me, however, there is only one overriding source for fear; the ocean. That largest wellspring of primordial terror here on Earth—both metaphorically and physically. Even today, less than five percent of it has been explored. Since the dawn of the human race it has represented such: it has challenged and terrified us.

And there is truth to that fear. For all our arrogant self-importance as a species, we don't really know what unknown terrors yet await us, lurking in its vast, unlit depths. Waiting to devour us.

-Dr. William Vanek, "The Terror of What Lies Beneath"

PRELUDE: SE OF BLOCK ISLAND, 1783

"Fall off a point, Mister Redding, *steady now*."

The speaker, First Lieutenant Trent Somersby, stood by the quarterdeck rail with his spyglass trained forward. The ship, the 32-gun frigate HMS Tryton, glided through an eerily calm sea under minimum sail. An air of dread had fallen over the ship and crew: except for the officer's orders, they were dead quiet, as if every man-jack among them was holding his breath.

Around them came the creak and groan of shifting timbers, the sigh of rigging and the sluice of water along the hull. The occasional desultory snap of canvas only seemed to underscore the uneasy atmosphere.

The crew was already spooked at six bells, when dawn broke in a spectral light layered with drifting fog across the water, lending the sensation they were sailing into some supernatural realm. It hadn't helped that there'd been several omens and by nature, sailors—even this battle-hardened crew—were a particularly superstitious lot. First there had been the comet observed in the east the night before they'd set sail out of New York Harbor, then the unusual number of crows that arrived on the rigging and yardarms the following morning. That had set the old-timers in the fo'c'sle whispering and the officers on the quarterdeck exchanging uneasy glances. Then had come the uncomfortably warm weather for September as they made their way east, accompanied by the menacing flicks of lightning on the horizon from a passing storm, hinting at deadly consequences should they venture further.

Overnight, the wind out of the Northwest had been weak and combined with high temperatures and a falling barometer, teeth were even more on edge.

And now this.

The very air had taken on a bad vibration.

Typically, Captain George Moulder didn't put in an appearance until they were well out to sea, trusting his officers to handle the first leg of a voyage. This particular trip however, had already begun under a cloud, omens aside: the evacuation of the British forces occupying New York with the conclusion of the 'War of Independence' for the American colonies.

Whether it was that or the insufferable heat in his cabin, Captain Moulder had appeared on deck in full uniform at first light, his bold features set in an even grimmer cast than was usual. His officer's jacket hung loosely on his gaunt frame, its blue and gold trim dulled by the eerie light, as if the very atmosphere was draining the vitality of his command. His beaver-skin captain's hat, with its prominent brocade, looked beaten and threadbare after many years on occupational duty.

Lieutenant Somersby had served under Moulder for many years and was overdue for a command of his own, a prospect that was looking dimmer now with the war in the colonies over. Still, the two men had served so long together they could practically read each other's thoughts. Captain Moulder stood quietly, hands clasped behind his back, waiting patiently for his first officer's report. The only outward sign of anything amiss was the thin trickle of sweat threading down the side of his face.

From the forward decks and rigging, the crew—most of the 205 of them—watched nervously at the odd mass in the water that had been spotted roughly half an hour before, roughly a hundred yards off their stern quarter at the visible edge of the fog. Every so often a few would steal glances back at the quarterdeck where the captain stood, taking their cues from the man who was treated and viewed like a God in their floating world.

Lieutenant Somersby felt the captain's unspoken request all but hanging in the sultry air surrounding them. He had no idea what the answer was. The thing out there in the ocean before them wasn't like anything he'd ever seen before. Initially it hadn't seemed to be more than a clump of underwater debris a couple meters across. But within a quarter of an hour it had expanded, or perhaps simply shown more of itself. Now it suggested something much more massive, an amorphous, crab-like shape just under the surface of the water ahead of them. It was peculiar how it maintained its distance, even matching small corrections in their course, like some sentient entity.

Somersby, a dark-featured twenty-five-year-old Falmouth native who'd come up through the ranks the hard way, was acutely conscious of not just the captain, but the other officers on the quarterdeck with them. Men who wouldn't hesitate to exploit an opportunity to take his position if he were to make a fool of himself, or demonstrate he was incapable.

"Mr. Somersby?" the captain finally asked, unable to control his impatience. He wanted to get past it and on with their voyage, particularly with a storm approaching.

Somersby kept his spyglass trained on the mass. *Did he see some movement within it? Something suggesting a writhing, tentacle-like form? What the hell was it? An unknown sea-creature of some sort? Perhaps one of those giant squids rumored to roam the oceans? Or a floating mass of seaweed and debris?*

He didn't think so. Still, he'd ordered the stern chaser in the lower officer's cabin be loaded with grape shot as a precaution. Next to it, Midshipman Hawks would stand, awaiting his command.

Water continued to sluice along the hull. Several of the crew shifted their positions uncomfortably. Someone coughed.

"I'm not quite sure, sir," the Lieutenant responded. "It's not anything I've ever witnessed before. It appears to be following us."

Rather than respond, Captain Moulder raised one brow slightly.

"We could hove to and send out a crew in the launch to investigate. I'd be happy to lead it if you so desire, sir."

Nearby, 2nd Lieutenant Percy, a hatchet-faced young man whose upper lip seemed perpetually set in a sneer, let out a chuckle and muttered something under his breath. His disdain for Somersby's more diplomatic approach to situations was well known. He was an aristocrat's son and bully—both things the captain despised—but because of his connections had wheedled his way aboard.

"Something to offer, Mr. Percy?" the captain asked.

Percy raised his chin. "Yes sir, I do. Recommend we cease this lollygagging and get on with our voyage. Let the damn thing have a taste of His Majesty's cannon if it continues to dog us."

Captain Moulder grunted.

Normally he would have deferred to Somersby but on this occasion, he had to admit Percy had a point. The crew was nervous. It wouldn't do to have a display of indecisiveness.

"Have Mr. Hawkes fire the stern chaser then."

"Sir?" Somersby looked apprehensive.

"You heard me, Mr. Somersby. I'm not in the habit of repeating myself."

Percy looked away, barely hiding his smile.

Lieutenant Somersby straightened his back and lowered the spyglass. "Aye, sir! Fall off to port another point," he addressed the helmsman. Then in a louder voice: "Fire when ready, Mr. Hawks!"

From the cabin below, the midshipman yelled back, "Aye-aye sir!"

A resounding *bang* followed, quickly swallowed up in the oppressive air.

The ocean behind the ship erupted with foam and splashes as the deadly chain shot cut through the surface.

Then... nothing.

The water rippled away and resolved back into smooth wavelets again. Across the ship the crew exchanged relieved glances.

Perhaps it *was* only a cluster of flotsam.

And yet... Lt. Somersby felt weird images dancing at the edge of his vision along with that damnable sense of a low hum that made the pressure in his sinuses swell. He winced, a wave of dread stealing through him. He fought down a sudden urge to scream and leap overboard.

Down below, one of the canon crew, a swarthy able seaman named Cunningham stood up and let out a low chuckle, showing a mouthful of rotting teeth.

"I think it was just a—"

"Hoy there, what's that, sir?" one lookout perched up at the mainmast crow's nest said, pointing to where the mass had been.

The low hum increased, suggesting a heavier sound beneath it. With it, an odd scissoring noise. It seemed to come from every direction at once.

Brow furrowing, Lt. Somersby glanced over the gunwale. What he saw seemed impossible: the area where the mass had been darkened, as if absorbing all the color and light out of the water.

Or as if whatever they'd seen earlier was *growing*. Rushing *towards* them.

"Hard to port, hard to port!" he screamed, losing his composure for the first time in his three years on the crew. The spotter on the main topmast screamed, adding to the alarm and confusion. Lt. Somersby didn't wait for any further response—he stepped over to the helm and dropping his spyglass on its neck chain, reached and spun the ship's wheel the opposite way. For a moment, some thought they might avoid the collision.

Then the ship shuddered to a halt, as if it had foundered on a submerged reef. Masts and rigging shook and groaned. One of the foretopmen was thrown from his perch and went tumbling off into the water with a splash, another fell screaming to the deck with a hideous *thud*, arms and neck at impossible angles. Shouts filled the air and amidships, the marines fumbled with their arms while their commander drew his sword and tried to maintain order.

Midshipman Hawkes found himself sprawling on the cabin floor, his arm sprained, and what he saw made him turn pale.

Under his hands the wood decking began to *come apart.*

"Oh father, who art in heaven..." he whispered, lips trembling.

From the main deck hatch, a bunch of sailors came pouring out, the men yelling. The boatswain ran up to the quarterdeck rail where the officers were, trying to shout something. Something was wrong with his face—it appeared to be blackening, collapsing like a rotten fruit.

"What's happening!?" Lt. Somersby demanded. What he saw was impossible: the man's head had all manner of worms sprouting out of it, like a decayed apple the Lieutenant had found in an orchard near his house as a child.

From below deck came the sound of water rushing in. Alarmingly, the ship canted forward. To the crew it sounded like the ship was shrieking. Lines and stays parted, snapping like musket shots. The main topgallant mast toppled and fell to the deck below, trailing snarled rigging. The tip of it smashed the shoulder of the bosun's mate, but no-one noticed—they were focused on the horrific forms writhing up through the deck planking, the wood itself breaking apart as if losing integrity.

Men screamed in a way never heard aboard even in the throes of their worst battles—the screams of unbridled terror. On the quarterdeck, Lieutenant Somersby felt his gorge rise as he watched it all unfold: he stood paralyzed as the men around him appeared to rot and dissolve, consumed by the infinitely multiplying worms.

Captain Moulder didn't cry out, but Lieutenant Somersby did as the Captain's right eye erupted in a spray of wriggling forms even as he felt his own body swell with strange eruptions. They smelled of things long trapped deep underwater tinged with another, sharper odor: the metallic smell of his own fear.

The lieutenant felt his scream die in his throat as his vocal chords broke up... writhing, his jaw in agony as its tendons snapped. His legs were sinking through the deck.

The icy blackness reached him, enveloping him like a dead widow's cloak.

Then: nothing.

1. PRESENT DAY

"Just a sec!"

Barbara Holden put on one of her better smiles and looked over the rail into the choppy waters of the Atlantic, suppressing the shudder again. She'd always been fascinated by the ocean, even as a girl growing up in a rural, western Pennsylvania town, but on this particular bright midsummer day, she felt seized by a disturbing sense of unease—something probing at her deeper instincts.

A nagging sense that her sunny, youthful worldview might be threatened by darker, distinctly unpleasant things.

She shook her head and brushed back an errant lock of wavy, red hair.

At thirty-one and in the prime of her womanhood, she cut the kind of dazzling figure one associated with successful sustainability-minded entrepreneurs or moviemakers these days; the sunny, slightly attractive type marketing companies adored on their social media feeds.

She was neither, in fact, but after getting laid off from her Marketing Director position at Eco-World Technologies, had been working the past summer as a bartender in Bridgehampton while she reconsidered her career options.

Around that time, she crossed paths—and became smitten—with Ewan Vickers.

Ewan seemed everything the men that had been in her life to date were not: unflinchingly confident, sincere, and boldly committed to a purpose in life greater than himself. It didn't hurt that he had a surfer's body and was incredibly handsome in a Kennedy-esque way, with wavy sun-bleached hair and dimpled chin.

Not to mention five years younger.

"C'mon, Barb! We're burning daylight!" Never the vaguely demeaning *babe*, or *dear*, or *hon* like some of her exes.

She loved the way he addressed her: seriously. Like an equal.

Mostly.

Ewan stood at the stern of their boat, a sleek 41-foot Sea Ray he claimed he'd bought off a bankrupt local fisherman. Although when she'd teased him once on why they were tooling around in a gas-guzzling luxury yacht while shooting documentaries geared toward saving the planet, his face had clouded over momentarily as he'd replied: "In a *perfect* world, Barb, in a perfect world…" as if that explained it all.

A part of his charm, she'd decided: his ability to embrace anything in clear terms. It didn't hurt, she also realized, that Ewan Vickers seemed to live in a world where money was never any problem, a luxury she didn't have.

She made her way back to where he was standing with Toby Graham, his fellow surfer and videographer. Tall and black, Toby had the kind of open face and natural charm that would have had her swinging in his arms if fate hadn't handed her Ewan first. Even so, there'd been one or two occasions over the past couple of months when she'd caught him sneaking glances at her, only to turn away with a quick smile.

Today however, he was all business.

"Surfer Dude" appearances aside, one thing both men were serious and thorough about was their diving equipment. And today's dive, after what they'd unexpectedly discovered the day before, meant going deeper than usual. With it came an element of danger—this dive site was in a restricted zone, off limits to everything but surface vessels.

But opportunity was here.

When not running their deep diving business taking tourists to the various shipwrecks off Long Island, Ewan and Toby handled underwater photography for networks like Nat Geo and Discovery, though lately they'd been increasingly handling more assignments for GreenWaters' investigation and litigation division. Barbara wasn't sure, but she sensed there might be a few fraying edges around the two men's financial picture. Or something else, altogether. Ewan had been acting increasingly distracted, even in bed at night.

They'd been particularly close-mouthed about this assignment. She'd only overheard snatches between Ewan and Toby at their apartment overlooking Fort Pond—something about illegal dumping just southeast of the Montauk Shoal, right about where they currently were, in fact.

There were rumors of a source out of Star Island Marina, which was already on their radar for supporting charter sport fishing. Ewan said it was a blatant crime against the planet and its dying resources. He'd encouraged a lot of his friends with a local advocate group called 'PlanetJustice' to post scathing tweets and one-star reviews on social media as a way of putting pressure on them, even though they'd never actually been on the fishing boats or visited the marina. Barbara's comment, "But wasn't Montauk kind of founded on sport fishing? I mean, they're just trying to make a living too," earned a withering glare from Ewan: "*After* it was ripped from the hands of the Native Americans. Those bastards are making money destroying our natural resources, Barb. Killing sharks for fun? You call that 'making a living'?"

"Well, no—" she'd started to respond when he'd cut her off with "*—Don't go there.* You've got a lot to learn, yet. Times are a-changing, and we're spearheading that change!"

She'd been put off by his *mansplaining*, but as with all things, Ewan let it drop.

"Where's your backup dive computer?" Ewan asked, as they rechecked all their gear. They had the larger High Pressure 120 tanks laid out.

"Here," Toby replied.

"That piece of junk? It's a Sea Quod. We're going past 150 today, dude."

"The Oceanic Nitrox flooded on yesterday's dive," Toby said quietly. He still didn't feel good about it. Of the two of them, he had a superstitious streak and a bunch of things had been adding up over the last couple of days that had him spooked. One couldn't stay spooked around Ewan for very long, though. The man blew through everything in life like a charging rhino.

It was both inspiring and unnerving.

Ewan grunted. The light breeze coming out of the northwest ruffled his hair.

"Check the regulators again. Then let's gear up and get going. We should get two dives in today if the weather holds." He pulled up the rest of his dry suit and zipped up. "Barb, you good?"

"Thumbs up, hon," she replied, muscling her way into the heavy suit. Despite her misgivings, it was a fine morning to be out on the water. Sunlight glittered off the waves. Aside from a fleet of day fishermen scattered miles to the northwest off Montauk's shore, they had the ocean to themselves.

From below decks, Gus "Doogie" Stillwell emerged, carrying extra diving weights. Doogie was one of their many part-time helpers—one of those locals who did pickup work around the harbor. Mostly, in his case, as a deckhand on the Viking Cruise lines, though he could also be found at Uihlein's Marina helping with boat repairs off season. A horse-faced man in his late-thirties, he had the haggard, leathery features of a veteran fisherman and a smoker. If not overly burdened in the brains department however, he was doggedly reliable and methodical, two things invaluable as an anchor man on diving trips.

"What's the good word, Doogie?" Toby said, crouched over the tanks, re-checking the regulators.

"*Focus-mocus!*" Doogie shot back, one of his standard *Doogie-isms*. Only this time it came out a little flat, as if he too felt under par.

"That's right, pal, *focus-mocus*."

Ten minutes later they were geared up and on the dive platform at the back of the boat. Doogie stood to one side, arm outstretched so Ewan could read the oversized watch on his forearm. Barbara always hated this part—the scuba gear was incredibly heavy and the neoprene suit made her sweat.

She looked over at Ewan, who gave her a wink and a thumbs-up.

"Everybody in!" Doogie yelled when Ewan nodded.

The first plunge into the water always shocked her: the sudden, claustrophobic sensation followed an unreasoning flash of fear—the fear of dropping into a vast body of water (like the Atlantic) with an unknown multitude of strange creatures somewhere below. Even as a girl at camp she'd hated freshwater lakes, the ones with murky depths and trailing water grass... and God knows what else.

Today their destination lay 160 feet down in an odd little crevasse not far from where the submerged shelf dropped aside into the deeper abyss of the Atlantic. Just inside the government restricted dive area... where the two strange shipwrecks had been found the day before. One had been the remains of a nineteenth century square-rigger—a frigate Ewan guessed—but the main wreck had been a WWII Destroyer, wedged into the top of the canyon.

The descent line they'd secured on the previous dive still hung in place. It'd been left attached to a submerged buoy for easy retrieval—to Barbara it appeared to be little more than a path down into nothingness.

The three divers took a moment to check each other to make sure all their equipment was working properly. The dive plan they'd laid out had them descending first to one hundred feet for some general ocean shots, then down to the wreck for forty minutes. Factoring in time for decompression, the entire dive was set for 90 minutes, max.

Ewan was concerned about the deeper rip-currents which had kicked in aggressively the day before roughly twenty feet above the wreck. There'd been a few hair-raising moments when the three of them were forced to swim aggressively against it for a full five minutes. Today, everyone was under strict orders not to stray more than ten yards down-current from the descent line.

This morning however, the ocean seemed preternaturally calm, as if it had been waiting for them. One of Barbara's weaknesses Ewan constantly ribbed her about was her overly imaginative mind and a tendency to personalize everything around her.

With her breathing growing more regular, Barbara relaxed somewhat as they made their way down through the absinthe-tinted depths. Here and there schools of fish went about their dizzying course changes, occasionally pursued by an occasional nurse shark. She let herself become attuned to the uncomfortable sensation of breathing through her mouth; the odd taste of the rubber regulator between her lips, the constant chorus of bubbles chasing each other up to the surface.

The subtle tugs and rhythms of the ocean.

Ewan took the lead, with Toby following behind with the main camera. Barbara carried the secondary camera; a Backscatter Canon 5D Mark IV underwater rig. Toby might be a much more seasoned underwater photographer, but lately Barbara had been getting quite a bit of good footage and Ewan had hinted at letting her handle even more of the camera work on today's dive.

A movement out of the corner of her eye caught her attention—an adult Great White flitting just along the edge of their range of visibility. She felt an instinctive pang of nervousness but wasn't overly concerned. Sharks rarely went after divers underwater.

Another movement caught her eye—Ewan signaling urgently.

It took her a moment, then she saw it: a giant sea tortoise gliding ahead of them. She lived for these moments: the majestic creatures of the sea, glimpsed in their element. Checking her tether to the descent line, she glanced at the depth gauge on her wrist, then brought the camera up and began shooting.

It would be great footage, she knew, with the light beams from the surface bracketing the tortoise as it caromed and arced gracefully through the water, trailing bubbles. For a moment she forgot she was underwater—forgot herself even—as she became hyper-focused on her subject. The movement and colors were entrancing, hypnotic.

To be so free of worry and anxiety, she thought, *I bet that sucker is just living completely in the moment, thinking only of—*

Toby jarred her out of her thoughts, swimming right in front of her while tapping his wrist clock followed by the "okay?" universal finger sign.

She blinked, realizing she'd been sliding into a diver's cardinal mistake: letting her attention wander. She gave the "Okay" back, checking first her dive computer then the camera. Everything looked good. Then she realized she'd made yet another mistake: assuming everything was okay before actually checking it.

Toby studied her a moment, his eyes oddly magnified from the water and face mask, then nodded and gave the thumbs down, signaling they should continue.

As he always did, after alerting her to a shot, Ewan had already gone on to the next thing and worked his way down into the darkness. And as always, Barbara found this disconcerting—his way of pushing the 'buddy' system (and everything else for that matter) to the limits.

Today, however, she found it particularly disturbing. Fear seeped in around her thoughts.

Something's about to go wrong... can we call this off? Just go home?

The ocean continued to transition into deeper shades of green-blue. Down they went—100, 120, 140 feet... and there it was, emerging out of the gloom: the rotting, shattered hull of an old frigate, and past that, the WWII Destroyer half-trapped in a crevasse that ran southward twenty or thirty yards toward the edge of submerged shelf where the sea floor fell away into the deeper abyss of the Atlantic.

The top of the Hyborian Canyon.

It was a confusing scene at first. In addition to the shipwrecks, there was a trailing debris field of garbage, junk and most disturbing, piles of what appeared to be blue toxic-waste barrels—the current reason for their trip.

Someone had been doing some highly illegal dumping.

Further confusing the scene, several fishing nets had caught on the wrecks, lending the illusion the whole site had been snagged by the web of some giant underwater spider.

This was the first time Barbara had seen it—the day before it had strictly been Ewan and Toby. Nearby, the bottom was mostly sand except for the garbage and debris. More disconcerting was how the ocean past the wrecks deepened into a twilight horizon of deep blue-black.

A random thought popped into Barbara's head: *Beyond here be dragons*.

On the tail of that a flashing image of those nightmare angler fish swimming amidst larger, scarier predators.

The descent line had been secured to a spot fifty yards away from the wreck, just outside the restricted zone. The brightly colored ties showed a strong current coming in from the east, which made it easier to get to the remains of the ships—but harder to get back. Fortunately, however, a granny line had been rigged further up that would take them to a secondary line trailing off the boat as a safety precaution.

Ewan had been cagey about having Barbara along this time as she'd never been on a dive below 120 feet, but she'd persisted the night before, ribbing him how she needed to "get her feet wet" someday.

"Are you sure?" he'd asked, sitting in their room the night before.

"Abso-positively," she'd replied, one of her 'Barbarisms'.

But now, she wasn't so sure.

Something struck her as hinky about the whole scene. For starters, there was no record of an 18th century frigate going down at this location.

Nor a WWII Destroyer.

"It has to be a newer wreck, one that somehow isn't on the books," he'd insisted.

Ewan wasn't swayed. "Once we get the ship's bell, I'm going to prove you wrong, *buck-o*. That rig is old. I can't explain it, but my gut tells me so. We're not just going to nail this toxic dump assignment, we are about to make headline news!"

"There's nothing on any of the charts, dude," Toby had shot back. "This doesn't smell right. Whoever set up the restricted perimeter knows those ships are there. No way these were missed. No. Freaking. Way."

Ewan had patted his friend affectionately on the chin. "*Yes way, dudette.* You got to lay off the negative vibes!"

Barbara didn't know that much about sunken ships, but her hunches were with Toby.

Today's dive plan was twofold: document the illegal dumping going on here off the shoals and capture evidence of this new discovery.

Barbara re-checked the dive gauge on her wrist and forced herself to continue taking relaxed, controlled breaths. The increase in pressure at this depth gave her a headache, and she was beginning to regret that last extra glass of wine and bravado about her readiness for this. As they drew closer, she felt a growing sense of dread.

Stay calm. You can do this.

Ewan was already halfway to the destroyer, the high beam of his ScubaPro dive light probing through the tangled netting.

She also noted something else that struck her as odd: it was as if the darkness beyond the shelf drop-off had *grown.* Come closer in fact. It had to be an optical illusion.

She felt her teeth clenching tightly around the regulator in her mouth and for a split second she had a weird thought: what if she were sucking on the orifice of some strange sea-creature, like some hardened sea anemone... trying to force its tentacle down her throat?

She brought the camera up and took a sweeping shot of the wreck, zooming in on the stern, then slow-panning the scattered junk and garbage around it. It appeared someone had been dumping old electronics here: TVs and computer monitors, keyboards and stereo components. And more recently, those ominous-looking heavy duty blue barrels.

The same kind used to dispose toxic chemicals in. Ewan had figured that one out by scraping off the gray paint someone had covered the warning labels with.

So, the rumors were true.

No wonder Ewan and Toby had been outraged. And yet, they'd also been uncharacteristically quiet around her about it. In the past couple of weeks, she'd heard them arguing over it several times, but whenever she tried to bring it up, Ewan shrugged it off. A little too quickly, she thought.

She gave a powerful kick of her flippers, realizing she'd fallen back too far. Toby was pacing himself, but Ewan had focused on something either just in or beyond the wreck. Strangely, the darkness beyond grew closer—she became convinced of it.

Closing in, she saw something disturbing: now part of the incoming darkness had formed a large tendril of sorts. It looked maybe two or three feet thick and extended toward Ewan as if curious about him. As if with conscious intent. She wanted to scream something at Ewan—impossible at this depth and distance of course—but even more alarming, he was prodding his sample net toward it.

Even Toby seemed perplexed, as if not sure what to do. He paused in his approach, making a waving motion with his hand.

They had been on countless dives in this area and had dealt with all sorts of underwater dangers in the past, but this didn't seem to fall under any previously known category.

Then something even more bizarre happened.

As Ewan made a short scoping motion with the aluminum handled sample net, she saw something hideous flash out of the tendril—a kind of head, a *giant* head, like that of a deep-sea angler shaped vaguely into human-like features. It struck out and in an instant subtracted Ewan's arm from the elbow down, sample net and all.

Barbara registered a flash of needle-like teeth and luminescent, homicidal eyes that managed to be bright cyan, silver and dead black at the same time. Then it disappeared into the darkness. Her breath strangled in her throat, the regulator like a foreign cork. Behind the mask, her eyes went wide with horror.

This isn't happening.

Ewan floated, stunned, the blood pouring out of his severed limb inky black at this depth. He looked about, confused, as if saying: *do you believe this?* A stream of bubbles exploded around him. Then his body jerked as the thing bit into him again, this time taking half his chest cavity and hip. The scuba gear hung in tatters, the tanks tumbling down. The man who had been her mentor and first true lover, a vitality-infused male in the prime of his life, had instantly and inexplicably been reduced to a savaged chunk of inert meat, floating slowly to the ocean floor. His remaining internal organs spilled away. More bubbles from his severed air-hose erupted upward.

She choked on her regulator, dimly aware of the hot, squishy feeling in her guts as her bladder loosened. Irrational thoughts blossomed up: *Nopleasemommy, nomakeitstop.*

Toby swam toward her, pumping his legs furiously. Around him, tendrils spread out of the dark at an alarming rate. Barbara went into shock, her heart going like a trip hammer. The shark she saw earlier darted in, then it too was struck. One second she saw it accelerating relentlessly toward Ewan, the next it was headless: Twelve feet of apex marine predator turned into chum.

Toby came within ten yards of Barbara, still swimming hard and pointing frantically with one finger: up! He jerked, then stopped, trying to process why he'd lost momentum.

Both his legs were withered, blackened stumps below the knee, the feet and flippers flaking apart as if flash-burned. The last thing Barbara saw were his eyes flaring briefly in shock, then going half-closed as the lassitude of inevitable death rushed in.

Barbara completely lost it.

Ripping off her weight belt, she released her emergency float and kicking furiously, signed her own death warrant: she shot straight up 160 feet.

Doogie was relaxing half-drunk on the back deck with a cigarette and his fifth beer of the day, figuring he had another idle hour ahead of him, when Barbara broke the surface twenty yards from the boat.

He knew he wasn't supposed to drink on the job, but things hadn't exactly been going super-duper with his finances since the recession. A lot of people in Montauk might be enjoying the substantial financial windfall with the incredible upsurge in tourism these past few years, but Doogie Stilwell wasn't a member of that club. His obsessive Lotto gambling habit hadn't helped either, though he somehow managed to scrape together enough to buy a few packs of cigarettes a week.

Inebriated or not, one thing he became instantly aware of: something terrible had happened below the water on his watch and he would be in deep shit. Serious deep shit if it came out he'd violated his parole, even though it was minor felony. Besides, he'd never gotten this drunk before on a job (well, almost never) but something about the warm sun on his face and a calm lapping of the ocean had triggered an urge to cut loose a little...

A few minutes later, he manhandled her onto the dive deck.

"*Shitfuck*, this ain't good!" he kept mumbling to himself. "Shitfuck shitfuck!"

She looked bad. *Really* bad. He ripped the regulator out of her mouth and saw that it was all chewed up and bloody. He'd seen cases of the bends before, but nothing like this. And where were Ewan and Toby? What the hell happened down there? It was supposed to be a routine dive.

Doogie knew he should get on the radio and notify the Coast Guard, just as he knew nothing on God's Earth would save her now. Her face was a hideously bloated patchwork of bright red, with gaseous blisters.

Barbara gasped a single word. Seconds later, blood erupted out of her mouth as her internal organs ruptured. She died, writhing in agony.

Doogie stood there, crouched over her a moment. Except for the lapping of waves against the hull and the hiss of compressed air from her regulator, it was eerily quiet.

Then Doogie leaned over, shut off the valve on her tank. He quietly stood up, took a step to the side and vomited into the ocean.

2. ONE MONTH LATER.

The house at 2492 Chatsworth Avenue was one of those hulking 1920's Tudors which, like many residences in the neighborhood, hid its true size in a scenic landscape of dramatic rocky outcroppings, brooding trees and half-hidden staircases.

Even the house itself seemed to evoke a vaguely Tolkienesque fantasy; English-style casement windows with a façade of tan stucco and stonework that managed to seem simultaneously welcoming and foreboding. The entire impression was of a stoic, elderly edifice from another era, one solidly built to withstand the inevitable tide of change and uncertainty.

In that way it perfectly suited its sole occupant, William Vanek; for him it was his castle, an impregnable fortress to keep him protected from the outside world.

And isolated within.

The afternoon had settled into an overcast, unseasonably cool late August one. Vanek sat in his study toward the rear of the house: a wide, low-ceilinged room with doors that led out back to a flag-stoned terrace. From the stereo near the fireplace came the muted strains of Claude Debussy's 'La Mer'. He leaned over his antique oak desk, deep in thought with his forefinger to his lips, contemplating the contents of the yellowed report strewn before him. His other hand idly tapping the edge of the wireless keyboard. On the wide screen HD display in front of him was playing the eerie video footage of the HMS *Cerberus*, a doomed 19th century arctic exploration vessel that had been recently discovered by a Canadian team. The ship had vanished without a trace in 1849.

The footage was taken by a remote camera sent in through one of the hatches, revealing a perfectly intact interior that aside from silt, might have been abandoned just yesterday. The frigid waters of the Canadian Arctic had preserved everything.

In the ghostly reflection of the screen was a thin, striking-looking man in his mid-forties. Vanek had the strong eyebrows, pronounced cheekbones and chiseled features of his father combined with the intense brown eyes that ran in his mother's family. He had an efficient, impeccable air about him: the kind of man who looked like he rolled out of bed freshly pressed with his bristly dark-brown hair combed just right.

Such was hardly the case, of course, though his late wife had often ribbed him about being an 'insufferable neatnik', a compulsion that had only escalated after her tragic death eight years previous.

The study was a treasure trove filled with old sailing ship models, rare nautical paintings, prints and paraphernalia. It had the trim look of a captain's cabin, right down to the well-polished plank floors and antique brass telescope standing near the back windows.

Many Marine historians envied this room, which only made sense; for the last six years William Robert Vanek had established himself as a renown Naval and sea-faring historian. That was after his career as a Marine Archeologist professor at SUNY Maritime College in Throgg's Neck imploded during the fifteen-month mental break-down following the death of his wife and father.

These days, safely entrenched in the house that had originally belonged to his grandparents, he was a man who'd developed a reputation of being a recluse. And a neurotic crank. Except for a weekly visit from his housekeeper and a once-a-month dinner with his mother and younger brother, he rarely had visitors and only ventured out when absolutely necessary.

In addition to the recently discovered *Cerberus*, the research scattered on his desk before him included a current case he was consulting on for a colleague in London regarding several British ships that had been scuttled in the Hudson River during the Revolutionary War. Next to it, set aside for the moment, a bulging case file contained one of his ongoing hobbies and obsessions; the mysterious sinking of his grandfather's ship off the coast of Montauk during WWII.

Aside from that, the entire desktop was a paragon of orderliness. Even erasers were neatly lined up like little soldiers.

The vibration of the smartphone near his elbow stirred Vanek out of his reverie. He glanced down and *hmphed* at the name on the caller ID.

"Hello, Chuck," he said, leaning back as he answered the call. "Back from vacation so soon? Got tired of chasing down mermaids in Tahiti?"

That got a sheepish laugh from the other end. One of Vanek's old friends, Carl "Chuck" Gavin counted as one of the few people who still bothered to swing by and remind him there was still a thriving, living world out there.

"Nope, turned out to be a bunch of confused Korean cross-dressers with species-identity issues," Gavin quipped in his raspy voice. A pause followed. "Actually, I'm here on some other business I'd like to run past you," he added in an even tone. That got Vanek's attention.

"I'm a little *busy*. Where are you?"

"Right on your front step."

Vanek frowned. He hated surprise visits.

Vanek swung open the massive front door. It looked heavy enough to withstand a medieval battering ram.

Gavin, a wise-eyed man in his mid-sixties with the weathered skin of a veteran sailor, stood on the front step under an umbrella, a bulging leather satchel under his right arm.

"Come in," Vanek said with a frown, standing aside.

"*Busy*, are you?" Gavin asked, as they stood in the spacious foyer. Vanek took his jacket and coat and put them on a stand in the corner. To one side, an archway led into the kitchen; to the other, a front parlor/library.

"Yes, *very*. A dozen things on my plate, actually." The truth was he'd been half-bored out of his mind and going stir-crazy. For the last forty-five minutes he'd been talking to himself aloud about his frustration, not even aware he'd been doing so. The sunken frigates hadn't promised anything ground-breaking. The images of the *Cerberus* had cast a spectral gloom on his day and his research on his grandfather's disaster had been hitting dead-ends for some time. When Gavin had shown up, he'd been contemplating blowing the rest of the day off and heading to his shop in the basement to tinker with the scale model of the *HMS Hyperion* he'd been working on the past three years.

He realized Gavin was studying him in that cocked-head way he usually did when a game was afoot. The man's eyes were gray and cold as the North Atlantic. Gavin combined a taciturn demeanor that could quickly shift into a gruff "old-man" humor if the mood *struck* him but today the face was inscrutable.

Vanek stood with his hands in his back pockets and looked at him straight back. "So, what *really* brings you here?"

In response, Gavin patted him on the shoulder and nodded past the main staircase toward the rear of the house.

"I have something you'll be interested to help on."

"You sound confident," Vanek replied.

"I am."

Giving him a speculative look, Vanek gestured to the back of the house.

In addition to the desk and displays, the study featured overstuffed leather couches and chairs around a low coffee table before a broad fireplace with a stack of birch logs in the grate. Gavin flopped himself down on a couch, the battered satchel between his legs, and busied himself pulling out a bunch of documents and photos which he spread out on the table.

Vanek sat in the chair next to him, leaned back and crossed his legs, English-fashion. His fingers immediately began to drum on the chair arm.

'Officially,' retired from a career in the Office of Naval Research or 'ONR,', Gavin was one of those indispensable 'jack-of-all-trades' that had his hands in all sorts of things from carpentry, boat-building to gardening and celestial navigation. Rumor had it he'd done everything from working with classified salvage operations to a U.S. President or two. One story Vanek heard involved Gavin consulting with the Russians during the loss of one of their nuclear subs in the North Atlantic.

He also knew that 'retirement' was a subjective word. Gavin was still closely tied with the ONR.

When they'd settled, Gavin leaned back, hands clasped loosely between his legs. Vanek noticed a small crease in his forehead but waited for his friend to start. Of all the people he knew, he considered Gavin the most trustworthy and reliable—an anchor in turbulent times. He raised his brows in an expectant look.

"Kind of odd case," Gavin began, answering Vanek's unspoken question. "Have you been paying attention to the recent news out in Long Island?"

"More lane closings on the L.I.E.?"

Gavin snorted, "That's a given. No, this is much more serious. There's been a couple of strange incidents the past couple months. Around the Montauk and Block Island area."

"Well, you get a bunch of lug nut surfer dudes smoking too much pot and that's what happens. Stranger than that?"

"Yes," Gavin replied dryly, "Even by your standards."

"So, what's this have to do with me?" Vanek asked, uncrossing his legs. He had a hunch on that score. Only one reason came immediately to mind, but as with anything concerning Gavin, it would be a mistake to *assume* anything.

"Plenty, but I'll get to that in a second," Gavin said, his thumbs now tapping each other. "Here's the deal: two months ago, a fishing trawler disappeared on an overnight charter. They found it adrift a few dozen miles off to the SE of Block Island, its entire crew missing. No sign of foul play—all their gear and belongings were intact. Nothing in their log or on their instruments to indicate anything amiss. It was as if they'd simply all jumped overboard."

Vanek shrugged. "Not unheard of. Could be a dozen reasons things like that happen."

Gavin held up a hand. "Then back in July, two Eco-Documentary cinematographers vanished diving near a restricted area 30 miles off Montauk Point."

"What an awful shame. You see that as a problem?"

Gavin ignored him. "Yes. The third diver made it to the surface but died immediately. She panicked and raced up from 160 feet with no deco-stops. It wasn't pretty."

"*Ouch*. I'm sorry. Nothing funny about that. No other bodies washed up yet?"

"Nothing."

"Hmm. What else?"

Gavin leaned forward and tapped the remaining piles of reports and photos. "The Coast Guard and Marine Patrol are at a loss, though they have sent one ship to patrol the area. There doesn't seem to be any obvious connections to the various incidents. That's where you come in."

"For Christ's sake, Chuck, I'm a historian who builds ship models. You want me to give the police lessons on how to handle scale rigging?"

Gavin hesitated a moment before replying.

"That won't be necessary. The girl who died? They recovered her camera. There were images on it of a very interesting wreck down there they were photographing, quite illegally. In a highly restricted zone. A World War Two Destroyer."

"*I see*." Vanek's mouth went dry.

Gavin nodded toward the files on the table. Vanek's interest perked up.

Could it be?

The official version was that the ship his grandfather went down with had been testing out a new anti-submarine technology, ironically after tangling it up with a U-Boat south of Montauk. The project, code-named "*Neptune's Reckoning*", had been the subject of all sorts of conspiracy theories over the years: an ultra-secret government tampering with time travel, mind control experiments, secret alien technology including a chair used to communicate with them in deep space... the usual suspects Vanek found propagated by the fringe lunatic crowd. Still, the reports did always feel a little 'off' to him, in a way that had nothing to do with paranoid whack-jobs obsessed with the so-called 'Montauk Project' or 'Philadelphia Experiment' and other conspiracies that had gained traction in recent years. It was more in the consistent way *all* the declassified documents led into odd dead-ends…

"The U.S.S. Exeter."

Leaning forward, Vanek blinked, trying to process this bombshell.

"*Where?*"

"Thirty miles off the coast at the top of the Hyborean Canyon. In the restricted zone I mentioned."

"I don't understand. *That close* to shore? It was listed as lost out past the Atlantic Shelf. How wasn't it found until now? Every major wreck in that area has been charted. You don't just happen to overlook WWII Gleaves-class Destroyer!"

"*Obviously*. Yet there it was. Apparently, the position of the wreck and the terrain made it somewhat difficult to spot to non—"

"—military personnel. But the ONR must have known about it all along, Carl. They don't miss a major ship sunk in their own damn backyard." Vanek uncrossed his legs and leaned forward, the lines of his face growing hard. "What the hell is going on?"

Gavin picked up the file and untied it.

"Nothing I'm about to tell you leaves this room. I'm telling you this out of courtesy as a friend of the family. There won't be any Naval recovery team, public announcements or postings on that human fuck-fest called 'social media'. This whole thing will stay under tight wraps. For the moment at least."

Vanek was all but bursting with a hundred questions.

Gavin leaned forward, "There are things... *irregular* about this wreck. I can't say any more unless you agree to come on board."

He nudged a paper over. Vanek saw it was a non-disclosure.

This was a first. Vanek glanced at his desk then back at Gavin, his eyes narrowing.

"How *irregular*?"

In response, Gavin glanced at his watch and smiled. "*Highly*. Sign it and find out. Otherwise I'll leave you to your, er, *busy* work."

Vanek stared at him a full minute. Then with a grunt he snatched up the non-disclosure, gave it a once-over and signed it.

The form disappeared into Gavin's satchel. "Okay, then. For one thing, there's been illegal dumping going on at the site. Toxic waste. If *that* gets out, the press and environmentalists will be all over it. It'll be a fiasco. That's not the main issue, however."

"What is?"

"It's what's *on* that ship. The technology from a top-secret project code-named '*Neptune's Reckoning*', the one your grandfather was involved with."

"I've heard of it."

"Yes. But forget what you think you know. The program is still highly classified. In particular what could be described as the brains of it, known as 'The Anti-Magnetic Field Oscillation System' or 'AMFOS'. That's what your grandfather was working on when the ship sank. The ONR wants to recover it, discreetly. Then we can hand it off to the EPA and deal with the clean-up."

"What the hell would the ONR want with seventy-five-year-old technology? Besides, if it's so important, why *not* send a government team down to retrieve it? And why now?"

Gavin's eyes narrowed. "It's not that simple. The ONR doesn't want its hands dirty. This project your grandfather was involved with, it's still highly sensitive. There are a lot of odd aspects to this case and you'd have a hands-on opportunity to vet the results before it goes public. If it ever does. I've got a military diver and a marine sonar specialist who's also an expert underwater photographer out there now, and I'd like to bring you in as a third consultant. Your knowledge on the topic would be invaluable. Plus, you have a vested interest"

"What would I be doing?"

"Nothing too taxing. I need someone who can correlate the research and help figure out exactly what happened. You have an eye for details."

Vanek considered that. Still, there was always a catch.

"What the hell *is* really going on here, Chuck?"

"That's what you're about to find out. You've been asking that question all your life: what's the truth behind what happened to Lt. John Vanek? And why the cloak of mystery and 'Area 51' bullshit?"

Vanek considered that. "I'm in."

"Great. You've got two hours to get up to speed. And to get packed."

Vanek leaned forward, his eyes flaring in alarm, "*What!?*"

Gavin stood up. "You're going to Montauk."

"I... who exactly are these 'consultants'?"

"Arnaud Navarre and Dan Cheung."

Only two. Not like the old days. Since the recession, even postage stamps required a purchase order.

"Arnaud Navarre?" Vanek was impressed. Navarre was a well-respected French aquanaut who'd led salvage teams on many historic—and dangerous—military wrecks. He'd seen him on several documentaries and read the book on the Bismark that he'd co-written but had never met him in person. If Navarre was involved, Gavin had better connections than he thought. Cheung, however, he'd never heard of.

"Who is 'Dan Cheung'?" He had a momentary vision of a pint-sized Chinese CPA poking through his research data.

"*She* is an expert marine biologist who's been doing experimental work in underwater communications the last few years over at Woods Hole Oceanographic Institution. Also something of an artist with underwater photography. Cheung happened to be a close friend of the woman who died with the videographer team."

"*She*?"

"Yes, *she*. She had to head into the city for some replacement lenses at someplace called B&H in Midtown. She'll be coming by here to pick you up."

"*Pick me up?*" Vanek had an urge to smack his head. He felt like an imbecilic kid on his first day of class. "Oh *no*. I can't just *leave*. I-I have research to do. Besides, you *know* I don't work in the field! I work here, and here only!"

In truth he sensed the first rippling tendrils of an anxiety attack. The very idea of leaving the security—and confines—of his house, filled him with panic. Since the death of his wife, Michelle, and his subsequent breakdown, he'd never traveled again. Even a trip to the grocery store was an ordeal. He hadn't been diagnosed as a full-blown agoraphobe, but in recent years he figured that was probably a matter of semantics.

Gavin looked him in the eye, his stare unforgiving. "Will, enough is *enough*. It's high time you got out of your damned shell. You can't hide from life forever."

"What the hell does *that* mean?" Vanek shot back, hating the rising edge in his voice. "I'm a grown man, Chuck! I'm not hiding from a damned thing!"

"I'll see you out there." Gavin picked up his satchel and made to leave.

"*Wait*!" Vanek stepped in front of him. "Where, exactly?"

"One of the Navy's military houses is available while you do your research."

Vanek's heart pounded in his chest. He felt a hot flush run up his neck and brighten his cheeks, threatening to burst the left side of his head. His mouth went dry. Even that filled him with a certain self-loathing.

"This is a big mistake, Chuck, what you're asking is utterly impossible! There's simply no way I could—"

Gavin ignored him, "Better get cracking, sailor."

Vanek stood at the entrance of his study, fuming.

He was angry—with Gavin for throwing his neatly ordered afternoon into chaos, with himself for being so easily affected by it.

What in the hell is Chuck thinking!? And what in the same goddamn hell gives him the right to barge in here and turn my life on end? He knows damn well what I went through! I told him, told the same thing to everyone: I DO NOT TRAVEL!

His fist slammed on the desk hard enough to make the monitors rattle.

He despised the mental hang-wringing that had seeped into his everyday existence. His father would scoff at him, if he were alive. It was getting worse, he knew that, and yet felt powerless to counteract it. Not the numb, disconnected stupor he went through after the accident. That had been the horror of his soul free-falling into an unlit abyss. Like living with himself in the third person. No, this was more like old-maid behavior to him. With most of his family gone—except for his mother and brother—and the majority of his close friends (except Chuck) pushed away since the accident, one critical element had seeped out of his life without even being aware of it: his whole system of checks and balances.

As Vanek looked around the study, it occurred to him his housekeeper wouldn't show up for another day. Meaning, despite being neat as a pin (by any rational standard) the place was in his view an utter mess.

Damnit, I left the lunch dishes in the sink! he realized, remembering he'd planned on doing a bit more research before taking a nap, then tackling the dishes. Now it felt like his whole afternoon was in shambles.

Pack. Damnit, I have to pack! And what the hell kind of woman calls herself Dan Cheung!? Pack first. Dishes second. Blood pressure cuff—Christ, don't forget the damn blood pressure cuff! And medications! Did he have enough Xanax?

He hit the stairs to his bedroom two at a time, trying to remember where he'd last left his suitcase. Or if he even still had it.

The doorbell rang at 3:46.

Vanek was hastily drying the dishes and getting them put away in their proper cabinets. With its old pine décor and Formica countertops, the kitchen could pass for a set piece out of another century. Little had been upgraded in the house since his grandmother had passed away 12 years previous. The place had stood vacant until Vanek decided to move in after the boating accident.

The bell rang a second time, impatiently, making him clang one of the plates against the one below it. A small chip fell out and skittered across the counter.

Fuck!

Lips in a thin line, he marched out through the kitchen to the front foyer, throwing open the massive door for the second time that day.

This time he was in for a bigger shock.

"Er, can I help you?"

Vanek's brow creased in puzzlement. Standing in front of him was a tallish, exotically attractive woman with tousled, dark thick hair, strong cheekbones and what he could only describe as a classic silver-screen actress' smile; warm and dazzling. She had bold green eyes, with one brow arched as if amused. From the café au lait complexion and light freckles, Vanek guessed she was half-black. Not that he could tell anymore these days, or that it even mattered, he supposed. His mother was a different story. She was very clear about not rubbing elbows with *those people*.

One hand was raised in mid-knock. Her mouth was turned up on one side in a quirky smile.

"That depends," she said. "Are you William Vanek?"

Vanek drew himself up, aware he was about to get rapped on the nose.

"I *am* William Vanek, yes. I'm sorry, you are…?"

"*Dan Cheung*," she replied, as if anticipating his reaction. She dropped her hand and adjusted the strap on her purse, which looked heavy. Dressed in a black zip-up turtleneck, faded jeans and leather-strap sandals, she seemed more like a successful business exec on her day off than a photographer/marine communications expert.

Except for the watch on her left wrist, which he saw was a Tag Heuer. A man's watch, and one that had seen a bit of use from the looks of it.

"Dan Cheung," he echoed, deciding right then this was some practical joke. "Oh, *ah*! I get it. Chuck put you up to this."

He glanced over her shoulder, expecting Gavin to step out of the bushes, slapping his thighs.

Dan's eyes bored into him. Her unwavering gaze, her sheer *woman-ness* was daunting, challenging, even.

"Chuck who?" she asked, as if Vanek was the one now pulling her leg.

"*Carl? Carl Gavin?*"

"Oh, *Carl*! Yes, he asked me to come pick you up." Now her eyes looked him up and down, measuring him. "He mentioned you were a bit of a strange bird. He wasn't kidding, was he?"

Vanek frowned, "I'm sorry?"

Ignoring him, she looked past him into the foyer.

"Are you going to invite me in, or are we going to chit-chat on your doorstep all day?"

Vanek started to raise his hand, "I—"

Without waiting for his response, she pushed right past him and into the house, looking around the foyer before moving on to the kitchen. Vanek stood there, dumbfounded.

"Wow!" he heard her voice echo around the house, as she worked her way backward through the rooms. "This place is *so* retro! What a time warp! It's like a museum! Tell me that's not an original Fitz Hugh Lane."

Then: "Oh my God, *no way*! You must be kidding me!"

Alarmed, Vanek realized she'd already made it back to his study. Was she casing his house? That painting alone was worth a fortune!

He entered the room as she plopped herself down in the captain's chair at his desk, dropping her purse on the floor.

His chair.

She leaned back and crossed her legs, idly toying with something in her hand while her gaze traveled around the room. She didn't seem particularly impressed.

"Yes, it is an original. Arguably one of the more valuable paintings in my collection."

She made a soft snort. "Not anymore, I'd bet. 19th century art is in the tank these days. Mid-century is what's hot. You should have sold it fifteen years ago if you were planning on getting its original value."

"Yes, well I have no intention of selling."

He saw her eye come to rest on an 18th century frigate model that had been a gift from a director in the English Maritime Museum. Her gaze snapped back to him.

"Gavin said you were like a hermit living in a tomb. It's a pretty *nice* tomb though, I have to say."

"I'm glad you approve. Are you always this complimentary?"

She laughed and leaned back further, dangerously close to a display table with a mounted giant Nautilus shell trimmed in gold. "That's quite a—" she began, just as she overbalanced and the chair's castors caused it to shoot out from under her.

Vanek's reflexes surprised even himself—he managed to catch the shell in his left hand as it toppled forward and Dan's waist in the other before she hit the floor. The table went over with a crash.

"*Oh*," she said, her face close to his as he helped her to her feet. For a split second he thought the shell was a goner. It was a priceless antique his grandfather had found in a Paris thrift shop before the war.

"I'm so sorry—I'm such a klutz sometimes."

Part of him flared in outrage at the near disaster she'd nearly caused, another decided her laugh was a good one. A ray of possibility in this whole mess. Two more things he took in at that moment: she had great legs, and she exuded a bold, sexual energy about herself that he found simultaneously electrifying and intimidating.

Vanek had always been a confident, assertive type but looking at her sitting at his desk like she owned the place, and now this, he felt completely off his game. In his world, women weren't *supposed* to act like this, *Michelle never…*

As if picking up on this, she smiled at him as she stepped back, regaining her composure.

"I'm glad your shell is... all right. Here, let me help you clean up."

The small table was sturdy enough, but what threw him was in the shell itself. Someone had stuffed a rolled-up paper down deep inside of it. When he shook it out, he saw that it was a yellowed photo, torn on the corners as if someone had snatched it off a board in haste, along with a sheet of note paper with writing on it.

"What's that? Old love letter?" Dan asked.

"No, it's nothing," Vanek lied, hastily shoving it in his front pants pocket. He wasn't entirely sure, but at a glance he thought it might be his grandfather's writing.

Was that in there all these years? How?

He busied himself with getting the table put back to rights and the shell back on it, very carefully.

Dan slung her purse over her shoulder. "So, are you ready to go?"

"Go?" he'd almost forgotten. He shook his head, as if coming out of a trance. Another wave of panic seized him.

"Look, this is a big mistake. I don't know what Chuck told you, but I can't just run off to Montauk right now and…"

She stepped in closer. She was only an inch or so shorter than him, he realized, and uncomfortably near. Her perfume, he also realized, was something subtle, with a hint of rose and jasmine. For a ludicrous moment he thought she would lean in and kiss him.

What the hell!?

Instead, Dan lifted her chin, the quirky smile back as if enjoying his discomfort.

"We should hit the road. Traffic will be bad."

"Wait a sec, didn't you hear me?"

"I heard. Man-up for God's sake. Go or stay, but either way time's wasting."

He stared at her, annoyed. More so that she had a point.

Jesus! he told himself. She's right—*start acting like a man and rejoin the human race!*

Dan Cheung only seemed to underscore that. With a bold line.

"Dammit," he said under his breath, and went to grab his suitcase.

3. WHAT LIES BELOW

The fishing trawler *Sea Bitch* cut its engines as it approached the coordinates on the Wayfinder. It was a chilly, hazy morning with choppy water—the kind of morning tourists tended to avoid.

At the stern of the boat, ten seventy-five-gallon plastic drums sat lined up under a tarp. Two young men in fishing bobs—waterproof overalls—sat on the gunwale nearby, smoking.

The containers, their toxic warning labels obscured by flat gray spray paint, were filled with PCB laden sludge from D-Base Corporation's mandatory Phase-2 waste clean-up along the Hudson River. They were about to be 'disposed of' at a fraction of the normal cost.

"Hey boss," the first man called up to the pilot house. "Only ten barrels today? That's it?"

"That's it," came the reply. "I guess it's a good thing you can count, Al. Otherwise you'd have to go back to school and learn how to do a thing or two with that brain of yours. Now get this shit dumped."

The man up at the helm was on the tall side, with a face that immediately drew one's attention: he had an angry cast to his brow that suggested a predator that had just missed its prey. The dark eyes only enhanced the feral look, accented by arched brows. A local *restaurateur*, salvage business operator and conman by the name of Antony Scarpia, everything about him implied perpetual anger: his face, his posture, the impatient way he tapped his fingers. He was the guy on the expressway in the BMW always riding inches from your rear bumper, the one who arrogantly cut in front of you at the cash register while checking his smartphone, the neighbor at the BBQ telling salacious jokes with the guys by the grill while regularly describing women with such endearing terms like *pussy*, *fuckbunny* and *cunt*.

Scarpia nodded to the crewman next to him on the bridge, a stocky brute with a badly healed broken nose by the name of Salvatore 'Sammy' Vanossi, AKA 'Sammy V'. Vanossi re-checked their location on the GPS against a second set hand-written on a mole-skin notebook next to it, then gave Scarpia a thumbs-up. The GPS, which had been hacked by his 15-year-old nephew, had been altered to show their destination coordinates fifteen nautical miles from their actual location. Scarpia fired up a cigar, gave it a couple of tokes, then clambered down to the main deck. The two men sitting on the gunwale stood up.

Al Stanos, one of the dishwashers at Scarpia's seafood restaurant "The Lobster Trap", rubbed his chin, not sure if he had just been insulted or not. It was always that way with Scarpia. Even when he delivered compliments, they always came with barbed edges.

Jimmy Reed, the other man standing there, was a new hand. A rugged, good-looking guy with a mane of long, curly black hair that women adored, he'd been recruited last minute from Scarpia's remodeling company over in Amagansett when Stano's usual partner, Brad, had called in sick. Most likely the three extra tequila shots over at 'The Point' the previous night accounted for Brad's absence, but as Scarpia's father always told him: you made do with whatever tools were on hand.

Jimmy Reed, however, wasn't sitting well with any of this. A local surfer and fisherman, he came off as a badass at first, but was generally easy-going once people got to know him. Nothing had struck him right about this new assignment. First grumbling about the early hour they'd been forced to leave Montauk dock, his attitude hadn't improved during the course of the morning and by the time they'd arrived at their destination he'd gotten increasingly belligerent, despite warnings from Al to 'chill, dude.'

"Why is this shit so heavy?" he mumbled, pulling on his cigarette. The drums weighed close to 850 pounds and were tricky to handle with the trawler's boom crane.

Scarpia gave him a hard, sideways look, but Jimmy missed it. "I mean what the fuck? Why don't—"

Before he could finish, Scarpia had grabbed his hand and in one swift motion slapped it down on the stern gunwale. Jimmy's protest turned to a scream as Scarpia took the cigar out of his mouth and put the burning ember to the back of his hand. He tried to jerk it away but Scarpia's grip was like an iron vise.

"Next time, I put the cigar to your worthless testicles and see how long they take to burn all the way through, got it?" he hissed, his mouth right in Jimmy's ear. He flicked the cigar off the stern and gripped a handful of Jimmy's hair, yanking him in close. Despite Jimmy's cut physique, Scarpia's manic strength completely overpowered him.

Jimmy was aware of the agony transmitting from his hand, along with the nauseating smell of his own burning flesh. But he was utterly focused on Scarpia's dead, shark-like eyes inches from his own. The pain took a back seat to what he saw in that gaze.

When Jimmy didn't answer right away, Scarpia's grip tightened.

"Is that a *yes*?"

Jimmy nodded rapidly, tears forming at the edge of his eyes. A dribble of blood ran down from his lip where he'd bitten into it.

Scarpia eyed him a moment longer, then let him go.

Back in the pilot house, Vanossi sat by the port view window, nursing a beer and a cigarette.

"You think that little shit will keep his trap shut?" he asked. They'd had a few problems with some of the crew over the past eleven months. One college kid they'd employed who'd started acting unstable after a couple of 'deliveries' wound up sealed inside one of the toxic disposal barrels on the ocean bottom, not far from their current location. He'd still been screaming when they'd dumped it over the stern.

"Not more than a week," Scarpia admitted.

"Do you want me to handle it, boss?"

Scarpia puffed on his cigar, then let it out in a long exhale that sent smoke writhing along the metal ceiling of the bridge.

"Sure. But not right away. Too many eyes saw him on our deck leaving the harbor this morning and he's known around town. Give it a day or two. And this time make fucking sure the body doesn't turn up anywhere near here. I don't want any more cops nosing around at my restaurant asking a bunch of stupid questions."

Vanossi knew better than to answer. In the six years he'd been working for Scarpia, one thing he'd learned was that Scarpia didn't put much of a premium on talk. While Vanossi wasn't the brightest bulb in the box—he'd dropped out of school at 16 after a stint in Suffolk Juvie—he possessed a survivor's instinct when it came to observing people and adjusting his actions accordingly.

The trawler drifted as the barrels were unloaded. Far off on the horizon, a few heavy tankers plied their way toward New York Harbor but this particular spot, not known for successful fishing in the past few years, was deserted.

Stanos watched the last barrel disappear under the waves with only a spreading slick of smooth water and bubbles to mark its passing. Next to him, Jimmy stood by the towing boom they'd used to hoist the barrels overboard, his eyes hard and distant, as if he'd instinctually picked up on his death sentence being issued nearby.

"Ever wonder what lies below?" Jimmy said, just to say something. The words rang as hollow and wooden as the feeling in his stomach. On the trip out, he'd been thinking about applying to community college in the spring, now he was wondering if he'd be around to see next week.

"Not really," Stanos replied. In truth, he thought seriously about very little, except making sure he did everything Scarpia told him and how he would blow his next paycheck.

Jimmy, however, *did* think about things a lot, and talked about them too, much to the annoyance of his co-workers at the construction company. The only reason he'd been recommended to Scarpia was his ability to figure things out and do them correctly.

As the throttles were engaged and *Sea Bitch* got underway, churning up the water beneath the taffrail, he couldn't help but think about the implication of his own statement. Like the tentacled, hideous creatures in those tattered, second-hand horror stories he kept on the sagging bookshelf in his apartment.

What lies below?

Jimmy shuddered and stepped away from the rail.

Thirty fathoms below the surface, in an area known by certain government officials as Restricted Zone 609, there was movement in the darkness. Not the typical movement one would expect to observe along the edge of the Atlantic Shelf; the infinite variations of sea life relentlessly asserting itself; fish, crustaceans, whales, planktons.

This area—one of many secret dump sites the public weren't aware existed—would in fact be considered a 'dead zone' in terms of most sea life. Not for the toxicity of the chemicals and illegal refuse that had been accumulating here for the past couple of decades, or the shipwrecks nearby, but because of the presence of something else.

Something quite old, utterly alien and unnatural that existed here.

As the plastic barrels with their deadly, man-made cocktail tumbled down toward the depths, the darkness in the trench where the wreck of the Exeter was wedged seemed to intensify and writhe, as if in anticipation.

If anyone had been there to observe, they would have seen a disturbing, terrifying sight.

Near the edges of the mass, undulating over the rim, in and around the old wreck of the destroyer and the British frigate, shapes formed and mutated with alarming speed.

Some appeared to be humanoid, if the distorted, screaming features with needle-like teeth and gelatinous texture (not unlike the decayed inside of warm-blooded bodies) could be considered such.

A thousand other forms materialized and mutated as well; sprays of tentacles, quivering antennae... luminescent eyes and black tendrils that suggested parasitic worms. It was an obscenity of nature—an '*un*-nature' as it were, defying all logic to process it.

From deep within the mass came fiery pulses of bluish-green light, cold and angry in the murky depths, their staccato flashes implying agitated hunger.

As if whatever this was, was growing.

4. THE L.I.E. 500

"Don't look so weirded out—I get it all the time."

"Sorry?" once again, just as he focused on one train of thought, she went off in another direction. And he'd only met her five minutes ago.

"My name. My maiden name was Danielle Evans, but somehow over the years 'Dan' stuck. I used to be quite the tomboy. I guess it didn't help I married a Chinese marine biologist."

"Ah, I see," Vanek replied, unable to deny a twinge of disappointment. *Of course, she's married, you dolt! The Dan—or Danielle's of the world are always married! Not that you were interested anyway, Will. She couldn't hold a candle to your Michelle.*

"*Look*, could you slow it down a bit?" he added.

They flew down Montauk Highway—Route 27—with the speedometer hovering around eighty-five in Dan's 2014 Ford Mustang GT500.

Dan flashed a grin. "This is a *Mustang*, Mr. Vanek. What would be the point?" she said, downshifting as they closed in on a lumbering landscaping truck.

Vanek was annoyed on too many levels. "Look, just call me William. I'm not some damn schoolteacher."

She glanced at him, "Alright then, *William*."

Vanek had been a little taken aback when he'd come out to find the sleek metallic-gray Ford in his driveway. With its custom wheels and black centerline racing stripe it looked like a veteran of several racetracks. His eight-year-old BMW in the garage seemed spinsterish by comparison.

When they'd merged onto I-95 South she'd laid on the gas, leaving him convinced he'd left his stomach back on the on-ramp. Dan quickly proved an expert, if unnerving driver. She wasn't necessarily aggressive in a tail-gaiting sort of way: her driving technique was more fluid, smoothly avoiding bumbling drivers the way a veteran commuter would skirt slow walkers in Grand Central during peak hour.

It'd been years since Vanek had driven out to Long Island, but he was willing to bet the time it took them to cross Throgg's Neck Bridge and out onto the Long Island Expressway set a world record.

Also grating on his nerves was the indie-rock music she had blasting through the car's speakers. When he asked about it, she turned it down briefly and replied, "Courtney Barnett. Isn't she the coolest?"

It was *kind* of catchy, he decided grudgingly.

Despite the sleek comfort of the Mustang's interior—it had a vaguely James Bond flavor to it, American Style—the knuckles on the hand gripping the door handle were white.

When in the hell did I become such a goddamned old maid? he wondered, with dawning horror. *Next thing I'll be wagging my finger at her like my grandmother used to do*. As a younger man he'd been pretty much a speed demon himself. But like many things, since the death of his wife, all those tendencies had slipped away unnoticed into the featureless gray zones of his current existence.

At the same time, there was the cautious exhilaration of being forced out of his shell. As if in agreement with this, the gloomy overcast in Westchester broke up as they headed east, becoming a brilliant summer evening. The broad open sky of Eastern Long Island, with piles of cumulus clouds scattered every which way like random flak bursts, seemed put there to emphasize this abrupt shift from the safe clutches of his home.

Dan kept mostly to the HOV lane along the endless ribbon of I-495. He found her as bold and confident as her driving; throwing out random questions like a boxer tossing test jabs, while occasionally letting on about herself.

Vanek thought it odd when she told him how Gavin had contacted her about coming to Montauk: it had been at the funeral service for Barbara, the diver who had died back in July. Barbara was an old friend of hers going back to college.

"We hadn't spoken in recent months," Dan said, "so I was shocked to find out she'd willed her cameras to me. Last I heard she was still running a marketing group. That Canon is a great camera. Still had the footage on it from her final dive. Of the, *um*, destroyer they found."

"The police didn't confiscate it?" Vanek asked.

"They did. But there was no reason to keep it. That was how I got involved—Gavin was tracking down leads on what happened. When he found out I have experience photographing shipwrecks, he offered to hire me."

"I wonder why he didn't mention that."

Dan gave a little shrug. "Why don't you tell me? Gavin is *your* friend. What's with all the 'secret science cloak-and-dagger' shtick? He showed up at my office in Cape Cod with a heavy-duty I.D., a non-disclosure thick as a phonebook and an offer to make double my normal day rate. And perhaps get some answers on what really happened to Barb. Damn her. What was she thinking?"

"It must have been a shock. Were you very close?"

"Back in college, yes. We kind of drifted apart. A real sweetheart, but kind of unfocused."

"You don't have that problem, I take it?"

Dan smiled. "Nope."

"Gavin mentioned you also do underwater sonar work?"

"Yes. At Woods Hole."

Vanek nodded. Woods Hole Oceanographic Institute was one of the best for marine scientists in the world. Bob Ballard—the acclaimed oceanographer who'd discovered the Titanic and was now President of Rhode Island College, made his career there.

"Yet they cut you loose at WHOI without a fuss?"

"It's not as big a deal as you think. I'm an 'Adjunct Scientist' on their rolls, and money is always tight. They don't know where to keep me—my work falls between both the Biology and Applied Ocean Physics and Engineering Departments. Underwater communications are interesting, but not exactly a hot money-maker at the moment."

Vanek considered this. "Gavin sought you out. I'm sure it wasn't just about photography."

"He also seemed interested in my work on the NOAA's Automated Hydrophone array and some of the unexplained sounds it's recorded in the past few decades. Quite a few recently, in fact. Come to think of it, the only person who's shown any interested in that. Except for the usual crazies."

"What kind of sounds?"

"Pretty spooky ones. I'll play some for you when we get there."

That sounded a little shaky to Vanek, so he dismissed it. "This whole business with the U.S.S. Exeter strikes me as, well, *peculiar*. Particularly finding it was this close to shore all this time."

"Good way to put it: 'peculiar'. Arnaud thought so, too."

When she didn't elaborate, Vanek let it drop. He sensed something off—a certain edge in her tone.

Vanek fell into his own thoughts. He focused on controlling his growing agitation at the thought of being out at the far reaches of Long Island, surrounded by ocean on all sides.

Where a tidal surge could wipe out everything.

You sound like a little old lady! Christ!

Vanek pushed himself back into his seat, forcing himself to regulate his breathing and relax.

It wasn't working. His lower digestive tracts growled in protest.

When Dan sailed past a puttering white Cadillac (Vanek caught the white-haired driver fluttering like a terrified bird as they did) he finally spoke up, wanting to smack his forehead an instant later.

As Dan smoothly shifted back up into fifth, she challenged him with a smile and raised eyebrow.

"A little nervous?" she asked, changing the subject.

Vanek grunted dismissively. "Of course not," he replied.

"You should be. I've been in a dozen car accidents this year alone."

When he gave her an alarmed look, she reached over and patted his knee.

"Just kidding." She swerved around an aging baby-boomer moseying along in a Porsche convertible before adding: "It's only been ten."

Surprisingly, they caught a break in the traffic once off the L.I.E.

"Gavin told me you're one of the top Naval Historian's out there. Is that true?"

They had navigated through the Hamptons and broken out onto the open, arrow-straight stretch of Montauk Highway which, being midweek, found themselves momentarily with the road to themselves. To the right, through the clustered pitch pine and red cedar trees crowding the highway, he caught snatches of the Atlantic, an expanse of slate gray in the early evening light.

Despite the undeniable *woman-ness* of Dan which had him both simultaneously attracted to her and on his guard for the past two hours, he wasn't inclined to confide much. Unusually attractive women tended to make him wary and even more standoffish than usual.

"Chuck can be as full of malarkey as an Irish sailor on shore leave. Take anything he says with a grain of salt."

She let out a short laugh in return. *Definitely a good one*, he thought. The kind that made you want to hear more. On the heels of that: *Rubbish. She's young and reckless. Keep your distance.*

"Carl Gavin doesn't exactly strike me as the 'malarkey' type."

"You don't know him as well as I do," Vanek replied. Even as he said it though, a strange thought crossed his mind: how well *do* you know him? Or *anybody* for that matter?

"Perhaps better than you think."

Vanek turned to her, "Really?"

That got another laugh. She downshifted as they approached the garishly striped roof of "Lunch", the iconic roadside eatery known for their lobster rolls and old-Montauk décor. The last time Vanek had been there was with his wife, posing next to the old 50's cars parked out front. One had been an aqua-blue Chevy Bel-Air, he recalled. As they went by, he saw that, like his wife, the cars were long gone. The parking lot however, was full. He absently noted a large black GM truck with tinted windows creeping around, looking for a spot. It was the glint of sunlight off the windshield that drew his attention.

"... nothing like *that*," Dan replied. "I've seen his type before."

"What type is that?"

"The kind that—"

"Look out!" Vanek yelled as the truck shot out of the parking lot right in front of them, its tires spitting gravel. Dan veered to the left, into the oncoming lane, where a large semi-tractor trailer was bearing right down on them.

Dan spun the wheel left, flooring the gas pedal. Reflexes and the Mustang's powerful V8 engine saved them.

Barely.

For a moment, his world was reduced to the massive Ryder radiator grill filling his vision and the deafening honk of the truck's air-horn. Then the Mustang leaped off the highway and fishtailed onto the sandy shoulder as the truck barreled past, inches away, buffeting them hard enough to rattle the windows.

The truck skidded and accelerated down the road. A moment later the only indicator of their brush with certain death was a dust plume on the highway and the fact they were on the wrong side of it. There wasn't any sign that anyone over at the restaurant had even noticed.

Vanek looked over and saw Dan staring straight ahead, expressionless. The knuckles gripping the Mustang's padded steering wheel were white. Surprisingly, outside of a little tremble in his kneecaps, Vanek felt nothing at all. It had simply happened too fast.

The car grew quiet except for the ticking of the engine.

"God-damn Long Island drivers!" Vanek finally said, his temper kicking in. He threw a hand up. "Where in the Sam hell did he *buy* his license? *Sears & Roebuck!?*"

Dan released the steering wheel and turned the ignition over. The car immediately rumbled to life, as if wipe-outs were a normal occurrence. She closed her eyes and opened them again, slowly.

"I'm fine," she said, turning to look him in the eye. "Sears went bankrupt, though." She pulled up a smile and reaching over, squeezed his hand. It was an oddly intimate, yet reassuring gesture. "Thanks. I didn't even see him."

Another sharp rebuttal or two came to him, but it came out as a mumbled curse.

"Shall we get going?"

Her forced nonchalance made him laugh. But it broke the spell.

"Sure. I'd keep an eye on the parking lots, though. Damn shithead tourists are on the upswing since I was last here!"

"That wasn't a reckless nitwit," she replied. "That guy knew exactly what he was doing."

"Ex-husband, maybe?"

She shot him a sharp look. "Not likely. He's dead."

Vanek mentally kicked himself. It would have been natural to ask *how*, but it didn't feel right. Instead he said, "Guess that rules that out. Whoever was driving that pickup looked most definitely alive.

"Well, that narrows it down somewhat, doesn't it?"

It was Vanek's turn to laugh. It felt odd. He wasn't sure how long it had been since he'd last done that.

Too long, he decided.

Something else bothered him though. Something about that truck.

A decal? A symbol? A trident?

He couldn't remember.

If her mood was shaken after their close call, it didn't last long. She took the detour down the Old Montauk Highway where the road dipped and rose like a kid's roller-coaster, giving Vanek a few goofy moments where he rose out of his seat. Signs with names he hadn't thought of for years drifted by: Hither Hills Park, Gurney's Inn, Surfside Inn, Hartmann's Briney Breezes Motel.

Slowing down, she turned back onto Route 27 and past the old IGA supermarket, the beaches and rolling Atlantic along their right. From there, they entered the strip of the village proper which, aside from a handful of trendy eateries, was more-or-less the same as Vanek remembered. The old Memory Motel was still there—and still the tough-edged customer eulogized in the classic Rolling Stones song nearly half a century back—and just past it, Pizza Village and the Corner Store stood like relics of a *seaside town past*. 'The Point' Bar and Grill sat across the street, still a scruffy local's hangout. Overlooking the central circle known as 'The Plaza' was the 1920's residential building known appropriately as 'The Tower'. Continuing down the strip on either side were faux Tudor-style buildings from the same period. Dominating the traffic circle to the left, White's Pharmacy's mid-century façade still promised its endless variety of beach supplies. Murphy's Irish Tavern had disappeared and the strip of clothing stores on the other side of White's had gone *Hampton's-upscale*. White's Liquor was also still there and looking as charmingly weathered as always. To the right were stubborn holdouts like 'Herb's Market' and 'Shagwong's Tavern', though the old Fish and Tackle store at the end had been replaced by a coffee shop. The biggest difference was the propagation of surf shops that hadn't been there a decade ago, fueled by the opening of Kai Constanza's 'Kai-Kai' sandal stores. When Vanek had been here last, Montauk had still had the air of a rough-around-the-edges blue-collar fishing town that scoffed at the white-washed pretention of the Hamptons. Now it appeared to have been overrun by surfer dude culture and Hampton's *wannabes*.

Then they were past the old Montauk Fuel Gas station and squatting hulk of the Community Church, heading out along the 4-mile ribbon of Route 27 to the Montauk Lighthouse, known on every local sticker, T-shirt and coffee cup as: 'The End'.

"Where exactly is this place?" he asked, after passing Ditch Plains. For an absurd moment he thought she would tell him it was the lighthouse.

They came up behind a slow-moving oversized white Lexus SUV. Dan looked annoyed. As soon as they crested the hill, she hit the gas and passed, muttering something under her breath. Vanek glimpsed a strange, slightly plump woman driving, her face painted in bright white makeup and wearing oversized 'Jackie O' sunglasses. Next to her sat a saturnine, middle-aged man with a ponytail wearing what Vanek first took as a priest's raiment, except at the white square of the collar was some sort of odd glyph or symbol. Both stared at him as they drove past, as if he'd affronted them somehow.

The Mustang's V-8 rumbled, and the Ford shot forward like a thoroughbred breaking it out a bit. After cutting back into their own lane, Dan glanced over at Vanek.

"Afraid I'm going to kidnap you?" she asked.

"Hardly," he replied, flabbergasted. "I'm not worth that much."

To his shock she reached over and gave his kneecap a squeeze. "Maybe my plan is to tie you up in the basement and keep you as a sex slave."

Vanek was at a loss how to respond. He blinked and let out a nervous laugh.

"That would certainly be a first," he said, finally.

At the bottom of the hill before the final slow rise toward the lighthouse where the Deep Hollow Horse Ranch sat, Dan slowed and turned off onto a section of the Old Montauk Highway Vanek had no idea even existed.

"Highway" was something of a stretch. It was more of a rural beach road winding through endless walls of Scrub Pine, with occasional driveways and mailboxes appearing randomly along the way. The ocean waited just out of visibility, but Vanek could sense it to the south, like a siren's call.

Dan slowed down to a respectable clip with all the blind curves until eventually they ran out of road. An old, half-collapsed gate blocked their path, while to the south the road forked into two separate driveways.

Dan took the one on the left, which was blocked by a much more modern, re-enforced gate with a slim, card-reader post before it. Two 'Private: No trespassing' signs were affixed to the crossbars. Rolling down the window, Dan pulled out a keycard and slid it in. The smell of sea-air and sunbaked vegetation drifted in. After a pause, there came a hum and a click.

The gate swung inward.

Here the drive was recently maintained, the asphalt newer, and the vegetation trimmed back on both sides. After a hundred and fifty yards or so, the road opened to a series of drives where a cluster of pricier vacation homes were nestled discreetly among the hills.

It was a neighborhood Vanek hadn't seen before, or even guessed at. The world was so often like that, he realized: even the most seemingly familiar places had hidden sub layers and levels that were alien and eerily strange.

Not unlike the landscape of our own psyches, he thought.

As she turned up into the driveway of a large New England-style house with dark clapboard siding and a sweeping porch overlooking the ocean, he realized the yard must butt up against the westernmost border of Camp Hero.

Which brought with it a whole host of conflicting thoughts: the unresolved loose ends of his grandfather's disappearance, the true tangle of mysteries underlying whatever operations had been happening out here versus the more public conspiracy tales cooked up by fringe lunatics and pseudo-science theorists. It also occurred to him how, unconsciously, just how adroitly he'd avoided the very source of the mystery surrounding his grandfather's last mission. He'd been out to Montauk perhaps half a dozen times when Michelle was alive, but never once set foot in Camp Hero.

Maybe because he *didn't* want to find out—the mystery was much more appealing.

Or was it something else? He had a vague feeling of unease: of unpleasant truths shifting in their graves.

Waiting.

The house was large, but not ostentatious. A patchwork yard of sand and grass led past a tennis court to the top of the bluffs dropping away a hundred feet or so to the ocean. Several other houses shared the area, including a flat plot of hardscape with only a stonework chimney remaining, the outlines suggesting where a large mansion once stood.

"If this is a 'military house', I picked the wrong career," Vanek said as they stood inside the front door. The place had an open, upscale Hampton's flavor to it: dark hardwood floors, wainscoting, and a lofty ceiling with polished wood beams. A stone fireplace was at one end of the main room surrounded with overstuffed chairs and sofas. The furnishings and décor all suggested old-fashioned nautical, possibly from a pricey interior decorator with a taste for the New England Coast, but not in the last decade or so.

Dan walked in and dropped her purse on the couch. "Belonged to a retired officer who passed away last year. Beats one of their usual hotels, trust me."

Vanek nodded in grudging approval. If he had to be stuck some place that wasn't his house for the next few days, this might as well be it.

"You can have your pick of bedrooms upstairs, but I had the maid clean up the back one—thought you might like it as it's quieter. Let's get you situated and then I'll give you the ten-cent tour."

"Fine," Vanek replied, picking up his suitcase. *Figures. Quiet room for the old man, is it?* It occurred to him then that he hardly had any recollection of what he'd packed in it.

Whoever the naval officer had been, he clearly favored comfort over austerity. *Definitely overpaid*, Vanek thought, as he looked over the bedroom Dan had left him in. His suitcase, looking even more banged-up and out of place here, sat propped in the corner. The room was slightly narrow with odd angles to the ceiling but had plenty of windows and a curved porch overlooking a landscaped backyard and a full-sized in-ground swimming pool. It had a queen-size Georgia-pine bed with a mattress thick enough to make him wonder if he'd need a stair to clamber up into it. The matching yellow-pine furniture looked barely used—presumably this was a guest room. The room also had a private bathroom with an equally odd-angled ceiling. It somehow contrived to look modern and cozy at the same time. A framed ocean shore print reminiscent of Andrew Wyeth adorned one wall. There was a modern flat-screen TV on the dresser and a bookcase that had mostly hardcovers and a few coffee-table sized books. The hardcover titles included the complete set of Hornblower novels by C. S. Forester and Alexander Kent's "Richard Bolitho" series, along with a few dog-eared Melville novels. If nothing else, he'd have some good reading to occupy his visit.

Dan waited in the doorway while Vanek looked it over.

"A little old-fashioned, but comfortable," she said, one hand on her hip.

"Who else is here?" he asked.

"Just Arnaud and myself. I claimed the master bedroom in the front. He preferred the smaller downstairs side room with a study." She looked at her watch. "He ran into town to get some dinner and liquor for tonight. He seems to have this thing about hospitality and guests. Whatever the maid keeps stocking the fridge with just seems to piss him off. Particularly the wine and cheese. Come on. I'll show you the downstairs."

The dining area had been converted into an *ad hoc* operations room. Against one wall hung several bulletin boards covered with sea charts of the coastal region surrounding Montauk and Block Island, while past one end of the dining table was an oversized smartboard with notes scribbled all over it. The table was cluttered with stacks of reports—some yellowed with age—along with a couple of laptops. A brand-new HP printer-copier had been shoved into one corner. Based on the empty 'Monster' cans and coffee mugs, someone here was a serious caffeine junkie.

Picking up on his gaze, Dan chuckled.

"Navarre. You'll either love him or want to kill him. He hates everything American but secretly consumes everything here like a maniac. Soda. Chewing gum. Hot Pockets."

The rest of the place was pretty much as expected. The house had an open layout typical of large beachfront properties—an open kitchen worthy of Architectural Digest, a spacious den with a HD flat screen large enough (in

Vanek's eye) to rival a movie theater, and a back mudroom filled with assorted scuba and surfing equipment.

The front porch offered a panoramic view of the Atlantic Ocean. With its set of teak deck furniture and overstuffed cushions, Vanek figured it would be a prime spot to watch the sunrise from or kick one's feet up for an evening cocktail.

Dan led him back to the dining room.

"Need anything to drink? Coffee? Juice? Something stronger?"

"Water is fine."

He glanced over the other bulletin board, which to his surprise was covered with printouts of a mix of both strange (and some outright terrifying) deep-sea creatures with artwork of fantastic sea monsters, some quite photorealistic.

They reminded him of images he used during his old college teaching days. Particularly the course based on his book, 'Myths and Monsters: sea-faring legends in the age of sail'.

The kind of thing he scoffed at these days.

Toward the left were a bunch of glossy color photo prints tacked up from an underwater dive - all images of the sunken wreck of an old destroyer.

The U.S.S. Exeter.

Vanek cocked his head. For a split second he was filled with an inexplicable twinge of fear, as if the image evoked a recent bad dream.

"So that's it." His mouth felt dry.

"Navarre visited it during one of our dives yesterday. Just past an older shipwreck we think dates to the 18th century."

From all the archive information he had, this should be impossible. This was the ship his grandfather had died on. His *tomb*, most likely.

"What can you tell me?" he asked.

5. THE ONLY TIME YOU NEED TO BE AFRAID

"It's *fine*, honey. Trust me on this."

The speaker was Craig DeFranco, a middle-aged man who easily passed-off as the modest sailing type: tousled hair with crows' feet at the corner of his eyes, a trimmed beard with the first threads of gray in it, docksiders and a heavy-duty windbreaker.

The girl he was speaking to—his daughter Kellie—was a 13-year-old on that confusing cusp of womanhood. The jury was still out whether she might become a tomboyish, self-sufficient woman or one of those pretty girls hanging out at the Star Island Yacht Club, though her father was betting on the former.

Either way, unlike her brother, she didn't seem cut out for sailing. This was their second summer on the Ericson 25 he'd scrabbled enough together to purchase, and she was still terrified of the water. Whenever the boat heeled over while picking up speed, Kellie's hands would lock on whatever line she was holding for dear life. If the lower edge of the foresail started skimming the water, a tight moaning sound would issue between her clenched teeth.

Sounds like our dog, Patches, when that big mastiff shows up at the dog run, her Dad thought. He was determined to have her beat it, somehow.

Ronny, her brother, sat out on the foredeck, one hand on the rail, eyes squinted, and chin tilted up as if contemplating a particularly good moment. It was Ronny who'd come up with the new name for the boat: *Lost Horizon*.

Craig was proud of his son, proud of the fact he was able to get him out of the house and away from cell phones and video games to savor the taste of the world, or in this case, sailing.

It's about being alive, Craig thought, relishing the ocean breeze on his face. He nudged the tiller, adjusting their course just slightly and eased the backstay half an inch to get the overbend wrinkles out of the main sail. The wrinkles disappeared and the vast expanse of canvas above was once again perfectly smooth. Satisfied, he glanced about, reassuring himself that they were in the clear. The nearest boats were some fishermen anchored offshore and a lone tanker plodding its way along the horizon.

It was a quintessential late afternoon off Eastern Long Island, a light but steady wind coming up from the southwest with sunlight glimmering off the ocean. A perfect day for some light sailing. Mrs. DeFranco—Alice—would be back at their summer house prepping dinner. Increasingly, Craig had noted with some irritation, she seemed less interested in boating and more preoccupied with editing her blog on home decorating.

Mentally prepping herself for the day we're empty-nesters, he thought, though it also occurred to him they hadn't had sex in quite a while and there was something about that which bugged him.

His head jerked up as something heavy *thumped* against the hull, causing the whole boat to shudder.

"Daddy?" Kellie whimpered. From the bow, Ronny blinked and looked around, as if coming out of a reverie.

"No worries, Kel. Probably just driftwood." Craig glanced side to side, but nothing was visible in the slate blue-green water. They were just inside the Montauk Shoal. The forecast was excellent, but Craig preferred to keep them reasonably close to shore, knowing from experience how unpredictable the ocean could be. He always insisted all of them wear life jackets no matter what the conditions were.

Still, something bothered him, like a deep, ominous sound just out of earshot.

Kellie clutched the metal rail post like she was about to be tossed overboard.

"Kellie?"

His daughter looked over her shoulder at him. He put on his best fatherly expression.

"The only time you ever need to be afraid is if *I'm* afraid. And just so you know, I—"

His words were cut off as the hull struck something again, hard enough to force the boat to slew sideways. From the forward pulpit, Ronny glanced back at his dad.

"Anything?" Craig shouted. The first seeds of doubt crept into his thoughts.

That felt... *deliberate.*

Ronny craned over the rail, looking backward along the hull.

Strangely, the surrounding water was *darkening...*

Wham!

This time the Ericson tilted sideways, the telltale sound of water rushing in below. Kellie screamed as the deck canted alarmingly, waves rising over the lee rail.

"Ronny, hold tight!" Craig shouted, grabbing the stern rail and jamming his foot up on the traveler. He narrowly missed getting his head clipped by the boom as it slackened back at him from the boat's momentum, then snapped to port again as the boat tilted further.

Craig couldn't process what was happening—it didn't make any sense—and could only think to reach out to grab his daughter as the yacht went over and began to sink.

The main and fore sails should have acted like a brake, but whatever was below struck them so powerfully that the boat completely rolled. Craig and his daughter found themselves catapulted overboard while up front, Ronny became tangled in the bow, screaming.

Kellie's own screams were cut short as she plunged in face-first, her mouth filling with seawater. For a moment her entire world was eclipsed by the shock of cold water and chaos of seething bubbles. Then the buoyancy of the lifejacket won out, and she popped upright to the surface.

She took in several things at once; the capsized, damaged hull of their sailboat, surrounded by debris and lines trailing in the water, her father several yards away, blood streaming down from a gash in his scalp, the frantic splashing from her brother, who was still entangled in the rail of the bow pulpit.

What's happening!? she wondered, filled with dread. The water seemed to be vibrating.

Something surfaced just beyond her dad, an amorphous blue-black shape that suggested a bloated dolphin corpse. Kellie tried to cry out but erupted a mouthful of seawater instead. As the realization of her condition set in—she was floating in the ocean—a cascade of terrible images crossed her mind: swimming in the ocean five years previous off Cape Cod and finding herself surrounded by jellyfish. At first, she didn't understand what they were, until one brushed over her arm, making her skin feel like it had been lathered in molten fire.

She'd run screaming out of the water, convinced she would die. She'd read somewhere about a jellyfish that could kill a human with its venom, stopping one's heart cold. That these were a completely different species (and considerably smaller) was lost on her 8-year-old mind. The overwhelming pain broadcasting from her arm overrode all rational thought.

It had taken a good twenty minutes for her dad to calm her down, caking her arm with damp sand and distracting her by running his hand across her brow. Since that day, any attempt to get her into the ocean had been met with hysterics.

Now here she was. And her father was in a bad way.

She looked back and forth between her brother and father, unsure what to do next. She focused on the blob which even as she gazed, was *changing*.

Even worse, more of them were surfacing.

"*Daddy*?" she whimpered.

Her father groaned in response, eyelids fluttering.

"What should I do, Daddy?" Ronny's struggles were growing weaker. Part of her knew she should go help her brother first, but she was crippled with fear and indecision.

Jellyfish! her mind shrieked.

Because now there were more of them…

Behind her father, a seam rippled and opened along the blue-black blob, revealing a bloody maw rimmed with teeth... and tentacles, translucent and worm-like. They writhed out and latched onto her dad.

"Daddy!" Kellie cried, her feet kicking into action of their own accord.

Craig DeFranco moaned again as the things engulfed him, sinking into (and under) his flesh—tearing. Over by the bow of the boat, Ronny's hands slapped at the water as one of the things engulfed him as well, accompanied by an odd *scissoring* sound which Kellie realized was the sound of his flesh being sliced.

Behind her the boat began to shake, more bubbles escaping from below as something incredibly massive seized and pulled at it. What looked like black eels broke the surface nearby, eels with odd growths and bleeding tumors. Several moving quickly toward her.

Before she passed out, Kellie saw her father's face torn open, his mouth gaping in a rictus of agony... then blackness.

Below, in the twilight murk of the ocean, the amorphous thing—roughly the size of a giant squid—seethed and undulated. To any passing underwater life (which were conspicuously absent in the area) it would have presented a confusing, difficult to comprehend entity. At moments it appeared to be one thing, like a hideously proportioned squid with a rash of tentacles writhing through the water, yet just as rapidly it became something else, such as a giant multi-headed shark. The one consistency was the darkness near its core, and the battery of iridescent silver-blue orbs that might be eyes.

Nothing could withstand the alien malignancy of those orbs—to gaze directly at them for any length of time meant insanity and terror; disintegration of coherent processes, even for simpler life forms.

It was a thing not of this world, though it had existed here for nearly three centuries, drawn to the surface initially by the first terror-ridden sailors braving the unknown.

Those early feedings had been simple and limited, just enough to sustain it through its lengthy dormant cycles.

Soon, however, more men came. Their fears and terrors even more varied.

The approaching burr of twin diesels drew its attention. Its senses picked up not only the static composition of the hull, but the living form aboard it. Something about it was off, its fear muted.

Curious, the creature withdrew to observe.

Kellie came to as she was pulled up, coughing and sputtering out of the water.

She couldn't make sense of the powerful hands and forearms of thickly corded muscle in her vision as she was roughly hauled atop a gunwale and into the stern of a fishing trawler.

A shadow blotted out the sun, and she found herself looking up at a bold-featured man with gray-blue eyes. She found the intensity of the face mesmerizing; it was as if every contour had been chiseled out of rock, even the eyes, though they were somehow both hard *and* kind. His gray hair was thick and wiry, suggesting something you could scrub your pans clean with.

"Miss? Are you okay?" he asked in a clipped, Slovakian accent. He noted her lips were blue and her skin deathly white.

For a moment, all she could do was stare at him, shivering. He ran and retrieved a blanket from the cabin and wrapped her in it.

Her face crumpled. "Daddy."

"Daddy?" he replied. "There's no one here. I just happened to spot you floating in the ocean. The sun is going down - you're very lucky!"

"Ronny—my brother too! I think it ate him."

"*Ate* him? Was there an accident? You were in a boat, yes?"

"I don't know what happened... my *daddy*!" she said, sobbing. She began to shake uncontrollably, like she was having a convulsion.

The man, a veteran Polish sailor named Les Gorecki, was no stranger to disasters and survivors at sea—he'd survived five shipwrecks in his 54 years on Earth, including one that left him stranded at sea for two weeks with a dead crewman. He'd ended up purchasing a charter fishing boat at Montauk for the sport fishing opportunities but in recent years the surge of tourists overwhelming Montauk were more interested in parties, selfies and surfing. This past year alone his charter business had received dozens of one-star reviews attacking what he did as environmentally wrong. He didn't mind the criticism, but what bugged him was the self-righteous tone of the comments. From what he heard, probably written on iPhones by the same company creating toxic wastelands in China.

The problem here was there wasn't a boat, just an unconscious girl adrift in the ocean.

"Hold on," he said, wrapping the blanket around her tighter. Whatever the situation, he knew he had to get her to a hospital soon. She was rapidly losing her color. He clambered up the ladder into the pilot house and flicked on the sonar at the communications console. It was an older SeaQuest model and took a moment to warm up, but in a few seconds the display lit up, revealing the ocean below in varying shades of green.

There it was, a sailing boat thirty yards off the port bow and hovering upside down twenty feet below the surface.

Something else was down there as well, but the sonar wasn't processing it correctly. An amorphous shape that suggested... *what?* Gorecki's brow furrowed, and he smacked the side of the sonar unit.

It was a nebulous shape that altered its contours as he looked at it, like a school of fish mimicking a whale, then a squid, then maybe a giant cloud of writhing eels.

Gorecki didn't like it. Didn't like it at all.

Next to the sonar unit was a pad of paper fixed to the desk and a pencil on a string. He jotted down the coordinates and picked up the handset of the VHF shortwave. He set the channel to 16—the Coast Guard.

"Mayday, mayday, mayday," he said, "Over."

"Roger," came the response. "This is Montauk Coast Guard. What's your emergency?"

"This is Les Gorecki, Captain, 'Catch-22' out of Montauk. Latitude 41.0203° North, 71.7092° West. I have a submerged yacht off the port bow, unidentified, one known survivor, two missing. Require assistance. Over."

"Say again your position?" The radio let out a squawk.

Gorecki repeated the coordinates.

"Can you hold your position? Sea Rescue is on another call. We can get Marine Two out there, ASAP. Copy that?" Marine Two was the East Hampton Marine Patrol's new patrol boat, also kept at the Coast Guard facilities.

Gorecki shook his head. That meant the nearest helicopter, from Suffolk County Police, was tied up. Waiting for the Marine Patrol's new launch—fast as it was - would waste time. Plus, he had a hinky feeling about this situation, a distinct sense of dread and unease alien to his unflappable personality.

A squid? A school of fish?

"Roger. Sorry, can't wait. Passenger requires immediate medical assistance. I'm heading into port. Submerged yacht isn't going anywhere. No sign of other survivors. Over."

This was highly irregular, and Gorecki knew it, but his instincts were telling him to hightail it back to the harbor.

There was a pause on the other end. Fortunately, the dispatcher was on top of her job and filled in the blanks, "Roger, Marine Two will meet you on the way. Medical team will meet you in the harbor."

"Roger."

Gorecki hustled back down to the deck and carried Kellie into the main cabin, then returned to the bridge and rammed the throttles forward. The trawler surged as the twin diesels engaged, sending up blue smoke as the sea at the stern seethed and churned.

Catch-22 swung northward at full power.

Behind it, several shapes broke the surface, obscene-looking things with gaping wounds and tiny mouths that tasted the air.

6. NEW FRIENDS

"Here he is," Dan said.

They were sitting on the front porch when a green Outback appeared on the road and skidded to a stop in the driveway. The door popped open and a tall, powerfully built man with close-cropped hair and wrap-around Ray-Bans eased out of it. He had on a black windbreaker, cargo shorts and sandals. The way he jangled the keys in his hand and raised his chin toward the ocean spoke of a soldier's confidence with a dose of impatience.

Even at a distance, he was every bit impressive as Vanek guessed.

Dan was reluctant to discuss any details of the *Exeter* wreck—that area was Navarre's—and instead played him the strange underwater audio signals picked up by the NOAA Hydrophone, along with increasingly odd activity by a pod of killer whales she'd been tracking for months. The sounds were oddly disturbing to Vanek's ears. Like a writhing metallic sound in an echo chamber.

Inexplicably, it made him think of agitated insects slicing flesh across a chalkboard. After a minute he asked her to stop.

Vanek was more interested in details on the *Exeter* dive but didn't press her. She was less evasive about the artwork.

"Gavin put those up as a joke. He said you had a thing about sea monsters," she told him.

Vanek frowned. It was a reference to a book of sea stories he had written years back during his professor years. Was Gavin that cock-sure he would be out here?

When she wouldn't elaborate, he busied himself going through the reports Gavin had left with him earlier. The references to the '*Neptune's Reckoning*' project only raised more questions than they answered.

The papers outlined a top-secret technology which included instructions on the use of experimental equipment and wire-mesh hull surfacing that the U.S.S. Exeter had been outfitted with over the previous five months, an anti-submarine technology aimed specifically at drastically changing the course of the war in the North Atlantic.

A technology developed by a Hungarian by the name of Anton Kovac.

According to the short bio, Kovac, one of the pioneering scientists in electromagnetism and acoustic weaponry, had been successfully smuggled out of the Nazi weapons program by partisans a year earlier in one of the more daring operations of the war. Kovac had been brought in specifically because of his advances in the application of low-frequency sounds for potentially lethal military purposes.

Specially, using sound to inflict fear, panic and at concentrated levels, induce death.

Lieutenant John Vanek—Will's grandfather—had been brought in from Naval Intelligence partly due to his engineering background, but also because he spoke fluent Hungarian. Vanek knew his grandfather had been on the team cracking the Enigma Code—the German's top-secret encoding computer. Those records were now in the public domain.

But how that program was linked to the installation at Camp Hero was a mystery. There were several reports on the shakedown cruise of DD-505—the U.S.S. Exeter—to try out the technology as a new anti-submarine technology but those didn't add up either, unless, as Vanek had begun to suspect, they were misinformation.

Maybe what the Exeter's crew were told they were testing out was something else altogether.

The photo Vanek found back at the house and the notes offered tantalizing clues as to what that might be.

Gavin had handed him a teaser.

They'd had about twenty minutes of enjoying the sunset view of the Atlantic when Arnaud Navarre arrived.

The Frenchman sauntered up the steps with a large bag that clinked. Taking off his glasses, he grinned. Up close Vanek could see he had a distinct Mediterranean look—a swarthy complexion and hook nose, along with a deprecating smile and small, almond-shaped eyes. With a classic knit 'watch cap' and razor stubble he might have just stepped off the *Calypso* as one of Jacques Cousteau's crew. He had a smooth power about him that made Vanek think of a leopard.

"You must be William Vanek," he said, offering his hand. Vanek stood up and clasped it. It was calloused, warm and dry. He exuded the no-nonsense air of an ex-military who'd seen his share of scrapes, which made Vanek both like and dislike him. The former for the way he inspired confidence, the latter because it also underscored Vanek's own lack of assertive masculinity these days. He'd had it, once. But that seemed like another lifetime. Another person.

Before what happened to his Michelle. And his father.

"Arnaud Navarre," Navarre added, bringing Vanek back in the moment. His accent was distinctly French.

Dan stood as well, giving Navarre the classic 'double air kiss'.

Navarre nodded and held up the bag, "I found a passable Single Malt, if you're interested. Along with some proper French wine. But the bread... *Je suis désolé.*" he ended the statement with a shudder and a sad shake of the head.

"Arnaud has an issue with the local wines," Dan explained.

"*Ah...* grape juice. Good for punishing your cooking," Navarre offered, though it had the tone of a good-natured joke. Vanek wondered if there was something going on between the two. *Not my problem,* he thought.

"Come, let's have a drink! Then... then we talk business," Navarre said. "You like our little seaside cottage, yes?" he asked Vanek as he led them inside.

"Not bad for a Navy shack," Vanek admitted.

Navarre laughed, "Yes, nice *'shack'*."

Clapping Vanek on the shoulder, he led them into the kitchen where he unloaded the bags on the counter.

Vanek still wasn't quite sure how he fit into the picture, even after Dan's brief update, or fully understood what that picture was.

Any attempts to broach the subject were brushed aside.

"First!" Navarre held up the scotch to make his point. "Then we can talk business." He plucked a couple of fresh glasses from the cupboard and filling them halfway with a 16-year-old Aberlour, handed one to Vanek. The other he offered to Dan.

"No thanks, I'll stick to beer for now," she replied, holding up her bottle. Navarre gave an amused shrug, then clicked both their drinks.

"*À ta santé*," he said.

"*À la tienne*," Vanek replied right back. The scotch was a mellow fire spreading down his throat.

"*Salut!*" Dan added.

"*Ahhh*!" Navarre said, with obvious relish.

Dan leaned against the island with the beer in her hand like a microphone. "We can't get anything done around here without a glass of wine and some dish riddled with *Herbes de Provence* materializing."

Navarre snorted as he pulled out a baguette, some olive oil and truffle-infused cheese and laid them out on the counter reverently. "Ha! *Herbes de Provence*? That's just some overpriced dried weeds we sell to you Americans so you can feel cultured!" He picked one of the larger knives from the cutlery stand and pulling a hefty cutting board from the lower cabinet, went to work with relish.

"So speaks *Monsieur* 'Hot Pockets'," she shot back. "Face it, Frenchie, you're an overinflated phony!"

He waved the knife in her direction, a brow raised, "Careful! This *fone-ee* is dangerously armed!"

Navarre carried everything into the dining room and cleared a section on the table. Picking up a slice of bread with cheese, he walked over to the giant wall map. It was an enlargement of a NOAA Coastal Survey Chart of Long Island and the area south past the Continental Shelf, marked with depth readings in fathoms and call outs for underwater hazards, restricted areas and shipping lanes. Various numbered notes and photos had been pinned to it. To the right was a dry erase board with numbered lists correlating to the pins along with scribbled notations, many with question marks after them.

Vanek and Dan joined him.

For a moment, Navarre said nothing. He sipped his scotch, chewed bread and studied the wall map.

"I was able to triangulate the sound captured from the Hydrophones," Dan said. "They also lead us to the wreck site."

"It suggests something is still active on the ship," Navarre added.

"The NOAA and the Coast Guard didn't find it this entire time?" Vanek asked, sarcasm edging his voice.

Navarre tapped his head with a finger, "Very odd, no? One can see how the outcroppings at the top of the canyon might mask the contour of the wreck. Still, Navy divers were down there at some point setting up the restricted perimeter. It would have been impossible not to have seen the wreck. Yet it was never reported. Not even leaked out. Difficult not to conjure up all kinds of conspiracy theories...

someone in your government, people like Gavin—or those behind him—do not want the Coast Guard or even NOAA to know what is on that ship."

"What do you know for sure?" Vanek asked.

Navarre nodded toward the map, "Only that something quite bizarre has been going on right under the public noses. The last major marine disaster in the area was Labor Day of 1951," he continued, tapping a spot just over a mile north of the lighthouse, "When the fishing boat *Pelican* capsized off Montauk Point. Around the Endeavor Shoals. Only 19 of the 64 people on-board survived."

Vanek rubbed his chin. "I know about the *Pelican*. The boat was dangerously overloaded, and the captain didn't think to have the passengers distributed properly. Squall came up with fifteen-foot waves... ship rolled, people went in. The Coast Guard rewrote a lot of regulations after the hearing. Especially on so-called 'party boats'." The thought of it, and his own brush with death at sea, made him shudder. He'd heard that when they'd opened up the cabin of the *Pelican* where many of the doomed passengers became trapped, they'd been jammed together like wrestlers trying to frantically escape. Some had hair ripped out. One man had another's torn ear clutched in his fist.

Navarre continued. "Since then, unless you believe in kooky books about secret time-travel experiments and alien abductions, nothing much exciting happens here. Heart attacks and the occasional drunk ramming other boats are pretty much it, aside from the occasional drowning. The rip tides are tricky. But the last headline event the harbor master recalled here was the search for John Kennedy Jr's plane back in '98. Until now. A missing ship from WWII turns up, a bunch of people die, and your friend Gavin hires me to retrieve some old technology from it. Something is strange out here at Montauk."

"You mean, other than surfers and Jersey tourists?" Vanek offered, then added, "Never mind. I thought the job here was simply to get the core of this '*Neptune's Reckoning*' technology off the ship, document it and call it a day."

Navarre tapped the photo of the *Exeter* thoughtfully. "Yes. *Simply* that."

"So, the two of you dove on the wreck... yesterday?" he asked.

"Correct," Navarre replied. "Two short dives. I wanted to get a sense of what's down there. It's a restricted area due to unexploded ordinance, so we have to be very careful. No touching or searching debris on the ocean bottom. The destroyer will have plenty of live munitions. Also, we discovered the remains of a sailing ship I have reason to believe is the *HMS Tryton*, reported lost in the area around the time of the American Revolution. I would love to get a proper salvage team involved once I can get the permits."

Vanek thought about it. "If it *is* the *Tryton*, maybe. But the *Exeter* would be considered a war grave. I still don't understand—what is the Navy hiding out there?"

"We were hoping you could shed some light on that," Navarre said.

Vanek was about to blurt out an answer but checked himself: *of course. The Neptune's Reckoning cloaking technology. But was it still active? What could it possibly do, especially after seventy-six years? It didn't make a lick of sense.*

Vanek took a sip of his scotch, "Not just yet. Did you discover anything else unusual down there?"

"No," Dan said. But that wasn't completely true. At one point in the dive she swore she saw something in the gloom along the deeper side of the destroyer wreck that resembled a giant Bobbit worm. She'd always found the things repulsive, with their multiple toothed pincers, rippling mouths and five undulating feelers resembling something straight out of a nightmare alien movie. Whales and dolphins struck her as beautiful—streamlined evolutions of nature. The predator Bobbit worms, hiding in the sand and growing up to ten feet long, waiting to snatch its prey and yank it into its equally nightmare burrow made her want to scream.

She wrote it off as a hallucination, of course. A side-effect of narcosis. Bobbit worms were large, yes, but what she saw suggested something a hundred feet long—not ten—which was absurd. Unless it was the custom wetsuit hoods the ONR required them to wear while out at the site—Gavin insisted they neutralized any vibrations from the destroyer's experimental equipment.

She suppressed a shudder and took a sip of her beer.

Navarre shrugged. He thought about his own disturbing moment, when he thought he saw a giant cloud of sea spiders racing toward him. He was horrified of the damn things ever since, as a kid on his first underwater swim in the Mediterranean, he came up out of the water with a cluster of giant ones clinging to his shoulder. At first, he thought it was just seaweed. Then they started squirming.

What he'd seen yesterday was impossible, though. The commando side of him had kicked in, forcing it out of his mind. Still, it unsettled him.

Vanek sensed some of this, but let it pass.

"So how can I be of any use?"

Navarre indicated a pile of documents that included printouts of the ship's deck plans. "Go through those. Dan and I already have, but you may have some insights about this device and how it worked."

"It can't be *that* complicated. It was 1943. You can't just go in there and take it out?"

Navarre's face took on an odd expression. "It may not prove that easy. Gavin doesn't think so. In fact, he seems quite nervous about it. I'm hoping you can tell me why."

7. LIKE A SUSPENDED GHOST

An hour and a half earlier, Rob Vincent stood on the stern deck of Marine 2, also known as the *John L. Behan*, checking his dive gauge. Fifty feet below him, now resting on the sandy bottom, was the DeFranco's Ericson 25. According to the vivid, amber-hued image on Marine 2's new side-scan sonar, the ship was resting upright. Sails intact. This far out from the shore was Coast Guard jurisdiction, but the new *Silver Shi*p patrol boat had been gassed up and ready to go and with a top speed of 30 knots, could respond faster than any other emergency response vessel in the area.

Vincent was one of the Marine Patrol's more experienced divers and after being hauled off his shift—all of the department's eight divers were also regular patrol officers—had been dispatched along with Vern Jacoby and Gabe Duvall to search for survivors and assess the state of the wreck.

Gabe was piloting the launch while Jacoby sat nearby checking his own dive equipment, including a new underwater Ultra HD camera the department had recently acquired.

A slight-but-muscular man with black hair, piercing eyes and a mustache his wife was on his case the past five years to shave, Vincent wasn't perturbed about this dive, though he was thorough. The weather was still calm and the tides normal. He expected to be in and out in fifteen minutes, enough time to check for the bodies of the father and son and give an assessment of the state of the boat. Sea Tow should be arriving within half an hour with their salvage crew to re-float the yacht and get it back to the harbor.

With any luck, he could be cleaned up and sitting on his back porch with a cool beer by seven.

Unpleasant business, he thought to himself, thinking about his own two sons. After pausing to transfer two EMTs to Les Gorecki's trawler, which they'd intercepted *en route* just past the point, they'd high-tailed it to the GPS co-ordinates where the girl had been picked up. Due to drift, it had taken the better part of fifteen minutes to locate the boat.

There was no trace of any survivors.

By that point it was clear to everyone this was now going to be a recovery, not a rescue mission. Suffolk County was sending one of its search-and-rescue choppers as a protocol, but Vincent figured that had a snowball's chance in hell of finding the father and son alive.

Sure, last year they found a kayaker off Connecticut who'd survived seventeen hours in the water, but Vincent doubted that would be the case here. Accounting for the location of the girl, the boat, and the current, they should have located them by now.

"Ready?"

Jacoby was right behind him, suited up and ready to go. His rectangular features and charismatic grin made Vincent think of a young Denzel Washington.

"I was born ready, pal," Vincent replied. "Last one back buys the first round."

The spectral rays of the early evening sunlight gave the wreck an even eerier appearance, like a vessel caught in an otherworldly transition. The effect was enhanced by the full sails lightly rippling in the currents, as if even resting on the bottom the yacht was still attempting to make headway.

Vincent, typically a pragmatic officer to the point of dullness, was spooked.

As they played their underwater flashlight beams across the hull, the extent of the damage was obvious. The bottom half of the hull was smashed-in, yet also partially *dissolved.* That didn't tally with anything in his experience. Vincent had seen all sorts of hull damage over the years—usually of the 'drunken boater ramming a fishing boat' variety—and even one yahoo once who had crashed his speedboat into a submerged rock shoal off the point, succeeding in shearing off both legs at the knee.

But nothing ever like this.

Just what the hell happened out here?

He felt a tap on his shoulder and jerked involuntarily.

It was Jacoby, signaling he would swim around the other side and complete his filming of the boat. Vincent gave him the 'OK' sign and indicated he was going in for a closer look himself. He realized, despite the cooler temperature at this depth, he was sweating inside his wetsuit. The regulator felt stale and gummy in his mouth.

Christ, why am I so damned jumpy?

He checked the time on his dive gauge and saw that he'd only been down here five minutes.

Kicking his fins, he forced his breathing back into a regular rhythm and headed toward the largest impact, which was just aft of the bow.

This wasn't no goddamned whale, he thought. *Hell, not even Jaws.*

The fiberglass was smashed inward, leaving a ragged hole roughly two feet across by a foot or so high. The hull was punched clean through past the inner lining, leaving ragged tufts of fiberglass along the edges. He could just make out what must be the back of the forward berth. Part of a torn cushion was visible, and even more disturbing, a reddish substance leaked out in the current.

Blood?

That didn't seem possible. According to the report, all three boaters were out in the water.

Was it possible there was a fourth person trapped in the boat?

Of course, it was possible.

Aside from a few slim brown cunners darting here and there, with a few Sea Ravens feeding along the bottom, the area seemed devoid of much sea life. Still, he couldn't shake the feeling of something *off.*

An odd, dense feeling of dread that raised his heart rate.

What was it? The damaged hull made him think of *Jaws...* the largest opening was sickle-shaped, like a Great White's mouth.

Adjusting his weight belt, he approached the hole carefully, probing the beam through it. The light seemed to lose strength inside the hull, as if the shadows inside absorbed it.

There seemed to be a kind of movement within.

Near his flipper he spotted a large Sea Raven working its way along the sand, noting its squat, Scorpion Fishlike appearance: the bulbous eyes, excessively broad mouth. This one had purplish red markings with yellow stripes, making him think of an infected muscle. He'd always hated the things.

Something gently brushed the side of his mask and he snapped his head to the right, a flurry of bubbles escaping from his release valve.

His mouth muffled by the regulator, he screamed.

It was the head and partial torso of a young boy—just about his eldest son Derek's age—that had drifted out of the opening like flotsam. The eyes were wide open and filmed over from being submerged, and the mouth was stretched in a rictus of a scream. From the trailing streamers of flesh and protruding bones, it was as if something massive (JAWS!) had bitten off the rest of him, yet even that didn't seem to add up: the lower part also seemed blackened, shriveled.

The arm—torn off just above the elbow—was what had bumped into him. It drifted away to the right, even as another movement from within caught his eye. From the shadows inside the hull came a faint, bioluminescent glow, with the suggestion of undulating, writhing forms like coiled tentacles or heels lurking there.

For perhaps the first time in his entire life, Vincent was completely terrified. Yet he was seized by compelling curiosity. Like the first time he'd visited the George Washington Bridge as a teenager and looking down from the waist-high rail to the three-hundred-foot drop below, felt a powerful impulse to keep leaning until he tumbled over.

A strange mix of both lassitude and terror that bade his bowels feel loose and squishy.

Get away! Now! his instincts screamed.

And yet... what was that? So strange and alien!

He leaned toward the opening, the underwater light beam revealing something glistening and repulsive uncoiling within... and saw too late that what he originally mistook for ragged tufts of fiberglass lining the opening were in fact a flesh-like substance concealing rows and rows of gleaming teeth.

He had time to think briefly of his mid-century ranch over in Hither Hills that morning, his two sons standing on the side deck with Gloria, his wife, behind them, and in that split second was consumed by the terror that he would never see them again.

The yacht lurched toward him and the opening snapped shut momentarily, cutting off the next scream before it escaped his mouth, along with his head.

Jacoby was roughly five yards off the port side of the yacht making a slow pan of the damage with his camera when he felt a current surge through the water, a vibration that filled his head with terrible images. For a bizarre moment the yacht's sails rippled and billowed as if filled with air and trying to sail off. Instead the ship suddenly rolled away from him, skidding along the sandy bottom. Clouds of sand erupted in the water... and from the opposite rail on the ship, a darker cloud.

One that Jacoby thought looked suspiciously like blood.

Oh no!

He released the camera to its tether and pumping his fins, started swimming as fast as he could.

Even before he came around the stern of the boat, he saw that it would be bad.

"Jesus fuck!" Gabe Duvall said as he helped Jacoby up onto the deck. "What happened down there!?"

Jacoby had surfaced minutes before with Vincent's head in his hand, the body having already surfaced by itself. Thinking quickly, Jacoby had released the weights on Vincent's body and forced the regulator past the ragged neck stump into the wetsuit to fill it with air. Before surfacing he'd swum over to the side of the boat to make sense of what had happened. Best as he could tell from the shreds of flesh and the jagged metal cross beam along the top of the largest opening, Vincent must have had his head inside the hull just as it rolled. A freakish accident, but the only one he could formulate for the moment.

Vincent was a close friend—close enough they frequently shared family cookouts and fishing charters out of the harbor—but fifty-feet underwater was no place to let emotions derail one's training. He shot some quick footage of the opening for the report then headed for the surface.

"Fuck if I know," Jacoby replied, setting the gruesome remains on the deck. He had a strong urge to vomit his guts out and start crying but fought it down. Gabe had only been on the force a couple of years and it wouldn't do him good to see a veteran officer losing it.

He pointed to Vincent's decapitated head. "I'll put that in the cooler. Right now, you call Ed Michels and tell him we have a fatality."

"What's the code for that?" Gabe said, staring in horror at Vincent's head.

"I don't think we have one for this situation."

8. ANOTHER STRANGE ACCIDENT

"I'm not quite sure how much help I can be," Vanek said, hedging around the truth. "There's nothing in the papers here to specifically explain what this 'The Anti-Magnetic Field Oscillation System' they were testing did, or how it actually worked."

Navarre set his drink down and leaned against the table, crossing his arms. Once again Vanek was aware of the strength and vitality the man radiated. Dan too, in her own way.

Both of them exist in the real world. I live in a box with a bunch of moldering books, for Christ Sakes!

To his surprise, Navarre snorted dismissively.

"*Bullshit.* Gavin said you've been researching this for years. Whatever it was, this technology had deadly consequences for the crew of the *Exeter* and is still giving off something that has the ONR spooked. It cannot be electro-magnetic. Not after seventy-six years underwater."

Vanek wasn't sure how to respond. "My research hasn't turned up as much as you seem to think. That's why I'm here. For answers. But to answer your question: no, it can't be anything electrical. And I'm beginning to question this whole narrative that a U-Boat sunk the destroyer."

Navarre grunted. "No. I don't believe that's what sunk the *Exeter*. What I glimpsed of the wreck suggested something much, much different."

"*Like what*?" Vanek was annoyed at what he saw as a bunch of mumbo-jumbo.

"Something very peculiar has been happening at the site of these wrecks, over time, though hell if I can make any sense of it. It reminds me of a dive in the Mediterranean—"

He was interrupted by the stomp of footsteps on the front porch, followed by someone hammering on the front door.

Navarre went to open it, his stride economical but quick.

Vanek and Dan exchanged glances as he returned.

The stocky, gray-haired man with him was flushed as if he'd just run a race. Dressed in a sailing jacket and worn-out jeans, Vanek immediately pegged him for a fisherman.

"You must come with me *now*, Arnaud" the man was saying to Navarre, in a thick Eastern European accent. "There's been another accident!"

"Les! What? What has happened?" Navarre asked, his hand on the man's shoulders.

"I rescued a girl this afternoon—she was adrift in the ocean. Apparently from on a yacht that sank. But it was strange—a 25-foot sailing boat capsized and sank for no reason! And one of the police divers was killed trying to search it."

"Where?" Vanek asked.

The man stared back at him with hard-yet-kind gray eyes. Without hesitation he marched over to the wall map and stuck his finger at a point twenty miles southeast of Montauk Point.

"Right there! Ten miles from yesterday's dive site! My sonar showed the boat floating upside down twenty feet below the surface! There was something down there with it—something, I don't know—something very odd! Now a diver is dead. His head cut off, I heard."

Navarre looked at the map, the pattern of post-it notes tagged on it. "That is not good, not good at all."

9. THE ING-THING

"So *that's* the 'Ing-thing,' huh? Most hot, dude. Most hot indeed!"

Jimmy Reed nodded, leaning back and taking a sip of his beer. He was sitting with Brad Hodgekiss at one of the outdoor tables at Gossman's Dock, right near the entrance to Montauk Harbor. The same Brad Hodgekiss he'd had the misfortune to fill in for on Scarpia's boat a few days previous. Hodgekiss, one of those tawny-haired, all-American high-school jocks whose life had transitioned from all-star senior to barstool flunky in the space of a season was still decent enough company when he was sober, or at least not high.

Unfortunately, those days were becoming increasingly rare.

Tonight was an exception.

Reed had graduated two years ahead of Hodgekiss in the increasingly improbable era of *ten years ago*. The two had hooked up through a series of local jobs and the fate that snagged so many young people once out of the contained world of the school system: hobbled by an underlying inability to face what life might really have in store for them.

The 'Ing-thing' in question was a twenty-two-year-old student from Malmö, Sweden, who'd picked up a summer gig as a waitress at Gossman's. Slim, tawny-haired and possessing sharp features matched with an equally sharp wit, she'd made it overtly clear she was interested in Reed the first time she'd laid eyes on him, sipping a beer at the back bar where customers usually killed time waiting for their tables to be readied.

Reed wasn't there for dinner—Gossman's Restaurant was a little out of his current meager dining funds—and had been nursing the beer for the better part of twenty minutes waiting for a yacht owner from the Jersey Shore who was looking to score some weed. The guy never showed up, but the evening wasn't a total loss.

Reed had ended up getting acquainted with Inge Eklund.

Three weeks and more than a dozen passionate evenings later, he still couldn't quite figure her out. Most of those late-night love-making sessions had been at his one-room apartment on Navy Road over on Fort Pond Bay; a run-down place with 1960's pinewood paneling that was either charmingly rustic or hopelessly outdated, depending on one's viewpoint.

Inge didn't seem to care either way.

Her straightforward and uninhibited approach threw him. Their first night together he thought he was putting on the charm at maybe fifty percent—just to warm her up a little—and instead found himself going hot and heavy in his pickup parked over at Navy Beach Pier, while the sun set on the Long Island Sound. When he'd asked her if she wanted to head back to his place her response had been to stick her tongue in his ear and murmur: "I think yes!"

Like many angles of his life, he kept their relationship under close wraps.

Tonight, however, when Brad had rung him up to talk over 'something else', he decided to share the news, if only to get his mind off other matters.

Reed was a popular guy in the area, more so in the summer, but there was still that invisible demarcation line between *locals* and *visitors*, though the latter were less often aware of it. A bunch of surfers might frequent the area enough year after year to think of themselves as local, familiar enough with guys like Reed to clap him on the shoulder and call him by first name and drop seven figures on houses that cost a fraction of that decades ago, but they were always going to be *visitors*, no matter what they thought of themselves. Unless your Dad came home with his hands reeking of fish, sweated out the mortgage year after year and had your ass bussed over to East Hampton High School where you looked like a blue-collar hayseed compared to privileged ranks there, you were a *visitor*.

Of course, the times were changing, for those smart enough and forward-thinking, at least.

One of his high-school friends, Lou Conners, had been harped on as a loser for living with his father in an unremarkable split-level ranch off Flamingo Avenue ever since graduation. Lou had made a career specializing in odd dead-end jobs. When Old Man Conners had kicked off the previous year from a heart attack, he'd added pot harvesting to his resume.

When Reed crossed paths with Lou again recently at *The Point* he found out the house had just sold for a cool 1.4 million. By total fluke too—Lou had run off to Patchogue for building supplies and accidentally left his cell at home, causing the prospective buyers to get into a frantic bidding war when he didn't return their calls right away.

Lou Conners, a guy who struggled with basic division and flunked English, was a fucking millionaire!? While I'm struggling for rent in this dump?

It made Reed want to smack his head against the wall repeatedly.

For the moment however, all that simmered in the background. It was a beautiful evening in Montauk, he was having his third beer (the last two comped by Inge), he was hanging out with a bud and the prospects between the sheets later were looking good.

Only one thing was really troubling him.

Scarpia.

Two, counting the burn on the back of his hand and the implications that went with it.

Over the years, Jimmy Reed had solidified himself as a solid, no-nonsense kind of guy who, while a little rough and tumble, played fair and didn't take shit from anybody.

Until the other day.

The truth was, the incident with Scarpia out at his boat had rattled his self-image and self-confidence more than he cared to admit. Arguably, Brad Hodgekiss was to blame. Sure, missing the gig and handing it over to Reed might have been providence in another time and place, but in this case, it had landed Reed on the edge of a—or perhaps deeper—shitload of trouble.

He'd heard about guys like Scarpia before, but this was his first direct run-in with one, and it'd left him feeling odd.

Scared.

That was a new sensation for Jimmy Reed.

On the heels of that came something else he was struggling with: the fact that he knew whatever Scarpia was up to exactly, it wasn't just illegal, it was outright dangerous to the environment. *Our* environment. Reed wasn't exactly a card-carrying Green Peace type, but the idea of someone like Scarpia shitting in his own swimming pool (while making a load of money doing so, no doubt) brought on a second emotion: *rage.*

Chalk up two, he thought, taking another sip of his beer. Fear *and* Rage. *That asswipe thinks it's perfectly cool to take someone else's toxic waste and dump it right off our little place here for profit.*

Which brought with it another disturbing and depressing realization: that there were guys like Brad who obviously had no issue with that. Guys who would sell the shirt off their own mother for a buck. Guys he *thought* he knew.

"Yep, that's the 'Ing-Thing'."

"Wow," Brad said, unable to keep the envy out of his voice. "Does she have a sister?"

Reed cocked an eyebrow, struggling not to laugh. Still, he couldn't resist. "Dude, have you looked in the mirror recently?"

Brad had a confused look on his face, as if unable to process the bluntness with which he'd been insulted.

"Jeez, bro, I thought we looked out for each other…"

Yeah, the way you looked out for me right into a dangerous lunatic's hands. One whom I have a hunch may not want me on this planet much longer.

Reed cut him off.

"Stow it," he said, leaning forward. All pretense of niceness left his voice. He caught Inge's attention and signaled her for a new round. "Here's the deal, *Brad*. I have a bunch of questions and you better be in the mood for fucking straight answers."

Hours later, Reed lay in bed, staring at a water stain on the ceiling.

In some ways it was like a metaphor for his life: functional, yet defective. And a long way from what he envisioned it would be in the overconfident, exuberant years of his youth. The vision he'd had for himself had been vague, true, but still much more successful than how it'd panned out to date.

Thought I'd be running a surf shop, maybe, with a decent-sized power boat, enough to attract enough deep-pocketed tourists to keep me in lobster dinners through the winter season. Instead, I'm doing pickup work for a one-man environmental disaster, living in a cut-rate studio and picking up waitresses.

Way to go, bucko.

That wasn't the worst of it, no-sir. Not by a long shot. What really began eating at him this evening was what Brad had told him. About Scarpia's deal with D-Base Corporation. With that knowledge came another frightening certainty: Scarpia was probably going to have them both eliminated.

He glanced over as Inge shifted in her sleep, the sheet falling away to reveal a small, but supple breast. A rueful smile tugged at the corner of his mouth.

She has no idea. How I envy her.

She's young, the world an endless landscape of possibilities, little more to worry about than her grades next semester and a little extra cash in her bank account after this summer.

Reed chuckled. Self-pity and introspection weren't his usual suits. One thing was, however. His father, for all his faults as a merchant seaman, didn't raise him to suffer fools.

Especially assholes like Antony Scarpia.

It was hours before Reed finally got to sleep. When he did, it was with the first outline of a plan.

10. I BET SHE'S GOT A LITTLE BALD-HEADED PUSSY

"Who the hell listens to this shit, anyway?" Sammy Vanossi said, just as his third beer arrived and Billy Joel broke out of the speakers, singing about drunks at the bar. Vanossi was strictly an Iron Maiden man, though he always had a soft spot for Sinatra, because that's who his mother loved. If there was one thing Vanossi obsessively adored and fixated on, it was his mother.

He stood with Scarpia by the front window of *The Point Bar & Grill* overlooking the main drag of the village as their waitress, Carmelina, came up. An anorexic Filipino woman who favored skin-tight pants and low tops that maximized her silicon-injected assets, she usually took her sweet time when Vanossi came there alone. When Scarpia was with him, he suddenly became gold-plated.

Scarpia scowled out the window at the usual tourist parade with their expensive cars as if he expected a hit squad to arrive any moment.

Which is probably not far from the truth, Vanossi thought, as Carmelina slid a full rocks glass of bourbon in front of his boss. She gave both men the full-wattage waitress smile and sauntered away, putting a little extra swing into her hips. She had a couple of bad teeth, which knocked a few points off her 'fuckability quotient' on his mental scorecard. Vanossi could always find faults with women (except his mother) and wasn't shy about pointing them out. He suspected she once had a little thing going with his boss, though he knew better than to ever ask. Scarpia rarely shared anything personal with him, other than the usual nasty barbs about his wife and two daughters, who lived over on the North Fork. People who got too much personal info on Scarpia usually didn't live long enough to share it.

Without looking, Scarpia took a hit of his bourbon and said, "He's the fucking Bard of Long Island, you got a problem with that?"

Vanossi ran a hand over his balding head, then unconsciously pulled on his nose with his thumb and forefinger. It had been broken sometime in the past and never set right.

"Not really a fan," Vanossi said, taking a chance. Depending on the night, that could get you a surprise bonus or planted in the ground. Tonight, he felt gutsier than usual.

"Me neither," Scarpia replied. "Guy's a fucking bald-headed pussy."

Vanossi took a pull off his beer, feeling emboldened. Looking over his shoulder, he said, "I bet *she's* got a bald-headed pussy. What do you think?"

Scarpia remained stone-faced. His thoughts were elsewhere. "No," he replied, "She doesn't. Besides, who the hell would want that? That's critical intel—like the fucking DMZ: you need to know exactly where that territory begins and where it fucking ends."

It took a moment for Vanossi to comprehend that Scarpia had just made a *joke*, it was that much of a rarity. But at least he got one bit of info confirmed: *The Point's* sexiest waitress was doing more than just serving Scarpia bourbons.

Vanossi considered that. As far as he was concerned, any female was fair game. Which reminded him of something else: the young girl that had been found in the water this afternoon. Halfway between their secret dumping ground and the point. Sammy Vanossi knew he wasn't the sharpest tool in the shed, but to paraphrase his favorite actor—Christopher Walken—*he wasn't no dummy* either. Word had been getting around the docks that something bad was happening out there. Even a couple of Vanossi's tougher sailing acquaintances were acting spooked.

Spooked wouldn't begin to cover it if they really knew what was going on, he thought. *They'd probably tie us up, wrap an anchor around our necks and toss us into the deepest part of the Atlantic. After they filleted us first.*

He planned to be long gone before that ever happened, though. Scarpia said the plan was to take off to Greece once the last two loads were finished. He claimed he had some relatives on a remote island there, where they could live like kings. Vanossi wasn't keen on that plan, however, though he was smart enough not to let on. He had his eye on a seaside village down in Costa Rica, where he would sit on the beach sipping Dos Equis and buy as many little *senoritas* as he wanted.

"They've found a girl out in the ocean today," he said, leaning against the window bar.

"I *know*. So?"

"And word just came in a cop diver just got killed trying to assess the wreck of the boat she was on."

Silence.

Vanossi glanced around to make sure no-one was in earshot. Aside from two regulars over at the bar watching the game, they had the place to themselves. "You think it might be wise to hold off those two last dumps for a bit?"

Scarpia was about to take another hit off his bourbon. The glass paused mid-air.

"You've been doing some *thinking*, that it?" he asked. There was an edge to his tone Vanossi didn't care for.

Still, Vanossi wasn't in the mood to back down. Scarpia may be a dangerous fuck, but Vanossi was no slouch in that department either. He'd once cracked a man's skull like an eggshell against a truck bumper in a Jacksonville parking lot, grinning as his brains leaked out over the asphalt.

"There's talk about some people interested in some wrecks near our dumping ground. Word is they've hired someone to take them diving there in the next few days. That's what's got me thinking," he said.

"A bunch of ONR shits, with their heads up their assholes," Scarpia snorted, taking a pull off his bourbon. "But nothing we can't manage—I already gave them a little scare the other day. You think I'm that fucking stupid? I've been getting inside dope from a source. Which is why we're going to make the next drop a double, finish this contract and get the fuck out of here. We'll be sipping *ouzo* on a Mediterranean beach surrounded by topless babes before they even get a whiff of what's been happening. All those surfer fucks will be eating Toxic Tuna Sushi while we live it up. Serves 'em right, bunch of pansy eco-pussy assholes."

Vanossi squinted. "You have contacts in the ONR?"

"I got fucking connections everywhere," Scarpia snorted, implying he was part of some far-flung criminal network. The reality—which Vanossi suspected—was far more mundane. Most of Scarpia's 'connections' were small-time crooks.

"When?" Vanossi asked.

"Next Tuesday or Wednesday. Depending on how the weather holds."

"What about Reed and Stanos?"

"What about 'em?"

Vanossi checked the bar again. The regulars were still manning the bar. Carmelina was standing at the waitress station, texting.

"You said you wanted me to—"

Scarpia put his hand around Vanossi's neck and yanked him in close. His breath smelled of bourbon and peppermint gum.

"I got a new plan for those three limp pricks. Somewhere further out in the deep Atlantic."

Vanossi's brow furrowed, "Three? We're not just bringing Stanos and Reed?"

Scarpia released his neck and clapped him on the shoulder. "You forgot about Hodgekiss. Make sure he's aboard too, if you have to drag him by his ears. We're tidying up loose ends."

"You mean...?"

"That's right, bucko. It's time to blow this little pop stand for good."

11. SOMETHING'S WRONG WITH HER

They arrived at Southampton Hospital just before eight. Even with Navarre's reckless driving it took them forty-five minutes. There was simply no way to speed through East Hampton even on a weekday night. Route 27 was the only main road along the South Fork and it was the height of tourist season.

Navarre introduced Vanek on the way over, explaining he was a naval and seafaring expert brought in by Gavin to help investigate the recent rash of occurrences happening off Montauk. Gorecki had been hired on retainer by Gavin to help them out as needed. Navarre had requested a local ship with the ability and availability to handle heavy diving equipment. Gorecki and his ship fit the bill nicely.

At the ER entrance they ran into one of the East Hampton Marine Patrol officer's Gorecki knew, who saved them the trouble of figuring out where the girl was. The officer, a tall man with a saturnine face, was just leaving with two others when they entered the lobby. All three were still decked in their patrol gear.

"Hey Les," he said, coming over to clap the Pole on the back. "You did the right thing today."

Gorecki nodded, his face grim. "Hi Aaron. I heard about Vincent. He was a good man."

"Yeah," the officer replied. "That he was."

"No sign of the father or brother yet?"

"Nothing, but that's not unusual. Tide may have swept them down the coast. May take a few days. Or not. Sometimes they never come back." He shook his head. "The yacht was a piece of work though. Looked like Godzilla had swatted it around."

"What do you mean?" Navarre spoke up.

The officer gave him a 'and-who-the-hell-are-you?' look, before Gorecki intervened.

"Sorry, Aaron. Danielle Cheung, Arnaud Navarre and William Vanek. They've been brought in to look into what's been happening around here. Everyone, this is officer Aaron Graves. Sends me my best clients."

Graves shrugged at the compliment and gave the three of them a cop's once-over. "What's your interest?"

Navarre ignored the question. "Tell us about the boat," he insisted.

Graves glanced at Gorecki, who nodded.

"It's a little odd. A *lot* odd, actually."

"Can we see it?"

Graves mulled this over. "Tell you what, swing by Star Island Marina tomorrow morning. We hauled it out of the water earlier. It's drying out right next to Cory's yacht, in fact."

"Can we go see the girl? Kellie?" Gorecki asked.

"Check with the nurse's station. She's on the fourth floor, SW. The mother's still in shock, she's under heavy sedation. Some friends are on their way up from White Plains to help her out." He raised his chin at Navarre. "Don't I know you?"

"No, I do not think so," Navarre replied.

"Yeah, I *do*. You're the French diver guy on TV. The one who claimed he found the *Bonhomme Richard* a year or so back."

Navarre bristled. "That's what I thought at the time," he said, his jaw tight.

Graves snorted. "Guess that turned out to be balls-up fuckfest, didn't it?"

"Thank you for the reminder."

They rode the elevator up in silence. Vanek made the connection now: Navarre had made a splash in the news a year and a half previous when a salvage expedition led by some over-zealous French investors claimed to have discovered the wreck of the *Bonhomme Richard*—the Revolutionary Warship commanded by John Paul Jones—off the east coast of England in the North Sea. After the audacious four-hour battle with the HMS *Serapis,* during which the British Captain's request for the American's surrender was met with Jones' much-quoted rebuttal "Sir, I have not yet begun to fight!" the *Bonhomme Richard* sank from its damage.

The true wreck had never been discovered due to the fact it was interspersed with so many others. Over the years there'd been many attempts to pinpoint it, including a failed mission by the U.S. Navy in 2011. So, it was something of a bold claim when the French announced they had at a sensational press conference at the Hague two summers back. Navarre had been in charge of the expedition but had been pushed into making the claim, even though there were immediate questions as to its veracity.

When the so-called 'evidence' fell apart under scrutiny, Navarre was publicly skewered in the press—particularly by the Brits—and he seemed to drop off the radar after that. Vanek had been preoccupied at the time with a previously unknown U-Boat wreck outside of New York Harbor, which had been discovered with its hatches sealed. Later when he'd read up on the French incident, he dismissed it as another headline grabbing claim shot down to pieces by flimsy facts. He'd completely forgotten Arnaud Navarre took the brunt of it. Not for the first time he mused at how quickly fortunes can change, how one could be at such heights one minute and in the next swirling down the toilet.

But what comes undone, can be redone, he thought, as the elevator doors opened, though that all sounds nice and easy when it's a well-polished platitude coming out of a psychiatrist's mouth.

The Southampton Hospital was modernized and thanks to someone doing their job in the wayfinding department, intuitive to navigate. The impassive, fierce-eyed head RN entrenched at the nurse's station was another matter. When neither Gorecki nor Navarre made any headway, Dan stepped up to the plate and dialed up a winning charm Vanek hadn't seen up to that point.

The nametag on her breast read: 'Vera'.

He didn't catch exactly what she said but Nurse Vera went from a narrow-eyed guard dog to giggling schoolgirl in the wink of an eye. Even Navarre did a double-take. A minute later, as they were being escorted down to the room, Vanek whispered in Dan's ear, "What on earth did you say to her?"

Dan gave him a cryptic smile, "Girl's stuff," she said.

"*Girl's stuff*," Vanek echoed, as if that explained everything.

Vera had them wait outside the room while she went in and talked to the mother. A moment later she came out.

"Make it brief," she said. "They've been through a lot today. I'll be right here, so no funny stuff."

The room was semi-private, with a curtain separating the two beds. Like all the others on this ward, the décor was a non-offensive creamy yellow with pale green furniture. A pastel print of a vaguely 'Hampton-ish' beach scene adorned one wall. Vanek found it ghastly.

On the other side of the semi-private room, a white-haired, German-looking man lay propped up in a bed, his right hand swathed in bandages. Sitting next to him, chastising him harshly, was his wife.

On their side, Kellie DeFranco sat upright in her bed, knees to her chest, staring blankly off into space. She looked gaunt, pale and haunted. Vanek could relate to that. The mother, a slightly pretty blonde in her 30s, sat in the chair in the corner, a magazine held upside-down in her hands. She seemed to be staring at some place past the inverted images on the paper, a place, Vanek presumed, described by the colorless, endless void of grief. He could relate to that too.

She glanced up briefly as they entered, her eyes glassy with medication.

This time, Navarre stepped up to the plate and took charge.

"Kellie?" he asked, "Do you remember Mr. Gorecki here? The man who rescued you earlier today?"

Kellie remained motionless, vacant-eyed. On the drive over, Gorecki had told them all he knew, which wasn't a lot. She didn't speak a word the remainder of the boat ride into Montauk Harbor except one odd comment as they eased into the berth where the EMT's were waiting.

"They scream with the bream at fifteen fathoms deep. *They scream with the bream at fifteen fathoms deep.*"

The words came out of Kellie's mouth in an odd, wet whisper, as if reciting a children's rhyme underwater. The four visitors exchanged glances, as if not trusting their ears. Kellie's eyes swiveled to the right in slow motion—*just like a ventriloquist dummy's eyes,* Vanek thought—until she was staring at Navarre.

Vanek felt an icy pinprick of fear in his gut. He knew that phrase... for a split second Vanek thought she was about to say something more horrible, something awful none of them would want to hear, then her eyes softened, and he saw only an exhausted, grief-stricken young girl.

"The giant black jellyfish ate daddy," she said, in a normal voice. "They ate Ronny too. They had big mouths and *lots* of teeth."

"The *giant black jellyfish with teeth*?" Navarre prompted quietly, as if finding this only mildly curious.

"*Mmm hmmm.* It attacked our boat first... it..." she trailed off, as if the words disappeared from her thoughts.

Navarre leaned forward, "Tell me about this jellyfish, Kellie; we need to figure out what exactly happened to your father and brother." If *nothing else*, Vanek, realized, *Navarre would make an excellent grief-counselor*. He had a calm, fatherly way of speaking that made you want to unload everything you had in your basket.

Kellie's eyes once again took on that opaque, doll-like quality.

Dead-eyes, Vanek thought. With it, he realized they had swiveled back and were now zeroed-in directly on him.

"*Him*. I have a message for him *only*."

Dan and Navarre both looked at Vanek, who shrugged in response.

When she said nothing further, Navarre waved him to the bedside and stood away. Unsure where this was going, Vanek stepped over and sat on the edge of the bed.

"Closer," Kellie insisted, leaning toward him.

Even before she continued, he had an icy sensation again that it would be bad.

"You know exactly what I mean, don't you, William?" she said, again in an odd, watery whisper. "Michelle screams with the bream... fish-white flesh rotting in the deep dark..."

And for a moment, Vanek could see, feel and hear it too, as if her words had slithered into his mind with oily black tendrils: Michelle's final panicked thoughts as she sank, the searing pain as something tore into her abdomen and the last precious lungful of air erupted out of her mouth—the cold terror of death enveloping her like a caul. His father too, trying to scream as the seawater filled his lungs…

Vanek snapped out of it, hands balled into fists, realizing someone was screaming and at first, he thought it was himself.

It was Kellie. It sounded like shards of splintered

[bones]

metal erupting from her throat.

Everyone was shouting at once: the room erupted into chaos as two nurses came running in, Gorecki and Navarre tried to get out of the way and the mother folded over, dropping the magazine and clamping her hands over her ears.

Just before they vacated the room, Vanek locked eyes with the girl and nearly screamed himself: they were glowing blue-silver, the eyes of a homicidal angler fish the moment before its battery of needle teeth bit into you.

I ate them all, William, those eyes said, *and I'm going to fucking eat you too!*

Five minutes later, the four of them were out in the front entranceway of the hospital, in the balmy, late summer air. To the south a distant storm out in the Atlantic sent ominous flashes of lightning.

Navarre skipped the cheroot and broke out a pack of Marlboros. He had an air of forced calm about him.

Vanek had the jitters. He'd never smoked cigarettes but like his father, had been into pipes for many years. It'd been maybe a decade since he'd last smoked. Right then, however, he could have popped the entire pack in his mouth and lit all twenty.

Dan put a hand on his shoulder and looked him in the eye. "William, are you okay?"

Vanek was quite a few neighborhoods away from *okay*, but he wasn't very good at expressing these things.

"You look awful!" Gorecki added, unhelpfully. "And when she put her lips to your forehead—how very odd!"

"She put her... she did what?"

"You don't remember that part?" Dan asked.

Vanek stared at the ground and tried to marshal his thoughts, and half succeeded. "No. Not at all," he replied.

"That was *interesting*," Navarre said, blowing smoke up at the sky. "Michelle. You know this person, yes?"

The muscles in Vanek's jaw clenched. He didn't answer.

To his surprise, Dan did.

"His late wife. That's right, isn't it, Will?"

Vanek looked at her, uneasy.

"Do you *know* her? This Kellie?" Gorecki asked, brow furrowing.

"Yes, do you?" Navarre added, toking on his cigarette with his thumb and middle finger, like a gangster.

"*Will*?" Dan asked, searching his face.

Vanek thought about the girl. The dead eyes. He shook his head.

"I never saw her before we walked into that room. Ever."

He became aware of the weight of three pairs of eyes on him, sizing him up like a jury. A hot sensation flushed the left side of his face and neck: the first sign of a full-blown anxiety attack.

"You're absolutely sure?" Dan asked.

"One hundred percent," Vanek replied. "I've only been out here before with my wife and that was over eight years ago. We didn't exactly get chatty with any kids."

"Perhaps your wife did? That you weren't aware of?" Navarre offered.

"Not likely. Michelle wasn't big on kids. Strictly a career woman. And that girl in there would have been what? Four? I don't think so."

They were interrupted by someone coming out of the front entrance, shouting at them. Vanek turned to see the woman who had been sitting on the other side of Kellie DeFranco's room marching toward them. Despite her age—and from the anemic complexion and bald head under the summer hat, someone recovering from Chemo treatments—she looked fit to be tied.

Uh-oh, Vanek thought, *here comes trouble.*

She pulled up short, hands on hips, as if deciding who to go after first. Her lips were compressed into a thin line. Navarre turned out to be target #1, as she stepped forward and in one motion snatched the cigarette out of his hand, threw it to the sidewalk and ground it out with one sandaled foot.

"Smoking in front of a hospital? Are you out of your mind!?"

Navarre stepped back and blinked, his lips in a puckered frown like a big kid caught cheating on his homework. Then she wheeled about on Vanek, her finger pointed in accusation.

"And *you!* What did you do to that poor, traumatized little girl!? She's in hysterics! I'll have you know I'm an RN and will take this up with the director of the hospital! What were you trying to do, upsetting her like that!?"

Dan tried to intervene and instead found herself in the crosshairs, "Look, Miss—"

"Don't 'look Miss' me young lady! That girl just survived hours of floating alone in the ocean after watching her father and brother die! Drifting northward all that time from that sunken ship. In fact, she told me—"

"—told you what?" Vanek said, interrupting her. "*Wait*, did you say, drifting *northward? From a sunken ship?*"

"I'm well aware of what I just said!" the woman snapped back. "The chemo targeted my chest, not my brain!"

"That's not possible," Vanek muttered to himself. "The currents don't work that way. And the..." He looked at the woman again, "Are you sure she said, 'dumping ground?' Did *she* say that? Or one of the Marine rescue?"

She drew herself up. "Of course, it was *her*. She spoke with me while my husband chatted it up with the rescue team. He's a retired City Firefighter, you know! They're all like peas in a pod. We came here today after one of those heavy-duty fishhooks went into his hand during his stupid fishing charter. Said all he needed was a pair of pliers and some band-aids. You don't know how many times I told him not to—"

"Ma'am, you've been extremely helpful," Vanek interrupted again, growing exasperated. This time she seemed thrown off, then pleased by the compliment.

"Well, once a nurse, always a nurse!"

Vanek turned to Dan and Navarre, "Can we get back to the house? I need to see the notes on the map again."

Navarre already had the car keys in his hand. "Ready when you are," he said. Then he smiled at the woman, "That is a most wonderful hat! You look lovely in it!"

"Why, er thank-you," she smiled back, her eyes saying *I know exactly what you're doing. But a little more would be nice.*

"*Bonne soirée!*" he replied, saluting his fingers off his forehead with a slight bow.

They left her there, bemused and slightly confused, while the ocean breeze picked up and plucked at her hat.

Three hours later, Vanek still couldn't get to sleep. The Sandoz watch on his wrist read just after 12:30 a.m. The same watch his father had given him to wear the night they stepped on the boat for what should have been a quiet night-sail off the coast of Connecticut up to Cape Cod.

His *lucky watch*, he called it.

Vanek had accepted it... and lived. His father hadn't. He could still vividly recall seeing the halyard tangled around his throat as the boat capsized...

He'd helped himself to the scotch in the kitchen and stepped out on to the porch.

His thoughts were in a maelstrom. Behind everything lurked the specter of Michelle, dead these seven years now yet still pervading his thoughts: the musical sound of her laugh, her slender neck and jawline, the way she pinned her hair up in the careless-yet-sexy way certain women possessed. The sense that after all his troubled bachelor years he'd finally found his incredible woman, with her wry smile, soulful blue eyes and sharp wit to share his life with.

He thought he'd hit the Lotto. The big payoff. Eight years of wonder, of making plans and talking about children and then... gone. The love of his life, snatched away by a cruel twist of fate. Or a brutal whim of Mother Nature, if he were to point fingers.

She still haunted his dreams, usually in some blissful scenario slowly going awry as the dream progressed, with Vanek losing her in some vast mansion or a station with a dizzying array of trains coming and going.

Mostly though, mostly the dreams ended with her drowning, slender hand reaching feebly toward him in a stormy sea, desperately trying to tell him some message he could almost but never quite grasp.

If that wasn't enough? The cruel double-blow of losing his father that same night. A man he both feared and idolized, whose intense and unflinching nature he would always live in the shadow of.

The years had slid away as he'd eased into a comfortably numb existence of articles, research, facts, numbers and figures. Safe, tangible things he could control, tabulate and file in their proper places.

Until this.

In the last few hours he felt increasingly like an actor who'd been shoved out onto the stage with no rehearsals or even a script to work from.

What in the hell am I doing here? he wondered for the umpteenth time. *I'm a naval historian! And what in the hell was Gavin thinking, damn him? That this would be some bullshit therapeutic experience to get me out of my shell after all these years?*

As he stood there gazing out at the darkness of the Atlantic Ocean—punctuated by a few glittering ship lights way out toward the horizon—the first trembling waves of a full-blown anxiety attack came on. Pain shot down his arm, then doubled back along his chest. The sense he was on the precipice of a massive heart attack or stroke. With it came random angry thoughts:

Tore me from my home to die of a heart attack!

I'm just going to drop dead here at this house. Stroke, then heart attack! My blood pressure has to be close to fatal!

What was with that girl? Death! She's marked me for death!

Does Gavin secretly enjoy torturing me? Set this whole Goddamn thing up!? Is that what this all about—good old Gavin just fucking with me!?

Vanek took a stiff pull of the scotch and shook his head, letting the warm glow smooth the edges off his anxiety. That was ridiculous, of course. Gavin had been a good friend of his fathers, and one of the most reliable men he knew. No, if anyone here was going to mess with his head it would be—

"—penny for your thoughts?" came Dan's voice, so close behind him he gave a start.

"It'll cost you more than that," he shot back, not thinking.

To his surprise she leaned into him, invading his personal space. "Really? What kind of price did you have in mind?"

Vanek's brow went up. It was either a bold invitation or a harmless tease. His handbook on these things was hopelessly out of date. These days one perceived misstep could find you instantly crucified in the public eye. Welcome to the 21st century: the age of sexual McCarthyism. Confused and annoyed, he said nothing.

Dan nodded toward the ocean.

"I've always found the ocean endlessly fascinating. The mystery of it all, the secrets it keeps... the allure. The folklore, sense of imminent danger and the possibility of romance, *no*?"

She stared at him, her hazel eyes luminous in the night, a glass of red wine in one hand. For a moment it seemed she would add something else, then didn't.

"There's nothing out there but a lot of ocean, shipwrecks, and dead-men's tales," Vanek said, nodding toward the sea. "And corpses: a graveyard for the over-ambitious and arrogant."

"That sounds rather cynical," she replied.

"It's the truth."

Vanek was aware of her closeness, catching a slight hint of musky perfume before it was whisked away by the breeze.

Everything gets whisked away eventually, he thought. *Even this*.

After getting back to the house and sending Gorecki off, the discussion in the map room had escalated into a heated discussion between Dan and Navarre. Dan speculated the evidence pointed to a more sinister explanation—possibly some other life form or creature wreaking havoc off the coast. An unknown 'sea-monster' of sorts. Navarre dismissed her as being ridiculous and over-imaginative, adamant it all had to do with whatever technology was still on the ship—that it was inducing hallucinations.

"Giving off some kind of frequency. Isn't that your department!?"

"You mean some kind of 'fear frequency'?" Dan pointed to the map, pasting a new note where Kellie had been rescued. "Perhaps. That might explain the wetsuit hoods the ONR insists on. But it wasn't a 'frequency' that sank that yacht. No, I think there's something else there, a species of unknown predator. What if the two wrecks are in some way connected? And what if now, for some reason, whatever it is, it's what? *Active*? Why now?"

Navarre shook his head with a derisive snort. "*C'est des conneries!* There is something on that ship that has agitated the local marine life. Whales are right off the coast here—do you know what one of those can do to a small yacht? A Great White? No? You've seen it before, perhaps? I didn't think so!"

"He has a point," Vanek added. "I've seen all kinds of strange things come up out of the ocean first-hand, but never anything that couldn't be biologically explained. Even around here. Back in '08 a decomposed animal washed up at Ditch Plains that had conspiracy idiots spouting crap for years, spawning an asinine 'Montauk Monster' legend that persists to this day."

Vanek well remembered the 'Montauk Monster' spiel, it had been part of the 'Michelle' era of his life. They'd joked about it that summer at the beach house they'd rented. Along with what they were going to name their kids.

The ones they would never have.

What Vanek couldn't fathom was the whole mess out at Camp Hero and how it might be tied into his grandfather's disappearance in WWII. The reports Gavin had given him read like X-Files loony-bin stuff—they described experiments going on at the base that were a key part of the *Neptune's Reckoning* project. So, it wasn't just about the ship! But they were short on specifics, and no mention of the 'chair' the conspiracy nuts kept going on about... except, the old photo of a chair from the house. And the note. He'd looked at them briefly while unpacking. The chair was certainly odd—like something out of a mad scientist laboratory from an old 1940's Universal monster film. But nothing *alien* about it, that he could tell. The note appeared to be a bunch of meaningless mumbo-jumbo.

Or, more likely he suspected, written in code.

Still, he wondered if the electromagnetic pulse technology used on the ship's hull had triggered some kind of unexpected effect, either on the sea life or the crew or both. Which made a certain amount of bizarre sense: what if the inspiration behind the whole 'Montauk Project—Philadelphia Experiment' legend had a grain of truth? Except that instead of time-travel and aliens there had been Kovac's trippy anti-submarine device? Was Navarre right? Had it triggered some kind of unprecedented attack by marine life?

Every corner of this thing only turned up more questions. What really happened at Camp Hero? And why were there no records from the German archives of an American Destroyer being sunk here by one of their subs?

He'd stared at the map, convinced the answer stared back at him. But he couldn't see it.

After another ten minutes of back-and-forth, the argument had gone nowhere and Vanek had excused himself to bed, agitated and vaguely depressed.

Now here he was—unexpectedly—sharing a moment with Dan.

He had to admit she had an intoxicating side to her. But hardly his type. A party girl, he figured. Not a highbrow, and if like most younger people he knew, a bossy know-it-all. Probably boring as hell in the sense of humor department. In short: *not Michelle.*

"Came out here to try and convince me about giant sea monsters again?" he asked.

An introspective smile crossed her face. "I think I'm sea-monstered out for the moment. Whatever's out there, it'll be there tomorrow. What about you? How are you doing? That was so creepy what happened with that girl!"

Vanek nodded. "It was... *odd.*" Although it was a lot more than that. He couldn't shake the uncomfortable sensation something weird had happened when her lips touched his forehead, as if the contact had penetrated his skull into his brain. Looking in the bathroom mirror afterward, he could have sworn there were reddish pinpricks in the skin, though that was ridiculous.

Suppressing a shudder, Vanek changed the subject.

"So, what's the deal with Navarre?"

"Oh, he's all right!" she replied. "He thinks he's right about everything, very *French*." She touched his shoulder. "He can be a real SOB at times. Like you, I bet."

Vanek *hmphed*. His father had been quite the SOB too. A hard man. *I remember the time I finally reached the boiling point after years of it—right after that disastrous Thanksgiving Dinner over at Mom's sister's house. Dad was on a roll that day. Taking nasty pot-shots at everything—the stuffing, the turkey, his French-Canadian in-law's country. It was the first holiday after Michelle and I got married. I found Dad out on the back patio puffing on his pipe like a PO'd Popeye, walked up and said to him point blank: "Dad, you know what? You really suck at having fun. And you're an ace at making sure no-one around you does either. Congratulations on being such a first-rate asshole."*

Maybe he hadn't fallen that far from the tree.

He realized Dan was still touching his arm. It made him uncomfortable and somehow thrilled. How long had it been since a woman had done that?

Did she... stop it, you God-damn nitwit! You just met this woman today!

"Well, he's good at what he does. Took the fall with all that *Bonhomme Richard* business, and paid dearly for it," he said to distract that thought.

"*Hmm*," Dan dropped her hand and walked over to the rail, the ocean breeze plucking at her hair. She rested on her elbows, cupping the wineglass in both hands.

Vanek hesitated a moment, then joined her.

"It's beautiful here, isn't it?" she said. "Beautiful and terrifying at the same time. Like looking off into the edge of the world. 'Beyond here there be dragons'. Like on the old maps."

He gazed out at the ocean, not saying anything.

Out on the pitch-black horizon, one of the lights winked and bobbed, as if disturbed. Higher up, clouds churned across the starlit night, straining to obscure the heavens. Even at this distance, one could feel the impact of the waves rolling in. The hiss as they receded. A relentless cycle spanning eons they were experiencing an infinitesimal fraction of. On a spinning orb in an impossibly vast cosmos filled with... *what*? A nearly infinite panorama of wonders and horrors we couldn't possibly conceive of.

Was that what awaited them tomorrow?

Dan turned to him, her eyes unreadable in the dim light.

"You should get some sleep. Tomorrow is going to be a big day."

With that she left.

Vanek stood there at the rail for a while longer, nursing his scotch and his thoughts. It wasn't until he went through the sliding doors, he realized the anxiety attack had slipped away for the moment, unnoticed.

12. JUST WHEN A DAY COULDN'T GET STRANGER

Vanek awoke Thursday morning to bright rays of sunlight probing through the blinds of the bedroom window. He had a moment of complete disorientation as he rose out of a lucid dream to find himself sprawled in a king-sized bed, tangled in the sheets.

The dream had been vivid—Michelle had come back and with her an overwhelming sense of yearning—yet something wasn't right: everything she said was laced with sorrow. She kept trying to warn him, but the words kept getting jumbled. He snatched her up in his arms and tried to kiss her, then realized it was Danielle, completely naked. Yet just as she bent forward and whispered in his ear, he rose into consciousness, the dream falling away in tantalizing shreds.

From just outside came the animated *cheep-cheep* of an over-eager bird and with it a cool breeze of ocean air against the distant boom and hiss of the surf. He realized he'd woken with a painful hard-on, like some high-school kid.

That brought a little smile.

He'd gone to sleep in just his underwear which was unusual, as he'd gotten in the habit of wearing pajamas since Michelle's death. Partly out of insecurity, he supposed. But as he'd set out his toiletry wet bag in the bathroom before turning in, he realized he'd completely forgotten to pack them, giving him another few moments of cursing at Gavin and the hastiness of the situation.

He always planned everything, carefully.

Kicking away the sheets, he took a moment to relish the soothing coolness of the morning and the deep cushion of an expensive mattress. He had half a notion to pick up the Hornblower novel off the nightstand and spend another ten minutes in bed.

A light knock at the bedroom door interrupted further thought.

Even as he sat up and scrambled for the covers, the door swung open and he found himself staring at Danielle, fully dressed in jeans and a denim shirt with the sleeves rolled up.

"Morning!" she said, then glancing down at the tent at his crotch, raised a brow and smiled, "Someone's *up* for roll call!"

His cheeks going red, Vanek snatched the sheets and covered himself. "Christ!" he snapped. "Don't you believe in privacy around here!?"

Dan let her gaze linger a moment longer, then laughed.

"You can get dressed and join us for breakfast when you're ready, cowboy," she said, before backing out and quietly closing the door.

Vanek smacked his forehead.

"Goddamnit!" he said to himself. *How the hell can she make me feel like a thirteen-year-old in an instant!?*

Fifteen minutes later, Vanek had showered. Dressed in a navy-blue polo shirt, worn jeans and black boating shoes, he sat at the kitchen island with a cup of strong black coffee in one hand. Navarre was impatient to get going to the Coast Guard Station and had pushed for a light breakfast, but Dan was having none of it. She insisted they sit down and eat the scrambled eggs, sausage and fruit dish she'd made.

"*Zut*! You Americans and your big breakfasts!" Navarre said with mock derisiveness, an unlit cheroot dangling from the side of his mouth as he reached for his coffee.

"And you and your stupid smoking!" Dan shot back, snatching the cheroot out of his mouth as she plopped a plate of eggs and sausage in front of him. In one contemptuous motion she pushed the lower cabinet door release with her knee and tossed it into the trash bin concealed there.

Still embarrassed, Vanek kept his mouth shut and dug into his own plate. The eggs were a little runny (not dry and fluffy, he noted, like *Michelle* always made them) but the sausage was nicely crisped and the toast—repurposed baguette from the night before—worked great with fresh butter and blueberry preserves he discovered. The coffee tasted strong and mellow. A Hawaiian blend he guessed. Kona, probably.

The bright kitchen with its 'country classic' décor was a welcome change, he grudgingly admitted, from the gloomy one back in Larchmont. Vanek made a mental note to look up some interior decorators when he got back and make an effort to bring it into the 21st century.

To the right of the island was an alcove with an iMac workstation at it, along with a shelf of cookbooks and a calendar. Next to it lay a copy of "The Montauk Experiment": Preston Nichols' rambling (and in Vanek's estimate, certifiable 'loony-bin' quality) account of secret government experiments involving time-travel, alien technology and weird sexual activities at Camp Hero, the same old army base near Montauk Point.

He wondered which of his housemates was reading it. Dan, most probably.

As if on cue, Dan sat on the stool next to him with her own plate. Navarre looked on with horror at the ketchup she poured on her eggs.

Oblivious, Dan dug into her breakfast with gusto.

"Gavin texted earlier," she said, reaching for her orange juice, "while you were in the shower. He wanted to make sure you'd settled in all right."

Vanek appeared hyper-focused with his breakfast. Dan gave him a sideways glance.

"I told him that as of this morning, at least, you appeared up for anything." A smile tugged at her mouth as her eyes turned up at the ceiling. Vanek's lips went tight as he chased a sausage around the plate with his fork. Navarre looked at both of them with the suspicious air of someone who just missed the joke.

After a few seconds where nobody offered anything further, Navarre made a show of checking his watch.

"It's a quarter to eight. We leave in fifteen minutes, yes?"

"Works for me," Dan said, biting into her toast.

When Vanek came out the front door, Navarre was leaning against the SUV, smoking a cheroot. By the cliff stood two oddly dressed people. As he walked down the front steps, he realized it was the strange couple they'd passed in town the day before. The plump woman faced the ocean with her arms and hands raised, making mystical-looking gestures while her priestly partner moved around her, jingling a clutch of tiny bells.

Near them was a pile of weathered rocks.

"Good God, what are they doing here?" Vanek asked as he approached Navarre.

It appeared to be a kind of new age ritual. The breeze carried an atonal chant to his ears. It sounded like a badly misinterpreted druidic soundtrack.

Navarre half turned and nodded. "Ah! *That* is the 'High Priestess of Taured' and her assistant 'Om'. They're staying at the property next to this one."

"They're staying at the property *next to us*?" Vanek echoed. Looking to the west, he noted the garish, ultramodern beach house sharing the same drive as theirs. Sited at an oblique angle and half concealed by scrub pine, he hadn't really paid it much attention the day before. The house was even larger than the Neville House. The white Lexus was parked out front.

A moment later, they completed their ritual and started toward the house. The woman, Vanek noted, wore a flowing white outfit of expensive yet indistinct design—the type of clothes one might find in an overpriced woman's store in East Hampton. She still wore the white cream pancaked on her face and had the 'Jackie O' sunglasses, though Vanek saw she also wore a curious necklace with an octopus-like pendant that seemed to be made of precious jewels and from the sharp glint in the morning light, diamonds.

The man who trailed behind her wore a pseudo-priest's raiment, with the same strange glyph at the collar. He walked with his hands clasped together solemnly, chin down as if contemplating some deeper truth in the sandy ground. The effect was thrown off by his cheap sandals.

Instead of walking toward their house however, they veered straight toward Vanek and Navarre, the woman twirling the fingers of her right hand in the air. A scarf trailed from her wrist flowing in the wind. Vanek thought she looked like an extremely strange, overweight alien mime imitating Stevie Nicks.

"Why good morning to both of you fine gentlemen!" she said as she approached. "May the Goddess smile up on you!"

Oh no, Vanek thought, *we're in for it now.*

She stopped in front of Navarre and put out her hand bent forward, palm down, as if she were visiting royalty. He half-expected Navarre to tuck one hand behind his back, take fingers in his other and bow to kiss it like some old-fashioned courtier.

Instead, Navarre inclined his head and smiled back.

"*Bonjour, Madame!*" he replied.

"Ahh, such a gentleman!" she said, apparently pleased, though Vanek noticed the sideways shift of her eyes toward her companion, as if suggesting he might learn a thing or two from this Frenchman's behavior.

She swung her full attention to Vanek, measuring him up with brows raised.

"And *who* do we have here?"

"This is—" Navarre began, but was interrupted by a raised hand.

"No-no! Let me guess!" She took off her glasses, revealing the most oddly beautiful and violet pair of eyes Vanek had ever seen. The lashes were long and black, accentuating what must have been movie-star looks in her youth. Her face was puffy and made stranger by the bright white foundation.

The eyes *were* captivating, however. He found them hypnotic in their strangeness. She stared at him a full minute.

"William Vanek," Vanek offered.

"Of *course*," she said, appraising him. "You're a Taurus—it's written all over you plain as day—and a lineage of mystery runs in your veins... does it not? Death and disappearances. Tied to the ocean, and the Ley lines that converge here. Do you know about the chair?"

Vanek kept a poker face. "Uh, *Chair*? *What* chair?"

"Hmm, perhaps you are not ready after all," she said, with a dismissive air.

Vanek felt his hackles go up. As a well-respected historian, one of his major weak spots was his vanity. Nothing triggered it quicker than dismissive behavior.

"I'm sorry, *who are* you?" he blurted out, mentally kicking himself: *never engage the crazies*!

She drew herself up. "I am Aduba, the High Priestess of Taured." She spoke as if stating a self-evident fact. Then she gestured toward the man with her, "And this is my companion, *Om*."

'Om' looked vaguely uncomfortable. He managed an awkward smile and nodded.

"Greetings," he said, his voice thin and reedy.

"Greetings," Vanek replied, feeling like he'd stumbled into a *Candid Camera* version of Star Trek. He was at a loss what to say next.

What do you chat about with card-carrying members of the Loony Tribe? Astral Projection? Alien visitations and abductions?

"Well, we shouldn't keep you," Aduba said. "I sense you have a very busy day ahead of you." She glanced up at the sky as if seeking a divination there. "Oh... your stars are certainly crossed. You have very interesting and... challenging times ahead! Be…"

Without warning she reached out and grabbed his arm.

"... *No*! There is a death about you! The mark of the creature runs in your veins! Terror of the Universe! Blood and screaming death!! Oh, *dear God*!!" The back of her hand flew to her forehead in a dramatic swoon, her double chin trembling as she turned her head away.

She staggered, but Om stepped in and caught her by the elbow.

"She's psychic, you see," he offered, by way of explanation, "sometimes she gets these episodes."

I bet, Vanek thought, *these types are always full of melodrama. Hopefully it's not contagious.*

Still, he couldn't deny a sense of unease; 'psychic' episode or not.

"So, you've met our neighbors," Dan said, coming up to the car as Om guided his charge back toward their house. A Canon MKIV 5D camera was slung under one arm. She stopped next to Vanek, hands in her front pockets.

Navarre chuckled, taking a last pull off his cheroot before stubbing it out on the gravel. "Definitely not playing with a *full dick*, those two," he said.

Vanek blinked, not sure if he'd heard correctly. Then Dan burst out laughing.

"Their real names are Donna and Edward Rawson," she said, composing herself. "Gavin ran a check on them. According to the records they're from Greentown, Illinois."

"In which *dimension*?" Vanek asked.

Dan laughed.

"Good question. But one you might not want to ask. They're harmless, though. Bizarre, yes, but harmless. Yesterday she said she was concerned about my aura, and that my chakras needed adjustment."

Vanek shook his head, "I bet."

The drive to the Coast Guard Station at Montauk Harbor would normally take the average driver eight minutes. Navarre did it in three.

If Dan liked speeding in her Mustang, Navarre drove his SUV like he was on a Formula One racetrack. With his large frame hunched over the steering wheel, the bored expression on his face was in direct contrast to the havoc they were wreaking on the road. Several times he scared the wits out of bicyclists along the Montauk Highway, nearly clipping two of them as he zoomed past. Riding shotgun, Vanek glanced into the side mirror to see the one cyclist careen off the shoulder and wobble into the scrub bush while the other stopped to flip the bird at them.

They tore up Old West Lake Drive past the half-hidden luxury summer homes nestled along Lake Montauk. A couple of elderly joggers yelped and leaped into the tall grass as they zipped by, then they were heading northward on County Road 77 where the old money estates were, with their imposing gates and hedges, dozing under canopies of oak in the early morning sunlight.

After half a mile they looped right onto Star Island, zipping past the Montauk Yacht Club on the right and the Star Island Yacht Club and marina to their left. Immediately beyond stood the Coast Guard Station with its trim colonial-style buildings, white painted cladding and brick-red shingle roofs looking smart against the sea-toned palette of the harbor.

Navarre parked in the gravel parking lot of the marina next to where several large boats undergoing repairs were up in cradles. Past the Remark Charters building they could see a bunch of people standing near the taped-off area around the recovered yacht which had been hoisted into a berth. The boat still had its sails up, torn as they were. Even at a distance he could see the severe damage to the hull. The whole thing struck him as an affront, like seeing a rare collector's car mangled after an accident. Nearby towered the giant Marine Travelift crane used to hoist boats out of the water, a few gulls perched along the top gantry like watchful sentinels. To the left was the Yacht Club building and Marina Store, overlooking the sprawl of the yacht basin, which except for a single Catamaran, consisted exclusively of motor yachts. Most of the hardcore sports fishermen had left the docks hours ago, but a few owners could be seen poking around their boats in the bright August sunlight. A light breeze tugged at the pendants and carried with it the unique ocean marina aromas of brine, diesel oil and from somewhere nearby, breakfast cooking.

From the looks of it, it was the start of a promising day.

He could just make out several men in marine patrol uniforms in a heated argument with someone obscured by the boat. Nearby, a handful of onlookers stood, some taking photos with their smartphones. It didn't look like the press had shown up yet, but Vanek figured it wouldn't be long.

As they drew closer, he saw, with some surprise, one of the men arguing was Carl Gavin. Even more surprising: he was livid. Vanek tried to think if he'd ever seen Gavin angry before and drew a blank.

He's been my icon for coolness under fire since I can remember, he thought. On the tails of that: *If he's pissed, there's a damned good reason for it! And if those damned cops think they can push a friend of mine around...*

Vanek's hackles went up. Just as he picked up his stride however, Navarre reached over and touched his shoulder, "Wait," he said quietly.

Vanek was about to shrug him off, but something gave him pause. Perhaps it was the oddness of the situation. Or just his body language. Gavin had one hand at his side, curled into a fist. For a crazy moment, Vanek thought he would slug the closest officer.

"I'm afraid you don't have the authority to make that call," the officer said. Vanek recognized him as Graves, the policeman they'd run into at the hospital the night before. Standing between Gavin and the sailboat, he had his fingers splayed on his hips and looked ready to stand there and hold his ground all day if necessary.

"Like hell I don't!" Gavin shot back. "I paid the docking fee on that boat. And I have the full authority of the United States Navy on this one. We're taking it back to the hangar at Breckenridge Labs for analysis, and that's final."

Graves shook his head. "There's nothing *final* about it. Right now, this boat is officially a crime scene and we'll hand it over to you when we're good and ready. One of our divers is dead because of it."

Gavin wasn't budging either. "Son, that boat was taken thirty miles out—well outside *your* jurisdiction. Federal waters, in case you forgot."

"What I *didn't* forget is that the Coast Guard called us in to assist, since they don't maintain divers of their own—in case *you* forgot. Just to make my point, I'm putting this crime scene under 24-hour guard until we've finished our investigation. And that *is* final."

Gavin stood fuming a moment, the lines of his face more granite-like than ever, then his eyes took on a cunning squint Vanek didn't care for. He grunted and turning away, nearly ran into Vanek.

"Oh—hello, Will!" he said. He glanced over his shoulder. "Might as well get in there if you can." Under his breath he added: "Little pricks."

"Everything all right?" Vanek asked.

One moment Gavin looked ready to turn back and take up the fight again, the next his features smoothed over and he was the congenial father-figure again. Vanek found the instantaneous change unnerving.

"Yeah, fine, fine. Jurisdictional BS. Nothing you need to worry about." He turned to the cops again. "Any issues with my friends here just having a look at least?"

A muscle twitched at Graves' jaw, but he'd already agreed to it at the hospital. Both groups became distracted as Gorecki pulled into the parking lot with his run-down Ford Explorer.

"Morning!" Gorecki said, clambering out while balancing a cup of coffee in one hand. His gaze traveled past the whole group and settled on the yacht. "I, *uh*, Holy Hell, now that is one fucked boat, isn't it?"

It wasn't a particularly funny statement, but something in the childlike way he said it diffused the tension in the air. Gavin's fist relaxed and a ghost of a smile touched Graves' lips.

Gavin acknowledged the three of them with a nod, then leaned in as he walked past Vanek. "I'll meet all of you back at the house after lunch for an update, yes?"

"Sure," Vanek replied. The boat grabbed his attention. He'd never seen damage like it. He was just wondering how they were going to deal with the police when Dan stepped forward and put on a concerned smile for Graves.

"I'm really, really sorry to hear about your diver," she said. She looked up at him with her head slightly tilted, one brow up.

Graves rubbed his jaw as if getting the tension out. "Yeah."

"We'll be quick?"

Graves considered it a moment, then nodded toward the yacht. "Make it fast. And don't touch anything."

The Ericson was in rough shape. The hull had been perforated in several places and still leaking water. Vanek had never seen anything like it. From the expression on Dan and Navarre's faces, they hadn't either.

Dan popped the lens cap off her camera, checked her settings and started snapping shots along the length of the hull and around the other side. Navarre stood with arms crossed, eyes traveling across the damage, measuring, calculating.

Vanek focused on the gaping hole in front of him.

It transfixed him. Something about the jagged contours of the fiberglass and the inner structure that reminded him of a Great White shark's mouth, yawning, just before it bared its gums while doing that hideous slow-motion one-two chomp.

A curious sensation overtook Vanek while he stared—like being drawn into a long tunnel, a roaring in his ears like the wind of a cyclone, followed by a telescoping sensation. He was only vaguely aware he had reached out and lightly touched the edge of the hole with his fingertip, like a lover's afterthought.

An immediate blackness struck him, an impenetrable Stygian ink accompanied by a bone-numbing cold, the kind of draining cold of too much time deep underwater.

And then…

A bright flash: an impact, or rather a high-speed projectile in the distant murk, the color and nature of it suggesting a violent, foreign penetration—an alien bullet containing a horrid seed.

Vanek didn't know this explicitly (in the same way he had no reference for distance), he simply knew it in that accept-it-at-face-value way one does in dreams. An interval followed—minutes/months/years possibly—when he became aware of a distant spray of lights.

Chernobyl Blue, he thought.

Violent and radioactive.

Approaching.

With them... ahead of them... tendrils of some sort. The impression formed in his mind was of writhing, whipping worms. Yet it was even more insidious than that. With it came a deep resonating sound that filled him with dread, accompanied by scissoring sounds at a frequency that he found strangely repulsive, like tiny metallic screams screeching across tormented flesh.

Death and insanity accompanied whatever was approaching, of a magnitude and power that threatened to eclipse all rational thought.

Vanek tried desperately to pull himself back, away from whatever the hell this thing was, but couldn't. He'd become non-corporal, suspended in the ether, a floating bit of flotsam waiting to be devoured... or torn to pieces. At the same time, it became aware of him and with that awareness came *change.*

The worm-like appendages became jointed, spider-like.

Like that first truly spider nightmare he had as a child after finding that nest of them poking around his maternal grandmother's basement at the old house in Irvington. His late grandfather—a mad inventor of sorts—had left boxes filled with 1920's and 30's electronics in moldering boxes stashed in the cabinets of his workshop. He'd pulled the box out under the dim light, squatting on his haunches, and like many kids stuck his hand in there to grab something without thinking much about it. Something must have died in it—a mouse perhaps—all he knew was that his fingers brushed something mushy and furry, followed by the dozen things he felt crawling up his bare forearm immediately. Heavy things, with dry, leather bodies. Then he saw them: squat, bloated spiders racing up his arm with horrifying speed.

He'd run out of the basement screaming.

That night he'd dreamed of them, scrabbling all over his room with dry leathery bodies, spinning sickly webs and dropping onto him with their undulating, quivering legs, malignant eyes and alien mouths…

Vanek saw them multiplying and growing on a scale that made him nauseous.

He glimpsed something else too—shrapnel bursts of imagery: some kid of alien tower reaching for the sky of an alien world... spawning mucus-like spoiled green egg-sacs that had been injected into screaming living hosts, the spider-worm things devouring each other in a cannibalistic orgy, and something else—a tantalizing clue that plucked at his deeper consciousness….

His whole viewpoint jarred, as if by a rumbling explosion, even as the spider things arrived, bursting all over his (incorporeal?) body... tearing, devouring.

The agony of millions of serrated, poison-laced jaws ripping at him dissolved along with the overwhelming image of the things swarming his vision.

"Snap out of it!" Navarre hissed in his ear.

It took Vanek a moment to register the powerful hands gripping his upper arms, shaking him violently. He took in a whooping gulp of air—as if he hadn't breathed in minutes—and wrenched himself away, staggering over to the weeds along the fence and vomited up his breakfast.

"That went well," Navarre commented.

They were sitting around the stern on Gorecki's deep sea yacht *Catch-22* at its berth at Uihlein's Marina. The boat, a classic 1966 65-foot *Rybovich* had been modernized and equipped with a crane at the back, though it still suggested a glimmering era of James Bond drinking martinis: shaken, not stirred. Gorecki had upgraded to it when the previous owner unloaded it (before skipping town) during the recession ten-years previous. He'd gotten it for next to nothing, thanks to a tip from the marina's owner, Henry Uihlein.

After Vanek had tossed his breakfast at Star Island, the Marine Patrol first thought he'd discovered something they'd missed in the damaged hull. When they found out it was some inexplicable mental 'episode', they'd been less than impressed. Gorecki intervened by recommending they convene over at his boat across the way.

But not before Navarre stopped in and quizzed the Coast Guard about the location of the *Ericson* and what they had on any other unusual marine related incidents in the area, including Cory's yacht.

Vanek was still pale as a ghost when they met on board the *Catch-22*.

The morning was still one of those photo-perfect eastern Long Island ones where powder-white clouds drifted lazily across a bright cerulean-blue sky. But the latest weather reports were warning about squall-lines coming in from the Northeast by early afternoon.

Gorecki surprised Vanek by handing him a steaming mug of Blue Mountain Jamaican coffee minutes after arriving.

"*Keurig* coffee maker," he said by way of explanation. "Not like the old days. Now most of my customers demand gourmet coffee for their charters. Bunch of *siusiaks*." He all but shoved the coffee into Vanek's hands. "Here, you look terrible. Expensive coffee fix everything."

"Thanks," Vanek replied, unable to suppress a chuckle. When he'd first come out of the 'episode' (as he now thought of it) his heart had been hammering in his chest and he would have bet the bank his blood pressure was through the roof. Even a whiff of anxiety set it off like a runaway flywheel these days.

Strangely though, once on the boat, he'd calmed down a little.

This is how you lose your mind—not with a bang but with a blabbering whimper! he thought.

But that wasn't quite it either, he knew. Something else was still going on. Something deeper and disturbing.

Somehow, that girl had opened the door on it. In his mind.

Dan sat on the bench next to him, legs crossed, alternating between giving him concerned glances and thumbing through the shots she'd taken on the Canon in her lap.

"Too bad Will didn't target their shoes," she said. "That Graves guy seems like a total prick. I thought he was going to arrest all of us."

"Nah, he's okay guy," Gorecki replied, "Losing that diver, Vincent, was hard on him. And the press showed up just as William here lost it. Whole thing is bad mess."

Navarre lit up a cheroot and blew smoke over the stern.

"We should get out on the water. We're running out of time," he said.

"Not *today*," Gorecki said. "Storm's coming. Besides, we haven't gotten the 3D scanner and float bags yet."

"They will be here tomorrow. *Then* we dive."

"Three-D scanner?" Vanek asked.

"Trimble T-X series," Navarre replied. "Not even on the market yet. Allows us to do a high definition 3D LiDar scan of the ship and pinpoint the parts we need to extract. Very important. According to Gavin, it's called the 'Anti-Magnetic Field Oscillation System'. That ship is loaded with live munitions and from our first look, highly unstable. One wrong move and *ka-boom*."

For a terrified moment, Vanek thought they would ask him to go along.

"If there's nothing on the schedule, I wouldn't mind visiting the library," he said. "And the Historical Society."

Navarre raised his brows in response.

"You'd be surprised what you can find in either place," Vanek added.

Dan finished her coffee. "If we're not going down today, I may join William and take a spin into town. The bookstore there just re-opened under new management."

Vanek had regained enough composure to look annoyed. When it came to research, he always preferred to go it alone. Dan shot him a flirty smile.

Damn the woman!

"Why not?" he relented. "I guess we could investigate what passes for literacy in these parts."

Navarre chuckled and blew smoke in the air again. "You see?" he said to Dan, "I'm not the only snob on this team!"

"Marvelous."

"So," Navarre continued. "Snobs or not, tomorrow we head out first thing in the morning. You still good?"

Dan pursed her lips. "I'll be fine. What did you find out from the Coast Guard, by the way?"

"Not much. As we discussed, there hasn't been much here in the way of a major marine disaster since the *Pelican*. Now all at once they have at least five deaths at sea here and the ONR poking sticks up their skirts."

Dan looked up. "Shouldn't the NOAA get involved? They have the best underwater equipment."

"Oh, they are! There's no question about the illegal dumping. Their new research vessel—the *Robert D. Ballard*–is back in port over at Davisville, Rhode Island, getting refitted after their last assignment. It should be here the next day or two. Which doesn't give us much time."

Gorecki rubbed his hands together. Vanek noted he always had an intense, concerned look about him, like a man bracing himself for a car accident. By contrast, his body language was relaxed, as if by the same token he'd survived enough crashes not to worry about it.

"This is *Złe wieści*," he said, "Not good at all. Those marks on the hull? I saw something like that once, a long time ago."

"You *did*?" Dan looked up at him.

"Yes. Off the coast of Greece, near the Calypso Deep - the deepest part of the Mediterranean. The merchant ship I was crewing on came across an abandoned Greek fishing trawler. It was still afloat, but barely." His voice trailed off and his eyes took on a sad, faraway look.

"*Abandoned?*" Vanek prompted.

"Well, not *completely*. We found the upper part of a man's skull on the foredeck. But that was it. Some blood, but not enough to account for the entire crew."

"Pirates?" Navarre offered.

"No. The damage to the hull was very similar to that sailing boat. Pirates wouldn't do such a thing. They'd take the boat or sink it."

Vanek shook his head. "Not if they were interrupted."

"True, but this was not like that. We found residue on the ship—the type of stuff from deep down, and clumps of seaweed. Parts of the hull looked *chewed*."

Dan didn't look convinced. "So... what? Are you saying it was attacked by some kind of sea monster?"

"Perhaps. As if we know all of that which hungers below. One of the crew—from Haiti I think—called it '*Jagad-b'ya*. He wouldn't elaborate, though."

Vanek was skeptical. "Didn't you take photos? What happened to the vessel?"

"We let it sink. No pictures. Our captain... was *przesądny*. Superstitious. We pulled alongside and looked, but he forbade us to go aboard."

Navarre flicked his cheroot over the stern. "Well, that's not an option. Our job is to get what's on that ship and get out. Sea monster or not."

Dan turned left out of the marina and drove over to the parking area at the northern tip of Star Island, past the Coast Guard Station. It offered a postcard view of the harbor, framed by a couple of scrub pines and a small beach. Toward the right, a pair of old fishing trawlers were moored at a rickety wharf while across the water toward the left stretched Gossman's Dock where the main fishing fleet crowded together. Due North was the harbor entrance where a vintage *Chris Craft* was motoring in.

For a space she didn't say anything, simply sitting there with her fingers resting lightly on the steering wheel, her eyes introspective.

"Tell me what happened back at the boat," she said, after a minute.

Vanek didn't reply at first, instead looking out over at the endless expanse of ocean. Thinking about it, ever since the incident with Kellie something had opened in his mind, in an unpleasant way. Like a hidden door he'd always been vaguely aware of but studiously avoided.

That's a lie and you know it! Michelle's voice spoke up.

Being aboard Gorecki's boat in the harbor hadn't bothered him as much as he'd anticipated. Sitting here thinking about what was out there, even from the safety of their vantage point, filled him with dread.

His right hand toyed with the armrest.

"What do you mean?" he said.

She twisted in her seat and made a 'gimme-a-break' face.

"You went white as a sheet, bug-eyed and slack-jawed for minutes. I think policeman Graves was about to speed-dial Montauk EMT. It was *spooky*. Now give."

Vanek couldn't gauge how much he wanted—or even *could*—reveal. It was like being flash-bombed with a horror movie. He decided to hedge his bets and tell *some* of the truth.

"I'm not sure, really," he said. "It was like being seized by a daydream, or rather a day-nightmare. I'd rather not discuss it."

"Why not?"

"I'd probably sound like a complete lunatic."

Her hand went to his and squeezed it.

"Just so you know, you don't have to worry about sounding like a complete lunatic with me. I had a manic-depressive grandmother who was in and out of mental hospitals most of her adult life. Trust me, I can talk *lunatic-ese* with the best of them."

"That's comforting," Vanek replied dryly. "So why exactly did we stop here? The bookstore and library are downtown."

"I also wanted to ask you about this Camp Hero business. In private."

A yellow caution flag went up in Vanek's thoughts. How much did she know? What did Gavin tell her?

"It's just an old Air Force base. The conspiracy stories didn't start until the early 1990's. Right around the time X-Files became popular on TV."

That wasn't completely true, but close enough.

"A coincidence?"

Vanek considered that. What if they were? *No. Ridiculous*!

Instead, he replied, "Not at all. You should stop reading Preston's book. Urban legends. He was a card-carrying member of the lunatic fringe."

"You think the whole 'Montauk Experiment' stories are just that, *urban legend*?"

Vanek hesitated. That's *exactly* what he had thought—the whole Montauk Project, time travel and Philadelphia Experiment tales were a bunch of horseshit cooked-up by a bunch of certified looneys with way too much free time and money on their hands.

The chair photo said otherwise.

He chuckled, "Well, not completely. The *Neptune's Reckoning* project was tied into a program conducted at Camp Hero. At least according to the files Gavin gave me. They were experimenting with low-frequency sounds to induce fear in enemy interrogations, but I can't make sense how that ties into the AMFOS unit on the destroyer. But I think we can safely rule out any supernatural or alien causes."

"Gavin mentioned the key to what happened to your grandfather could be here."

"He *talked* to you about my grandfather?" Vanek found that odd, even vaguely annoying. Gavin was notoriously tight-lipped about everything.

"Not in detail," she responded, a little hastily. "Only that he went down with the *Exeter*."

When Vanek stayed silent, she gave him another searching look.

"Was his... was he ever recovered?"

Vanek's jaw tightened. "No."

"*Oh*. So, he may still... I'm sorry." Dan leaned back against the headrest and looked up at the roof. "Look, I'm wondering if there's something *here* connected to what's happening out there."

"Then why isn't Gavin here with the ONR team tearing it all up? Why the hell drag all of us out here?"

"I don't know, except maybe he thinks you know something he doesn't."

Vanek snorted. "Why the hell would he think…?" he let the thought trail off.

Yes... why would Gavin think that? And exactly what is all this cloak-and-dagger business with salvaging Kovac's device off the U.S.S. Exeter?

But he *did* know the answer to that, didn't he? Starting with that first unclassified document that had arrived from the Navy Department twelve years after he'd formally requested it. It hadn't revealed a lot—most of the pages had been redacted—except the name, dates and location of the top-secret project his grandfather had been involved in. That's where he'd first heard about *Neptune's Reckoning*.

The name itself struck as having more than a whiff of the over-dramatic, like one of those ridiculous conspiracy spy-novels forever populating the NY Times best-seller lists. Written (he surmised) by over-weight middle-aged white men whose most exciting adventures were the ones they watched on TV at three in the morning eating cold pizza with a cat in their lap.

Except there was nothing far-fetched or amusing in the matter-of-fact sentences (those not blocked out) that he read in the official documents he'd received.

That was before the picture of the chair. Three by five inches, with no caption on it.

A chair, sitting in the middle of an empty chamber. Not just *any* chair, he saw, but a modified version of those vinyl-cushioned, high-backed ones with padded armrests commonly found on a WWII-era Destroyer bridge, except this one was mounted on a hydraulic lift instead of a fixed metal post. Leather restraining straps had been fixed to the arms and footrest, with some wires and a medieval metal-strapped head piece dangled to one side. It looked like a vintage mad-scientist's contraption. It was situated inside a metal cage with copper screening perhaps eight-feet square. Little else could be discerned in the image, as the lighting was a single overhead bulb in a cage and the walls of the main chamber were smooth, resembling lead sheathing if Vanek were to wager a guess.

The picture quality was sharp—Kodak Double X film he figured. On the back of it was penciled: "B 18". Below that was a single symbol:

Ψ

Looking at it made him queasy, though he couldn't articulate how.

A trident? As in Neptune's Trident? Or the Greek letter for 'psi', as in: 'the study of'?

Or both?

And the note with the encrypted message. Should he share it with them? Was he being hyper-paranoid?

Before he could follow that train of thought further, Dan started up the Mustang.

"Why don't you just ask him after lunch?" she said.

"Who?"

"*Gavin*. As in '*Carl*'? He said he'd meet us at the house at four. That gives us plenty of time to hit the library, bookstore, and grab some lunch. Have any issues with seafood?"

"If I did, I guess I'm in the wrong place."

"Glad to hear it. How about Duryea's Lobster Deck?"

13. A SURPRISE VISITOR.

The parking area next to the Montauk Harbor entrance was one of the more picturesque locations in the area. The channel was defined by two man-made breakwaters of brown rock extending out into the Block Island Sound with light towers at their tips—a view that tended to frame the incoming and outgoing parade of boats in such a way that only the most incompetent of photographers could take a bad shot. Partly it was the palette: the green-blues of the ocean against the ochre browns of the boulders with tawny strips of beach on either side. Partly it was the gateway it represented: both physically and metaphorically.

Like many things here, however, it was a man-made construct. The harbor was called Lake Montauk for a good reason: prior to 1927 it was a land-locked body of water. During that year, Carl Fisher—the man responsible for developing Montauk into something more than a rickety fishing village on Fort Pond Bay—had the channel dynamited open and ushered in the current era of a modern tourist destination.

This particular afternoon the parking lot was only partly full, with a few desultory strollers and a half-hearted fisherman or two. The elderly man at the mobile concession trailer was spending more time with the games section of the East Hampton Star than serving any customers.

Dead in the middle of the lot, Jimmy Reed sat in his Tacoma pickup truck, arm out the window, a lit Marlboro dangling from his fingertips. A pair of pretty girls in string bikinis sauntered by, unabashedly checking him out as they did (with matching smiles) but Jimmy Reed wasn't ogling beach-bunnies this afternoon, even if these two—upscale Manhattanites guessing from the gym-toned figures and Park-Avenue dental work—were all but wearing sandwich boards.

Jimmy Reed gazed at some point past where the tabletop-flat horizon of the ocean met the maverick-blue sky, contemplating his next move. Which he figured better be a good and careful one, after the text he'd received from Al Stanos a few minutes earlier.

"Sat 7p Mr. S want u onbrd—finish dis job and we r done," it read, followed by: "Mr. S. aint ASKING got it?"

Jimmy Reed didn't know which struck him as more depressing—Al's sub-idiot-level skills with the English language or the implicit threat in the note.

There was no way in hell, of course, he was getting on Scarpia's boat again. Jimmy Reed might not be the brightest of bulbs, but it didn't take much to figure out that getting back on the trawler was as what his dad would call a 'shit stick of a bad idea'.

A snatch of ocean breeze buffeted through the open window, bringing with it a hint of the more innocent aromas of his life here—brine, sand and suntan lotion. He remembered the cigarette in his hand and took a final pull off it before flicking away the butt. For a moment he took in the panorama (including the two women now flashing him disappointed smiles) and could pretend the cold knot at the bottom of his stomach wasn't there.

Then he fired up the Toyota, knowing it was time to pay that visit he had been contemplating since the night before.

Back at his apartment, Inge had just stepped out of the shower when there came a knock on the door. She stood in front of the dresser mirror, toweling her hair, confused. Jimmy never had visitors in the afternoon. Sometimes in the morning and definitely late at night (if a few of his pals were looking to hook up for a beer, some weed, or both) but afternoons were a dead-zone at the Reed crash pad.

The reflection looking back out of the mirror was one of those exceptionally pretty women utterly nonchalant about herself in a way only certain Scandinavian females possess. Inge Eklund could have easily landed a career as a fashion model, but the thought had never even occurred to her.

As she wrapped the towel up around her head and slipped into her clothes, her eyes went first to the clock on the dresser then to her smartphone charging next to it, frowning as she saw the discrepancy.

The clock was off again—which meant she would be late for work. She picked up the phone and was about to call her girlfriend, Rachel, when someone pounded on the door again.

Must be the landlord, she thought. She'd run into him a few times—an unsavory, overweight bulldog of a man by the name of Dick Thayer. On each occasion his disconcertingly blue eyes seemed to crawl all over her as if they were an extension of his stubby, restless fingers.

She took a moment to make sure she was presentably dressed, fastening the top two buttons on her blouse.

Still focused on the idea it was Thayer, she didn't think to fasten the chain latch as she opened the front door.

Standing out on the balcony was a brutish man she didn't recognize.

"Well *hello* there, little ray of sunshine," said Sammy Vanossi.

"I'm sorry, can I help you?" Inge replied, nonplussed. She may have been college-smart, but streetwise she wasn't.

A greasy smile spread across Vanossi's face.

"I was looking for Jimmy, he in?"

"No, he went out."

She tried to close the door but found she couldn't. Glancing down she saw his foot was blocking it.

"Even better," Vanossi replied.

Inge's eyes widened in alarm. "I'll screa—"

She was cut off as Vanossi lunged forward, one hand quickly closing around her windpipe as he shoved her back into the apartment.

A seagull let out its shrieking cry as it soared overhead, as if speaking out for her. A muffled yelp and thud came from the apartment as the door slammed shut.

The neighborhood went quiet except for the distant call of the surf and a pink tuna taxi scooted past.

14. ANOTHER CLUE... AND LUNCH

The bookstore on the lower half-circle of downtown Montauk had changed owners (and names) since he'd last visited. He'd called the Historical Society en route only to find they were closed for renovations, so this seemed as good a place to start as any. As they pulled into one of the angled spots in front of it, he shook his head. The wood signboard declaring its current incarnation out front said: 'Neptune's Nook'.

He chuckled, "Seriously?"

"*What*?" Dan asked.

"Never mind."

The bookstore was a cozy set up that immediately struck him as not just the kind of place you'd want to *buy* a book but pull up a chair and enjoy it slowly. Page-by-page. The dimly lit front room featured rustic wood cases and overstuffed leather chairs that made Vanek think of an upscale Hamptons retail crossed with an old-school British bookstore. Framed oil paintings of moody, impressionistic seascapes hung on the walls, nautical pieces and sculptures accented the displays of coffee-table books and a cleverly staged section of bestsellers and top-ten beach-reading material.

The back room was filled up with gleaming wood bookcases, a small reading couch and table, with a fluffy gray Maine Coon cat lounging on it like a queen on her divan. Bridging the two rooms sat a small cashier counter with a register. Behind it sat a man who could have passed for a dark-haired version of the late Tom Petty. With his scuffed jeans, Keith Richards t-shirt and sandals, Vanek pegged him as more rock-star than vacation bookstore owner.

"Hey there," the man said, looking up from a book he was reading. He did a doubletake as Vanek walked straight past him to the back room.

"Hi," Vanek replied absently. Even from a distance he could see the more serious literature was kept there. It was a classic (and sensible) set-up: eye-candy up-front for the beach-going masses and interior decorators, a secondary area for the bibliophiles and more serious literature enthusiasts.

Naturally, he gravitated to the clearly marked 'seafaring' section, his eye traveling to the end of the alphabet on the bottom shelf. His brow furrowed as he dug his hands in his back pockets.

As if they would really carry that old book...

"Will, do you know who this is?" Dan asked behind him. She'd paused by the man at the register. A young woman perusing Michelle Obama's biography nearby glanced up, as if wondering if she'd missed something.

Vanek held his hands up in a 'you got me' gesture.

"It's *Nick Carr*. As in *the* Nick Carr who wrote 'Leviticus Tree'?"

Vanek still drew a blank. He shook his head.

Dan gave him a dismissive wave. Carr leaned back in his chair with a slight smile.

"Never mind him," she said. "I loved your novel! One of the best horror stories I've read in ages! The whole thing with the moldering corpse under the deformed apple tree... *ugh.*" She shuddered. "But *um...* like what are you doing sitting here behind a cash register here in Montauk? That book was a major best-seller."

Carr chuckled. "Well, I kind of *own* this store. I was out here visiting last year and saw it was going out of business. No way I could let that happen. I went ahead and bought it."

"Wait, so you work here full time and you're still a famous writer!?"

"Well, that novel *was* a year and a half ago. I'm covering my bets. But I'm only here part-time. I have a couple people helping me out. It's quiet, I get to support the community and hey, worse case I have a guaranteed venue to sell my next book."

Dan didn't look like she was buying it. "Oh, come on, you must be joking. At the very least you should be cruising East Hampton in your Jaguar or something."

Carr chuckled again. "Not my style, I guess."

Vanek walked up to them, unable to resist a little poke. "What he's saying, Dan, is that being a 'best-selling author' doesn't necessarily mean you're using hundred-dollar bills for Kleenex."

"Definitely not in this era," Carr agreed. "Just don't tell my legions of female fans. You're a writer yourself?"

"Of sorts," Vanek replied.

Carr grinned and wagged a finger at him. "I thought I recognized you. '*Myths and Monsters: sea-faring legends in the age of sail'*?"

Vanek shrugged. "Yes. That book was published, God, ten years ago."

"Yeah, but it's a great collection! I usually keep it in stock. Wasn't there one back there?"

"Um, I didn't notice."

Carr stood up, stepped over to the back room. "Nope. Damn! I'd love to get you to sign a copy!"

"Maybe next time."

He realized Dan was eyeing him up and down. "You are *so* busted! Here I thought you only wrote magazine articles."

"Like I said, it's an old book," Vanek offered lamely.

Carr looked amused. "Yeah, but a really *good* one. It still sells. That chapter on the ship with the skeleton crew found adrift in the Sargasso Sea? Wicked cool. And loved the way you described the tale of the battle with the dead French crew at Trafalgar. It had me half-convinced I should run off and join the Royal Navy, just to hear the 'sing-song clatter of swords through the smoke' as you put it."

"I think you'll find they stick to high-powered firearms these days."

Carr laughed, 'No doubt. Still, it's a terrific read! The descriptions really put you in the thick of it." He stood up and offered his hand, "Nick Carr."

Vanek took it, "William Vanek."

"I'm Danielle Chung," Dan butted in, extending her hand.

"A pleasure," Carr said, with a little bow. "Wow. So, what brings the two of you into my fine establishment this morning? Anything I can help you with?"

Dan was still sizing Vanek up, arms crossed and one forefinger tapping her lips. "Yes," she said, "as a matter of fact maybe you can. Do you have anything about Camp Hero by any chance?"

"There's a small table in the back section next to the paranormal, if you're looking for the funny-farm conspiracy literature. No historical accounts, I'm afraid."

"It was a long shot. Any copies of '*Leviticus Tree*' in stock?" Dan asked.

"As a matter of fact, yes. In the back."

"Paranormal section?"

"Naturally."

"Will!?"

Vanek started, "Oh, er, of course!"

He found it easy enough—Carr had put an extra copy on a display stand atop the bookcase. A nod to himself but not obnoxious. Vanek snagged two and gave them a once over. It had the standardized NY Times best-seller cover art (Vanek often wondered if there was an app that simply auto-generated these things), though he wasn't a big fan of horror. At least it didn't have the pretentious self-proclamatory '*a novel*' added to the title. It didn't make him feel any better this young kid was a hot seller and Vanek hadn't written anything in a decade. His eye, however, went to the bookcase occupying the corner, filled with various old and antique books.

There were several early editions in there from Melville, Milton and Christie, even a few old John Dickson Carr mysteries (Vanek wondered if there might be a connection); books that a decade or two ago might have been under lock-and-key.

A dying market these days, he thought glumly. It did, on the other hand, up his estimation of Nick.

Back at the register, Vanek handed him the book along with his credit card. "You'll have to sign them for us, I'm afraid. One for each. I'll pay for both."

That got an amused smile from Carr. "Deal," he said, handing over Vanek's own book, "But only if you'll come back and sign one of yours. I can have it in two days."

Dan looked back and forth at the two of them as if unable to process this exchange. "You can make mine out to Danielle Cheung," she said, spelling it out for good measure.

Carr signed the copies and rang them up.

"One thing, you might check the library. They have a pretty good reference section with a lot of oddball documents in there. You might be surprised. Last year I was looking for some documents on the *Pelican* disaster and they had all sorts of odd things in there."

"Already planning on it," Vanek said. "We didn't have any luck with the Historical Society."

"Great place. But the new crowd out here doesn't seem much interested in local history."

Carr was about to add something else when the bell over the door jangled and five young tricked-out 40-something women jostled their way in, three of them talking loudly on smartphones. Vanek took that as their cue.

"Stop back!" Carr said, rocking on his heels. He glanced at the women with something approaching alarm.

"Absolutely," Vanek replied, then as they turned to leave, looked at the new customers and added, "Good luck."

Outside, Vanek glanced around the circle. The sun ducked behind darkening clouds, but the main drag remained busy, the wind plucking at hats and batting shopping bags about. Much of it was familiar to him, but then again so much had changed. At least Montauk Liquors and the Bake Shoppe were still there, the latter known for its deadly pastries and long breakfast queues. The saltbox Chamber of Commerce Building still sat across the street, largely ignored like a neglected aunt at a vacation party.

I still remember the time Michelle...

The thought was cut off as his gaze came to rest on Dan standing there, staring at him with arms folded. A touch of a smile curled the corner of her mouth.

"*What*?" he asked, nonplussed.

"*What*!? We just walked into a local bookstore and found not only a bestselling author behind the cash register, but one who wanted *your* autograph. That's '*what*'!" She looked at the signed copy in her hand in disbelief then back at him.

Vanek felt a pang of professional jealousy. His stab in the literary market lay in the past: a *has-been.* To shake it off, he pulled out his cell phone. A moment later he was speaking with the clerk at the Montauk Library.

"We might be in luck. The library has a small reference section on Camp Hero, including maps."

To his surprise, she hooked her arm through his. "Come on, sailor. This'll be my first lunch with an author. I want to hear what other secrets you've been keeping."

Vanek hadn't been to Duryea Lobster Deck since his parents had taken him and his younger brother out to Montauk when he was a kid.

Out past the LIRR terminus at Montauk along Fort Pond Bay, in his mind's eye was the quaint, roughshod seaside restaurant and fish market with cluttered white picnic tables on a deck overlooking the section of the bay that once served as the original center of the Montauk fishing charters.

The upscale eatery as they eased into the parking lot only underscored how much his nostalgic vision was out of touch from the reality of the present.

At a glance, structure was fundamentally the same, with its red lobster plaque over the fish market and the white-painted flagpole to the side of the gravel parking area, but the stylish teak decking and Restoration Hardware-looking outdoor dining furniture took him by surprise. It was as if the Montauk of his youth had been overrun by the Hamptons. A cursory glance at the menu only rammed this home: the prices made Manhattan restaurants look cheap.

"Thirty-one-dollars for a salad??" Vanek choked. Even by his Larchmont standards, he found this absurd. "Who eats here? The Rockefellers?"

"Google employees. Come on Mr. Writer, it's on Gavin's nickel," Dan replied, dragging him in by the arm.

Fortunately for them the restaurant was slow—perhaps on account of the weather—and the waiter showed them to a table overlooking the broad expanse of the bay. Just below them was one of the few remaining docks from the old days, with a handful of motor yachts moored there. The breeze ruffled the stretched overhead awnings and tugged at Dan's hair. Blue-gray storm clouds drifted over the water.

"That was pretty amazing," she said after they'd ordered, giving him an appraising look. "Wow, *Nick Carr*. That made my day. And *you*. Gavin didn't mention you had books out there."

"Book. Singular. It's not that big a deal. It was a long time ago. Can we talk about something else?"

"Hmmm. Maybe. I heard this used to be the main fishing docks," she said, arms on the table, contemplating the view. At least she didn't pull out her smartphone and compulsively check it. If she did, he would get up and walk out.

"No, those were over there, where the Rough-Rider's Landing condos are now," he said, pointing to a second dock three-hundred yards away along the southern curve of the bay. "Started out as a Navy base for testing torpedoes during the Second World War. After they closed it a few entrepreneurs struck on the idea of developing it into a sportsman fishing mecca and called it 'Fishangri-La'. They ran a special express train out of Penn Station to funnel city-folks out on weekends—reached its peak by 1951. The train would unload them over there behind the condos and there'd be a stampede to get on their favorite charter boats with their favorite skippers. After '51 it all ended."

"With the *Pelican* disaster."

"Yes, the *Pelican* disaster."

"Could that be connected to what's going on now?"

"I doubt it. Sometimes... well, sometimes just awful things happen."

"Like to your family?"

Vanek stiffened, the bluntness of the question like a slap.

Dan reached over and touched his arm.

"I'm sorry, that wasn't right of me to say that."

A cold knot tightened in Vanek's gut. His urge was to yank his arm away, yet at the same time it felt, well, *nice*.

Christ, did Carl put her up to this? Take pity on the old man?

He glanced over and saw Dan studying him intently.

"I lost my older brother," she announced abruptly. Her gaze went out to the ocean.

"I'm sorry," Vanek said, not sure if he was or not.

"Don't be. You had nothing to do with it. He died of an accidental gunshot to the head. At a college party. That's what they said, anyway."

"What about your husband?"

"That was different. It was a college romance thing—he was an artist exiled from Guangzhou I met while at school. An amazing talent. Took a nasty fall hiking Breakneck Ridge along the Hudson just after graduation. Took him four days to die."

Vanek didn't know how to reply to that, so he didn't.

The waiter arriving with their drinks broke the chain of thought. Dan had a Ginger ale. Vanek, iced tea.

"Tell me about your work," Vanek said, changing the subject. "Gavin mentioned your photography, but very little about Woods Hole."

Dan sipped her drink. "It's not that big a deal. I'm not exactly the rock star employee at Woods Hole everyone wants to hang with. The sonar research I've been doing there, while interesting to those in specialist fields, isn't a hot topic right now. Same with my side research into fear with marine life, particularly killer whales. Not necessarily flooded with big budgets."

"So why do it?"

"Because it interests me. Like my underwater photography. And I believe it's important."

"So is socio-economics. But there's probably better money in it."

Dan gave him a narrow look. "Is that why you gave up a career as a writer for researching obscure marine magazine articles? For the money?" she said, testily.

Vanek snorted and sipped his drink to mask his discomfort. He didn't care for anyone poking around near that dark period of his past. Or the extended purgatory that had become his life afterward.

"Hardly. It's not the glamorous jet-setting lifestyle everyone makes it out to be."

"I bet. I've seen your 'jet'. It looks like a museum."

Now it was Vanek's turn to be annoyed. "That's my grandfather's *house*!" the right side of his head and neck went hot with anxiety.

Dan reached over and playfully tugged his cheek. Then she leaned in and whispered in his ear.

"Lighten up. It's one of the coolest museums I've seen."

Vanek was rattled. And confused. He was beginning to question if any of this was a good idea.

"You still didn't answer my question," he said, pointedly. "About your work at Woods Hole."

Dan leaned back as their food arrived. She'd ordered the fried calamari with a house salad while Vanek had gone for the Fisherman's Platter, which looked like it had been created as an art installation. He wondered how much they were paying the chef and decided it was probably a lot more than he made poking around old maritime archives.

"It's interesting," Dan replied, spearing a large oval of squid meat, "and sometimes dangerous. Especially working in the ocean."

"With killer whales?"

"*Orca*. They're not that dangerous. They don't attack or eat humans in the wild. They're actually the largest of the dolphin family."

"Really? So: 'Flipper' with lots of teeth?"

Dan laughed. "*Yeah*. If you put it that way. But their brains are quite impressive and like humans they have well-developed amygdala, the region of the brain—"

"—associated with emotional response. Yes, I know a bit about it," Vanek interrupted.

"Right. I forgot. What you may not know is that like other dolphin species, they have a complicated system of sounds they use for communication and navigation - whistles, echolocation clicks, pulsed calls, low-frequency pops, and jaw claps. Most of my work involves using hydrophones to capture the data, but it also involves interpreting it. Not just Orcas, either. I've researched a variety of other species as well. This last year I've been focused on the comparative analysis of ocean mammal communications—it seems that humpback whales have changed the frequency of their calls from bass to tenor to avoid the frequency of shipping sounds, which were interfering with their communications."

"So, why are you at Woods Hole? I thought most killer whales are in the Pacific Northwest."

"They're anywhere their food is, though they do favor the higher latitudes. I spent four years shuffling between Hawaii, Seattle and Alaska. The last three have been at Woods Hole under Dr. Koltenbach, though he recently left and is now in Scotland. He pioneered the study of whale sounds. But back to your question. I think it's the work on cataloguing marine sounds and fear responses that got Gavin's attention. In particular, some odd interspecies communications I've been observing lately."

Vanek began working on the snow crab claws. "What do you mean?"

"Starting a couple of months ago, around the time the Navy picked up on those strange sounds I played you before. We recorded our own."

Up until this point, Vanek had been lobbing balls to keep the conversation going out of politeness. As someone focused in his own silo of academics—and human equation—of marine history, science wasn't something he expended much mental energy on outside of understanding the mechanical aspects of ships and the sea. This time, despite his dismissive attitude toward Dan, he found his curiosity genuinely piqued.

"Tell me more."

Dan took a few more bites of her calamari, then leaned back with her beer. She gave him a direct look.

"You're not going to laugh at me?"

"Not unless it's a joke."

"It's not. Or if it is, it's not a funny one. We first noticed it during a routine scan off the coast. We were monitoring whale communications between distant pods—those are groups of whales—when the hydrophone arrays picked up a series of signals past Block Island that didn't match anything we'd recorded before. At first, we thought it was some distortion of man-made shipping signals, but quickly ruled it out. Plus, it was too bizarre—we considered whether it might even be some practical joke, perhaps put on by some Navy boys from a submarine out on maneuvers."

"And?"

"We ruled that out as well. For one thing the sounds were originating out of one localized area—the same area as the wreck of the *Exeter*. It's too near a major shipping lane, so the Navy tends to avoid it. Plus, Gavin checked through his contacts and was able to verify there were no active operations in the area."

"They did sound... *strange,*" Vanek said, recalling the sound clips from the day before. The raw oysters on his platter suddenly didn't look so appetizing.

"Yes, they *were* disturbing. I've spent years listening to this type of thing and never heard anything like it. For example, typically, when whales communicate at a distance, it's relatively easy to isolate their signature and guess the nature of their language—looking for mates, sounding off for a food source, location of other groups. Within a pod is much more difficult—you can't tell who is who. It becomes more like a conversation in a crowded room. Compounding matters, whales—like people—compensate when there's a large number of them, talking and raise their volume."

"You mean, they start *yelling*?" He found the idea slightly ridiculous.

"Basically, yes. But that's not exactly what was happening here. At first, the sounds we picked up resembled mating calls—low frequency songs like humpback whales, but accompanied by clicks similar to dolphins or sperm whales. But these were... *bizarre.* The clicks were more like angry chattering and the song-like calls odd frequencies we've never seen before. Almost like something imitating marine mammals. It was weird; at one point they resembled cooing and in another, a... well like a hissing growl. Then we picked up on a series of low-frequency sounds—below 20 Hertz. They call those the fear frequencies—they can do odd things to the human brain—triggering fear response. Predators use them in the animal kingdom. And these, quite frankly, scared the hell out of me. I know that doesn't make sense, but there it is."

Vanek mulled this over. Was it really a coincidence the source of the sounds were in the area of the *U.S.S. Exeter*? Where his grandfather now rested? His brow clouded over as he considered the implications. It was beginning to feel like a vortex was swirling around Montauk, one that threatened to pull them—including the past and present—into it. What would Mich—

"Penny for your thoughts?" Dan interrupted, breaking the spell.

"Huh?"

"Your face just went cold as marble." She reached over and touched his forearm again. "Let's talk about something else for a moment, shall we? There's plenty of time for this business. I rarely get to have a relaxing lunch with such a nice view and a handsome man, no less."

Vanek mumbled something incoherent into his iced tea.

Dan poked him and sat back, smiling. "Oh, come on now, don't be modest, Mister Author. I bet you have all sorts of bored Larchmont housewives chasing you down at the local grocery store! Or country club. I have no idea what people do there to socialize."

Vanek found himself thrown off. Not the turn he would have expected the conversation to take. The truth was far bleaker, though. Aside from a random lunch date or two, he hadn't been in the company of another woman since, well, since Michelle had died.

"I'm not much for country clubs, I'm afraid. Nor chasing down married women in supermarket aisles."

"Seriously? You need to get out more. Well, maybe not to country clubs. I had a boyfriend once who swore by them. Not my thing. But what *do* you do for fun? Gavin made you out to be a recluse. Tell me it's all an act!"

"It's not."

Dan finished off her beer with a gulp. "Time to fix that. Come on, I'll settle up the tab so we can get out of here. We still have a library to visit."

Over the bay, the skies had darkened even further, the breeze picking up and the low clouds roiling like bruised cotton.

15. THE SWEET TASTE OF FEAR

"Good day for a boat ride," Gorecki said as they sat up in the cabin of *Catch-22*. It was one of Gorecki's stock phrases. To him, *any* day was a good day for a boat ride, barring a full-blown nor'easter in January. Even that was up for debate. He *lived* for the ocean.

Navarre sat next to him in the cockpit, gazing out the windows at the harbor while toying with his sunglasses with what appeared to be calm indifference. Behind the calm, however, he was turning over all the details and possible contingencies of tomorrow's dive. One thing he'd learned the hard way over so many years was that if something could go wrong, it would. Sometimes without any logical explanation. Like when a veteran diving partner of his swam off into the deep blue during a routine dive and was never seen again. They'd been exploring a 17th century Spanish wreck off the Canary Islands. Presumably it was narcosis, that insidious enemy of all divers, but who knew? The ocean kept far more secrets than the paltry answers she offered up.

He didn't care much for the way the barometer kept falling. Gorecki wasn't shy about heading out in the weather, but Navarre wasn't sure about Dan. While she struck him as competent, he had only tested her out on the two quick dives. For this type of thing he had always had nothing less than a team of divers he knew implicitly were seasoned—ones he could size up practically with a glance.

Those days were gone, as sunken as the rotting timbers of the ship he'd been forced into misidentifying as the *Bonhomme Richard*. For now, at least. Fame was a fickle mistress, he well knew, but she could also show up unexpectedly again.

And there was more to the story than he had let on with either Dan or Vanek.

This wasn't the first time Navarre had done a 'High Priority' job for the ONR or any other military operation. It was the first, however, where he wasn't permitted to bring in his own team. Which suggested two things: extracting the *Neptune's Reckoning* device was somewhat straightforward (and something a single diver could manage) and they wanted minimal exposure on this. It also made him think the two divers—himself and Dan—were expendable. What he didn't quite understand was William Vanek's role in this. On the surface, it meant more complications all around. Unless he had a purpose Navarre (perhaps even Vanek himself) wasn't aware of.

One thing he did know, Gavin struck him as a devious sort.

That was neither here nor there, and if nothing else, Navarre was pragmatic. Fate had dealt him Danielle Cheung and William Vanek. And Gorecki. Gorecki was the only one he figured he could rely on if things went south.

Gorecki nodded toward the northeast, where the wall of clouds had taken on an even more ominous appearance, with intermittent patches of greenish hues, suggesting something diseased heading their way.

"On the other hand," he said, "it's probably a good thing we didn't dive today."

***

Thirty-odd miles away, in the murky gloom of the ocean depths, the darkness around the wreck of the *U.S.S. Exeter* gathered itself again and began to move.

Of itself, it had little in the way of formulated conscious thought, at least in the same way creatures it encountered did: its mental processes were more alien to them than was a deep-sea tube worm to a human. Even more so as this environment was unnatural to it, let alone what it had been spawned out of; a different fabric of time and space entirely.

And yet, there were similarities.

It *hungered*, for one.

Disrupted out of its usual dormancy pattern, it was both hungry and in its own odd way, *irritated*, the way a wolf spider might be if pushed prematurely out of its winter hibernation stage.

It was becoming *awake*.

After a millennium of regular cycles, this had been the second time this had occurred. Both because of *man*.

This wasn't the first time it had encountered the human species—that event could be traced back to the first intrepid ocean-going travelers in the area nearly a thousand years previous—but those encounters had been on its own terms.

They had also altered and redefined it, the way coming in contact with a quantum particle will alter its state. Unlike the marine life it had encountered up until that point, which while nourishing in a straightforward, natural cycle sort of way (though there was nothing natural about this creature), its first encounter with man had awakened a latent thirst it hadn't experienced before: fear.

Not that it hadn't encountered fear before—the whale and dolphin species possessed it—but with humans it was at an entirely new level; the difference between, say, an average clam on the ocean bed and a sweet mouthful of caviar.

While dolphins, whales, and killer whale species knew pain, loss and sadness, mankind brought with it the limitless permeations of imagination; specifically, the infinite (and deliciously colorful) variations of its ability to generate *terror*. That terror gave a whole new, unbridled form the creature which had arrived through the far-off reaches of time/space much like some spiders cast their filaments and sail off with the wind until a distant tree catches them.

It wasn't the only one to arrive on Earth, but it was one of the few that survived. Those that arrived on land died in short order. The chemical composition, lack of light and inherent pressures of deep ocean were similar enough to its place of origin to facilitate surviving the early larva stage. Once in contact with the local living organisms it began to assimilate rapidly—yet their shape shifting, chameleon-like substance (at the cellular level) meant it was crucial that it encountered the most resilient species from the get-go. Those that encountered weaker ones were doomed from the start. Some did survive, for a time at least, to terrorize seas where they nested. They went by several names in old myths: *Vyatha, Ghora* and... *Jagad-b'ya*, which translated to: *Terror of the Universe*.

This particular creature first encountered a remnant species of marine dinosaur modern paleontologists would have been shocked to find were still in existence some two thousand years ago—a small but aggressive apex predator in the twilight canyon off the continental shelf where it landed (or rather materialized, as the solar system had just crossed through a subtle wrinkle in time-space at that juncture).

It wasn't until it encountered those first early ocean crossers—a group of Vikings that had gone way off course during a storm—that it evolved into an entirely new type of entity. It didn't so much assimilate other species' DNA, (though it did that too), it assimilated their consciousness. In particular, their fears.

The small group of survivors on that first boat had been rife with it, half-dead and half-mad with terror at finding themselves in such an unknown part of the Earth. But that was nothing compared to what they were about to encounter coming up out of the ocean.

So, a new version of itself came into being.

As did the more recent arrival of the wooden ship whose bones rested not far from its nest.

Then came the planet-engulfing event known as the Second World War and with it a device that woke the creature from its hibernation prematurely. That too was a first—by accident, it made its first attempt to host part of itself in another.

It almost worked.

The next interruption wasn't as singularly dramatic but was the confluence of several recent things: warming ocean temperatures, an overabundance of underwater noise at depths and a chemical change in the content of its environment due to toxic pollution.

Extreme toxic pollution, in this case.

Once again, drawn by the proximity of live intruders—human intruders—it began to move, spreading northward in an amorphous, black shape, accented by the string of silver-blue orbs that served as a sort of eyes. They were of little use at such depth—its main sensory apparatus appeared all but invisible to the naked eye; hair-like filaments that could stretch out considerable distances, questing, probing.

Tasting.

What they were drawn toward this time was something that was more of a vague echo of an element it had encountered

[*before*]

the way a human might encounter a hint of a smell that drew its consciousness back through time, spanning decades in a millisecond to a memory one hadn't realized had been forgotten.

The sensation aroused a much deeper yearning, almost a blind hunger.

With a *connection.*

Two-hundred yards to the east, with an abrupt sideways roll, a killer whale veered its course away from the wreck and the thing coalescing around it. Its partner, however, continued on. The male killer whale - which Dan would have recognized immediately from the blue NOAA tracking tag on its dorsal fin and its emitter signature—had been following a pod of minke whale with its mate down from Newfoundland, while sending occasional clicking signals to their own pod, fifty miles to the east-northeast. Minke whale were its preferred food source in the North Atlantic and these orcas had broken off from their small transient group and gone off hunting one on their own.

The male killer whale, which had been tagged U47 by the NOAA Fisheries Service, was better known by Dan and her immediate group of marine biologists as *Günther*. Named after one of the scientists she realized its tag number was the same as the once infamous German U-boat Commander Günther Prien, whom as fate would have it, died in combat not far from where this killer whale was initially spotted.

Günther had also demonstrated unusual levels of communication and intelligence, which was why he had come into Dan's purview within the previous year. To preserve the battery power in the tracking tag, it was set to activate on specific times of day, the signal being picked up on GPS by satellite and fed into the NOAA's master tracking program.

The female, assessed as being fertile, hadn't been tagged as per NOAA Fishery policy: any whale considered to be contributing to the population wasn't to be tampered with.

Günther was thought to be too old and had been tagged the previous year.

It had been months since Dan had studied this orca, which had last been seen off the coast of Cape Cod. Günther let out a series of agitated clicks and headed northeast back toward its group east from Block Island.

The one minke whale they were following wasn't so smart—it continued on, drawn by what it thought was a minke calf in distress, though something in that call was peculiar. It wasn't concerned about the two killer whales. It took at least three or more of them to take down a full-grown minke. Usually an entire group of Orcas working in tandem, switching in relays to tire out the minke before finally holding it under and drowning it.

This minke, while nervous, didn't feel in immediate danger. It was more concerned about the calf and its odd distress call. What it found when it approached the edge of the shelf where the wreck of the *HMS Tryton* lay was yet more puzzling.

Its vision wasn't the best, but it was able to make out what registered as a large minke calf surrounded by a growing, nebulous cloud of darkness. The signals it gave off were even stranger—transitioning into the alert calls of an endangered pod... but deeper, a heavy sound.

The minke whale did a slow zig-zag approach, confused. Behind it, the female killer whale appeared, having left Günther behind. It too had heard something unusual, more like one of its own calfs in distress.

As the minke whale closed in, the darkness expanded even as the 'calf' began to alter its form, its glowing silver-blue eyes multiplying from two to four, then to six. Instead of a mouth full of baleen, its jaws were lined with savage, translucent teeth like that of an angler fish.

Before the minke whale could do little more than let out a whimpering call, the mutated calf shot forward and bit most of its head clean off, leaving blood and shreds of flesh dangling in the water. The killer whale veered left and pumped its tail frantically but before it got more than three meters, a spray of tentacles shot out of the gloom and seized it, wrapping around its sleek black and white torso in a vice-like grip.

The whale screamed.

The tentacles tightened, causing the orca's internal organs to rupture. Blood and gore ejected from its open mouth as it died.

To the east, Günther swam a tight circle, agitated. Killer whales were the apex predator—it had never heard such a thing as it did now. Its instinct urged it to come to the female's aid, but its acute sense of self-preservation warned it to keep away.

For the first time in its existence, Günther knew fear.

With a flick of its tail, it bolted eastward.

Away from the blackness.

Sixty miles away over at the Woods Hole monitoring lab, Libby Eastman, the technician on duty, leaned into her monitoring screen. Both hands were on her headphones, a deep cleft of concern appearing between her brows. After a moment, she took the headphones off and leaned back.

"What is it?" asked Aiden Powell, the intern helping her out.

Libby blinked a couple of times. It had sounded like a scream coming through the relay buoy off Block Island. She couldn't be sure because in her entire career at Woods Hole—which had just passed the 9-month milestone—she's never heard anything like it. She knew it was possible but *knowing* and *experiencing* it were two different things.

It sounded like a siren of sorts—a panicked crescendo dropping off into a pulsing throb.

Libby knew she should try to stay emotionally detached from the test subjects the way Dan Cheung did; she envied how Dan was all business and confidence when it came to dealing with anything in the field, like some veteran ER doctor.

You do this, I'll do that. This is how it'll be handled.

Libby's professional façade lasted all of about five seconds.

In fairness, it was a particularly anguished sound.

Her hand went to her heart and she let out a sob, the other hand scrabbling for the smartphone on the desk next to her.

"Oh, God!" Libby exclaimed. "Something terrible is happening!"

It took her three tries to call up Dan's contact profile.

16. WE DON'T GET A LOT OF REQUESTS FOR THIS SORT OF THING...

Tucked-in off Route 27 just east of town, the Montauk Library was an unobtrusive, stucco-and-glass modern building nestled in amongst the scrub pines.

Dan pulled into the parking lot—which was all but empty despite the overcast that begun moving in—and slid into a spot opposite the main entrance.

"Let's see what their so-called 'reference section' on Camp Hero consists of here," Vanek said as he unbuckled his seatbelt. "Who knows? Maybe today is our lucky day."

"Such an optimist," Dan replied.

"Can I help you?"

At a glance, the woman sitting behind the circulation desk was like any number of non-descript, vaguely friendly middle-aged librarians found across the country. In this case a black-haired version with a neutral smile, square glasses and a square face to go with them. But as Vanek knew from decades of researching in such places, these types were often the best kind.

The eyes behind the glasses possessed a sharp intelligence as keen as any Harvard professor and seemed to say: *See, I'm just your average, busy-body librarian who will give you only enough help to get what you need and not an ounce more and that's exactly what I want you to think.*

"Well, I'm *hoping* you can," Vanek replied, dialing up the charm. "I'm William Vanek and this is Danielle Cheung. We're out here on behalf of the Office of Naval Research doing work on Camp Hero and rumor has it, you have better reference files than Uncle Sam on the subject. Is that true, Miss....?"

"... Mrs. *Pritchard*, Elma Pritchard," the woman replied, her face instantly warming up. "Aren't you the... oh, yes! You're the one that called earlier?"

"Guilty as charged. May I call you Elma?"

"Why, yes," Mrs. Pritchard said, a hint of color coming into her cheeks. "I believe Miss. Riggs—she's in charge of the reference section—set aside some materials she thought might be of interest."

"Is she in?" Dan asked.

Mrs. Pritchard blinked and looked at her as if seeing her for the first time.

"No-no, I'm sorry, she's over in East Hampton at the book fair today." The polite librarian smile was suddenly back.

"What kind of materials?" Vanek prompted, sensing the shift. "Secret underground maps? Confessions and photos of captured aliens? That sort of thing?"

Mrs. Pritchard let out a small laugh and stood up.

"Oh, nothing *that* interesting I'm afraid. Here, why don't you follow me?"

The rest of the library, like the circulation desk, was of a vaguely modern, sleek design done in a neutral palette dominated by light pine. Vanek tried to pinpoint the style but found he couldn't. The climate-controlled air and acoustic-muting materials only furthered the sense of oddness, as if he and Dan had walked out of the blue-collar seaside resort town and into an experimental eco-friendly neutralized environment. It made him slightly uncomfortable.

Mrs. Pritchard led them down past the stacks to a bay-window alcove containing a worktable and a semi-circle of wood shelves neatly filled with books and thick binders.

"Make yourself comfortable," she said. "I'll be right back."

"*Comfortable*?" Dan said, looking around. Glancing down the stacks to make sure the librarian was out of earshot, she added, "I think Little Miss. Muffet has the hots for middle-aged academics."

Vanek gave her a squinted eye, "*Thanks*."

Dan responded with a quizzical look. Again, he was aware of her magnetic attractiveness. And that she seemed to enjoy teasing him.

Don't read anything into it, Michelle's voice spoke up in his head, *she's young enough to be your daughter!*

A minute later, Mrs. Pritchard came back pushing a roll cart loaded with a bunch of books and thick binders.

"We don't get a lot of requests for this sort of thing," she said. "But as it turned out, someone from your office was asking for the same materials just the other day."

"Really…?" Vanek said. "Do you recall who it was?"

"No, I'm afraid I wasn't here. Miss. Riggs spoke with them. If you check back tomorrow, you can ask her yourself."

"Thanks, I'll do that," Vanek replied. "So, what do you have here?"

"I'm not sure, really. This is Miss. Riggs' domain."

"Do you have a copier here?"

"Oh yes! It's right next to the circulation desk. It's twenty-five cents a copy for color, ten for black and white. We can make change for you, if you like. Nobody seems to carry coins much anymore."

"Thanks, Elma. You've been a tremendous help."

"I *have*?"

"Absolutely."

Vanek reached in and picked out a folder overflowing with 8x10 photographs, his brows raised at her.

Taking the hint, Mrs. Pritchard wished them luck and bustled off.

Dan came over and pulled out a stack of spiral-bound documents with 'Declassified' stamped on the blue covers and began leafing through them.

The photos were old black-and-whites, most dated from the 1940's and 50's. The images were of Camp Hero, some of them of the original construction of the complexes during WWII but others included the building of the iconic AN/FPS-35 SAGE radar tower in the late 1950's. Some were duplicates of the photos he'd seen in Gavin's files. A few were not: snapshots of the two coastal batteries with their 16-inch guns being tested, random images of the underground facilities.

"Anything interesting?" Vanek asked.

Dan shrugged and laid out the bound documents which were about an inch thick and contained several fold-out plans of the installations.

"You tell me. Sonar and fish are my thing."

Vanek fanned through them quickly. "These are just standard installation drawings and reports. Nothing that exciting unless budget allocations and naval cannon firing procedures float your boat."

When she lifted the last one out of the box however, several inserted pages fell out.

"What about these?"

Vanek took one and unfolded it. It was an old plan on blueprint paper that might have been either new extensions or at least proposed ones. He was about to toss them aside when a yellowed piece of paper slid out with a pencil-drawn floor plan on it. In the lower corner someone had written in block letters:

Bunker 18

"What is it?" Dan asked, catching his puzzled expression.

"I'm not sure. Probably nothing."

He looked at it more carefully, noting the call outs on the rooms, particularly the square one with what appeared to be a chair in the center of it. The hair rose on his arms. At the same time, he felt overcome by an odd sensation... a roaring in his ears, a vertigo.

Blood... screams... the screech of bending metal followed by a choking, gurgling sound... a hissing, chittering like that of an agitated insect... or of clicking: a battery of cobalt-blue eyes and the shrill scream of a man in utter terror and pain... gibbering voices and the vivid image of a man's torso being ripped open, intestines flopping out like bloody sausages... another of empty, burned eye sockets and a gory visage of another face with its lower jaw torn off... a muffled explosion that sounded wet and revolting.

And the worms... writhing. Seething. Seeking.

Vanek snapped his head up, blinking.

"Will? *Will*? Ground control to Major Will?"

Dan was shaking his shoulder.

Instantly the bland, neutral-pine world of the library reasserted itself: the bright sunlight slanting in through the bay window, the cheap roughness of the report cover under his fingertips, the insistent tug on his shoulder.

"*Huh*?" he said.

"The color went out of your face. Like you saw a ghost. Are you all right?"

Vanek grunted. He felt a neighborhood or two shy of all right... yet, he wasn't entirely sure what he *did* feel. Or what was happening to him.

Two for two today, bud. Maybe this is how it all starts: your mind slips its moorings and heads down the rapids and cataracts of mental instability until whoosh—over the precipice you go and down to the bottomless well of insanity! Great timing too! Just when you get roped into a critical situation you fold up and implode like one of those cheap birthday-greeting balloons at the Dollar Discount Store! What in the Sam hell did that girl do to him? Some kind of contact hallucinogen?

He looked down at his right hand and saw that it was trembling. He realized something else: part of him didn't want her to know. That was the Vanek way: *everything's fine. No problem.*

"Um, do you think you could go get me a glass of water?"

Dan studied him with concern. "Of course. Let me see what I can find."

Vanek waited until she was out of sight, then he glanced at the papers again. No strange reaction, though looking at that square little room made him uneasy, as if the angles were disturbingly off. From the drawing there seemed to be additional call outs about the interior lining of it, along with an extraordinary thickness to the walls.

Was it a bomb shelter of sorts?

He didn't think so. Still... he folded the paper in half, then glancing around to see if he was being observed or if there were any visible cameras, carefully slid it sideways while simultaneously moving the report over with his other hand, covering the fact that he'd deftly transferred the sketch into his notebook.

It wasn't anything he could fully articulate—partly it was an old researcher's habit of not sharing anything until he was sure of what it might contain, the other was that, despite how attractive he found her (*she's not Michelle*!), he didn't quite trust Dan either. Or anyone, for that matter. Except maybe Gavin, whom he'd known for decades.

Yet how well do you really know him? The devil's voice spoke up again.

Come on, it's Carl for chrissakes!

Dan returned a moment later with a bottle of water.

"Technically, this isn't allowed, but I convinced Mrs. Pritchard to make an exception. The place isn't exactly overrun with visitors."

Vanek glanced around, noticing it for the first time. Except for an elderly man poking around the shelves the next aisle over and a small group of kids over at one of the reading tables, the library looked empty.

"What did you find?"

"Oh, this?" Vanek held up the other two blueprints. "Nothing, really. I think it was something I ate... and maybe a little too much scotch last night."

Dan smiled and stepped closer, "*Hmm*. And along with that load of BS I bet you have a bridge in Brooklyn you'd like to sell me."

"You're too young to know that kind of saying."

"Really? You're too old to get away with lying to me."

Vanek realized with a start that yet again she was close enough to kiss on the lips.

Damn the woman!

As if sensing his discomfort, she inched in even closer.

"And a little too old to be stealing papers out of a library like a high-school delinquent," she whispered. "Give, or I start screaming my head off."

Vanek tried to put on a poker face, but decided it wasn't worth it. He had to force himself not to make a pass at her. After taking a sip of the water, he unclipped a couple of the original maps from the binder and handed them to her.

"All right then," he replied in a quiet voice. "Do me a favor and make photocopies of these. Eleven-seventeen, black-and-white. We're going on a little field trip."

She stood in close a moment longer, enough that he could smell her breath (which had a whiff of mint), then stepped back, one eyebrow arched.

"It better be a good one."

This time Vanek asked if he could drive. For one thing, he hadn't driven a Mustang since his college years and was curious to try it out. For another, and perhaps it was the air out at Montauk, he felt an urge to try something different. Dan didn't object—she tossed him the keys and said, "Knock yourself out!"

He took them east out along Route 27 back toward the house.

Instead of turning off on the Old Montauk Highway at the Deep Hollow Ranch, however, he continued up the first of the hills that rose along the final stretch of Long Island.

The view from this elevation was breathtaking, with the rolling breakers of the Atlantic to the south and the calmer gray-blue swells of the Sound to the north. Due east rose the maroon-and-white spire of the Montauk Lighthouse while from Hither Hills the giant SAGE radar array towered over the trees; a hulking, rusted framework of a lost Cold War era against the eternal sun-bleached blue skies of Eastern Long Island.

"What did you find in the library?" Dan asked, as he pulled into a parking area overlooking their house to the south and Camp Hero to the left.

"An original plan of the old base, drawn by hand," he said.

"Why steal it? Why not just make a photocopy?"

Vanek weighed his answer. He sat back and put the SUV in park.

"I did it on a hunch."

"And…?"

"Someone else has been poking around in this business and my instinct tells me I don't want anyone else finding out about this just yet. When all this is over—if it's over—I'll find a way to get the blueprint back to them."

Dan crossed her arms. "So, it isn't all *bullshit*. Spill. What's on the drawing?"

Again, Vanek hesitated. But at this point he decided to come clean.

"A part of the installation I'd never heard of before, or not before two weeks ago, at least."

Her brows raised in response.

Vanek stared ahead. "A place called 'Bunker Eighteen'. I found a reference to it going through some of my grandfather's things."

"*Hmmm*. This is starting to sound like one of those 'Montauk Project' conspiracy tales…"

"I think we're well past the *starting to* part."

"That's an about-face! What do you mean?"

Vanek took a deep breath.

He retrieved the paper from the back seat and spread it out on his lap.

Frowning, he ran his finger over the various call outs, trying to make sense of what he was seeing. In researching his grandfather's story, he'd spent countless hours studying the bunkers and installations at Camp Hero, but this was something completely new. "What do you have back at the house in the way of equipment? Flashlights? Crowbars? Hammers?"

"What, are we breaking into a bank?"

"Close. We have to break into a bunker."

"Between the two of us we have a bunch of stuff. Arnaud arrived prepared for a full-scale invasion, I think."

As they pulled into the drive, Vanek saw with some alarm that their neighbors had been joined by more people. Alongside the Lexus were several Cadillacs and Buicks, including (oddly) several banged-up vehicles which Vanek thought of as "Brooklyn Beaters". Two VW buses sat towards the back like a couple of surfer-dudes late for the party.

"What the—?" Vanek said as he got out of the car.

The words trailed off as he saw—to his horror—that the 'High Priestess Aduba' had spotted them and was marching over, her sidekick, Om, trailing behind with a worried expression. He reminded Vanek of an overwrought rescue dog not quite sure if he was still being taken home or not.

"Ah! You've returned!" she said, hands raised as she approached. "The Goddess smiles upon you! Indeed!"

Vanek glanced around, weighing whether he could sprint to the front door of their house before she was too close. Even as he considered it, he realized he was too late: Aduba was upon them in a flurry of flowing chiffon, a cloud of jasmine and lavender arriving with her.

"Er, hello," Vanek said.

Dan drew up her best smile and echoed him, saying "Hello!" with an indulgent tone that was entirely missed by their neighbors.

Oblivious, Aduba stood, hands still raised, the tops of her eyebrows just visible above her glasses, as if awaiting a follow-up response from Vanek of reality-altering magnitude. When none came, she stepped forward and cupped her hands around Vanek's chin, to his further alarm.

The roundish head with its white make-up turned to Dan then back to Vanek.

"*Lovers*! Two lovers—Taurus and Virgo! Such a beautiful thing!" She glanced at the sky. "Star-crossed, I'm afraid, but such is your fate. You can still join us! We are of the Age of Aquarius, and our time is now!"

"Many have arrived already," Om added helpfully, inclining his head and waving back toward their house.

"It's *coming*, you know. The nightmare of a thousand faces! But we are gathering our forces. Our *love*."

Something about this prickled Vanek's nerves.

"Who's coming? Donald Trump? The Easter Bunny? This isn't some magical convention! You're two confused people from Illinois!"

For a moment, Aduba looked affronted. She regained her composure immediately.

"I told you: I am Aduba, the High Priestess of Taured. This is Om!"

"What you are is *delusional*!" Vanek felt his blood pressure going up. By nature, he was polite. Except toward people who insisted on persistently barging into his life with what he thought of as 'loony-logic'.

Aduba plowed ahead. "We're *interspatial*, dear—our molecules cannot be confined to just one time and place. Also, we're a-material. I wouldn't expect you to understand."

"*A-material*? You drive a *fifty-thousand-dollar Lexus SUV*!"

Unperturbed, Aduba looked at her husband, then back at Vanek. "Because the goddess has deemed it necessary. We are of the Age of Aquarius, for two-thousand years, but our time is *now*."

Realizing he was trying to speak rationally to a person who, best he could tell, was operating in a different solar system, he put a knuckle to his forehead and smiled to himself, the dials on his temper edging into the red zone.

Thankfully, Dan intervened. Stepping in between them, she took Vanek's hand in both of her own and pulled it to her chest.

"That's just incredible!" she said to the High Priestess. "Perhaps we can join you later? We have much *loving* to catch up on!"

Aduba turned to her. Despite the over-sized glasses, Vanek could sense her eyes narrowing.

"Do not seek to mock me, child. Terrible things are yet to pass and both of you are in the crosshairs! Soon you will seek out aid, mark my words! Soon!"

With that, she left.

"Well, *that* was interesting," Vanek said, once they were safely back inside the house.

Dan peered out the curtained window at the activity over at their neighbors.

"My God, it looks like a California Cult convention is getting underway over there. Next thing they'll be holding candles and singing *Age of Aquarius*."

Vanek was surprised. "A little before your time, isn't it?"

"You didn't know my parents. They were nuts about the Fifth Dimension."

Vanek spread out the blueprint of 'Bunker 18' and compared it to the map of Camp Hero tacked up off to the right of the sea charts.

"Well, in the meantime I think we need to figure out something in this dimension. Is this the only map we have of Camp Hero?"

Dan dropped the curtain and walked over, hands in her back pockets. "Hmm. We had a few, I think. Gavin dropped off a bunch of them the other day along with the sea charts. Arnaud didn't think we'd need them, so he left them on the table."

She stepped up to the table next to him and shuffled through the pile of loose printouts there.

"Here, what about this one?" she said, pulling out a black and white map from the 1960's.

Vanek looked it over and shook his head, "Too recent. Anything older?"

"Here." She handed him a construction plan from 1943.

"Perfect."

As he took it from her, their fingers brushed and yet again, he found himself inches from her face. The air between them seemed electrically charged.

"What?" Vanek asked. He realized his mouth had gone dry, and he was having difficulty getting his lips to work. The left side of his neck went warm with the first flush of anxiety.

A smile tugged the corner of her mouth.

"Do you think she was telling the truth?"

"About what?" he replied, knowing full well what she meant.

"That we're…?"

"I…"

Michelle's voice spoke up in his head and not in a friendly tone:

Wake up, Will! I told you: she's young enough to be your daughter! Our daughter! The one we never had!?

He pushed it aside and was about to kiss her anyhow—Michelle be damned—but realized his hesitation had cost him the moment. Dan blinked and stepped back, as if coming out of a trance.

"*Oh*," she said.

Vanek turned away, looking at the map in his hands as if it was the most fascinating thing in the universe.

"Look," Vanek said, eyes on his feet, "I'm not sure what's going on here, but I, *er*, we need to really focus for the moment—"

He was interrupted by a heavy knock at the front door.

"Carl?" Vanek asked, as he stood in the entrance. He'd completely blanked on Dan mentioning he'd be by after lunch.

"Hello, Will."

Without waiting to be invited, Gavin shouldered past with his usual bluster. He was dressed in chinos and a chambray shirt, as if he'd just walked off an upscale yachting party with wealthy boat-owners who disdained looking as such.

"What have you been up to?" Gavin added as he walked into the dining area. Vanek followed him in and acting on instinct, put himself between his old friend and the hand-drawn plan on the table. Chiefly it was his old researcher's precaution to protect a new tidbit of information until he'd had time to fully assess it. While Gavin looked over the wall, Vanek leaned back and deftly flipped the paper.

Gavin grunted, hands clasped behind his back like a commander surveying his battlefield.

Dan glanced at Vanek and an unknown agreement seemed to pass between them.

"No new developments yet. Navarre is over at Uihlein's Marina with Gorecki waiting to get some special 3D scanner for tomorrow's dive. I've been going through the files you gave me. We were about to review what we do know and what our next move should be."

Gavin grunted. "That's it? Why aren't you out there now? Salvaging the wreck!?"

"I'm sorry?" Dan replied.

Gavin zeroed in on her. "The *wreck*? The *U.S.S. Exeter*? I thought I made it clear the urgency on this matter! Why the hell aren't you down there right this minute with Navarre retrieving the *unit*!? That Goddamn Trimble scanner was supposed to be here today! We paid a fortune for it!"

Vanek was taken aback. The last words came out with flying spit. Gavin was acting like a lunatic, a side he would have never suspected. He also didn't care much for the bullying tone he was taking with Dan. Nor did he like the effect on himself: a hair-trigger reaction to someone's anger that let his anxiety run riot. A hot flush went up his neck into his hairline. His heart began to hammer.

Despite that, he stepped between Gavin and Dan, raising his palms up.

"Carl," he said in an even voice, "Easy."

Gavin spun on him, "*Easy*? God damn it Will, I brought you out here as part of the solution! Or are you going to be part of the problem!?"

Vanek tried to ignore the throb in his temples. *What on earth was up with the man?*

Fighting his temper down, he forced himself to take a diffusing approach. "Carl, I've only been here a full day. I'm still getting up to speed. Navarre and Danielle can't dive on the wreck until tomorrow. We were just about to go over what we do know from the files, *again*. What the hell is going on, anyhow? I've never seen you like this."

Gavin started to say something, then checked himself. He looked around. "I-I," he started, shaking his head. "Never mind. I'm under a lot of pressure from the ONR to wrap this thing up before the NOAA gets here and starts poking their noses up our skirts. *Christ on a stick*, is there anything to drink around here? I could use something stiff."

Vanek turned that over in his mind and came up short. "There's some scotch in the kitchen," he said. "Dan, anything for you?"

She put on a terse smile and glanced down as her phone began to ring.

"No, I'm fine for the moment. Let me take this."

Over in the kitchen area, Gavin took a stiff pull of his scotch, standing by the breakfast nook window while gazing out over the ocean. He hadn't bothered to raise his customary *salut*, which was also highly irregular in Vanek's experience.

Vanek leaned against the island, not saying anything. He'd settled for a glass of cold water. The left side of his face stayed hot and flushed. The upscale kitchen only underscored his sense of dislocation. Like standing on a stage. Still, he couldn't deny the view was spectacular. More so with the stormy clouds scudding across the ocean.

"Have you ever been out to Camp Hero?" Gavin asked abruptly, intruding in on his thoughts.

"No."

Gavin kept staring out the window.

"Your grandfather was there."

Vanek gave a start.

"He *was*?" He thought about the recent documents and photos he'd found. *Of course*. The clues were all right there in plain sight.

"Yes. The second phase of '*Neptune's Reckoning*'. It wasn't really an antisubmarine technology. It was one of those loony fringe science experiments, designed to induce fear—even death - through low-frequency sound. Then they discovered they were tapping into something else."

Vanek hesitated.

To tell him about the blueprints... or not: that is the question.

How much did Carl know? How transparent should he be?

Vanek settled on what his father used to refer to as 'navigating around the truth'.

"What kind of '*something else*'?"

Gavin frowned. He appeared to be weighing up how much to divulge.

"Initially it was a top-secret program conducted during WWII. On paper it was an experimental cloaking technology for ships to avoid detection by both submarines and magnetic torpedoes. A game changer given how badly things were going for us in the Atlantic in those first couple of years of the war. I don't have to lecture *you* on that. I suppose you've heard of the 'Philadelphia Experiment'?"

"Lovely movie."

"Utter load of Hollywood horseshit. But that's where the premise came from—then someone piled on a bunch of time-travel garbage on top of it. It never ceases to amaze me the amount of ridiculous crap people actually believe in!" He took another drink of his scotch, then shook the ice cubes.

"Your grandfather was part of the original program out of Philadelphia. He flew up to Rhode Island with the test unit for a trial run on the *U.S.S. Exeter*."

"The *Exeter*?" Vanek echoed.

Gavin chuckled. "The very same. Something happened on that test cruise—something strange. The captain and crew were told the destroyer's hull was coated with a special mesh paint that allowed it to be activated by an electromagnetic field oscillator—supposedly that was the device your grandfather delivered."

"That much was in the files you gave me."

"Yes, but that's not what it *was*. And this report reveals your grandfather showed up at Camp Hero *after* the ship sank."

"That doesn't add up," Vanek said. But the strange image of that destroyer chair in the room sprang to mind. "They listed my grandfather as 'Killed in Action' with the *U.S.S. Exeter*. I understand the program he was working on was being monitored by the Coastal Defense Station here, but I've never heard of anything tying him *directly* here."

"Yes, that's the *official* record."

Vanek set his glass on the counter and crossed his arms.

Gavin swiveled to face him, his eyes hard and direct. "So, the mystery deepens. The report I was recently given shows the whole 'anti-magnetic' technology was a cover. Dr. Anton Kovac's fringe science technology was about highly focused low-frequency acoustics. They were testing it on various subjects out at Camp Hero before that 'mad' Hungarian, Kovac, convinced them—based on a technology he'd 'acquired' from Nicolas Tesla just before he died—that it could be tested out on an entire *ship*. Use it against Nazi submarines."

"That sounds... pretty far-fetched."

"It did even then. But either he talked a good game or convinced them with a workable prototype. Regardless, the Navy forked over an obsolete Gleaves-class destroyer for it to be tested on. Something unexplained happened out there and the ship sank with all hands. *Except* your grandfather."

"Except…? Then what the hell happened to him?"

"That's just it—no one knows. After the wreck, the report showed he was involved in experiments that were conducted out at Camp Hero for several months *after* the sinking of the *Exeter*, but it doesn't give the exact dates of *when*. I was hoping maybe you might have some leads on your end. Ever come across anything like that? Anything your grandmother might have said? Anything in your grandfather's personal effects, maybe lying around the house?"

Vanek looked him back straight in the eye and said, "No, can't say I have." He didn't know what prompted him to tell such a bald-faced lie, it just popped out of his mouth. Partly it was something about Gavin's urgent prodding into his family house and history. "What is this document? Can I see it?"

"I'm getting to that," Gavin replied. "It's still classified. But my suspicion is that it may be relevant to what's happening out here."

"How so?"

Gavin's lips compressed into a thin line. "Just *because*. I'm not sure how to divulge the details just yet. Except to tell you I believe the answer lies somewhere out at Camp Hero. In one of the bunkers."

Vanek coughed to cover his surprise.

"I'm not sure I follow," he said.

Gavin continued to stare at him. For an absurd split second, Vanek thought he was about to blurt out: "Liar! Liar! Pants on fire!" Instead, Gavin looked down at his scotch and nodded at it, as if in affirmation.

"There's been rumors over the years about the experiments there. About a special *chair* used for interrogation and possibly *other* sorts of testing, the kind they don't like to keep traceable records on."

"Seriously?"

"Oh, come on Will, you're not that naïve. What happened at Guantanamo Bay was hardly a first. UltraMK? The Stargate Program? There's plenty of shady crap under the government's skirts. What I can't figure out is how what they were doing out off the coast of Montauk in 1943 was connected to the interrogation program at Camp Hero. Or why it was all closed down in short order and hushed up so thoroughly. I call that serious damage-control in action."

"So why not call in the cavalry, a back-hoe and start digging around?"

Gavin set his glass down next to Vanek's and pulled a few folded pieces of paper out of his pocket. He held it in front of Vanek's face.

"Because of this."

Vanek raised his brows in response.

"This is a copy of the report. The one you never saw and never got from me, clear?"

"Got it."

"The thing is, there's *still* pushback coming from somewhere in Naval Intelligence, to answer your question. Someone or some group—very high up it seems—wants to keep this all dead and buried. That's why *you're* here. I want to get to the bottom of this just as bad as you do. But I have to do this discreetly. Hence all the subterfuge with getting Dan and Navarre out here, then you. You need to get out there, into that wreck and get Kovac's equipment out of there within the next twenty-four hours. This report will narrow your search somewhat."

He glanced across the kitchen to make sure Dan was still on the other side of the space, then placed his hand on Vanek's shoulder like he'd done in the past whenever he was about to give some fatherly advice.

"I should get rolling. Don't show that to anybody. Not even to your partners here. And Will?"

"Yes?"

Gavin nodded toward Dan. "She's a hot ticket but keep your distance on that one. I need both of you focused one hundred percent on the job. Are we clear?"

"*Crystal*," Vanek replied, unable to resist the classic Tom Cruise line.

The reference blew right over Gavin's head. "Good," he replied, not smiling. "I'll be running errands, then over at the ONR next couple of days if you need me. And call me immediately if you find anything out at Camp Hero."

Vanek nodded.

Guess we're going on a little expedition, then.

After Gavin left, Vanek stood for a moment, then pulled a folded paper from his wallet—the note he had found back at the house. Something had occurred to him while Gavin had been talking.

The 'Mad Hungarian'.

Of course! His father had spoken fluent Hungarian. He took out his smartphone and photographed the 'gibberish' word by word. A minute later, he had his answer through his image recognition app.

The words weren't gibberish—they were abbreviated Hungarian numbers.

Not just any numbers, he suspected.

Coordinates.

"What happened?" Vanek asked, dropping into the chair. Dan sat on the living room couch, head in hands, her phone on the coffee table. She reminded him of a frazzled editor he'd walked in on once, just before she lost it. Though he'd only known her barely a day, he wondered how much of the fearless go-getter was an act.

Dan leaned back and regained some of her composure.

"I'm not quite sure. I just got a call from my colleague at Woods Hole. One of the orcas we've been tracking for some time... it sounds like something terrible has happened. Either to it or one of the whales it was traveling with."

Vanek had a bad feeling about this. "Where?"

"Right near the wreck of the *Exeter*."

16. "I HAVE A LITTLE PROPOSITION..."

"*Whoa*, this will break the internet, dude!"

The speaker was a mop-haired black kid named Jax Pierson that Jimmy Reed knew from the area. Jax had a reputation for organizing meet-ups, Tinder parties and more importantly, was a key member of an Eco-advocate group called PlanetJustice that went after anything they saw as unsustainable or environmentally unfriendly practices in the area, or anywhere in the world for that matter.

Jax was part of a recent wave of 'eco-tourists' (as Jimmy Reed thought of them) that had overrun Montauk in the last five years; generally upscale, highly motivated millennials from wealthy family's hell-bent on changing the world.

While in public he got along well enough with Jax and his friends, Jimmy Reed privately thought of them as a bunch of breathtakingly self-important spoiled brats who saw no irony at all in the fact they lived highly entitled lives while attacking others doing the same. At one party, he'd found himself being lectured by a high-schooler on how crucially important it was for Jimmy to develop his personal brand and monetize it. Jimmy thought it was some kind of prank, put up by one of his drinking buddies.

It wasn't.

Locally, PlanetJustice spent a fair amount of energy trying to shut down the sports fishing industry for what they labeled as 'totally barbaric, unsustainable business practices bent on crushing a critical life-giving food source'. On one hand, Jimmy agreed with them. He knew first-hand what was happening with the depleted fisheries on the eastern seaboard. On the other, he grew up with a lot of those same fishermen and knew them as a level-headed bunch who worked their asses off while the people attacking them mostly lived—as far as he could tell—off little other than their parent's bank accounts. He didn't fully understand how, but they always seemed to have plenty of money and no issue with spending it.

Welcome to the *New Montauk*. Over-run by people you just want to strangle.

Still, they also had their uses.

Jimmy had gone over to the house Jax shared with his fellow PlanetJustice pals—a one-point-two million-dollar pad in the neighborhood of Soundview Drive.

Inside, the place looked like a cyclone had just ripped through. Empty food cartons, surfing gear, computer and gaming equipment were strewn everywhere. Though hardly a candidate for 'Good Housekeeping', Jimmy couldn't help but wonder if he'd stumbled into a simulation of one of the disaster areas Jax claimed they were always sending aid to.

Fortunately, except for a couple of Jax's roommates wrapped up in a game of 'Gods of War' on the living room Playstation 4 system, they had the place to themselves. Jimmy wanted to fly this by Jax in private first, before making an announcement to the world wide web. He waited until they were in the back room which had an open kitchen on one side, before giving him the quick version of the story.

"So, you say you *worked* for this Scarpia dude? I mean like, helped dump the goods?"

"Yeah," Jimmy admitted. "I was just filling in for a friend. Hell, it's not like I knew what the job was."

"And now you're *woke*, so things are now, you know, *real*?"

"Yeah, *real*. Whatever. Look, do you think you can get the word out, blow this thing sky high?"

Jax responded with a self-righteous snort. "Oh yeah. Just chill. We knew about the dumping, but now we have a name to go with it! Fucking fascist! Scarpia and his little operation are about to get crushed. But you have to get on there. You know the deal: pics or it didn't happen."

Jimmy shook his head. "Did you hear a thing I said? I can't go back on that boat, or I'm dead. And what do you think—I can just whip out my cell phone and start snapping away once I'm on board?"

"*Whatever*. Look, without anything concrete it's just a lot of vaporware. Can't do much unless he keeps at it. You said after this next drop he's gonna swerve out of here for good?"

"Yes. That's what I think." Jimmy wasn't sure how much was getting through. Even while he talked, Jax's fingers tapped out a staccato on the keys of his tablet.

"Problematic."

Jimmy rubbed the bridge of his nose with his thumb and forefinger. An unconscious gesture his father used to do when his patience had run out. He stood up.

"Look, forget about it," he said.

As he turned to leave though, Jax held his hand up.

"I said problematic, dude, not *impossible*." Jax flashed him a Cheshire smile. "Netflix and chill, my man. I got you on this. Team PlanetJustice is about to slay these mothers."

"Seriously?" Jimmy asked.

"Most," Jax replied. "No-one fucks with the environment anymore without paying for it. Scarpia and company? *Destroyed*."

As if to make his point, from the other room came a yell and the sound of a mace crushing someone's head through the surround-sound speakers.

Five minutes later, Jimmy pulled up in front of his apartment building, wondering if he'd just made a monumental mistake. Then again, he didn't have a lot of options.

It wasn't until he got to the top of the stairs and looked up that he saw the door to his apartment was wide open.

"Inge?" he said as he entered, trying to keep the edge out of his voice. Jimmy wasn't the sort prone to panic, but he didn't care for the sharp prod in his gut. Something about that open door wasn't right. Inge *always* locked up after herself. She was nothing if not methodical.

He made a full circuit of the apartment before he came back to the door and saw the damp towel on the floor.

Stepping out onto the landing, he scanned the neighborhood, even the beach along Fort Pond Way as if perhaps in a whim of fancy she cast off her towel and decided to go for a swim.

Nothing. Other than a few desultory strollers and a maid service car ambling along Navy Road, it was quiet.

The phone vibrated in his cargo short's pocket.

A 718 area-code. He didn't recognize the number.

"Hello?"

There was silence on the other end, followed by what might have been a heavy cloth getting shuffled around. He was about to hang up when he heard a muffled shriek.

A woman's voice.

"*Hello*?" he repeated.

"Listen up, little lover boy…"

"*Who is this*?" It took a moment, but he recognized the voice: the illustrious Mr. Vanossi: Scarpia's muscle. It wasn't a stretch to figure out he wasn't calling to invite Jimmy over for a non-GMO popcorn rom-com slumber party

"I have a little proposition for you." Vanossi's voice had an undeniably oily quality to it. The kind that made you want to wash your phone after he spoke through it.

"Go on."

"Make sure you're on the boat next Tuesday, on time, and you get your little Swedish meatball back with all her parts intact. On the other hand, if you talk to anyone—and I'd like to put special emphasis on that exact word—I'll mail her back to your apartment one piece at a time, starting with her perky tits. After I've gotten to explore all three of her orifices, with rigor. How does that sound?"

Jimmy felt a mixture of rage... and fear boil up within. Outside of an occasional run-in with a drunk local or the testosterone-brimming visitor out to prove himself (like that one college boy at Shagwong's one night), Jimmy had never been threatened before.

Not until his last run-in with Scarpia.

He had a lot of friends here. Hell, this was *his* turf! Who the fuck was Scarpia and his cronies to show up and threaten *him?* Here in Montauk!

A momentary flashback of the malice-riddled eyes of Scarpia just as he ground the cigar into the back of his hand hit him: *careful.*

"I don't believe I hear an answer…?" Vanossi prompted. This was followed by a blunt smack and a muffled scream. Then came the unmistakable *snick* of a knife.

"Okay! *Okay*," Jimmy replied. "Deal. I'll be there."

"And…?"

"And... not a word! I swear! Leave her alone, Goddammit! She's just a foreign exchange student."

Vanossi must have put the phone very close to his mouth. The next words came through close and intimate.

"Hmm. I kind of like the taste of foreign pussy. Maybe after all this is done, we can *share*. How about that, lover boy?"

Jimmy felt his gorge rise.

"Sorry, I don't roll that way. You lay a finger on her though, and I'll rip your fucking balls off with my bare hands. How's that suit *you*?"

Vanossi laughed, "Oooh, tough guy now."

Jimmy didn't know about that, but he thought there might have been a little nervousness in Vanossi's voice. Or maybe it was just wishful thinking.

He hung up.

17. BUNKER 18

The guardhouse to Camp Hero was empty when Vanek and Dan pulled up and the gate stood open. Easing past onto Camp Hero Road, which Vanek noted was recently paved, he drove them in the general direction of the radar tower, which seemed the likeliest starting point based on their map.

The unmistakable centerpiece of the Montauk Project conspiracy theories, the high-power AN/FPS-35 radar tower had been built in the late 1950's and went fully operational in late 1960. The combination of its complex Cold War technology and sealed-off underground bunkers made it perfect fodder for people with little knowledge and a lot of excess imagination (in Vanek's estimate) but for his purposes, the location and its dates of construction didn't tally up.

Still, it was impressive: the squat, concrete base structure with its massive, oblong radar array 126 feet across and 38 feet high looked right out of a movie set. The lattice work was now rusted and had fallen away in chunks, but the local boaters still preferred it as a landmark as it was easier to spot than the lighthouse.

As if to add ominous drama and urgency to their arrival, storm clouds lanced with occasional flickers of lightning rolled overhead, chasing cat's paws across the ocean to the south.

Dan pulled the Mustang into the parking area. A few tentative raindrops splatted at the windshield, but the jury was still out if this was a passing squall or a lengthier downpour.

After Gavin's odd visit, Vanek had compared the plan of 'Bunker 18' to the various above and below ground installations but none seemed an obvious match. Dan seemed a little distracted, rattled by the news she'd gotten from Woods Hole.

Whoever had covered up the location had done a thorough job.

Wherever it lay, Vanek figured it had to be a spot no-one had poked around too closely in. And likely some place close to the command center. The latitude and longitude numbers narrowed it down considerably, but even with the GPS app on his phone, it still left a large area. It took the better part of half an hour before he found a potential site, just southeast of the original Headquarters building on the 1943 map. The tricky thing was the 'original' map of the base. It had been drawn up in 2000 by the U.S. Army Corps of Engineers and was missing several key details, either deliberately or by oversight. Still, he only had an educated guess. There were no surface details on the blueprint except for exits, which he'd attempted to align with both the 1943 map and the 1958 map. The closest he could get to the estimated entrance location was the parking and picnic area near the SAGE Radar tower. It was looking like a wet walk. Fortunately, Navarre had extra foul weather gear stashed at the house that was a close enough fit for Vanek. Dan had brought her own.

The two of them unloaded a couple of waterproof backpacks containing flashlights, a few ropes and tools, water, and power snacks. The rain jackets were a little heavy-duty for summer weather—they were sailor's gear—but they'd do.

After unloading everything from the trunk, Vanek glanced around to get his bearings.

"What are we looking for?" Dan asked.

Vanek shrugged. "Not exactly sure. Some kind of entrance that hasn't been used in a while. Presumably on or around a rise or hill."

"Easy then," she replied, glancing around. Aside from the trail they were on, the terrain was nearly impenetrable with a tangle of pitch pine, beach grass, summer grape and thistle. "We should be done by next month."

"Hopefully not," Vanek replied, looking warily at the game trails splitting off from the main path.

Probably infested with deer ticks, gnats and God knows what else. I'll have Lyme disease before I walk ten feet.

He had used repellent on his clothes and shoes at least, and both of them were wearing jeans as a precaution.

After thirty yards or so, he spotted a trail on his left heading up a low rise.

"This way," he said.

The path appeared to be a game trail and forked off in short order. He chose the left path again, but after a hundred yards of winding up and down, it dissolved into a tangled mesh of scrub bush he would need a machete to hack through. The right fork didn't seem any better. They made their way along it for twenty minutes before it ducked under an intertwined tunnel through huckleberry, creepers and staggerbush.

To get through it they'd have to crawl on their hands and knees.

Vanek cursed under his breath. He'd become hot and sweaty in the foul weather jacket.

This is a lunatics game, you nitwit! he told himself. *You're a 46-year-old man on a snipe hunt for a mystery bunker you could spend the next twenty years looking for and never find! For Christ-sakes, grow up!*

"No good," he said aloud to Dan.

They crawled back and stood up.

"This is pointless," he said, wiping the sweat off his forehead. "We'd need a whole search party to have a chance of finding this damn thing." Checking his watch, he saw they'd been at it close to an hour.

"What about that?" she asked, pointing to what appeared to be a game trail further to their right.

Vanek crouched down on his haunches and tried to peer through. It didn't look promising. Just as he was about to stand up and turn around, however, something caught his eye.

At the base of a gnarled scrub oak he spotted a rusted metal tag stapled to the bark. Closer examination revealed it to be a tin path marker.

The kind the military used to use.

It wasn't much, but as good as any other lead. As far as he knew, there weren't any poisonous snakes out in eastern Long Island. As he got down on his hands and knees he wondered.

"Um, Will, are you sure about this?"

"Hell no," he replied. "But... let's just see where it goes."

"Sure." Dan didn't sound overly confident.

Vanek paused, taking a deep breath. Although he'd never had claustrophobia before, the old anxieties were quick to pluck at his thoughts: *what if you get trapped? What if there are snakes in there? Spiders? A rabid fox? Or rats—there could be rats there!*

He squeezed his eyes shut for a second, forcing the voices—which sounded suspiciously like his late wife's—into silence.

"Damn you!" he spat out. "Shut up!"

"Sorry?" Dan asked behind him.

"Er, nothing." Vanek hadn't realized he was talking out loud.

Before he could reconsider, he made himself crawl forward, hands and knees digging into the sand and pine needles, the backpack ungainly on his back.

Within twenty feet the trail tunnel dipped and turned into damper soil with a narrow, trickling stream. Even as he cursed himself though, he caught a glimmer of gray through the branches. More importantly, the trail opened up ahead. Ignoring the chafing of the backpack and the sweat trickling from his armpits, he kept going. The air was suffocating and humid.

Scrambling forward he broke through onto the side of a hill. The bushes were still dense, broken by an occasional stubby pitch pine and scrub oak. The trail wound up and over the hill. To his right he could see the concrete spotting bunker thirty yards away.

"Come on!" he said, helping Dan to her feet. He could almost sense it: something close by.

At the top of the crest, he paused, disappointed. The trail skirted the top and continued down the other side, toward the west. A few raindrops pelted them. To the south, the surf had picked up considerably, sending rolling breakers crashing along the shoreline. The scene seemed to mock him: *nice try, buckaroo! Only three hundred more hills to go!*

The trail below went into a swampy area. Vanek frowned.

For a moment he'd been sure...

As he stepped forward, his hiking boot snagged something, and he nearly fell flat on his face.

"Will!" Dan said, catching him just in time.

"Dammit!" Vanek repeated, then looked down.

Near his foot was a concrete lip, perhaps an inch and a half thick, sticking out from under the tangled brush. Crouching down, he pulled at it, revealing a circular lid perhaps three feet across. He looked up at Dan, who shrugged.

He worked his way out of the backpack. Setting it down, he pulled out a folding military-style shovel. He dug backwards into the soft earth around the lid, using the shovel as a lever.

"Give me a hand."

Dan got down on her knees and pushed.

At first, it didn't seem the lid would budge. Then, abruptly, it did, sliding off to one side as if eager to comply. Dan nearly pitched into the revealed opening, but Vanek grabbed her shoulder and hauled her backward.

It appeared to be a ladder access, a circular tube of concrete leading straight down into darkness. Rusted iron rungs ran down along one side. Cool, musty-smelling air wafted up, old and stale.

Vanek pulled out his flashlight and shone it down.

The pipe went down roughly eighteen feet with the rungs continuing down to a cement floor strewn with detritus. From what he could see, it looked like a chamber down there with puddles of water. The question was how stable the rungs were.

Vanek grunted.

God knows what's down there, not to mention mold, bacteria and knowing the military, a lovely cocktail of toxic substances.

Why the hell didn't I think to bring a mask? What am I doing here? I should be back in my study, comfortable, working on that next article for Maritime History and worrying about dinner!

Michelle? Care to weigh in with a helpful insight or two?

His dead wife remained silent.

Damn it! he muttered under his breath and hoisting himself over, tested his weight on the first rung. A few flakes of rust fell away, but it felt solid enough. There was just enough space to accommodate himself and his backpack.

He glanced up at Dan.

"Secure one of the ropes around the hatch and toss it down, just in case. I'll go first and see what's there. If I start screaming, call Gavin and the cavalry."

"Very funny," Dan replied, already pulling a coil of nylon rope out of her own backpack. She hunched down and tied off a slip knot (with the practiced ease of a veteran sailor, Vanek noted). Coiling the loop around the concrete cover, she added, "Seriously Will, be careful, okay?"

"Roger," he said, snapping off a mock salute. "Keep your light pointed down so I can see. Thanks."

Vanek worked his way down gingerly, testing each rung twice before moving to the next. One or two protested but held. He kept one eye on the rope dangling next to him, just in case.

Stepping off at the bottom, Vanek aimed the flashlight around, revealing an eight by ten-foot chamber with a ship-style steel door. Aside from the debris on the floor and a rather ominous-sized spiderweb occupying one corner of the ceiling, it was empty. All four walls were covered with graffiti, ranging from highly skilled taggers to clumsy spray-painted messages with such clever sentiments as 'suck my dick', 'Rachel fukz sharks' and more oddly: 'Welcome home, Crimson King.'

"Anything?" Dan called down.

"Not much."

He gave the wheel on the door a yank. After the third try, it gave with a screech, the hinges protesting as he pushed the door inward. Beyond was a corridor extending in both directions, with piping and conduits running along the top. In some places parts of the ceiling had collapsed, but a string of light bulbs mounted in cages in between the pipes were intact.

To his left, the tunnel ran for fifty yards before opening into a larger chamber. An old metal desk was visible along with a toppled chair and trash strewn all over the floor. To his right, was a damaged stone block wall. It looked as if someone had made an unsuccessful attempt to break through it with a sledgehammer.

Dan appeared next to him, flashlight ready.

"What took you so long?" Vanek asked, checking his watch. It had taken her a good five minutes to join him.

"Got another call from Woods Hole," she replied. "My intern is pretty upset. Plus, I didn't care much for the look of those ladder rungs."

Vanek played his beam down the corridor where the desk sat. There must have been a ceiling vent as gray light filtered down from above. From the graffiti along the walls and amount of debris, it was obvious a few generations of kids had beaten them to it. Vanek couldn't mask his disappointment. He'd been hoping for a stroke of beginner's luck.

If 'Bunker 18' had been discovered here, it would have been all over the conspiracy wire. Unless he could find what generations of trespassers had missed.

They'd come this far. It was worth a look.

The area with the desk must have been a checkpoint of sorts. The remains of a wooden filing rack leaned against one concrete wall, with a couple of old Bakelite telephones laying smashed on the floor. Remnants of other broken furniture lay strewn about. Here, overhead light came from a couple of ventilation grills in the ceiling, overgrown with foliage. Beyond the desk the tunnel continued about twenty feet then formed a 'T' with a perpendicular tunnel. Midway down was a shallow alcove.

The bunker was muted and quiet, a wrecked relic from another era where German submarines prowled off the coast and 16-inch cannons were considered necessary to protect American shores.

The alcove was curious—in the floor they found an access that had been filled in with concrete. Based on the missing chunks, someone had given up trying to chisel through it.

Behind the desk they found a shallow closet, boxed-in when the space behind it was walled-up. The doors to it had been torn off and lay nearby, smashed.

The other corridors both ended in solid walls of concrete, filled in when they decommissioned the base, Vanek figured. Two more access points were visible near each end, but also plugged with concrete. It would take a month with a jackhammer crew to get it out, if that. A further investigation yielded little else; the bunker, whatever its original expanse was, had been sealed up tight. Aside from debris, the desk and a lot of graffiti, the place was empty.

Still, Vanek couldn't shake the sensation he'd overlooked something.

"Doesn't seem like there's much here," Dan said, once they'd circled back to the entry door.

"No, it doesn't," Vanek agreed. He pulled out the blueprint again and looked it over in the beam of his flashlight. Two of the access points seemed to line up which meant that whatever secrets 'Bunker 18' held, they were right on top of them. Or maybe right in front of them.

So close, yet so far.

"Where do you usually find a secret... never mind, follow me!" he said.

Using his feet, he measured off the depth of the closet against the depth of the surrounding wall. At a glance it wasn't obvious, but the side wall of the closet was eight inches deeper than the sealed area.

Vanek pulled out a hammer and steel chisel.

"Hold the flashlight," he told Dan.

It took half an hour to break through. The wall was only a couple of inches deep here and to make matters easier, water had been seeping down the opposite side, leaving the concrete porous and crumbly once Vanek had chiseled through the first inch. He widened it a bit further before pausing to shine his own light through the opening.

Beyond, lay a pristine corridor, stretching a hundred feet. He could make out several doors on either side, with a set of iron doors at the far end. Aside from some water stains and a thin layer of dust, it might have been used yesterday. Even the military gray-blue paint on the walls was intact.

What Vanek first noticed was how stripped-down it was, even by military standards. The second thing he noticed was the lack of any signage, which struck him as ominous, somehow.

"What's there?" Dan asked.

"A tunnel. With some doors along it."

Once he'd made the hole, he found it much easier to enlarge it. Within twenty minutes the opening grew a foot and a half across, ten minutes later it was double that. Using his hammer, he knocked away the roughest parts, so they could climb through.

A minute later they were standing on the other side, flashlight beams playing across the space. The silence was disconcerting, as was the atmosphere. It felt dead and chilly. Like a tomb.

"What do you think?" he asked.

"I'm not sure," she replied. "It looks like any old bunker that's been sealed up. What makes you think this is Bunker 18?"

Vanek's light fell on the wall immediately to their right, where there hung a small rusted metal placard with the numbers '18' on it.

"Just a hunch."

There was more to it than that, though Vanek wasn't sure how to articulate the feeling without sounding like a lunatic. He sensed a *residue* here, the mental equivalent of catching a hint of tobacco smoke in a room someone smoked a pipe in decades previous. In this case it was something cold and terrifying. It made him think of Wolf's line from the old Stephen King novel "The Talisman": *Bad smell here, Jack, bad smell*!

The four rooms on either side of the corridor yielded nothing but there was something peculiar about the iron doors at the end: there were several massive dents from the *inside*.

Vanek and Dan exchanged uneasy looks. The size of the dents suggested a fist the size of a giant—easily two or three feet. Also, there appeared to be dried blood spatters on the floor and walls. Quite a few of them, in fact. Vanek also noted quite a few gouges in the concrete floor (and ceiling), as if raked by large talons.

It wasn't a giant leap to conclude something incredibly violent had transpired.

Vanek looked at the heavy sliding bar lock that had been thrown in place.

What in the hell had happened here? he wondered. And on the heels of that:

Do you want to open that door and find out?

Having come this far, he realized, he really had no choice.

"Give me a hand," he said.

The steel bar put up a stubborn fight at first. After a few judicious whacks with the hammer though, it loosened enough for the two of them to lift it up out of the hangar, jumping aside as it fell to the floor with a deafening *clang*.

Using his foot as leverage, Vanek hauled back on the right door until it slid back along its track with an ear-splitting screech.

Dan let out a scream as something fell in from the other side of the door.

The flashlight beam revealed a desiccated skeleton—military, based on the uniform—its jaws wide open in its final death scream. The fingers were splayed as if its owner had tried to claw their way out of the chamber beyond, if the broken nails and fingertips were any indication. More disturbing was the ragged tears across the uniform shirt and what looked like several bite marks out of the right side of the torso.

The uniform and patches were classic WWII vintage Navy, which suggested several other things in Vanek's mind.

"Do you think whatever did this... is still in there?" Dan asked.

Given the sealed door, that made a fair amount of sense.

"A good possibility," Vanek conceded. "Though the odds of it being *alive* aren't. That corpse is probably seventy-five years old."

Still, he couldn't shake the feeling that *something* was in there. His heart rate was up—he could feel it hammering away in his chest. Yet at the same time came an acceptance. A sense of resigning to the age-old human compulsion *to know*.

Beyond the door was a spacious room, roughly square, with another massive door at the opposite end and a smaller one to the left that appeared to lead to a small control room. The second set of doors—also steel—had burst wide open. The smaller door on the side clung by one bent hinge.

Half a dozen more bodies occupied this space, some dismembered and torn apart. Mold-stained papers and broken chairs were strewn about, many with gouges and bite marks in them. One body had been smashed into a wall with such force it had been flattened into the concrete. Next to it lay the remains of a radio control station, also destroyed by some major force, while from the ceiling hung loose wiring and piping. Against the opposite wall was a line of large cages, some which appeared to have the remains of animals (and one human) in them.

Vanek and Dan played their flashlights around this grisly tableau, both unsure what to make of it.

Whatever had occurred here was right out of an extremely violent horror movie.

Vanek's flashlight beam probed the inner chamber.

Carefully stepping around the bodies and debris, he saw that it was a smaller room—a plain concrete cube—with a control room window to the right. In the center sat a cage of metal mesh perhaps ten-foot square, with a door on the back side. Parts of the mesh were blown out as if a dozen cannonballs had been fired out from it. Heavy electrical cables wired to the top of it now hung loosely like dismembered snakes. Inside of the cage was a single seat on a pedestal (Vanek recognized it as the same hideous one from the photo), except this one was larger and set in a semi-reclining position.

In the seat was a corpse.

All kinds of red flags were going off in Vanek's head. Including one particularly big one.

"Holy shit," Dan said, looking around. "This is like that movie *The Thing.*"

"With Kurt Russell?"

"Who's Kurt Russell?"

"The star."

"No, he *wasn't*. Mary Elizabeth Winstead was."

Vanek shook his head, realizing there wasn't any point in discussing it further: *Generation Gap*. Besides, either way, whatever happened here wasn't a Hollywood concoction.

He walked up to the cage and touched it lightly with his fingertips, as if wary of a shock. The corpse inside was bound to the chair by heavy leather straps, with a wired metal helmet right out of a 1940's sci-fi movie still secured to its skull. The hands, blackened bones with shreds of desiccated flesh gripped the armrests with curled fingers, as if bracing for an impact or in the throes of agony. Whether through the process of decay or from its final state, the lower jaw hung wide open, perhaps mocking its tormentors in the control room.

The narrow, oblong strip of window—which Vanek guessed was armored glass—had been holed through in several places, the edges oddly melted and wrinkled. For a wild moment a crazy thought passed through his mind: *it's all true! The damned lunatics got it right! The Montauk Project conspiracy, the chair, the testing... and the aliens!? You want proof? Here it is Will! In full, living technicolor!*

"It's a Faraday cage," Dan said, joining him.

"A *what*?"

"A *Faraday cage.* Used for electromagnetic shielding. Neutralizes the electromagnetic shield inside of it. They had one over at the University of Rhode Island." She scratched at the mesh. "Copper mesh, of course."

She spoke like it was nothing more unusual than a car battery or sewing machine.

"Whatever they used it for here, it doesn't look like it worked too well. I wonder who that guy is?"

Vanek wondered the exact same thing. One fact seemed apparent—this was ground zero for whatever had transpired here. He stepped over to the door and throwing back the three locking slide bolts, opened it slowly.

The corpse was dressed in a naval officer's uniform. The corroded lieutenant bars on the collar were a giveaway. So was the leather name tag sewn over the left breast pocket.

The silver type had been eaten away, but enough remained for Vanek to read.

"*Jesus Christ*," he whispered.

William Vanek was staring at the remains of his grandfather.

18. PROGRESS, MR. GAVIN?

"Hi Carl, how are things shaking?"

On one hand, the wet, gravelly voice speaking through the disposable cell phone was undeniably creepy, as if the speaker were trying to speak through mud or slurry. On the other, the words were often cheerful in Midwest 'neighbor-chatting-over-the-fence' sort of way. Which creeped-out Gavin even further.

'Dave' (if that was his real name) was his contact for a right-wing shadow group *within* Breckenridge Laboratories, the quasi-government-owned research facility out on Long Island.

"Oh, they're shaking just fine, Dave," he replied, forcing himself to keep the tension out of his voice. Dave and whoever was backing him possessed an uncanny ability to pick up on the tiniest nuances of his conversations, almost as if they were psychic. Based on some odd comments he'd noted on more than one occasion he wondered if the whole secret 'right-wing' group was also a sham itself.

Maybe they were ultra-*Left* wing.

Gavin didn't care one way or another. His only concern was keeping the cash flow coming into his accounts through various bogus contracts with non-existent distributors. Because right now his finances had grown dangerously overextended, and he'd yet to provide any tangible results for the so-called 'mind control' technology he'd promised.

The technology he'd stumbled on referenced two years back while at the ONR.

"Well, 'just fine' doesn't explain why Kovac's electromagnetic wunderbox isn't sitting on my desk right now, old friend."

"The last effort didn't pan out. The new one is looking excellent, however. I'll have it to you within twenty-four hours."

"I'm awfully sorry to hear about that, Carl. Awfully sorry. Should I send Chuck over for a friendly little visit?"

Gavin wasn't typically impressed with threats, but the last time he'd screwed up with this client a whole bunch of unpleasant things began to happen quickly in his life: first his Ecuadorian neighbors (and good friends) were arrested and deported, his taxes were audited, his daughter lost her job with the Department of Agriculture and one morning he came home to find an envelope down in his wood shop containing explicit photos of their 17-year-old Filipino nanny he'd had a brief fling with thirty years back. He had no idea where the photos came from but it hardly mattered—the implicit threat was clear, including the fact someone had slipped in and out of his highly secure household without being detected.

But there was nothing to be done about it. These days even a whiff of such a thing could derail his pension and put him in the ugly crosshairs of the press. Bad enough for him, even worse for his family, even if he was exonerated. For the moment, the more pressing thing on his mind was getting the second half of the money they'd negotiated.

"That won't be necessary, Dave. You got my attention the last time."

"That's good to hear, Carl. I hate repeating myself, I really do. Any luck with locating the bunker? And the chair? Time is of the essence."

Carl had no idea, but he wasn't about to say as much.

"They're working on it. Within the next forty-eight hours I would expect—it's not as critical as the wreck." Carl let out a smile. He often did that when the lies rolled off his lips.

"You have twenty-four."

Gavin thumbed the disconnect button on the screen and resisted an impulse to chuck the phone off his balcony, which Vanek would have been somewhat surprised to see, wasn't back at his house in Greenport but at a hotel not far from the Breckenridge Research Institute.

He'd first come across the ONR files on the research being conducted out at Montauk back in the 1990's after a passing comment from one of his colleagues there, Jed DeWalt. Over coffee one morning, DeWalt joked about the recent hubbub with Preston Nichols and his Montauk Project book: 'Another nutcase hits the bookshelves.' The funny thing is, in a way he was right even though he got nearly all of it wrong.

"What do you mean?" Gavin had asked, all ears.

DeWalt had lit up a cigarette—the second of his thirty-per-day habit that would cost him his life five years later courtesy of an aggressive lung cancer—and blew smoke up toward the cafeteria ceiling.

"Well, something kind of like it *did* happen, only long before the whole SAGE radar, and it didn't involve aliens or any of that time-travel UFO shit."

Gavin joined in with a casual *yeah, no-surprise-there* laugh but his eyes went as watchful as a cat's.

"No kidding? Just what kind of shit *did* it involve?"

"Something about an anti-submarine technology that was really a crazy telekinesis-thought manipulation program. As the story has it, they were conducting tests in a bunker at Camp Hero when it all went wrong. Bunch of people killed. All the technology was destroyed shortly afterward. Damage control. Funding was redirected into the Manhattan Project coffers so it all got swept under the rug."

Gavin had shrugged. "Sounds like typical urban legend BS to me. Are there any existing records to back it up?"

DeWalt took a pull on his cigarette. Gavin had never smoked, except socially. To fit in.

"If there were, they'd be in Section C down in the ONR archives. Why?"

Gavin pulled out one of his own cigarettes as a distraction. DeWalt acted like the average joe middle-class bureaucrat, but he had an uncanny ability to zero in on small things with laser precision. "No reason, really. You brought it up."

"Yeah, I did, didn't I?"

Gavin nudged the conversation toward other things—like how the Yankees were doing that season, but his mind kept ticking away. He knew of at least one person supposedly tied into just the same thing: the Vanek's over in Larchmont.

The next morning on his way to his office he'd stopped by to visit Leslie, the curator of the ONR archive division. With his badly combed hair and a tendency to stand way too close while talking to people, Leslie was like many gatekeepers of government archives, both overtalkative about inane subjects and fussily protective of anything in his domain. Gavin always found him socially awkward and just plain *off.*

Gavin had cooked up a pretense about looking into the history of the 'no-dive' zones off Montauk (which oddly, would come into play decades later) from unexploded ordnance when, as if an afterthought added: "Hey, is it true we have records on experimental projects out at Camp Hero conducted during the Second World War?"

"Why do you ask?" Leslie said, raising an eyebrow.

"Just occurred to me," Gavin replied casually, "Jed DeWalt mentioned it the other day—he was telling me about some new book called the Montauk Incident or something and I thought it might be funny to copy some papers, paste some UFOs on them and leave it on his desk."

Leslie nodded and gave him a knowing smile. Practical jokes amongst the ONR staff weren't common, but a few of them were known to consistently pull them. Gavin fell into that category. He saw that it had a way of putting his colleagues at ease... as well as cutting him slack when it came to poking around in corners he probably shouldn't.

"Ah. Well, I don't think there's much. Most of those documents and reports went missing long before my time here. Back in 1943, actually. The ones that remain only reference them. That's how we know they existed at all."

"Like a cover-up? Seriously?"

"I don't know if it was anything like that. More likely a bunch of money got wasted at a time when it shouldn't have. So, they got 'misplaced'. You know how it works."

"You betcha," Gavin replied. "Still, could I have a look?"

"Sure. Just don't expect any tell-all Area 51 stuff, that's all. They're over in the BB005-BB020 stacks in section C. Knock yourself out."

Gavin had. What he found in the in the file cabinets under "Camp Hero" was both intriguing and infuriating. There were references to a 'Bunker 18' in some documents and to an Air Sea rescue of a Naval personnel somewhere off Block Island, but the exact coordinates and dates were referenced on pages that were missing, as was any details of what had happened in the Bunker.

Several other papers gave building costs and equipment requests, which had been stamped 'denied'. It all looked like a dead-end until, just as he gathered up the papers to put them back in the manila folders, it occurred to him there was something odd about them.

They were too *new*.

He compared them to documents in several other folders dated to the same period and realized there was no question about it: the paper these documents were typed on, despite having 'stains', were of a different, newer stock. The type was crisper too, not the smudged characters one tended to see on old reports, or old mimeographs.

These were recent fabrications.

So where were the originals?

Gavin returned the files and stopped by the front desk on his way out.

"Find them all right?" Leslie asked.

"No problem," Gavin replied. "Nothing as exciting as I'd hoped," he'd added.

Leslie laughed, "That's pretty much what Jed DeWalt said too."

"Jed DeWalt?" *Why the hell didn't you say so, you dumb-ass whackjob*? he thought.

"A few days ago. In fact, he mentioned playing a little joke on you too, come to think of it."

Gavin chuckled and shook his head. "Guess I'll have to cook up something else. Thanks anyway."

"You betcha!" Leslie said, giving him the finger and thumb 'pistol' gesture. Gavin had to clench his hands to keep himself from throttling him.

That night he swung by DeWalt's house on the South Shore after ringing him up to discuss an 'urgent matter'. They were close enough friends—having worked ten years together—that DeWalt readily invited him in for a drink. DeWalt lived alone in a modest split level near Hampton Bays. Rumor had it he was gay and favored pool boys, but he'd never let on anything to Gavin. It wasn't the sort of thing you wanted to advertise in a government agency back in the 90's. Once they were out on the patio by DeWalt's in-ground pool, Gavin confronted him about the missing documents.

"Come on, what's the deal?" he'd asked, like they were discussing an old flame.

DeWalt had frowned and gazed toward the ocean. In fact, he looked downright scared.

"I really don't want to talk about it."

"What's going on, Jed? I've never seen you like this."

"I can't discuss it. Just drop it."

Gavin saw a quiver in DeWalt's lip. The man was weak, but still. What the hell?

"Jed," he said, putting a little iron in his tone. "Talk."

"Dammit, Carl. They threatened to expose me if I didn't. A guy was waiting for me when I got home after we talked. He had... photos. Of my, you know, *visitors*. *All* of them. Christ—they've been spying on me, Carl! He gave me specific instructions. That Leslie is a watchdog, though. He randomly rechecks the folders anyone takes out. I had to come up with a system to swap out the documents without removing them. Since they were in the classified section, I couldn't exactly photocopy them, you know. Not without any clearance.

"So, I used a camera. Photographed them, did my own edited reproductions, treated them with tea bags and swapped them out the next time I was there."

"I don't get it, why not just leave the originals?"

"Simple, they wanted the only copy. Otherwise anyone could just go and leak them out."

"And what *was* on there?"

DeWalt gave him a sideways look. "Nothing too much, but a few interesting snippets, nonetheless."

"How interesting? Come on pal, give it up. I've always played square with you."

Hardly true at all, but DeWalt didn't know that. But Gavin had spent years perfecting his 'tough-but-affable chum' act. He'd also made sure DeWalt was drinking double what he was.

DeWalt didn't respond right away. The silence dragged out. Gavin knew better than to prod him at this point—DeWalt was the obstinate sort who dug his heels in when pushed. The silence dragged on.

"Well…" DeWalt finally said, "Some of it was a little weird. The 'Bunker 18' stuff, for instance. Which was created about the time they rescued the only survivor from the *U.S.S. Exeter*."

"There was a survivor from the *Exeter*? *Who*?"

"An officer named Vanek. Lieutenant John Vanek."

"That doesn't make sense. Why would they do that?"

"Yeah, that's where the spooky 'Twilight Zone' stuff creeps in. Something very strange happened to Lt. Vanek out there... and to the ship. He was brought back to the base hospital at Camp Hero for medical treatment. But he wouldn't stop ranting about a giant sea monster that ate the ship. At first, he was dismissed as being delusional. Not for long."

The story DeWalt went on to relate *did* sound like something out of the Twilight Zone, or more like that new show, the 'X-Files'. What was in the government reports was very hush-hush and heavily redacted, but they did mention that the Navy had stumbled upon an incredibly powerful mind-control technology being tested there in a secret installation where the initial round of experiments had ended in catastrophic failure, resulting in the entire program being hastily shut down. The original reports appeared to have been destroyed, but there were several references to a top-secret program called '*Neptune's Reckoning*' and the 'Kovac's EM unit', which DeWalt was convinced were all part of the same thing. The tone of the reports was that Kovac's device had worked *too* good and might be uncontainable.

Typically, military reports were dry as dust and equally devoid of emotion, but these were an exception, or at least they had an element of color to them, as if written in haste.

"There's something there, Carl," DeWalt had added, "And someone within our organization wants it kept quiet, even forty years later."

"*Who*?" Gavin asked., "What department was this guy from?"

"Take some advice, Carl: drop it. Drop it like a nuclear potato and walk away. You don't want to get on these guys' radar. They... it wasn't just pictures, okay?"

"Come on, Jed, give me something. Nobody leans on a friend of mine and gets away with it. Do you still have copies of the documents?"

DeWalt wouldn't budge, however. From the hard, pale look on his face, Gavin realized no amount of coaxing or pushing would work.

He would have to find another angle.

Gavin was genuinely piqued. His interest wasn't simple curiosity—something this big could mean money—a lot of it... from the right party. But he would have to be extremely careful.

He did have one lead, however:
Lieutenant John Vanek.
Or his surviving family, at least.

19. "PERHAPS SHE NEEDS A LESSON"

Scarpia sat at a table nursing a bourbon in the back of The Lobster Trap, in the area usually reserved for large parties or other events. It was a slow afternoon (*all* of them had gotten slow lately) but it didn't bother him much. The restaurant—along with his house and family—was about to join the pile of uncomfortable ghosts in his past.

Like himself, the Lobster Trap had become a relic of the *Montauk of yesteryear*; frayed, worn, and coarse along the edges. It had never lived up to the 'premier seafood restaurant' it advertised itself as, but by this summer it bordered on derelict. For decades it had managed to acquire a certain level of 'quality' dining status with the sports fishermen crowd (though most locals avoided the place). With hipster eateries and boutique cafés reshaping the culinary landscape of Montauk like a kind of millennial terraforming wave, restaurants like his were either viewed with hostile disdain or ignored all together.

Scarpia looked over at the oversized fish tank separating the two dining areas and snorted. The old fishing nets, buoys, shells and clunky ship model decor more than ever looked like *kitsch* picked up at a tag sale for bargain prices, which much of it was.

"Augie!" he snapped. The lone waiter on staff sat hunched over on his stool at the bar, absorbed in texting. Scarpia could never figure him out—for a guy who seldom said more than two words, he apparently had quite a bit to text about.

Augie looked up, annoyed. Scarpia resisted the urge to draw the small .45 Colt Defender he kept inside his waistband and pop the sonofabitch. It would only create more of a mess than was already unfolding. He'd just gotten a call from a dockhand informant of his that a shipment was due to arrive tomorrow with specialized underwater equipment for a once-famous French military diver. Presumably the same one staying out at the ONR safe house.

It wasn't rocket-science to put two and two together.

Scarpia waggled his drink. Whether the restaurant was empty or full, getting Augie to do anything past the most basic waiter duties proved impossible. Just as Scarpia's temper was about to rise a notch, the waiter stood up and fetched a bottle from behind the bar. One of the top shelf bourbons. No sense cutting corners at this point, Scarpia figured.

When Augie had deposited the fresh drink in front of him (without a word, as usual) and resumed his texting spot at the bar, Scarpia pulled out his phone.

"Do you have her?" he asked. It had been hours since he'd heard from Vanossi.

"Right here in the barn," Vanossi answered, referring to the abandoned property on East Lake Road along the harbor waterfront. The place—once owned by the Van Eyckmanns of the Hudson Valley—had fallen into disrepair since 2012 and for one reason or another, hadn't found any buyers despite the real estate boon in Montauk in recent years. In addition to an old 1920's cottage on the property, it had a dock with a shingle-sided barn over the water. Scarpia had an in with one of the local realtors and had cooked up an arrangement that got the word out he was temporarily renting it for storage. The barn came equipped with a two-bedroom apartment on the upper floor and in addition to a semi-private access, was suited perfectly for storing questionable items.

Such as kidnapped waitresses.

"She's turning out to be a feisty one," Vanossi added. "Dumb bitch scratched my face."

"Added to your collection?" Scarpia replied. Vanossi always liked it rough with the ladies.

A muffled cry the other end of the line followed by a muted smack.

"Nothing I can't handle, boss."

"Perhaps she needs a lesson."

"Yeah?" Vanossi voice brightened up. "Can I have a little fun?"

"Knock yourself out," Scarpia said.

"What about Jimmy Reed?"

"Fuck him. We just need her alive enough to get him on the boat. More importantly, there's been a change in schedule. Got word our final delivery is coming through on Monday. Update your dance calendar."

"Sooner is better, boss, sooner is better."

Scarpia didn't bother to respond to that—he just hung up. Vanossi was right though. Scarpia was increasingly aware that too many noses were poking in his direction. The stinky Frenchman—Navarre, and that half-jungle bunny scientist from Rhode Island (at least she was a hottie—Scarpia gave her that much). The Navy. That snot-faced historian from Larchmont. God knows who else at this point.

There were a few minor things to sort out. His ex-wife would be in for a surprise when the alimony check didn't arrive in a few weeks and no doubt his two teenage sons would be put out. But he figured it was about time they grew up and learned to fend for themselves in the world. Like he did. No-one gave Antony Scarpia any easy ups. Certainly not *his* father. Antony Senior was doing hard time in Sing-Sing by the time Scarpia reached his son's age.

He checked his watch. The masseuse was scheduled to arrive in ten minutes. She was a young Filipino woman who always gave him a little 'extra' with her dexterous, powerful hands. He would miss that. But there'd be plenty more where he was going. Plenty.

One more dump and *hello money island.*

20. A SECOND ENCOUNTER

Vanek stood, thunderstruck.

Simultaneously, he *wasn't* surprised. It was like a form of déjà vu—from the moment he crawled into the sealed tunnel he knew something awaited him here. There were a few occasions—not many, but a few—back when he was in college and his mother would call, when he would pick up the phone and answer "Hi, Mom," without even thinking about it. A little spooky, sure, but hardly worth ringing up the local newspaper over.

This was like that, but in a much more ominous way.

Along with it, a whole slew of questions swirled in his head: *what the hell was this place? Why was his grandfather's corpse sitting in the midst of it?* And: *just what was behind the catastrophic state of everything here?*

He was also aware of another unsettling sensation—what appeared like flitting movements in his peripheral vision. The way one might catch a group of disturbingly large insects disappearing deeper into the unlit basement of an abandoned mansion.

A cold sweat blossomed on his brow.

Where had that odd visual come from? he wondered.

"Doesn't look like it worked," Dan said, intruding in on his thoughts.

"I'm sorry?"

"The Faraday cage. At a guess, they were using it to neutralize the electromagnetic energy around the chair, or whatever that thing is in it."

"That 'thing'," Vanek said in a quiet, terse voice, "was my grandfather."

"Oh my God," Dan whispered. Her eyes went wide. "You're not *joking*."

"No."

"But why…?"

Vanek glanced around at the cage, the burst patterns on the mesh, the carnage in the surrounding chamber.

"That's the million-dollar question, isn't it?"

Yes indeed. Because he had no doubt this was the exact same chair in the photo he found in his grandfather's stuff. Which didn't quite add up. The chronology he had pulled together had his grandfather going directly from Philadelphia to Newport, Rhode Island and from there to Exeter and his final mission where he was officially listed as lost at sea.

So how was it he had a photo of this same chair in this same facility, and how the hell did grandpa Vanek's corpse wind up sealed in here? At the epicenter of an event involving extreme violence.

In 'Bunker 18'.

Vanek stood before the door to the cage and its hideous occupant, seized by a complex surge of emotions and questions; a strange sense of different events and facts revealing a hidden pattern that teased his subconscious.

The U.S.S. Exeter's final mission.

The shipwrecks.

His grandfather.

The girl in the hospital.

The disappearances off Montauk.

From behind he distantly heard Dan say: "This looks like a power switch..."

There came a *click* and a *hum* and the lights came on, sporadically.

Then a deeper hum kicked in.

Vanek was focused on the headpiece covering his grandfather's skull... there was an empty circular socket at the center of the forehead, blackened and burned out as if it had held something the size of a robin's egg.

Before he realized what he was about to do, he reached out, unlatched the Faraday cage door and stepped in. In the lap of the corpse lay a charred crystal.

A key.

It spoke to him: *answers.*

He picked it up and inserted it in the socket, his expression identical to the one he wore as a five-year-old the day he took a fork and stuck it into a power outlet.

The shock wasn't painful - instead came images.

And horror.

"*Will*!" Dan screamed, "*Snap out of it*!" She had him by the shoulder, shaking it.

Vanek spasmed, feeling like a circuit had been closed then broken, trying to clear the visuals out of his head.

They weren't just in his head, however. They were coming out of his grandfather's mouth and forehead. At first, they seemed like tiny black octopi, but as they emerged and fanned-out, they grew; writhing and *squirting*. From the amorphous, thin tentacles to clusters of silver, misshapen eyes, there was something utterly repulsive about them. Their proportions were all wrong, for one thing, like witnessing an unnatural mutation never meant for humans to see.

The corpse began to shudder as more of the things erupted out of the gaping jaws, spilling over the chest in a revolting carpet. Vanek stumbled backward.

It wasn't limited to his grandfather. The other corpses nearby were twitching, giving off the dry snaps of old bones mobilizing, one near the entrance rising up in a hideous pantomime of life. Around that came an insidious *scissoring* sound, one that made Vanek recall an evening sail on the Chesapeake Bay where the crabs rose to the surface by the thousands to feed.

More immediate, was the groan of rusty metal: the doors to the chamber were starting to close.

Most of the lights flickered and exploded in a shower of sparks, plunging the space into a flickering gloom.

"I'm sorry!" Dan shrieked.

"Run!" Vanek yelled, grabbing Dan's arm.

They bolted past the burst steel doors just as one corpse staggered upright with clawing fingers. Its eye sockets were filled with the squiggly things, lending them a bizarre form of life. Vanek realized the hammer was still in his left hand. He swung it wildly as they ran past, smashing the skull with a crunch.

The flashlight Dan had in her right hand played ahead, revealing more of the dead personnel lurching toward them. Beyond, the massive dented doors were sliding shut. Quicker than they should have.

"We're not going to make it!" she gasped. They still had thirty feet to cross, and the opening was shrinking past a couple of feet.

"We have to!" Vanek shouted. Panic gave urgency to his feet. He batted aside another cadaver and shoved her forward as hard as he could. Dan stumbled through the opening at an angle, just as Vanek threw up the hammer crosswise as a wedge.

He almost made it.

Something snagged his ankle just as he pushed through the narrowing gap, causing his arm to snap up in reflex: the hammer, which was just a few degrees off from perpendicular, shot out forward with a *pop*.

Despite being two-thirds of the way through, Vanek felt the massive edge of the door press his ribcage and hip in, about to crush him. Dan crouched before him—*what the hell was she doing*?

She jumped up, a skull in her hands, and wedged it in lengthwise above his head.

The first body! Of course!

It bought him just enough time. She grabbed his arm and hauled him the rest of the way through, his pelvis banging painfully on the edge of the steel door. They tumbled to the floor, the flashlight beam dancing crazily in all directions. As he landed, Vanek twisted, just as one passing beam showed the nightmare wave of things coming at them along every surface, then the skull imploded from the pressure and the door slammed shut.

A second later, Vanek and Dan had the latch bar dropped in place, sealing the place.

Grabbing each other's hands, they stumbled to their feet and ran back down the corridor. Vanek had no idea if the outer doors were airtight, but he didn't want to wait and find out.

Minutes later they were clambering out of the access shaft and onto the ground. Together they manhandled the concrete cap back into place and stepped back.

Vanek was panting like he'd run a marathon. Much of that was as due to the adrenaline pumping through his system as it was physical exertion. Dan stood bent over with hands on knees, taking in breaths with big whooping gasps.

The wind had picked up speed, with oily gray-blue clouds riddled by intermittent flashes of lightning. The misty curtains of rain were coming at them out of the northeast; with it the ozone-charged aroma of an impending storm.

"What in the hell just happened?" Dan said, straightening up. She was in far better physical shape of the two. Most of Vanek's workouts had been confined to the gym in his basement. He was never more aware than right then that treadmills and sprinting for your life were seriously different aerobic exercises. If he got out of this whole mess, maybe he could start up a new fitness plan: *The NEW Will Vanek Run for Your Life System—burn insane calories, shed pounds INSTANTLY! Wait 'til we show you our 'other-worldly' motivation technique! Brings a whole new dimension to the term 'Fear Factor'!*

In the meantime, they had more pressing issues.

"Hell if I know," he answered. "We better high-tail it back to the car, though. Unless you want to stay here and see how secure this cap is?"

Dan seemed to go a shade paler. "*Car.*"

"Agreed."

"Do you think those things will get out of there?"

It was a very good question. He had no idea. And yet... maybe he did.

"Let's not find out."

As they climbed into the car, the clouds opened up and the showers came down in torrents, as if overcompensating for its delayed arrival. For a moment the two of them sat there. Neither spoke as the rain hammered the vehicle.

Vanek stared straight ahead, his thoughts a maelstrom. His entire nervous system seemed to be in shock.

After a few minutes, Dan turned toward him, "Will, what was that!? Tell me *something*, please. You dropped some LSD in my coffee this morning? Put me in a deep hypnosis without my knowing? Tell me I didn't just see those... those... writhing things erupting," she shuddered, "... and the dead coming to life like a SyFy channel movie or something. Just, just tell me that, yes?"

Vanek said nothing. What the hell *could* he say?

What came out was: "Now*, I will believe that there are unicorns*."

Dan stared at him, incredulous.

"*What*!?"

"Shakespeare. 'The Tempest'. Never mind." He turned the ignition and the Ford's engine came to life. "After today, I'm pretty sure I can believe in just about anything."

The drive back to the house went slow, the rain coming down in hammering sheets as if determined to knock them off the road. Fortunately, the Mustang seemed impervious, and she was able to navigate them back to their driveway without a mishap.

As Dan pulled in, the storm hit a momentary lull. The two of them sprinted up the stairs to the safety of the front porch. The ocean had transformed into a violent surf, rollers charging into the beach below as foam misted off the whitecaps and vanished in the wind.

Normally, standing on a porch watching a storm-whipped sea would have filled him with excitement. A backdrop fit for a battened-down square-rigger out of one of his historic articles, sailors clinging precariously to the yardarms while fighting to reef in the sails. Instead, the whole scene felt off, Vanek grappling with a worldview forever skewed, the merciless reality of a universe that tore his wife (and father) out of his life now looking comforting compared to what he'd just witnessed underground in 'Bunker 18'.

He felt blind terror seeping in from every angle.

What if those things erupted out of the shaft and just kept coming and coming, eclipsing everything in existence with their repulsive, undulating legs and malignant silver eyes?

Dan touched his shoulder. He saw she was shivering.

"Let's go inside. I don't know about you, but I could really use a drink."

Vanek nodded.

Back inside the house, Navarre looked up from the chair where he'd been perusing the Hampton Star, his amused smile at their appearance turning to alarm as he registered their expressions.

"What? What has happened? You go off to lunch, libraries and bookstores and come back looking like death? Is this the effect food and literature have on Americans?"

Vanek managed a grim laugh. "Something like that. Better get me a scotch."

Navarre tossed the paper aside and stood, looking them up and down before answering. "Go change your clothes. I'll get the drinks."

"What you're saying is simply not possible," Navarre said, ten minutes later. "There *must* be some kind of explanation. Something you missed." The three of them were seated in the couches around the fireplace, fortified with drinks. Vanek had done much of the talking, with Dan filling in the gaps.

"You're correct," Vanek agreed. "But that *is* what happened."

Navarre tapped his chin. "But what if it was staged? Projection lighting? Animatronics? You've seen these modern spook houses…"

"*Haunted Houses*," Dan corrected.

"... yes, *Haunted* houses. Very sophisticated. Quite convincing!"

"The place was sealed-up and had been for a long time," Vanek offered. "Besides, that wouldn't make a lick of sense."

"Ah! Only as far as you *know*. We're talking about a government installation. There could be all kinds of secret entrances. I say we go back and have a look." He glanced out the window. 'Well, not right now, perhaps."

Vanek took a stiff belt of his scotch. He had no intention of returning to that bunker. Not today, tomorrow, or a hundred years.

"I'm not going back there, Arnaud. In fact, between this morning and what I saw this afternoon, I don't want to have anything to do with this place: real, imagined, or otherwise. I'm finished. Tomorrow morning, I'm packing up and heading out."

"Just like that?" Navarre asked.

"Just like that."

He finished off the scotch, stood up, and walked out.

Upstairs, Vanek put what few clothes he had in the suitcase, leaving the wet ones draped over the glass shower door. He didn't care for the whiff of failure that came with his decision, but the truth of what happened today left him scared as hell, right down to the bone, and that kind of fear—naked, irrational, ball-shriveling—was something he'd never faced before. It spoke of a whole landscape of fear he never suspected existed.

And never wanted to encounter again.

But it wasn't just that. There was something even worse—a part of him *enjoyed* it. As revolting and horrifying as it was: a forbidden fruit... like a glimpse of something disgustingly perverse that left one slightly turned-on.

That disturbed him even more.

He grabbed one of the Hornblower books and stretched out on the bed, realizing he hadn't given any thought to dinner. Not that he was hungry.

When did you become such a skirt-wringing coward? came Michelle's voice. He glanced up from his book, annoyed.

"What?" he said aloud.

Hiding behind your logic, rules, your safe little articles and your ridiculous little ship models. Have you grown that blind and stupid?

Vanek's expression grew alarmed: *Where was this coming from…?*

A soft knock at his door distracted him.

"Hello?" he said, reluctantly.

"Can I talk to you?"

It was Dan.

"Enter," he said.

She stood framed in the doorway, dressed in a plush white bathrobe with a snifter of brandy in one hand. He was about to suggest one of the chairs, but she walked over and sat herself right next to him on the bed. It struck Vanek as oddly intimate. He put the book down and tried not to look uncomfortable.

Just as he was about to ask her what she wanted she reached over and grabbed his hand in hers. She turned and looked at him, and for a moment the brazen, confident marine biologist/photographer disappeared and a terrified young woman sat in her place. She took a sip of her brandy and looked away.

She let out a short laugh.

"You know, when I was a little girl, I used to be terrified of one of my dolls. Rebecca. That was her name. She was an odd thing. Something my Dad had picked up on one of his trips to the Caribbean. I think she was a gypsy, maybe. She had black hair tied into pigtails, ruddy skin with big rouge spots on the cheeks, and a white linen dress. With a corset, I think. Her eyes were big—black with whites all around them. Crazy-lady eyes. Something about her was clearly off. The whole package suggested a doll that was older. Deranged."

Dan sipped her brandy, more judiciously this time. "Anyhow, some mornings I'd wake up and find my other stuffed animals rearranged, as if they'd been tossed around during the night. Or sometimes at night, lying tucked up in bed, I might glance across the room and see her sitting there—if the light from outside my window was just right—I'd catch a glint in her big shiny eyes, as if she were watching me. Studying me. Malevolent and insane. One night I had a terrible nightmare, one where I woke up paralyzed. I could see every detail in my room–and with it an awful knowledge she was right there to my left, peering over the edge of the bed, keeping me paralyzed by some malignant force of magic. Her crimson lips wide open, revealing rotting, snaggle teeth. Somehow, I knew she was planning to possess me, take over my body and destroy my personality forever."

"Classic sleep paralysis," Vanek said.

"Yes, I know that now. But that's not all. When I woke up, my favorite stuffed animal—Big Bird—had a ragged tear across his throat and one eye was missing. Not only that—there were tiny bite marks on my forearm. I freaked out. It sounds ridiculous, I know, but that day Rebecca disappeared. I always assumed my mom and dad disposed of her after I woke up in hysterics. But now I'm not so sure. They never said anything. After a while, I *forgot.* I slipped back into the world where things make sense—garbage is picked up Tuesdays, summer arrives on June 21st, the dog needs to be walked three times a day, so on. A *safe* world. Kind of funny coming from a woman who studies killer whales, fear response and marine biology."

She leaned into him a little. "Will, I'm *scared.*"

He hesitated, then put his hand on her shoulder. He'd been expecting a pep-talk, a cliché 'don't-back-out-of-the-team-now' pitch. But not this.

"After today, you should be. The best thing is to step away and just let the ONR and Coast Guard deal with it," he said, the words sounding lame and patronizing even to his own ears.

"I don't believe that. Honestly, I don't think *you* believe that."

Vanek began to protest, but she twisted around and looked him directly in the eye.

"You look different," Dan said. Yet again, he became aware of her closeness, her intense... what? *Woman-ness*? That sounded vaguely ridiculous to him. But the whiff of lavender-scented bath oil wasn't.

"What do you mean?" Vanek glanced away.

She continued to study him.

"I don't know. More self-assured. You were acting like such a fussy old man the other day. Down in the bunker, you were... you were like something out of a movie. You saved my life. I can't believe we made it through that door!"

He looked back at her. "Well, you saved my skin too. Using that skull as a wedge was quick thinking."

Dan didn't respond. She continued to stare at him.

Now what? he thought, mentally kicking himself. *'Using that skull as a wedge?' You sound like a horse's ass!*

The thought was cut off as she leaned in and kissed him softly on the lips. It was an incredibly erotic sensation, heightened by the sweet taste of brandy.

She stepped back.

"I doubt that it will change your mind, but I want you to stay."

Vanek watched her as she stood up and went to the door, his thoughts in a maelstrom but unable to form any of that into words.

Dan rested her cheek on the door frame as she gazed back at him.

"Arnaud put some leftovers in the fridge, if you get hungry."

With that she was gone, leaving Vanek staring at an empty door and a headful of disturbing questions.

21. JUST A NIGHTMARE

Vanek squirmed in the grips of a horrible dream.

Through the eyes of his grandfather.

He saw it in hyper-lucid detail—the sinking of the *Exeter* and the horrific deaths of its crew, torn apart by a leviathan sea-monster that swallowed them into the ocean. Everything registered at once: the sickening crunch of the destroyer's captain bouncing off the navigation console with the AMFOS unit blinking as the bridge tilted, the tentacles bursting through the windows, escaping through the door on the bridge and the heart-stopping plunge out into the black ocean as the ship tilted up at a forty-five degree angle.

Then came the recovery in the infirmary at Camp Hero... and an incident as one of the doctors injected him with a tranquilizer while strange creatures burst through the windows, the doctor bizarrely taking the syringe and attacking his own face with it while laughing like a lunatic. A soldier burst in, clubbing aside several of the creatures with his M-1 Garand, then in an act of sheer intuition, struck Lieutenant Vanek with the stock, knocking him out.

When he came to, he was himself again, now standing in front of his grandfather in the lead-lined chamber with the Faraday cage.

His grandfather was young again—the clean-cut, confident youth he remembered from the framed service photo back at the house in Larchmont. Except for the eyes.

They looked normal. Almost. Except for the silver-blue glow of the pupils.

"There's no point in running, William," he said, his voice giving no room for argument. His upper lip was bared, his teeth showing—the way men with bad dentures do. "A mile, two, twenty or two-hundred. Won't do a lick of good. It's got its hooks in you, see. Like me."

He tried to raise his hands and to Vanek's horror saw the fingers had become chitinous hooks, like the teeth of a lamprey eel. Even worse, when he glanced up again, the teeth had also become hooks, the lips now rubbery and peeled back to allow the worm-like filaments out of the mouth.

Nearby stone-faced doctors with clipboards and cameras crowded in, men Lt. Vanek knew were from Intelligence with their dark glasses, cruel mouths and cigarettes. One stuck out against the others—tall and hatchet-featured, his eyes black and merciless.

"This happens four out of five times," the hatchet-faced man said, drawing on his cigarette. "And it just keeps getting better and better, Buster!" He grinned and blew smoke upward. "Just a few more tests! Besides, these things really turn you on, don't they?"

Vanek became aware he had a raging hard-on. Then he saw there were other *things* in the cage with them. More kept materializing.

The air was filled with clothes and flesh tearing, men screaming as the things ripped into them; the coppery tang of fresh blood and fear.

Vanek screamed.

He came to with Dan cradling him in bed, her hand running softly across his forehead.

"You were having a nightmare," she said.

Vanek blinked several times. For a passing moment he still could feel the needles going into his arms, the hot blood spattering across his face... the high-pitched shrieks of men being mutilated.

"That's an understatement."

He propped himself up on his elbows. The bed was all overstuffed pillows and comforter, the heat from his body filling it like a low banked furnace. No wonder he had slept so deep. He was lying in a sea of warm, white fluffiness.

"You were mumbling, too. You kept saying 'they're eating me from inside!' over and over again. What was that about?"

Vanek shuddered. It was a very good question. One he wasn't sure he wanted to probe just yet. Had he ever had such dreams before? In a strange way, he felt certain he had. Not since he was a teenager, though.

"Just a bad dream. What time is it?"

"Nearly three a.m."

Vanek let that sink in. The suicide hour. He forced the afterimages of his nightmare away for a moment and focused on his present situation: he was lying in bed, with a very attractive marine biologist who'd kissed him earlier. It struck him as absurd and invigorating at the same time.

And disjointed. Everything out of whack.

He felt her eyes boring into him.

"What?"

She dabbed at his forehead with her sleeve. "You're sweating. You want me to get some cold water?"

He shook his head no. That cold knot of fear still sat in his gut—the kind of cold knot that hinted at a much larger, seething terror waiting to burst through it. It was just a dream, he told himself lamely.

Vanek surprised himself by asking, "Would you mind just sitting here a minute?"

"Sure. Just don't get any funny ideas."

He thought about that kiss earlier, and the subsiding ache in his groin. He dismissed it. Probably just an impulsive thing... wasn't it?

"I think I'm fresh out of those for the moment."

22. OFF MONTAUK

Thirty miles off the coast in the twilight of the night ocean one hundred and eighty feet down, the amorphous darkness emerged from the top of the Hyborian Canyon, seething around the *U.S.S. Exeter*.

It had been sluggish (by its terms) to react, having been roused prematurely out of its sixty-year or so hibernation cycle, but it was increasingly energized by the new variety of prey the past few months. Now—through its delicate sensory filaments that picked up input beyond the limited range what the humans it encountered were capable of—it was aware of something so much *brighter* calling to it.

And *familiar*.

It was also aware that it had changed, its basic molecular structure (if it could be called that) altered by the infusion of toxic substances over the past six months, combining and recombining enzyme sequences. It had acted as a catalyst in a strange—even by this thing's definition—means; agitating, exponentially causing it to expand, hunger... for new and more.

Much more.

Around it, the ocean life receded away instinctively, even at a microscopic level, as if life at its simplest forms was repulsed by it. Those that couldn't withered and died in a blink, their life force feeding into the thing.

It had never ventured far from where it had landed into centuries back, just as a trapdoor spider was wary to head too far from the safely familiar contours of its trap, nor had it any reason to in the past.

Now, however, circumstances had evolved. Not just with its physiology and its immediate environment, but because something in the near distance had called.

Something *not* of the ocean.

In the past it had been capable of extending its manifestations for only brief moments outside its watery environment and to do so it needed a proper conduit. That had happened only once.

It yearned for that. Again.

New tastes... new flavors... new fears.

The tendrils surged forward, past the wreck, the cloud flicking northward. Questing.

Seeking.

22. INTO THE LAIR

Friday morning arrived with the expectant air it does so often out at Montauk in late summer; bleary-eyed crowds lining up at the bakery on the Plaza, the early riser families with their bickering kids packing into the Pancake Houses... the usual joggers, bikers and beach-goers braving the chill with steaming mugs of coffee.

The harbor restaurants were still sleeping off the night before while the late-straggler fishermen chugged their way out of the harbor into the growing light. Over by Star Marina, many of the leisure boaters roused themselves as the gulls crowded overhead, searching for scraps from the returning overnight deep-sea charters.

Aboard *Catch-22* it was all business as Navarre and Gorecki went through and checked the gear laid out in the cabin. The weather was shaping up good for a dive.

Vanek stood on the dock nearby, windbreaker zipped up against the chill, hands jammed in his pockets. The breeze that ruffled his hair had that invigorating aroma of the ocean.

He had woken hours earlier in the predawn, haggard, but determined. Not because of Dan's request, or because of the words the nightmare version of his grandfather had said, but something that crystalized in his thoughts as he gazed out into the darkness with his suitcase sitting next to his feet.

A basic need to *know*.

No matter how bad this thing was.

It was more than that. It was also the basic truth that everything waiting for him back in Larchmont—the sprawling Tudor house, the ship models, the unfinished articles on his desk... were, compared to that, a big hollow *nothing*.

A cold, dead tomb.

He had no idea how he was going to make it thirty miles out and back on the ocean today, facing God knows what, but he was determined to do it.

"Ready?" Dan asked.

A low flying gull arced in nearby, its hectoring caw goading him on.

"Yes. Let's go."

Vanek didn't care much for motor yachts but he had to admit the 65-foot *Rybovich* was a true classic and a fine piece of boat design. The yacht cut through the water like a thoroughbred, arcing out past the lighthouse and into the bright blue haze of the August morning.

Vanek sat up in the roomy forward cabin, going over photocopies he'd made of the '*Neptune's Reckoning*' documents at the main table while Dan sat on one of the built-in couches across from him, rechecking data on her laptop that had been downloaded overnight from Woods Hole. They estimated a fifty-minute trip to the dive site at cruising speed.

The cabin was a curious mix of late-60's wood veneers and more modern–if conservative–interior nautical design. Gorecki probably did most of it himself, Vanek figured. Everything had a distinctly ship-shape, masculine touch.

Navarre sat nearby, poring over the available deck plans and details of a Gleaves-class destroyer Gavin had provided.

"*Hmm*," Dan said, toying with her hair absentmindedly. "This is pretty weird."

Vanek reshuffled the papers. The only additional clues he'd uncovered was a report mentioning his grandfather in an evaluation at Camp Hero a month before the ship sank and another referencing debris found along the shoreline near the Point.

So, what the hell was his grandfather's corpse doing in the bunker out there? What was the deal with that helmet? And what the hell had they really used that room for?

He'd tried to raise Gavin before they'd left but only got his voicemail. Vanek was never one for leaving details in messages–he was old-school in that regard—so he only mentioned that they'd found an interesting 'development' out at the old base and they needed to discuss it.

"I'm sorry? What was that?" he glanced up. Navarre stayed immersed in the plans.

Dan angled the laptop toward him. On the screen, a three-dimensional object expanded and grew at an alarming rate, with random bursts of colors like flack-bursts; it was both mesmerizing and disturbing. She'd hooked it up to a speaker cube issuing that strange, scissoring whisper they'd heard down in the bunker. The sound too was three-dimensional, lending it an even more unsettling quality.

"What the hell is *that*?" Vanek asked. Goosebumps flared up along his arms.

Navarre looked up, brow knitted in irritation.

"It's a beta program we've been experimenting with that translates digitized sound into a 3D fractal animation—a way to visualize sound in three dimensions. My intern ran some hydrophone clips through it overnight. It's kind of creepy, isn't it? It's similar to ones we've seen come from whales when they're agitated or frightened. But this is on a whole other level of detail and complexity. It's like, I don't know, a *fear fractal*?"

Navarre chuckled. "I like that! Fear fractal. Like a new game!"

Vanek squeezed his eyes shut and turned away.

"Are you okay?" Dan asked, closing the laptop.

"I'm…" he couldn't say exactly. For a moment it teased something out of the back of his thoughts, like a tiny black explosion of ink... or fractals?

In a blink, it disappeared.

In its place was an even stranger sound, a resonating pulse that cut through his senses to his very core. On the screen the animation mutated, this one appeared to be traveling through space at a high rate of speed, the pulse synched with what he could only describe as a massive non-object 'beating' at its center.

"What the hell is *that*?"

Dan chuckled. "Makes you feel oddly good, doesn't it? It's the same program running a simulation of the primordial sound of the universe captured by the NASA Planck telescope. I downloaded it from their website. This sound cube works underwater—we tried it out with whales and strangely, they seemed to like it. It's like sound therapy. I use it for mediation. Cool, isn't it?"

Vanek didn't know what to think.

"I need some air," he said.

Gorecki cut the throttles ten minutes later as they arrived at the dive buoy. The sun shone full up in a cloudless sky and a warm breeze fluttered the mast flags. After checking the sonar, Navarre clambered down from the pilot deck and met Dan and Vanek by the stern.

"Today we focus on getting in and out of the *Exeter*, okay?" Navarre asked. "Five minutes to bottom, fifteen to thirty minutes to do what we need. The main AMFOS unit should still be on the bridge, by the sonar station. The second part of it is located in the sound room two decks down near the forward navigation compartment. That will be the tricky one to get in and out of." He patted the 3D Scanner, "That's why we have this. Given the state of the wreck it could be very dangerous—that sound room is just forward of the magazine of the forward five-inch gun turret, meaning it's likely there is live—and unstable - munitions to deal with. One wrong move and *ka-boom*. Mission over."

Laid out on the transom he had a marked-up diagram of the dive site with call outs including current direction, wreck locations and the rough topography that included the Hyborian Canyon. He already gone over this earlier in the cabin with Dan, but Navarre was nothing if thorough. Vanek had to respect the man's no-nonsense professionalism.

Gorecki joined them, going to the rack of scuba tanks as Dan and Navarre suited up.

Dan had both her camera and the speaker cube slung from a chord, Vanek saw.

"That works underwater?" he asked.

"Oh yes. It's a test model from Lubell Labs, rated up to 60 meters. They've been using them in underwater defense systems."

"Good for scaring the hell out of enemy fish?"

"Very funny. Actually, with its 3D sound projection ability, it can be used for a lot of things."

"Deep-Sea discotheques?" Navarre chimed in.

"That would *definitely* scare the hell out of enemy fish. And submarines," Vanek replied.

"Ha!" Navarre looked over the settings on the new Trimble scanner. It was surprisingly compact. "Based on our previous dive, I've marked several locations on the decks we can scan from. I'm not sure about this damn tripod. Still, with any luck we can capture the 3D data on the first dive, review it, then remove the equipment on the second."

Gorecki helped them into the buoyancy harnesses and scuba tanks. Vanek always found it the worst part of diving; trying to manhandle the tanks, weights, cumbersome gear. Navarre and Dan made it look easy. Vanek noted that all the equipment was Mares—arguably the best in the world.

Each checked the dive computers on their wrists and their back-ups while Gorecki lowered the dive sled over the stern.

"We'll make two deco stops on the way back up, with a little padding just to be safe," Navarre said. "Watch me carefully at all times. Stay alert. Let's have a safe dive, yes?"

Minutes later they both went down the dive ladder at the stern.

"Good luck!" Gorecki said.

After clearing their masks, Navarre gave the thumbs up and went under.

Vanek stood frowning by the stern, staring at the bubbles on the surface. He'd already reached a decision before they'd left the harbor.

He walked back into the cabin and returned a minute later in Navarre's back-up wet suit. It was a little too big, but it would do. He knew it was foolhardy, but he *had* to get down there. Plus he noted something else—those special dive hoods had been left behind. Why would Navarre do that?

Gorecki was incredulous.

"Are you crazy!? You can't *dive*!"

Vanek smiled.

"Actually, yes I can. I've had my PADI Open Water certification for over ten years."

"But Navarre said you were terrified of the water! He'd never let you on his dive without personally checking you out!"

"You're right, on both accounts, but I need to get down there. That's the ship *my* grandfather went down on, not his. I'll be right behind them on the dive line."

"No, no, I can't let you do this! Navarre will have my hide."

Vanek handed him the PADI certification card from his wallet. "Here—you can hang on to this as proof. Now help me with that harness."

Dan followed Navarre to the diving line and hooked onto it. He tested the tension and after hooking himself and the dive sled, gave her the thumbs up, then got close enough to her to look her in the eye then point at her rebreather. The hard rubber regulator felt stiff in her mouth, but at least the regulator was Navy class-A rated and would make breathing at depth a lot easier.

Getting her breathing into a set rhythm, she gave him the 'okay' sign and nodded. Navarre turned on the dive sled and let it pull the two of them down into the gloom.

Dan couldn't deny she was both excited and terrified. She'd been on hundreds of dives, many of them involving contact with dangerous—even potentially lethal—sea life. But this was different. Those encounters involved *known* things. Creatures with documented and (somewhat) predictable behavior patterns.

Adding up all they'd witnessed so far painted a daunting picture, suggesting whatever waited down there was on a level of danger outside anything ever encountered before. In fact, the more she thought about it, it was pure lunacy just the two of them doing this. How many people were dead already?

They should have an entire regiment of Navy divers.

And maybe a nuclear sub.

A quick look around, Navarre insisted. Any sign of danger, out of there immediately.

Then again, he seemed to gravitate toward it.

Too late now, she thought, one hand in front of the other. *Stay focused. Don't let your attention wander.*

Navarre focused on the changing light and sea life as they descended. He'd spent so much time underwater it was second nature to him.

Arnaud Navarre: *human aquanaut*.

As a kid he'd read all those Submariner comics, fantasizing that someday, he too would be one with the ocean deep, a creature of the sea, gaining control over its otherworldly minions. Even when he graduated to obsessing over Jacques Cousteau—and later became an expert commando diver—he never lost sight of that comic-book fantasy, hidden deep within himself.

He listened to the soft purr of the sled's engine, occasionally checking his dive computer. Bubbles occasionally burbled up and past him toward the surface. He recalled one dive on a wreck where one of his commandos got cocky and didn't hold on to the anchor line. A rip current kicked in halfway down and just like that he was swept away. They recovered his body a week later.

Navarre learned early on to be meticulous about safety.

It took about five minutes to reach the bottom, going leisurely. The dive line remained hooked onto a cement block dropped by the documentary crew. The bottom was sandy, with bits of debris floating around it. One looked suspiciously like a human finger. Scattered about were the various blue plastic barrels they'd seen the other day.

Navarre looked back. Dan unhooked her 'D' clip from the anchor line. She checked her gauge and gave him the thumbs up.

Both flicked on their HID Pro lights and probed the area in front of them as the tow-sled took them toward the wreck. The sled itself had a high-power LED headlight. The current seemed moderate. Their beams cut through the murk.

Navarre noted pieces of the *HMS Tryton* sticking out of the sand like the ribs of a prehistoric sea monster. Past that, out of the gloom, the stern of the *U.S.S. Exeter* emerged; a coral-festooned ghost from a war seventy-four years in the past. Before them, loomed a sign embedded in the sand:

Warning: Restricted Diving Zone
Live ordinance/ammo - access beyond this point forbidden
by the order of the U.S. Navy Dept.

Nothing here looked right. For one thing, aside from bits of debris flitting through their beams, the patterns of the usual sea-life looked disrupted and chaotic: schools of alewives, cunners and ling—jellyfish, shrimp and the occasional shark—their movements seemed odd.

Then there were the blue plastic barrels everywhere, some of them burst.

Toxic waste, he guessed, from the gray mud around them. But he would leave that to the NOAA and Coast Guard. Toxic dump or not, it wouldn't affect this large an area.

Navarre felt a chill.

According to the readout on his dive computer the water temperature was ten degrees cooler than it should have been.

Something else was at work here.

They swam along to the port side of the *Exeter*, lights playing along the superstructure. To Navarre there was always an unspoken accusation about shipwrecks, a muted testimony of the lives cut short and taken to a watery grave. In this case, a precarious one—southward, the absinthe-green water darkened into the primordial gloom of the Atlantic deep, the shipwreck poised to slide down into oblivion.

The destroyer showed significant marine growth—barnacles, anemones, corals and sea fans—the superstructure looking remarkably intact. One of the rear 5-inch gun turrets had tumbled off, lying thirty yards further to their left, and the two smokestacks aft of the bridge lay bent over as if swatted by a giant hand.

The life-boats—one webbed by a stray trawler net—still clung to their davits, indicating the ship had gone down too quickly for them to be deployed.

The front section of the ship had wedged itself into the top of the canyon, the front thirty feet of the bow disintegrated, as if all the metal had gone brittle and fallen apart. The destroyer was angled as if it had been caught attempting to slide down into the canyon as it sank, which Navarre figured about right. He estimated the angle at twenty degrees, which would make setting up the 3D scanner tricky.

But not impossible.

The forward gun turret hung precipitously over the missing section as if only attached by wishful thinking. Webs of snagged trawler nets covered sections of the wrecks. Perhaps that was how the overall shape would blend with the surrounding rock formations on a sonar scan.

Navarre pointed toward the open deck skirting the back part of the bridge. The oversized lifesaver ring still hung, affixed in place on the rail. Atop the bridge was the large radar housing which, when active, could cook a man in seconds if he stood next to it. Now, like the rest of the wreck, it sprouted an assortment of tufted growths and corals, lending it the appearance of an abstract mad scientist's skull, skewed as if listening with one ear what awaited in the abyss beyond.

He let the sled take them past the ring of circular porthole windows at the front of the bridge, then slowed down to hover on the deck. He saw the access door to the interior had been wrenched off, as if yanked by a giant (tentacle) hand.

Navarre also noticed that all the windows of the bridge had been shattered, smashed *inward*. Shards of glass still lined the circular portals. Yet one more disturbing aspect of the wreck—as far as he knew the glass was armored.

Dan paused nearby, taking shots of the bridge and down toward the destroyed bow. It was tricky business with the tangled fishing nets, any of which could snag and tangle an unwary diver.

Securing the sled's tether to the rail, he signaled Dan he was going in for a look.

Inside, the bridge was even spookier.

Easing himself in carefully through the ruptured door, he flicked on his hand lights and let them play around the interior. Even on a typical shipwreck, the very act of sinking tends to make chaos of the most ordered spaces. Navarre had seen plenty, including a few violent combat wrecks that were discreetly kept out of the papers.

But nothing like this.

Whatever had occurred on this bridge, was on a magnitude he'd never witnessed.

Consoles were torn and twisted, piping bent in bizarre shapes, instruments mangled. Human skulls and bones littered the floor, many smashed.

The bridge was a slaughterhouse.

Navarre couldn't begin to figure what did this. He moved over to the sonar console to where the AMFOS unit would be. A metal stand had been jury-rigged next to the sonar, but it was empty. A few torn cables fluttering in the current was all that remained. From the drawings (and one black-and-white photo in the ONR documents) it should have been relatively easy to spot—a distinctive round-edged cast steel housing with large Bakelite dials and two glass cathode-ray screens—but there was nothing resembling it on the bridge. Navarre did three sweeps of the entire cabin to be positive. He found similar parts.

Someone—or something—had removed it.

Outside, he gave Dan the 'no-go' signal and indicated they should proceed to the lower deck. Perhaps they would have better luck in the lower sound room.

The front end of the ship looked like it had been pinched and torn off—definitely *not* the work of a torpedo.

It took a few minutes to set the scanner up on the canted deck and calibrate it. Ideally, he would take scans from three distinct locations to get the best data cloud capture, but the way the deck tilted and the fact it was over a canyon only permitted two.

He took several scans from each position for redundancy, then decided to have a swim around the bow section to scope it out. There might just be enough room from the torn off forward compartments to go directly in.

Navarre waved to Dan and pointed toward the front of the wreck, careful to stay well above the scattered barrels, more (from what he could see) were on the verge of toppling over into deeper water.

What bothered him was the state of the marine growth on the bow. It looked odd... turning to blue-black as if the growths had become blighted, or *poisoned*.

Could toxic wastes do such a thing?

The marine growth, perhaps, but the metal hull?

He checked the dive gauge on his wrist: 167'.

As they came up on the front section of the ship, Navarre stopped short, taking in the damage. He'd never seen anything like it before. The hull had fallen to pieces. Inner piping, conduits and debris hung out. On the deck next to the toppled front turret lay several twenty-one-inch torpedoes. Navarre guessed they must have tumbled out from the launchers positioned just aft of the bridge when the ship impacted. He also noted the front turret seemed to have been pushed *up* out of its seating ring on the deck, as if something had punched through the hull from below.

Could a direct torpedo hit have done this? he thought, realizing—between what he was seeing here and the condition of the bridge—the absurdity of the question. The more he thought about it, the more spooked he became. His thoughts (like long-legged sea spiders) creeping around his brain.

Next to him, Dan aimed her camera—Barbara's Canon 5D in its SeaLife dive housing—and snapped more photos. As she did, Navarre noticed something else: an odd, iridescent glimmer of light down inside the damaged bow, roughly where the forward sound room would be.

A silver-blue glow.

Moving up toward the turret opening in the deck he could see the same glow issuing from directly below. It felt odd, as if the ocean here was filled with a heavy, dreadful background noise.

He signaled Dan by touching his face mask with two fingers then pointing down the opening: *Closer look*!

Dan felt a twinge in her gut and a sudden urge to pee. Worst case she would just go in the suit, but that wasn't what really bothered her. She'd been thinking about the hull of that yacht and how the damage on the destroyer looked like a larger version of it. The old line from the movie 'Jaws' came to mind: *We're going to need a bigger boat.*

What's bigger than a destroyer? A battleship? Did they even have those anymore?

Navarre was slipping ahead. Dan gave her flippers a good kick. As they drew closer, she saw the damage to the upper and lower hull looked truly weird. It suggested it had been *bitten* off, which of course was absurd. The beam of the destroyer measured thirty or more feet across.

Her unease intensified. The water felt much colder and there was a distinct current pulling downward.

Toward the canyon.

Past that, the darkness seemed to be intensifying. Growing.

All at once the rebreather felt stuck in her mouth, the air coming through it like trying to suck a milkshake through a straw. She tried to catch up to Navarre, to warn him.

Navarre checked his depth again as he approached. What he first took for sea growth around the gaping hole where the front turret sat was more like a pitch-black mold, spreading out like a cancer. Down through the ruptured deck of the 5-inch ammunition room his lights made out the top of a bulbous, fantastically strange blister shape, surrounded by nine flesh-like flaps suggesting a carnivorous plant. Inside he could see the flicker of the silver blue lights, waving, like clusters of a phosphorescent sea anemone's... or like one of the bizarre, pulsing jellyfish life forms that had been discovered.

It was hypnotic in a repulsive way.

Navarre also noticed the scattered oblong forms of five-inch artillery shells around it.

Even stranger, as he inched downward, the top of the blister appeared to be changing. Morphing. The opening now resembled a woman's labia and vagina. The current was drawing both of them right down into it.

He saw undulating filaments reaching out, as if beckoning him. And he *wanted* to get closer, to investigate... to feel them. *Strange*. Navarre felt an erotic, sexualized compulsion to go inside there, even as another part of him equally knew that death—and perhaps untold terrors worse than death awaited within. The urge to let them *touch...* and caress. He was aware of a painfully hard erection in his swim trunks, even as violent images flashed across his thoughts: body parts, human bodies being torn apart, visceral organs being ripped and gobbled by spider-like creatures. A light scissoring sound seem to come from behind his head.

Relaxing. *Beckoning*.

Navarre reached out.

23. A TASTE

Inside its cocoon-ship, what passed for the creature's mind flexed and coiled like a bundle of worms; alien electromagnetic strings altering the fabric of time-space like a sentient tumor throbbing through multiple layers of organs, or in this case dimensions.

The kaleidoscope of iridescent lights lining its pod brightening with anticipation as it altered to accommodate these minor life-forms approaching it. It held itself back the way a bloated trapdoor spider might hesitate over a curiously different prey outside its lair after already sating itself.

It sensed something else, as well.

A taste of something it was *drawn to*.

The field beyond the front of the ship began to darken as it drew energy and light from the mass of water there, any living matter in its proximity withering or winking out of existence, similar to the way a power source would draw energy. Except this energy came from converting life in the nearest dimensions. When the creature fully ramped up, the cost was enormous.

Even as the forms approached it, it began to radically change.

24. YOU'VE DONE A MAN'S JOB

"So, you've *finally* located the bunker, Carl?"

"Yes, I got the confirmation this morning," Gavin replied, gazing out the windshield at the Hither Hills State Park camping area below. Down by one of the trailer-tents, a tall black man was helping his two sons at their bungling attempt to get a kite airborne. A woman—the mother presumably—sat at the steps of the tent door cradling a cup of coffee. It reminded him of more innocent days long past with his own wife and son. When the summers at the beach were like the future: bright, sunny, full of endless promise.

Before slurpy-voiced bastards like Dave surfaced in his life.

"And the chair? You *must* have found the chair."

Gavin's eyes narrowed. Dave's usual 'Mr. Friendly' banter had a hint of an eager edge to it: *He hides it well, but the bastard's a junkie for this crap*.

"Yes, there was *a* chair."

"No need to be coy, Carl. What was in it? Was the crystal there as well?"

"What are you talking about... *Crystals*? Seriously? Is this bunker some kind of New Age storeroom?"

There was silence on the other end. Gavin had a cold feeling he'd gone too far.

"No, Carl, it most certainly is not." Dave's voice went flat and emotionless. "What's down there is dangerous. They were more than a little naïve back then and paid for it. Twenty-seven officers, scientists, nurses and enlisted men died before they sealed it up. Most were in pieces, according to witnesses. Do you find that funny?"

"No, I do not."

"I'm glad to hear that, Carl. There was a body, though. Photos?"

"No."

"Sloppy. But the room was still active? You're completely positive about that?"

"I'm not positive about anything except what I was told happened down there."

Silence. Then: "What have your clients found out on the water?"

"They're out there now. I'll fill you in as soon as I know."

"Yes, you will. Call in a clean-up crew for the bunker, stat. Enjoy the rest of your morning, Carl."

Gavin hung up without responding.

None of this sat well with him. For one thing, why hadn't Dave just sent his own team to locate the bunker? Didn't he have the missing files on 'Bunker 18' from ONR? He had assumed they were the same people who had threatened DeWalt all those years ago or were at least connected to them. If Dave and whoever he worked for didn't have the run down on what was down there, then who did? And who were these Breckenridge people, really?

Gavin took a sip of coffee from his thermos.

25. "WARP SPEED AHEAD, MR. SULU."

Easing out of the rather drab docking facilities at Davisville, Rhode Island, the *Robert D. Ballard* fell off southward toward the Atlantic Ocean in the bright morning. At two-hundred and twenty-four feet, the gleaming white ex-Navy vessel, loaded with two underwater Remote Operated Vehicles, the latest computers, lab and mapping equipment, a high-bandwidth satellite communications system capable of transmitting mapping and oceanographic data real-time, she was arguably the most advanced deep-sea exploration vessel in the world.

She was also the one available NOAA vessel close enough to respond to the latest events unfolding out at Montauk and Block Island.

On the bridge, Commander A.J. Hopper, sitting in the only chair on the bridge—the high-backed Captain's seat—surveyed the open sea ahead through the broad, forward-slanted windows.

A trim, self-efficient woman with dark blonde-hair and the no-nonsense air of a military personnel, Hopper was a master at projecting calm and confidence even when her internal workings were in turmoil.

This morning, her usual sense of self-balance was off, making unnecessary comments to the crew, unknowingly adding to the agitated air on the bridge. The crew were more than capable of taking the ship out of port on their own, but Hopper seemed to be all over them with minor course corrections, speed adjustments and critiques. Nothing too overt—they were accustomed to operating as strict as any Coast Guard ship—just enough to keep their teeth on edge.

The source of her unease had been the call on her cell while she'd been driving back from a quick breakfast over in Wickford. The call had been from Acting Chief Michelle Cabrales, whom she knew from back in Officer's Training School, giving her a heads up on the ship's next (somewhat odd) mission along with a peculiar warning.

"Official orders will be transmitted shortly, Commander," Chief Cabrales had told her. "*The Ballard* will be calibrating its new sonar scan equipment to update our bathymetric survey maps along the Long Island shelf."

"We *are*, Chief Cabrales?" Hopper was perplexed. The maps and charts for the area were current.

"Officially. *Unofficially*, you'll keep your head down and eyes open for anything unusual you discover and don't broadcast anything on live feeds. Anything you do find, report directly back to me. Understood?"

Hopper had just turned onto the flat stretch of Davisville Road. "Understood. Can you clarify 'unusual', Ma'am?"

"I can't really say. Only someone in ONR has been sniffing up everyone's skirts here in a way that's got many of us spooked."

"Terrorist activity, Ma'am?"

There was a pause on the other end. Chief Cabrales continued in a quieter tone.

"Nothing like that. Listen A.J., something's going on out there that certain people want to keep suppressed, at any cost. Watch yourself. And watch your back... do you understand me?"

"Yes Ma'—*Michelle*," Hopper replied, a little awkwardly. Then added, "I will. *Thanks*."

Cabrales had been a mentor to her during those uncertain years during officer training when she'd been trying to assert herself in what was still a male-dominated field. Michelle Cabrales was a one-person powerhouse: smart, unerringly confident and with an iron shod moral and ethics code.

This was a first, however. The slight tremble in the Chief Acting Officer's voice had been unmistakable. Michelle Cabrales had sounded *scared*.

By the time Hopper had boarded the *Ballard* and signed in she felt like a cloud had settled over the day's prospects. Hopper was an extremely pragmatic woman by nature, so this superstitious sense of foreboding was new to her.

And unsettling.

Hopper took a sip of her coffee and crossed her legs, forcing herself into an air of confidence.

Sometimes just acting the part enables you to become it, her father always told her.

After using the bow thrusters, the ship had steered away from the docking area and continued on a southeast heading through Narragansett Bay past Hope Island. The morning still looked promising and at least the weather report was good for the next twenty-four hours.

Over by the helm console, the executive officer, Lt. Commander Jackson Drake, was eying her expectantly.

Hopper gestured toward the horizon with her first two fingers.

"*Full warp speed ahead*, Mr. Sulu," she said.

26. A NARROW ESCAPE

Her scream muted by her rebreather, Dan caught Navarre's vest and hauled him backwards, just as the filaments from the opening nearly touched his fingers.

He instinctively tried to resist, twisting about and trying to back-hand her, only the density of the water slowing the blow enough to not knock her mask off. The flurry of bubbles escaping his rebreather disrupted the filaments, which lunged at them again, but Navarre regained enough of his senses quickly enough to beat a retreat, his flippers knocking them away.

Dan looked back and saw something worse: snaking out rapidly out of the darkness of the ruined deck compartments were dozens of giant Bobbit worms, a foot in diameter, with horrific barbed jaws and sensory antennae splayed wide. Their iridescent, jointed carapaces glimmered in the dim light. Even stranger were the tiny clusters of glowing silver-blue eyes, just inside the rimmed mouths.

Navarre saw them too. Realizing Dan was trying to haul them straight up to the surface, he angled them toward the bridge where the tow sled was still tied off. Both pumped their legs furiously in unison, trying to escape.

For a moment it seemed they had, then Dan saw the worms—continuing to elongate—snaking around the contours of the ship, coming at them from multiple directions.

Faster than they could possibly outrun them.

It didn't make sense—these worms were over twelve times the size they should be... yet there they were.

Navarre had his diving knife out in one hand, while guiding them to the bridge rail. One worm darted at them and he slashed at it viciously—it snapped easily out of range, as if toying with them.

Dan saw them spreading out past them in the murk, while realizing with a sinking feeling that whatever these things were, she and Navarre were about to die.

Very painfully, from the looks of it.

This can't be happening! These things can't exist!

She struggled to breathe through her mouthpiece, dimly aware she was hyperventilating. She heard a clanging sound and saw Navarre had abandoned the tow sled and was banging the back end of a large swivel device mounted behind the bridge—it was an array of five tubes perhaps twenty inches in diameter and twenty feet long. Even as he kicked, there was an answering clang and to her further horror, a twenty-one-inch torpedo tumbled out through its rotting canvas cover and bounced down the deck, debris and sediment clouding up in its wake. He kicked the firing hammers again and two more fell out, following the first.

She expected them to explode. Instead, several of the giant worms whipped around and plunged after them. Navarre grabbed her tank strap and shoved her away. Dan did understand until she saw his ankle was caught in a steel cable wrapped around the operator's chair on top.

Dan moved in to help but Navarre shook his head no, jabbing his finger repeatedly toward the tow sled: *get away!* She tried again but he pushed her off, his eyes angry behind his mask. There was no time to argue. She swam toward the stern. As she passed the ship's smokestacks, she saw more of them coming up and over the rails.

Her entire existence diminished rapidly to seconds.

She had only swum another couple of yards when she felt something grab her shoulders. Screaming, she twisted around, coming up with her dive knife. Another hand grabbed her wrist.

To her shock she saw it was Vanek.

Something banged against her hip, painfully.

She saw it was the speaker cube. Vanek tapped her shoulder to get her attention, pointed at the cube then down at the torpedo launcher where Navarre was tangled.

Maybe…

She unclipped it, depressing the *power on* button, followed by the *activate* button.

Then she flicked her wrist, sending it tumbling away, giving off the strange scissoring sound that while muffled, was very audible. The sound traveled in all directions at once.

Its effect was instantaneous.

The remainder of the worms whipped after it, some of them—quite strangely—seeming to wink in and out of visibility.

Vanek didn't waste any time. He swam down to where Navarre struggled to free himself, Dan following him.

To his surprise, once in the water Vanek felt a calm spread through his body. Partly it was the sense of self-sufficiency that came with having a scuba tank and equipment, partly it was his old diving instincts kicking in after all these years.

Clipping his 'D' ring to the dive line, he worked his way down hand-over-hand as quick as he could.

With the negative buoyancy it went relatively smooth. He'd checked the dive tables and estimated he had ten minutes maximum once he was down there if he had to get up in a hurry without a decompression stop. The tanks he had on were Navarre's back-ups—he hoped they were the same gas mix.

He hadn't told Gorecki the whole truth; that it wasn't just about the ship his grandfather had gone down on—his gut told him something far worse was waiting.

Heading down into the gloomy depths, he focused on keeping his breathing regular and his mind clear. It was easier than he thought. The combination of the amniotic sensation of swimming underwater, the gradually increasing pressure and the sense of vastness stripped away his ego, clearing his mind.

Hand over hand. Steady... breathe. Keep moving.

Within five minutes he'd reached the bottom. Checking his dive gauge and wrist compass, everything looked normal. Depth: 160. PSI good. Current moderate. Dive lights working. Pressure was giving his sinuses hell, but he'd cope. Unclipping himself from the dive line, he headed south.

It didn't take long to locate the *Exeter*. He'd just passed the remains of the *Tryton* when he saw the stern of the destroyer looming up out of the darkness.

It was here!

Of course, *why wouldn't it be?* Dan's photos told him that. But seeing it with his own eyes brought it home.

The source of so many questions. And mysteries.

As he swam up and over the stern rail, he paused as he felt the ship shudder, followed by a loud metallic *clang*.

What the—?

Then he saw the forms halfway down the deck.

And the giant worms undulating all around them.

He winced as the scissoring sound erupted everywhere around him.

The minute it took to cut through the straps and free Navarre's foot seemed like an eternity. The ship vibrated as the giant Bobbit worms chased the speaker down the length of it. At one point the wreck groaned and abruptly shifted downward a foot, causing all three divers to wonder if it would simply plunge down into the gorge, taking Navarre with it.

Then the three of them clung to the tow sled, glancing backward to see if death would bolt back out of the blackness and claim them.

The sounds grew fainter, then abruptly stopped.

Once they reached the dive line, there was a brief argument (with hand gestures) on how long they should decompress - for Vanek it'd become borderline. For Navarre and Dan, critical unless they wanted to risk a case of the bends. What were those things? How far would they come after them? And: how fast could they travel?

They had two dive knives between them, and little else.

Navarre made them stop in their ascent and wait thirty long, agonizing minutes. All three kept their masks trained below, waiting for the worms to come.

Nothing happened.

Vanek and Dan were working their way out of their cumbersome scuba tanks with Gorecki's help when Navarre climbed over the stern ladder.

"Never mind them, I'll take care of it," Navarre said to Gorecki, tossing his mask aside. He wrestled his tanks off along with his flippers. His right leg bled from where it had gotten caught. "Get us out of here, Les, *now*."

Gorecki nodded and bolted up the ladder to the pilot house. A moment later the twin diesels rumbled to life.

Once the tanks were safely stowed in their racks, Navarre limped into the cabin and came back out with a pack of cigarettes and a Zippo lighter.

He stood, his dive suit half unzipped, sat down and lit up. He offered one to Vanek, who shook his head *no* at first. Then he changed his mind.

"If you don't mind." He accepted a light from Navarre, took a pull and broke out coughing. It tasted like an old burning newspaper.

"I won't ask what the fuck you were doing down there, as you saved my life," Navarre said, drawing in smoke and letting it blow out the stern.

"Both of us, actually," Dan added, holding up the tether the speaker had been hooked to. From the intense look on her face, Vanek thought she was still processing what they saw down there.

"What in the hell was that?" he said to both of them.

"*Eunice aphroditois*," Dan offered. "Polychaete worms."

"Seriously?" Vanek asked. He'd never heard of such a thing. What he saw, though, was straight out of an alien sci-fi horror film.

"*Il n'est pas possible!*" Navarre spat out. "Such worms can only be an inch thick. Those... twelve, fifteen times as large!" Then to himself: "Could that be? No! She said 'jellyfish'."

After two puffs on the cigarette, Vanek felt light-headed and sick to his stomach. Making a face, he flicked it overboard. "You're right. It doesn't add up." He thought about what they'd encountered down in the bunker. And the girl's story... the visions... his nightmare last night. Everything out here was *not adding up*. What was the answer? There was the frustrating feeling of *almost* being able to connect the dots.

"What now?" Vanek continued. "Have you seen enough now? Enough to call Gavin and let him and the Navy deal with this whole mess? If they're some kind of giant, unknown sea creatures…"

Navarre rubbed the bridge of his nose. "*Bizarre*. But there was something down there inside the hull, like a... *Dan*? Your camera?"

Dan looked at the Canon sitting on the bench next to her as if coming out of a trance, "Oh my God, of course!"

"And with any luck, this Trimble unit should give us a clue what was down there!"

It took only a few minutes to transfer the data from the SD card to her laptop. Not for the first time Vanek marveled at the incredible *immediacy* of digital photography. In the ancient film years of his childhood it would have taken a week to get the images developed and printed.

Crowded around the table of the main cabin, the high-definition display made it seem like gazing right through a window.

Most of the shots were of the *Exeter*, including one of the stern, clearly showing the letters DD-452. Another showed the dead marine growths near the bow and there were half a dozen piles of toxic waste drums. The others were out of focus despite the highspeed setting—there was too much movement.

Except for two of the photos.

One was looking down into the crevasse below the severed bow. The curve of the pod was just visible along with blurred filaments stretching out of it. Its inner sparkle of lights could be seen, colors that suggested the cosmic spectrum of a distant galaxy.

The other was a clipped-off close-up of one of the worms, its vicious-looking barbed jaw whipping across the lens. A few of the mis-sized silver-blue eyes above the feelers glowed as if in a homicidal rage.

Vanek shuddered.

"Wow. I don't even remember taking that one," Dan said.

Navarre tapped his chin with his fist. "That's it?"

"That's it," Dan replied. "I didn't exactly have time to compose good shots and check the shutter speed."

With a HDMI cable, he attached the portable UHD monitor that came with the Trimble unit to the scanner. A minute later the point cloud data images came up, displayed in thermal false color gradients. The three datasets rotated independently, then after a few adjustments, came together.

"How does it reference the coordinates?" Vanek asked.

"GPS," Navarre said, smiling.

"What's the accuracy?"

"Plus-minus two centimeters. But watch this."

He hit a drop-down menu, clicked *Reconcile Datasets* and the screen went blank for a second. When the dataset reappeared it was incredibly sharp, with the rough edges of the data sliced off on the XYZ axis, leaving what looked like a clean section taken out of a real ship.

"You've used this sort of thing before," Vanek commented.

"Once or twice," Navarre replied. "This is 'top doggy' on the market. It makes best guesses on surface colors based on a preset database. The functionality is limited on this portable unit, but once on a full workstation I could manipulate it in all kinds of ways. Here we can only manipulate slice planes along the different axis."

"That's... something," Dan chimed in. "You've been holding out on us, Arnaud. I had no idea you had something like this up your sleeve."

Navarre manipulated the slice plane on the 'x-axis', which revealed the interior of the ship as he did. The lower decks were still 'gloppy' as if the scanner had difficulty registering the data, but the upper parts were as sharp and clear as a detailed physical model.

What was evident, however, was that something had forced its way up through the lower hull in a blister-like shape.

"What is that?" Vanek asked. "Some kind of outcropping?"

"No idea," Navarre admitted, scrubbing the slice plane back-and-forth. "Looking at the damage, it almost seems as if something forced its way up through the hull *after* the ship impacted bottom. See how the decks slant so, then curve forward and upward toward the penetrated decking? It wouldn't do that from that angle."

"It looks like... some kind of open blister," Dan said.

"Yes, an 'open blister'. How strange. You didn't capture any photos inside the ship?"

Dan didn't need to recheck her camera. "No, I was too busy trying to save your ass."

"Hmm. But you see that? That object in the sound room there? That looks like it—the second part of the AMFOS unit. We'll have to go back," he said after a moment of silence.

Dan and Vanek stared at him.

"*What*!?" Vanek said.

Navarre sighed. "I said, 'we have to go back'. Perhaps not *we*. I."

"But that... those mutant things... what if they weren't *from this Earth*?"

Navarre sat looking at the screen a moment. In the reflected light his face looked composed, yet sad. A man resigned to a deadly task.

"I have everything riding on this. You do not understand everything—my arrangement with Gavin and the ONR is to deliver the goods on this. When it comes to private military contracts, my reputation is first rate. I do *not* fail."

Vanek considered this. Of course. It made sense Navarre would be obsessive given the fiasco with the *Bonhomme Richard.*

"So, what's your plan?" he asked.

"I'm working on it."

With that he turned on his heel and walked out.

Vanek leaned forward on the table, hands clasped.

"Are you okay?" he asked Dan. Her hair was damp and matted from the dive and her face looked drawn, but he thought she still looked remarkably beautiful. She'd stripped down to her one-piece bathing suit when they'd first entered and was shivering. She had a swimmer's trim physique, he saw, trying to avoid sizing up her breasts and the effect the cold had on them.

For Christ's sake, he mentally kicked himself, *you just narrowly avoided death and all you can focus on is a woman's nipples.*

Dan's eyes remained locked on his, but he wasn't sure if she was looking *at* him or *through* him.

"I don't know. I think so. Those things scared the shit out of me. Whatever they were. I panicked. I should have never left Arnaud." She put her hand on his arm. "Will, if you hadn't come along, he'd be dead. We'd both be dead."

"More luck than anything else. The only reason I went down was to prove I could do it. Besides, I think it was your handy little speaker that did the trick. Those things went after it like cats after catnip."

She laughed, lightly, her eyes studying him. Then she reached over and snagged a nearby towel, wrapping it around her shoulders.

"You're full of surprises," she said.

Vanek wasn't sure how to take that. "*For there is no folly of the beast of the earth which is not infinitely outdone by the madness of men…*"

"Another quote?"

"Melville. Moby Dick. I just hope our Frenchman isn't developing an Ahab complex."

"I think what was down there really upset him. Deeply. And he has something to prove."

"The *Bonhomme Richard* fiasco," Vanek replied.

"Yes."

"He left those ONR hoods behind? Why?"

"They made us dizzy. He wants to stick with equipment he knows works. But something else troubles me."

"What's that?"

"What you just said. What if those things weren't *of* this Earth?"

Up on the flying bridge, Navarre bandaged up his leg, then leaned back in the chair next to Gorecki.

"You want to tell me what happened down there?" Gorecki asked.

"No," Navarre replied, resting his chin on his hand. His other tapped at his smartphone.

"You look very serious."

Navarre grunted. "What's down there is very serious. We're going to need some extra help. And equipment."

"You're going to ask Gavin for more money?"

"*Non.* I will call in some favors for this one."

***

The ocean around the pod and the wreck of the *U.S.S. Exeter* was in turmoil.

The mutated Bobbit worms the creature had become—triggered by the fears of the female life form—writhed chaotically at the tumble speaker box, snapping at it, batting it this way and that until one finally crushed it with its jaws.

The three-dimensional sound both confused and over-stimulated it; at first it thought it was another of its kind, invading its territory.

When the sound abruptly cut off, the creature began to lose cohesiveness. It began to deconstruct and morph to its natural state (which neither Dan, Vanek or Navarre would have found any less repulsive or horrifying): a writhing, somewhat spider-like mass with squid-like attributes. The agitated, scissoring sound it gave off reached a crescendo before resolving into a series of clicks and snaps.

It had been confused by this last encounter—one of the intruders left it curious... it felt *familiar*.

Still, it was ravenously hungry.

The filaments streaming out of the pod undulated and intermeshed with it, transferred some of its limited energy. As it did, more of the surrounding coral blackened and fell apart.

It needed sustenance. Lots of it.

From the east it sensed something large.

Filled with life forms.

27. TO PORT

"*Jagad-b'ya*," Vanek said.

"*Who*?" Dan replied.

"*Jagad-b'ya.* An old Sanskrit term meaning 'terror of the universe'. Similar to a Buddhist one: *Bhaya-bherava Sutta*. Which means: 'fear and terror'. Gorecki mentioned it, so I Googled it."

They were having lunch at one of the umbrella-covered tables overlooking the water at Gossman's Clam Bar, near the entrance channel to the harbor. It was one of Vanek's favorite spots. Everything about it was scenic: the view of the inner harbor docks with its mix of fishing trawlers and yachts, the sandy shallows just underneath their seating where alewives and the occasional jellyfish could be seen in the aquamarine water, even the seagulls with their cardsharp eyes (and shrill hawkers cries) sitting atop the wooden pylons. The parade of boats motoring by the beach, the scrub brush of the opposite shore under a vast blue sky completed the remote fishing village backdrop.

A light breeze tugged at the umbrellas and loose strands of Dan's hair. With it came the smell of saltwater and fried food. The smells of summer.

The remains of two lobster rolls and salad on paper plates lay on the table between them, weighted down by their iced tea.

"Why this just sounds like the start of a delightful lunch conversation!" Dan said, brushing her hair out of her sunglasses. She had changed into faded shorts and leather T-strap open-toed sandals before getting off the boat, with a light cotton shift over a floral-knit V-neck. There was something about sandals on a woman Vanek found quite sexy.

That was one thing Michelle *didn't* wear.

Once back in port, Navarre had dashed off to make calls and order equipment for the second dive tomorrow. Dan and Vanek had gone back to the house to shower and document what had happened, Dan adding her photos to the report. Gavin wasn't answering his phone. Vanek wanted to go to the Marine Patrol with everything, but Navarre insisted they keep a lid on it until the next afternoon. He was about to dial 9-1-1 when Navarre seized his wrist.

"*No*," Navarre repeated. The look in his eye had been cold. Merciless.

Two hours later, Dan had asked him about grabbing lunch. Shaken, but ravenously hungry after the dive, Vanek had agreed.

"I think I've gone *certifiable*," Dan said.

Vanek laughed. For a passing moment it felt like he was in a parallel dimension, one where he was another man simply on vacation enjoying lunch with a particularly attractive woman. Even stranger, he thought, was how *alive* he felt.

Like I've been dead for years.

"Fair enough," he said out loud. "Sorry, I keep thinking about what we saw down there today, and how it might relate to what happened down in the bunker. Perhaps even tie-in to the curriculum of my old teaching days."

"An old technology with new nightmares," she said, holding down her plate while picking up her iced tea to sip on.

"Something like that. Think about it though, every incident surrounding this thing is utterly different. How is that even possible? Today we saw some kind of giant Bobbit worms. The girl who survived the yacht sinking described a 'giant jellyfish'. The damage on the boat itself looked like neither. The footage recovered from the camera of that friend of yours - Barbara Holden—showed something that resembled a giant angler fish coming out of the murk. Then, down in the bunker my grandfather and those things, black. Squid-like. So, which is it?"

"On the surface of it, it doesn't add up," Dan answered, cocking her head.

"It sounds like utter nonsense," Vanek agreed. "Unless we're all hallucinating."

Dan considered it a moment, one finger toying with her sunglasses. "You're forgetting your 'episodes'. Did you ever have anything like those before?"

"No."

But that wasn't exactly true, was it? Because when he was a kid...

He shook his head to cut off that line of thought.

Dan gave him a sidelong glance. "Are you pondering what I'm pondering…?" she prompted.

Vanek let out a laugh. She had that effect on him, he realized. But it triggered a thought. Pinky and the Brain were always in a lab…

Next to them, an elderly man who struck Vanek as a silver-haired blue-blood, started arguing with his companion, a clearly effeminate young kid who looked like a college freshman. The older gentleman reminded him of a professor he'd once consulted with on the pathology of a certain sea—

"—of *course*!" Vanek said out loud, smacking his hand on the table.

Dan gave a start. "What?"

"The *pathology*! The evidence! There'd be tissue residue on the yacht they recovered! I didn't think of it until now, we were so focused on... we need to get back over there *now*. Star Island Marina."

He was already up and piling everything on their tray.

Less than ten minutes later they were pulling into the parking lot at Star Island.

Even as they neared the gate, it was obvious the yacht was gone. Nor was there any sign of the police officers. As Vanek and Dan approached the berth they saw there was little indication it had ever been there.

"What the hell?" Vanek asked, to no-one in particular.

"Can I help you?"

Both of them looked over to see someone climbing down the ladder against a vintage motorboat being restored nearby. A moment later a sandy-haired man with a bushy mustache and the muscled forearms of a sailor walked up to them, wiping his hands with an old rag.

"Ah, we were here yesterday with the ONR," Vanek said, hands on hips. "What happened to the DeFranco's yacht?"

The man shrugged. "Bunch of Breckenridge Lab guys showed up and took her this morning. Cleaned up real good after themselves."

"*Breckenridge Labs*?" Dan said, nonplussed. "Not the ONR?"

"Definitely Breckenridge. The Marine Police were none-too-happy about it either. The spooky Men-in-Black team arrived, carted the whole thing up and drove it away."

"You say they *drove* it away?" Vanek repeated.

"On a flatbed tractor trailer. Have to say they were quick and thorough about it."

"How do you know they were from Breckenridge?"

The man smiled. "That's easy, the truck was red with a big 'F; on the door. The same one my son drives for them."

"Thanks," Dan, said to him, then turned to Vanek. "Now what?"

In response, Vanek pulled out his smartphone and brought up Gavin's number. This time he answered.

"Carl, where the hell have you been? What's going on? We just showed up at Star Island Marina to find the DeFranco's boat is gone."

"I don't understand. What are you doing there?" Gavin replied.

"Looking for evidence."

"You won't find it there, Will."

"Tell me something I don't know."

There was a pause on the other end. "Fine. *Congratulations*, you've completed your mission."

"Sorry, *what*?"

"I don't like repeating myself, Will. But I know it's been a difficult two days for you, so I'll cut you some slack. The mission is a wrap. The ONR got what it needed. Take a day off, relax, but don't go anywhere just yet. They'll want to interview the three of you tomorrow afternoon. Location to be determined. Someplace nearby. And a reminder: not a word to anybody. Any violation of the NDA will be met with swift and maximum force. You did well."

"That's *it*?"

"That's it."

Vanek started to say something else but Gavin had already hung up. He looked at his phone in disbelief.

"*What*?" Dan asked.

"He told me ONR got what they needed. Stick around for an exit interview and we're done."

"Seriously?"

"Seriously."

Dan raised a hand, either annoyed or in resignation. "Well that's just great. But that doesn't make sense. What about the AMFOS unit? We didn't retrieve it. All we got were some photos."

"Yes…" Vanek said, half to himself. Something wasn't right. For one thing, Gavin sounded scared. That was a first, "... and those are back at the house. Come on, let's go."

***

A little more than two-hundred feet from where Dan Cheung and William Vanek were having lunch, Antony Scarpia and Sammy Vanossi sat in a booth at The Dock Bar & Grill, a hold-out from the older days that still drew mostly year-round locals.

A rough-around-the-edges tavern with low-light, plenty of rustic charm and amusing décor ranging from taxidermized animals and fish to boxing mementos, eclectic signs and even a moose-head wearing a sombrero, outside of Lobster Trap it was one of the few places in town Scarpia felt he could get Manhattan clam chowder, stuffed clams and a burger at a decent price.

Vanossi was working his way through an order of 'Dock Dogs' and Sauer Kraut, with a Cosmo to wash it down.

Though barely two o'clock, Scarpia was working on his second bourbon and coke.

"I don't understand, now you want to make the last dump *tomorrow*?" Vanossi said around a mouthful of hotdog.

"That's the new plan," Scarpia replied, looking around to make sure no-one was in earshot. The place was moderately full for Thursday, but no-one was paying them any particular attention and they had a spot at the very back.

"What happened to next week?"

"The Feds is what happened to next week. Too many poking around asking too many questions."

"Maybe we should just lay low until it blows over."

"Fuck that. It's time to wrap this up and get the fuck out of Dodge."

"Why not dump the rest of it somewhere else?" Vanossi said, sitting back. Years ago, he'd be able light up and have a smoke while he finished off his drink. These days you couldn't have a cigarette in the middle of the Montauk Highway without some fuckhead do-gooder driving by with a wagging finger and withering look.

Scarpia grunted. That was the first good idea Vanossi had coughed up in ages. He was annoyed he hadn't come to such an obvious conclusion himself.

Stupid, Antony, you're getting sloppy.

He looked up as their waitress, Ruth—the oldest one in the house—ambled up to clear their plates. She had the kind of weathered Irish features he thought of as 'a lot of hard miles and none of them good ones.'

Kind of the way his own wife was starting to look these days.

No matter, he thought. *Where I'm going after tomorrow the ladies will be all young, hot and probably topless half the time.*

"Will that be all, boys?"

"Just the check," Scarpia said.

Ruth already had it in her hand. She laid it on the table, picked up their plates and walked away without another word. A tough woman with a whacked-out sense of humor, normally she would exchange a caustic observation or two with the customers she recognized.

Not those two, though.

A couple of thugs on a greasy slide to the eternal firepit, her father 'Old Harry' used to say.

And the sooner the better, she thought.

28. PARTY LIKE THERE'S NO TOMORROW.

Just as Vanek and Dan were climbing back into her Mustang by Star Island Marina, a sleek black 46-meter Baglietto super-yacht was easing out of its berth at the Montauk Yacht Club for an evening cruise out past Block Island.

The ship—*Hatshepsut*—was owned by Ty Ekdahl, a thirty-year-old Social Media Czar and Claire Osterberg, darling of the Pharma tech giant *Asmari.* The two eschewed the older money of the Hamptons and embraced the hipper *nouveau riche* now overrunning Montauk.

Crewed by ten and typically with room for twelve passengers on an extended cruise, they'd invited a couple of extra people for an overnight party to celebrate their engagement. Most were friends from Manhattan but five were in from Ekdahl's company HQ in Palo Alto. The yacht exterior resembled more of an ultra-futuristic spaceship than a sea-faring vessel, while inside it was all modern Park Avenue hotel.

On the flying bridge, Osterberg sipped at a glass of Loire Valley *Sancerre.* Dressed in a colorful sun hat, Vera Wang silk Jersey top and linen pants with her raven-black hair flying in the wind and sharp cheekbones, she looked more like a model on a trip to Nantucket than a billionaire CEO. The latter was up for some debate these days with the SEC and lawyers sniffing around Asmari's heels after an exposé article in the Wall Street Journal claiming the company's technology was a complete fraud.

For the moment, however, it was a vista of clear skies and the promise of an exciting cruise on a luxurious yacht. Tomorrow would take care of itself. She felt young, exceedingly confident and excited about the future. Ekdahl was a slightly nerdy catch, in a deceptively rugged kind of way, and what he lacked in height he made up for in sheepish humor and unerring business instincts.

The future was theirs.

"*Pfennig* for your thoughts?" came a voice behind her.

She half-turned to see Ty standing behind her, a chilled glass of one of his designer vodkas in one hand. Referencing old sayings in obsolete currencies was one of his many 'Ty-isms' she'd found so amusing early on in their relationship. Now with ominous clouds gathering around her own finances, they were quickly losing their charm.

"Oh, just wondering what I should wear to tonight's party," she replied, pulling up a smile. The chilled vodka had been starting a little earlier each day.

"Not wearing the *Brunello Cucinelli* ensemble I picked out?" He'd made it clear with several recent jokes he considered her Vera Wang clothing 'slumming'.

"Tonight, dear, *tonight.*"

Ty smiled back. He couldn't recall ever being happier in his entire life, or at least happy in the *Ty-Scale.* Claire was everything he'd ever fantasized in a woman: brilliant, bold, exceedingly attractive and successful. Sure, he knew about some of the difficulties she'd been having with the press, but she'd assured him her board of directors were all over it. A good thing, he thought, as his company, SyDon, was sliding toward bankruptcy after miserable returns the past two quarters. The social media app (a play on the name of his obscure icon Syd Barrett) had early on been wildly successful in the disenfranchised teen dating market but had quickly fallen out of favor when word got through to its user base that most of its legally (and illegally) collected private data was being sold to not just corporate advertisers but the NSA. None of that was openly in the press yet as very little of the mainstream news was clued in to SyDon's demographic, but when the stock market caught up to the reality of their account books, it wouldn't be pretty.

He'd floated a bridge loan from a board member's research firm, Breckenridge Labs, but Ty was wondering if he might have to ask his bride-to-be to bail him out. Just for the short-term, of course. The meeting he'd had just that morning over at their offices had promised another tantalizing opportunity: a powerful new technology that could be used to manipulate social media users through their deepest fears, in ways that made what the Russians were doing look child-like.

But that was something he would worry about tomorrow. If nothing else, Ty Ekdahl was a survivor and possessed a ruthless streak few people—perhaps even his fiancée—would have suspected. If the going got really tough, anyone was fair game to throw under the bus.

Anyone.

"Cheers," Claire said, clinking her glass to his.

"*Salut*!" he replied.

"Life is good," she said, wishing it were so. For a brief moment she had a flashback of standing in front of her mom's mirror as a twelve-year-old, back in their old house in Johnsberg, Illinois. She'd dressed up as Queen Hatshepsut for Halloween. And now, here she was. Queen of the seas.

"Well, tonight at least, we'll party like there's no tomorrow!"

Over at his pad, Jimmy Reed sat on the narrow balcony, nursing an Anchor beer as the sun followed its arc toward the western horizon. An unlit Marlboro dangled from one hand.

He was meditating on the call he'd received minutes earlier from Sammy V and whether, despite his good friend Jax's assurances, this might be his last afternoon on Earth. He suspected if he could shake and hold up the old 'Magic 8 ball' he used to have as a kid, the answer on the floating icosahedron in the little murky window would be: "Outlook Not So Good."

Was it worth it, he wondered, getting your ticket punched for a pretty (but not overly bright) Swedish college student? *You could just jump in your nice Tacoma truck and start driving and keep driving until you were, say, out past the Rocky Mountains. Maybe sitting on a beach in southern California. Good surfing there, dude.*

In the end there really wasn't a question, he realized.

You got her into this mess. You have to at least try to get her out of it.

He lit up the Marlboro, took a long draw and let the smoke trail up and over the roof.

Maybe this is it. Maybe my entire life was leading up to tomorrow.

29. AN UNEXPECTED DINNER INVITE

When Dan and Vanek got back to the house, it was just after 2 p.m.

Across the way, the 'Aquarian's' (as Vanek now thought of them) party had escalated into full swing. Most of their followers, he noted, drove very expensive cars.

Navarre was waiting for them on the front porch, smoking a cheroot while reclining in one of the deck chairs. Gorecki sat on the chair next to him, drinking a soda.

"They took everything," Navarre said as they walked up the stairs.

Somehow Vanek wasn't surprised.

"Who? What do you mean 'everything'?" Dan asked.

"Gavin's friends from ONR and Breckenridge. They showed up at Gorecki's boat too, after you two left."

"Hell," Vanek said.

"Yes, *hell*," Navarre agreed.

"Then I guess you know, Gavin has pulled the plug on this whole thing. Mission complete. It's over."

Navarre seemed to find that amusing. He toyed with the cheroot in his right hand. "Yes, I know. He called and canceled my contract. Asshole. Strange, no? One moment the ONR is all hot to retrieve this AMFOS technology, the next they are not? Right after we dive and find not just that, but some odd life forms?"

"Yes, it *is* strange," Vanek admitted.

"And strange that you happened to find this bunker the ONR couldn't, and seem to be connecting all their dots for them?"

Vanek frowned. He didn't care much for the interrogator tone Navarre was taking. He felt his blood pressure go up a tick, then ease off. As if a light injection of fearlessness had entered his nerves. Along with his temper rising.

"Look, if you're insinuating I had anything to do with this, *any* of this, Arnaud, then out with it, Goddamnit. After whatever the hell happened down there earlier, I'm not in the mood for pussyfooting bullshit."

Navarre's eyebrows went up. Either in amusement or anger, Vanek wasn't sure. He stared at Vanek a long minute as if weighing him up.

"*Hmpf*! Perhaps you do but don't know it. Your friend Gavin is... what do you say, 'a slippery customer'. But no, this is not 'over'. Gavin told me I was to not go back to the wreck under any circumstance. Fuck *him*. You can go home to your nice house in Larchmont, if you want. And Dan? You too. Go back to your photographs and whales and research at Woods Hole. Or you can join us tomorrow, if you like."

"What are you talking about?" Dan asked, folding her arms.

"What I am talking about is doing what I should have from the beginning. Bring in a team who can do this the proper way. Since the *Bonhomme Richard* fiasco I have been running around *à moitié aveugle*—half blind! But I am in luck. Three expert divers I know well will be here this afternoon with... extra equipment. They were returning from a delicate 'salvage' operation off Mexico and on a layover in New York."

"Who's paying for them?" Vanek asked.

"Not for you to worry—I called in a couple of favors."

Vanek tried to get his head around this and came up short. "You're crazy. Why not just drop this whole thing? Besides, if they took everything, you don't even have the dive charts to work with. You'd go back down there blind?"

Navarre took another pull off his cheroot. "Not *everything*. Les here was smart enough to pocket the latest dive charts when he saw them coming down the dock. He left the old ones out to misdirect them. To answer your question, William, what is down there is something incredible. Perhaps even not of this world. They can do what they want with their AMFOS technology. I want a second look, a chance to document it, then get out. But this is *our* discovery."

"Yes. And a very dangerous one, in case you forgot."

Navarre chuckled. "No, I did not forget. Tomorrow, tomorrow we proceed with caution. And properly armed."

"Armed?" Vanek repeated.

"Yes."

Dan didn't look sold either. "They took my cameras, my laptop?"

"Yes," Navarre said. "They said they will be brought back to you within a week. After all relevant data has been stripped off, I presume. But the team tomorrow has several. You can borrow one if you like."

"I have to think about this," Dan said.

"Of course."

She stood there fuming for a few minutes, nostrils flaring. She turned to Vanek. "Care to go for a walk?"

"A *what*?" Vanek was confused.

"A *walk*. North, East, West. Anywhere."

"Sure. Of course."

Inside, the dining area looked odd with all the charts and photos gone. They'd taken the drawings of the bunker along with his grandfather's chair photo. It made him feel both rattled and irritated. And *violated*. The idea of strangers—particularly government agents—going through his personal things and taking what they wanted was a new experience.

One he didn't like very much.

Vanek went into the kitchen for a glass of water. Dan busied herself making some iced green tea. From the aggressive snap in her movements, Vanek figured she was pretty angry.

"So, what do you think?" she asked, in a tight voice.

Good question, Vanek thought. This whole second dive business was looking crazier by the minute.

"What I think is that this is very dangerous business we're getting into here. But I get Navarre's point. I'd like some answers. Especially where my grandfather is concerned. Besides, I don't like being pushed around."

There was more to it than that, he realized. It was the fact that ever since this morning—when whatever scared the hell out of him—he'd been feeling less anxiety. A *lot* less anxiety. Which was crazy. Yet there it was.

For the first time in years, he was starting to feel *alive*.

So that's the price, with irony: the more you run out of time to live, you feel more alive.

Great.

Dan stood by the counter, not saying anything, stirring the tea in a slender thermos she'd pulled out of the cupboard. With the afternoon sun slanting in through the windows highlighting her just so, she looked to Vanek like an artist's portrait; so alive in golden light while somberly gazing at the future.

Something else occurred to Vanek as he stood there: Gavin brought him out here for one reason only: to find the bunker. That was it. The ONR or Breckenridge boys might be in for a little surprise when they get down there, though. Either way, he'd decided to blow the whistle on this mess. But that would wait until tomorrow. What had happened on the *Exeter* all those years ago, 'Bunker 18' and what was happening now, were all connected. He was convinced the key was what they'd seen down there.

In the meantime, he had to admit Dan had grown on him. If he was going to die tomorrow, there were worse ways to spend his remaining time on Earth.

"Anywhere in particular you want to head?"

"The beach," she said. "I really need to blow off some steam. It's either that or start drinking, and it's a little early for that."

"What the hell," Vanek said. "We've done everything else. Let's go to the beach."

Ten minutes later they were sitting down on the empty expanse of sand. This stretch tended to be deserted as it was generally rocky, backed by eighty-foot bluffs that were only accessible by private stairs.

Dan found a sandier stretch a little way east where she and Vanek spread out the blanket and beach umbrella they'd found. Vanek dropped the cooler on the corner and helped get the umbrella set up. It felt surreal to be sitting here but Vanek decided to just go with it.

Dan stripped down to her one-piece bathing suit and ran down to the water with the buoyant excitement of a kid, pausing in the shallows to let the surf wash over her ankles.

Nothing kid-like in her figure, he noted. *Right there's a female in the full bloom of her womanhood and not shy about it. She's going to make some guy a very happy man.*

Then he remembered the kiss from the night before.

Don't read into it, pal. She's just flirting with you.

Still, no reason he shouldn't enjoy the view.

Dan's electric-blue swimsuit stood out like a bright gem against the sand and gray-green surf. She paused a moment, gauging the incoming waves, then sprinted forward, making a clean dive as she knifed into the breaker.

Vanek felt a pang of anxiety as she disappeared under the water. What if that damned thing was right there waiting? For a split second the horrid images plucked at his mind: hundreds of whipping tentacles snatching her and dragging her into the deep, the insidious scissoring sounds as the barbed jaws sliced. She surfaced, grinning, raising her arms in a victory salute. Vanek looked down and saw he was gripping a beach towel so hard that his knuckles were white.

A minute later she trotted up to him, spraying cold water drops as she snatched up a beach towel and dried herself off. She looked alive and fresh. The ocean seemed to have taken the edge off her anger.

"It's wonderful," Dan said, squeezing water out of her hair. "Why don't you take a swim?"

"I'm fine, Dan."

She looked him up and down. "You know, you really are awfully white for a white guy."

"Occupational hazard," Vanek replied.

She looked down at him with a half-smile. There was a sensuality to the whole situation. Vanek found himself staring at her nipples, which were very pronounced after the cold water, and immediately glanced away.

"I better get some sunscreen on you before you turn into a roasted potato," Dan said. She seemed to enjoy his discomfort.

"Great, so I can jump in the water and start killing off coral reefs?"

She squatted down and dug around in her purse. "Not this stuff. It's Sun Bum."

"Sun who?"

"*Bum*. Shut up and lie on your stomach so I can see yours."

Vanek shook his head, amused, but did as he was asked. A moment later he felt her cool hands spreading lotion over his back. For a moment he allowed himself to close his eyes and relish the sensation, the warmth of the sun, the grit of sand under his folded arms, the methodical impact of the waves with the accompanying hiss and sing-song clacking as the stones receded with the water.

He couldn't recall the last time he felt a woman's hands on him like that. In fact, he couldn't recall what it felt like until now, as if with Michelle's death a specific amnesia settled in.

She swatted his ass playfully and told him to sit up.

"Your turn," she said, handing him the bottle.

Without waiting, Dan positioned herself between his legs cross-legged with her back to him, pulling her hair to one side. Vanek squirted a dollop of sunscreen and worked it over her shoulders.

"Don't be shy," she added.

Again, he became painfully aware of her closeness and couldn't help but wonder if this was just some kind of teasing game or something else. As if sensing this, she inched backward even closer into him so that her butt was pressing right up against his crotch.

Vanek gave a start as he sensed himself responding.

After a minute of him rubbing her shoulders, Dan turned her head toward him. He realized her lips were slightly parted.

Why not?

He leaned in to kiss her…

... and his phone started ringing and buzzing like an angry alarm.

Vanek nearly smacked his forehead with his hand before realizing it was covered in lotion. Glancing down he saw the caller ID and grimaced.

It was his mom.

For a split second he felt he could have killed her.

"Hi mom," he said, after wiping his hand on the blanket and answering the call.

"Hi son," she replied, "I hope I didn't catch you at a bad time?"

Torturing him further, Dan grinned and gave his leg a pinch.

"Ouch!" he said.

"Are you *okay*!?" his mom answered, concern in her voice.

"Yes fine," Vanek said.

"Good." A silence followed. He sensed she was about to ask him a favor. She always got quiet before asking him of anything, which was rare. "Look, Will, I hate to impose on you and I know you're very busy, but I was wondering if you would join your brother and I for dinner tonight?"

"*Tonight*?" Vanek asked. "I'm uh, all the way out at Montauk."

"Oh, that's even better! We're out here too."

Vanek closed his eyes. They must be at his brother's summer place over on Shelter Island.

"You are? Well that's, that's terrific. Look, um, it's a little crazy right now, in fact I'm with a friend, Dan, and we're in the middle of—"

"—it's actually quite important, Will," she interrupted, sternness creeping into her voice.

Vanek stiffened. "What's going on?"

"Well, some men came and visited us today. Son, there're some things I need to tell you about your father. And your grandfather."

"What *men*?"

"They seemed to be associates of Carl's. They had Breckenridge Labs badges."

"Are you okay?"

"Of course, I'm okay. It takes more than a couple of government stiffs with sunglasses to rattle my cage. But we *need* to talk."

It was fortuitous when he thought about it. The Vaneks weren't the type to dwell on such things, but this might be his last chance to see her. And his brother. *Besides, just what in the hell was going on? What the hell was Gavin's game?*

"Okay, what time?"

"Seven?"

"Yes. Sure. I'll see you at seven."

"Thank you, son. I love you."

"I, er, love you too, mom," he replied. Now *that* was odd. He couldn't recall the last time she'd said that.

"Your mother is out here?" Dan asked.

"Ah, yes. My brother owns a summer house over on Shelter Island. I forgot they were coming out here this week. He rarely uses the place anymore."

"Younger or older?"

"Younger."

"So, you're going over for dinner tonight?"

"Yes. That's the new plan."

"That's sweet." She patted his leg and re-situated herself next to him. Whatever was about to happen, the moment had passed. Vanek wasn't sure if that was for the better or worse.

One thing he did know, however: nothing works like a bucket of cold water on your sex drive than a call from your mother.

"William?"

"Yes?"

Dan still sat close to him, close enough her leg bumped up against his, and he couldn't deny a certain intimacy, an unspoken agreement. It might have been all in his head, except she took his hand in hers.

"Could we just sit here for a bit?"

"Of course."

To his further surprise, she leaned her head against his shoulder. It was an oddly girlish gesture to him. He wondered if something else might happen between them, but it didn't.

They stayed another hour or so at the beach. It was an odd, yet strangely comfortable interlude, as if both sensed it might be the last before whatever would unfold in the near future.

Vanek lost himself in the Hornblower novel he'd nicked from his bedroom while Dan re-read 'Leviticus Tree'. It was quiet and peaceful in a way Vanek—who was never very fond of hanging out at beaches—found relaxing. Dan took several more dips and took a stroll up the shore, coming back with several smooth stones she found interesting, along with a couple of shells that wound up laid out in a pattern next to the blanket. A few fishing boats made their way along the horizon and a few gulls took up residence near them, anticipating food that never came.

Vanek found himself turning over everything from the last two days, the words in the book blurring into meaningless jumbles. There were still loose ends, but a distinct picture was beginning to emerge. After a bit he found his thoughts drifting toward Dan, contemplating the vagaries of fate and how this remarkable woman had dropped into his sedentary (boring) life like a bolt out of the blue, and the wonder of living in a universe where such things could even happen.

It wasn't until the sky deepened into early evening Dan finally set her book aside and rolled over to face him, propping her head on her hand. She had the languid expression one often gets after an interlude of sea, sand and sun.

"Thanks for coming out here this afternoon," she said. "You look different when you're relaxed."

Vanek set his book aside, one brow raised. "How so?"

"I don't know. *Handsome*."

Catching Vanek's flustered look, she added, oddly: "You must have really loved your wife."

"I... I, well yes. I did."

"And she really loved you?"

"Yes. As far as I know."

"I know you did. I can read it in your face. You're very lucky, you know that?" She turned her head slightly, her gaze shifting out toward the ocean. "I don't think I've ever really been in love before. Schoolgirl crushes, yes. But nothing like that."

Vanek let out a muttered, "*hmpf.*" He found her intensely feminine and strong—but also sad, he realized. And something else... an air of conflict about her, as if she was struggling with some inner decision. He had a sudden inexplicable urge to touch her cheek.

Instead she sat up abruptly.

"We should get going," she said, picking up her towel and shaking it out.

Back at the house, Navarre's friends had already arrived while Les Gorecki was about to get into his truck. From inside, Vanek could hear loud voices, all speaking French. It sounded like a family reunion.

"You look like you got sun!" Gorecki said to Vanek. He gripped Vanek's shoulder. "Do you good. Hey, just got word. That girl at the hospital? Kellie? She disappeared. Poof! Police are looking for her, just so you know."

"Thanks," Vanek said.

"I go grab some dinner, get the boat ready for tomorrow. See you two bright and early?"

"Yes."

"*Do zobaczenia*!" Gorecki said. If he was worried, he didn't show it. He gave Vanek a pat and climbed into his truck.

"Ah William! Dan! Come in!" Navarre stood at the kitchen island with three men, drinking beer. All three wore jeans and windbreakers with a distinctly European flair along with the boisterous energy distinctly *French*. Introductions were made. Vanek hastily put names to faces: Philippe had light brown hair and a beard with mischievous eyes, Michel large brown eyes, a beak of a nose and a weak chin, Yves had an aristocrat's chiseled features and a quick smile.

"You wish to join us for dinner?" Navarre asked.

"Actually, I have plans," Vanek replied.

"Ahh, hot date then?"

"With his mother," Dan cut in.

"Well, and brother. I just found out they're out at my brother's place in Shelter Island," Vanek explained. "But it looks like you gentlemen have some catching up to do, so I'll leave you to it."

In truth, Vanek always felt awkward with groups and hadn't socialized in years. The idea of getting drawn into small talk as an outsider filled him with dread. Still, he couldn't help but feel a pang of jealousy at how eagerly Navarre's friends greeted Dan.

They certainly aren't shy about it, he thought. *But it's not your business.*

Dan already had a beer in her hand and laughed at some comment Philippe made, so he made his way upstairs to shower and change.

He had just pulled on a heavy cotton shirt and was cinching his belt when there was an urgent knock at his bedroom door.

He opened it to find Dan standing there.

"Hi. Can I—" he started, but she walked right past him and sat on his bed.

"I'm going with you," she said.

"Sorry?"

Dan made a tight smile and shuddered as if trying to rid herself of something. "You can't leave me with those men! God, I feel like a slab of raw meat dangling in a lion's cage. *Ugh*!" From downstairs came more laughing. Someone called her name.

"But it's, well it's my—"

"Too late," she interrupted, standing up. "I'm inviting myself. Besides, I'll save you a cab ride. Give me ten minutes."

By the time he went back downstairs, Navarre and his friends had already decided they were heading over to the Surf Lodge on Edgemere—one of the more popular hangouts in the area—and Vanek was in the process of wishing them luck when two of the three visitors broke out in low whistles.

Vanek turned around and gave a start.

Dan stood in a form-fitting maxi dress in a striking peacock blue and gold print, slit up one side. The sandals accented her long legs. With the light touch of make-up and the contrast against her dark skin and hazel eyes, the effect was both dazzling and classy.

Where the hell she pulled this out of so fast, he had no idea. Dan looked secretly pleased.

Navarre grinned. "Somebody's mother should be impressed!" He raised his beer, "*à la vôtre*!"

Three glasses clinked with his.

Vanek walked her out to the Mustang. "If you wouldn't mind," she said, tossing him the keys as they approached the car. Taking his cue with a smile, he opened the door to the passenger side and closed it for her once she was in.

"Where on earth did you come up with that outfit?" he asked.

"I spotted it on a 37th Street wholesaler place in New York right before I came to pick you up. Next to the scuba shop. It really caught my eye. Nearly got a ticket double-parking to get it. You like?"

"It's an eye-catcher. Gustav Klimt would go crazy."

"Who?"

"A dead artist. Never mind."

Fortunately, the evening traffic was light heading west. Vanek felt a little absurd driving the Mustang with a woman 17 years his junior—like some guy having a mid-life crisis. Or some tacky Viagra ad. Once they were out of town, however, he opened up the throttle and forgot everything for a bit, just relishing the evening light, the implicit power of the car and its 8-cylinder engine, and the amusing thought of introducing the striking (and no doubt by their conservative standards, *outlandish*) woman to his mother and brother.

"What's your brother like?" Dan asked as they turned off Route 27 onto 114 North.

"Sweet kid. Or used to be. He kind of turned into a little old man after his wife left him. Now all he talks about is his job or the three antique cars he owns."

"Where's he work?"

"Engineering firm in Westchester."

"What's your Mom like?"

"Getting up there, but still an old battle axe. The kind that cracks walnuts with her teeth."

"Hmm. This should be interesting."

Vanek thought about his mother and brother's very WASP values and thought, *that may be a massive understatement.*

Half an hour later they pulled in front of a modest bungalow on Grand Avenue.

The house, a red shingled split-level, looked vaguely like a mid-century misfit amongst the older white-painted Victorian houses surrounding it.

Vanek's brother, Gerry, answered the door. To Dan he looked like a gangly Mr. Nye 'Science Guy' with mustache and double-knit slacks.

"Hi Will... and, er hello…?"

"Dan," Dan said, extending her hand.

"Gerald Vanek," he replied, blinking.

An awkward silence followed where Dan wondered if he was simply going to turn them away.

"Can we…?" Vanek prompted.

"Oh! Please come in!"

Inside, the cramped entranceway led into a quant front living room paneled in yellow pine. The furniture might have been set pieces from the late 1940's, though a flat screen TV sat tucked in the corner next to a small fireplace along with a modern mini stereo system. Tchaikovsky's Piano Concerto No 1 played through the mini speakers mounted high up on the wall. The rest of the décor—particularly the curtains and tchotchkes on the bookcases—had a distinct grandmotherly touch. Right down to the knitted afghan folded over the couch.

Sitting on the couch was a stately woman with wavy gray hair and the kind of features Dan would have described as 'handsome'. She was dressed in capris pants and slippers with a light sweater over her blouse. She set down the cup of tea she was drinking and stood up as they entered.

"Hi, mom," Vanek said, stepping over and giving her a polite kiss on the cheek.

"Hello, son," the woman replied with an equally polite smile. She glanced over at Dan and measured her head to toe in a single look. "Oh, so you're... *Dan*?"

"I must be," Dan said, dialing up the charm on her own smile.

"Well, I'm relieved to see you're a *woman.* When William here mentioned he was bringing a 'Dan' for dinner I was afraid he might have turned... well, *you know.*" She made a show of her wrist going limp.

Dan laughed, but it was a little forced. "I get that a lot. It's really *Danielle.* But everyone calls me Dan."

"That's quite a beautiful name, Danielle. I'm Ava."

"A pleasure," Dan said, shaking her hand.

"Please, make yourself comfortable," Gerry said, a little awkwardly. "Can I get you something to drink?"

"A beer would be fine," Dan said without hesitation.

"Make it two," Vanek added.

"I'll have some wine, Gerry. But with dinner," his mother said.

They had dinner in the small dining area off the living room, which also had a quasi-1940's nautical flavor to it. Dan wondered if she'd walked into a movie set of sorts.

Gerry had grilled rib-eye steaks out back ("I do hope you're not one of those new-fangled vegetarians!" Mrs. Vanek had prompted with a knowing look toward Dan, who shook her head *no*) along with a salad and a lobster mac-and-cheese, the latter which Dan suspected was store bought.

Most of the conversation went stiffly, with Gerry keeping the ball rolling with seemingly nonsensical chatter about everything from natural blood pressure cures (beet juice powder!) to the wonders of Walt Disney movies.

Vanek wasn't sure what to make out of all this. Gerry had been a sweet, shy kid growing up, but had grown increasingly into a fussbudget since his wife had left him a decade ago and sometimes so hyper-focused on his job that Vanek worried about him. Communication, however, was never their strong suit. But it was clear the visit from the authorities had rattled them: his mom kept talking more pointedly than usual. On several occasions, Gerry was on the verge of babbling. Dan played along like a good sport, at least.

Once dinner was over, Gerry cleared the table with Vanek's help. Gerry offered coffee but Dan went with another beer. Vanek opted for a glass of single malt while their mother opted for a snifter of cognac.

"So, William here mentioned you are some marine scientist?" his mom asked.

"Marine *biologist*, and photographer," Vanek corrected.

"Can you actually make a living at that sort of thing?" his mom plowed ahead, ignoring him.

"I'm not driving a Lexus, if that's what you mean. But it pays the bills. And I enjoy my work."

"Hmmm," Ava Vanek replied. "And how exactly did you two meet?"

"Mom, what did the ONR guys want?" Vanek asked, cutting to the chase.

Instead of answering, Ava Vanek picked up her snifter of brandy. She held it aloft as if it were of most unusual interest. Then she set it down again.

"Would you please excuse us?" she said to Dan and Gerry as she stood up.

Out on the small back patio overlooking a fenced-in flower garden was a wrought-iron table and cushioned chairs. To one side sat a gas grill, next to a chiminea that was rarely used. The outdoor wall sconces cast a warm yellow glow. From the nearby Azalea bushes a couple of crickets zinged. A lone firefly flitted by the fence.

His mom sat and crossed her legs, swirling the cognac.

"It's a Courvoisier Napoleon," she said. "At least your brother has good taste."

"He should. I bought it for him for Christmas two years ago," Vanek said. He sipped his scotch, savoring its mellow fire. An Aberlour. Come to think of it, he'd bought that too. But somehow Gerry always got the credit.

"I'm glad he has you," she said, but didn't elaborate. "Danielle seems like a very nice girl, with very bold taste I might add."

"Thanks, mom. But we're really just working together. For Chuck, actually. Or were, at least. He pulled the plug on our research this morning after dragging me all the way out here."

"About your grandfather's ship."

"Yes. Did he tell you they found it?"

She shot him a surprised look. "They did? *Who*?"

"Dan did. Well, with a French diver, Arnaud Navarre. I was brought out to verify it."

"Dear God. They didn't mention that."

"What did they want?"

"They wanted to know if you'd been by, and if you discussed anything about what you were working on."

"And?"

"I told them the truth. I had no idea you were even out here."

Vanek considered how much he should tell her about Carl. Or the weird turns this whole 'investigation' had taken.

Ava took a long sip of the cognac. "Good Lord, I wish they would have just let all this stay buried. Let the dead stay dead."

Vanek looked at his mother. "*What* are you talking about, mom?"

The silence dragged out. She stared off into space.

"Your grandfather. He was involved in some strange business during the war."

Tell me about it, Vanek thought. *You should see where he ended up*.

"It was... well, it wasn't the *usual* strange things: espionage, spying, counterintelligence. He was involved in some *special* programs. There was one in particular—the last one—that something terrible happened. Out here, or rather, out at Montauk. You see, your grandfather really didn't go down with that ship. Or rather, he survived the sinking."

Vanek stared at her. "Mom, how do you know any of this?"

She let out a soft laugh. "Oh, there's a *lot* I know I have never told you. But let me get to this one in my own way. As you may guess, it's not something I'm comfortable with. Especially as your father made me swear never to talk about it. You see, after the destroyer sank and your grandfather was rescued, well, something happened to him out there that *changed* him. In a bad way. The short of it is that he was being held at the base hospital and he *escaped*."

"Escaped?"

"Yes. *Escaped*. And in the process, several guards were killed. He managed to make it all the way back to Larchmont to see your grandmother before they caught him again."

"I don't understand. He came *back*? To my house?" Vanek rubbed the bridge of his nose. In a way, that would make sense. At least it explained the photo. And note.

"Well, it wasn't yours back then of course. He... well he spent that night, and that was when your father was conceived."

"*Okay*..." Vanek replied, not too sure he wanted to hear this.

"Will, I know this is awkward. What I'm trying to say is whatever... whatever changed your grandfather out there was passed to your father. A *darkness*. Your father was plagued by bad dreams his entire life, you know. And sometimes, sometimes he said he could see things. Like hallucinations. Only when he was near certain parts of the ocean. He saw doctors about it, of course, but the medicines didn't help any. We just learned to deal with it. And of course, we kept this from you and your brother. And it's one of the reasons your brother has always been so obsessed with surrounding himself with safe, *logical* things. But now with you out here digging around in your grandfather's business... I don't think any good can come of it."

"It's probably too late for that."

"It's *never* too late, William. Pack up your bags, take your lady friend and go home."

"What else are you not telling me?" That made him wonder about the accident. If that's what it really was.

"Do you remember when you were young, that time you got lost in the woods up in the Adirondacks?"

Vanek blinked. This was out of left field.

"That was a long time ago. I was only eight."

"You were *seven*. We were up visiting the Brandreths. You went off with your father's camera. You were gone for twelve hours. He was very upset."

"I think Dad was more worried about losing the camera," Vanek said, dryly.

"Nonsense. But do you remember what happened when you came back?"

"I got my ass whupped," he said. But that wasn't just it, was it? He'd been terrified for most of it, wandering aimlessly, knowing there were black bear and wild dogs near, lost like a dumb idiot even after his father had warned him not to do just that. But something had happened while he was out there, wandering the seemingly endless hills and animal trails, the quiet pine trees pressing in.

He'd lost his fear.

He hadn't been aware of it at first. But at some point he became aware he'd stopped running in blind panic anymore. That all that fear had leaked out of him: this was a forest. He was alive. He would use his internal instinct to find his way back. Simple.

And he did.

His father had given him a good spanking, but it hadn't been one of his worst. It was as if...

He realized his mother was staring at him, intently.

"I was fearless after that."

"Yes, you were," she said. "Like your father. And grandfather."

But that had only been true for a while, hadn't it? Somehow, over the years, the old fears crept back into your life like insidious little (worms) filaments, eroding your psyche and seeping into your nervous system like some kind of anxiety-drenched sewage.

A little of that had eased back in the last couple of days, but where did that leave him?

His mother was still staring at him. "I don't know what's happening out here right now," she said, "But you'd better find that again. You're going to need it."

Vanek shook his head. "I told you, it's over. Chuck says it's finished."

His mother let out a chuckle. "Nothing is over with men like Carl, son. Like with your father. Did you know he was doing work with Carl at the ONR?"

That was news to Vanek. As long as he knew, his father had worked as an engineer in design development at IBM. Exactly *what* he designed, he had no idea. Even to the day he died. But he was positive Dad had never mentioned working with Carl.

"I never heard that one."

"Well he did. He never told me anything specific. Your father was a private man. A *cold* man, and driven. Which is why I married him, I suppose."

Ava Vanek looked away, sipping her cognac.

"There was a *dark* inside to your father, William. It began to get the better of him near the end, I think. Just be careful of that. You carry a little of that too. And one other thing."

"What's that?"

"Carl? He's not the kind of man you want to trust. I know you think the world of him, but trust me, inside he's weak. He looks strong, but he isn't. Those are often the most dangerous people. Understand?"

Vanek looked at her in disbelief. "*Carl*? 'Chuck' Gavin? What are you talking about? Why this sudden about face? I mean, sure, he's only human. But the guy is a rock."

"No, he *isn't*. Now I've said enough. Promise me you'll leave tomorrow."

Vanek stood up. "I can't do that. I can't do that at all."

In response, his mother dropped her head and shook it slowly.

Ten minutes later they were on the road heading back to Montauk.

"Well, that was certainly different," Dan said, once they got off the ferry to the mainland.

"I tried to warn you, but you insisted."

"They seem nice enough. Are you okay?"

"I'm fine."

"If you say so."

30. ECO MEGA-SHITFEST

Jax Pierson took another pull off his Acai smoothie and sat back, cracking his knuckles. The word was out on all his social media channels about 'a shocking eco mega-shitfest event about to be revealed. He'd also gotten the word out to his contacts at various late-night radio talk shows on the conspiracy circuit, like the *Outer Frequency* and *The Kirlian Wave*. They were just empty teasers at this point, which was why he had to move fast.

The problem was he'd found *nothing* usable about Antony Scarpia on the web, even through his 'dark web' feelers. It was like the guy didn't even exist in the digital age, which was close to impossible. At least in Jax's worldview. There were three records of arrests over twenty years old in Kings County for minor things—one for larceny and two others for assault. Recent records searches coughed up little more than a rough age and home address in the North Fork, named him as the part owner of 'The Lobster Trap' (and 'Sheepshead Investment Corp' as the other, which Jax thought sounded phony as hell) but little else. Not even a damn photo!

The guy was like a relic from the dinosaur age.

Or a small-time mobster deliberately off the grid in the current one.

He had everything in place to skewer the man and his operation in a lightning strike—PlanetJustice had a long track record in that kind of social media lynching—except usable source material. Not even a still shot.

That would be remedied in short order.

Jax had set up an app that would flood several social media channels including Snapchat and Twitter at regular intervals, but first he had to drop in either photos or video clips for content. The preset captions were all ready to go and once the cameras were in place, they were programmed to automatically upload through PlanetJustice's servers.

Jax did this all with a speed and level of organization that would have a television network producer in awe.

One press of a key and Antony Scarpia would be getting a nuclear Armageddon across the net: PlanetJustice was about to play judge, jury and executioner.

The *coup de grâce* would be even more spectacular.

Three summer members—one whose dad ran an experiential design company in the city catering mainly to music festivals—had set up a spectacular projection lighting show on the SAGE Radar tower for tomorrow night. That involved a Tesla coil rig which—when activated—would set off a special effect that was going to slay everyone.

Jax felt that jittery sensation he always got before doing something big. The power of even one voice was awesome.

He looked over his shoulder at the two girls texting while sprawled on the couch. One was a honey-blonde named Megan while the other a striking black-haired Malaysian who called herself Kayla. He had it in for Kayla but had decided he'd settle for Megan, though neither girl had given him any indication they were even remotely interested. Sometimes they seemed more interested in each other, but not as much as their smartphones. "*Hello*? Ladies, you about ready? We gotta bounce. We're on a mission tonight."

"It's like, raining!" Kayla pouted, not looking up.

"I thought we were like going to the Hula Hut, dude," Megan added.

"Well, *yeah*, but later. I can't freakin' break the internet without even a single photo of Scarpia or his boat. This dude is totally evil."

"What's the deal? You seem to really have it in for him."

"He's a white-privileged fucking fascist! Dude is dumping toxic waste into the ocean."

"Hmmm, you gonna buy a couple girls some drinks?" Kayla said, looking up finally and giving him a curl of a smile. Jax felt part of his stomach go mushy. As usual, he was the one expected to bankroll the evening. Or rather his parents. At least until his remote job started with Google in the fall.

"Yeah, I guess," he said, sheepishly. "But I'm not kidding. We gotta bounce."

To his surprise, Kayla put her phone down and leaned back, tracing the line of her neck and jawline with her forefinger. One eyebrow went up. He thought she looked incredibly seductive.

"Got any tabs left?" she asked.

"Maybe."

She reached her foot out and brushed Megan's leg with her toes.

"What do you say, girl? Playtime?"

Annoyed, Megan finished tapping on her smartphone and set it aside. She picked up her e-cigarette and inhaled.

"Sure, what's up?"

In the end it took two hours to get them piled into Jax's Prius and on the road. Megan and Kayla spent the better part of an hour and a half getting their make-up and clothes just right. Jax's fantasy of some wild sexual tryst with the two of them became a desultory catch-up game on one of his three MMOs while they locked themselves away in the bathroom.

As they made their way up East Lake Road, the rain had eased off, but the traffic stayed light. Most of the action was on the other side of the harbor. That suited Jax—he wanted as few distractions as possible. It was hard enough to stay focused on what they were here to do with two hot girls in the car with him.

Just before they got to the Inlet Café he slowed down, turning off the lights as they came up on the gated entrance to the old Van Eyckmann property. The place was supposedly abandoned, but even from here he could see Scarpia's fishing boat moored at the dock. The barn looked dark and there wasn't any sign of activity on the property.

That was good. Jax's plan was simple: set up the dozen smart spy cams he'd brought to capture footage of Scarpia and his operation in action, then let the little mobster do the rest.

He crouched next to the stone pillar of the entrance gate and scanned the grounds with a pair of mini-binoculars.

To the immediate right was a large cottage—an 'old-fashioned' sort of thing with traditional shingle siding—while the main area consisted of a few modern gray-painted buildings and an open area to the right for storing boats. Ahead a stocky pier led out to the bay on which the faux 'old-Asian' style barn sat. Just before that was Scarpia's trawler, *Sea Bitch*.

A second sweep of the binoculars didn't alter his plan much; the place looked deserted. No cars or trucks anywhere. No obvious signs of cameras.

Perfect.

"Come on," he whispered to the girls. Skirting around the metal swing gate, he headed diagonally toward the cottage first. His wristwatch said: 7:43.

Except for the crickets and the gentle lapping of water along the shore, the compound was dead quiet. To the north, music could be heard from the Inlet Café, mostly lost in the breeze still carrying down from the northeast. The boat traffic coming in through the harbor entrance was particularly sparse, most of it veering to the crowded docks on the west side of the harbor where the restaurants were, or south toward Star Island Marina. Only one lamp post in the compound worked, out on the dock next to Scarpia's boat.

The storm clouds had broken up enough to let the dying sunlight break through intermittently, but most of the area lay cast in gloom.

"*Shhh*," Kayla said a little too loudly as they bumped into each other by the corner of the cottage. Megan giggled.

"Quiet!" Jax hissed. The cottage seemed deserted, but he couldn't be too sure. He plucked one of the spy cams from his pocket and placed it high up on the wall, in between two shingles. Jax was having second thoughts whether bring them had been a good idea. He should have nabbed Callum—another PlanetJustice diehard—but he'd gone back to Greenport for his cousin's wedding.

This didn't look like such a big deal. He figured they could get the cameras planted inside of ten minutes and be on their way to dinner within twenty. Grab a few drinks then hit the clubs by ten.

From the cottage he led them on a loop outside the light post past the first outbuilding where he could have a good view of the trawler. If anyone was around, he figured most likely they'd be on the boat. The interior cabins were dark, however.

Emboldened, Jax handed his binoculars to Kayla, who was busy vaping. "Hold these. And keep alert. If you see anything, whistle. Can you do that?"

"Like, *no*."

"Can you do this?" He made a *sssst* sound with his tongue and teeth.

"*Whatever*."

"Just do that then. And if anyone comes out of any of the buildings, run as fast as you can for the gate. Okay?"

"*Uh-huh*. Hey, this is kind of cool, *yeah*?"

"Totally. Be right back."

Jax went in a crouching run out onto the dock, pausing as the timbers creaked under his weight. He glanced around nervously, but nothing happened. His hands were splayed out in a subconscious imitation of Tom Cruise in Mission: Impossible. Jax even felt like an action hero; young, energized... engaged in something slightly dangerous. The dark gray camo pants and pseudo-military button shirt emboldened him. He placed one mini camera on one of the pilings at an angle that would capture anything going on or off the boat.

He paused to take out his smartphone to snap a few shots of the trawler including several from the stern where the name of it was clearly visible. Jax felt that tingling rush he always had when doing something like this; the sense of empowerment over the adult world—that he wielded the ability to make environmental crooks like Scarpia pay dearly. They'd been fucking up the world long enough. It was up to Jax and his generation to set things to rights.

Freakin' fascists still haven't figured it out! We're woke and running circles around them. They won't even understand they've been crushed even as the boulder comes down on them. Sorry-not-sorry, dudes!

Still in a crouch with hands out to his sides, Jax did a visual sweep of his surroundings. At least that's how they did it in the online covert operations videos. He glanced back at the girls and was annoyed to see they weren't watching him. Both were busy texting.

Shaking his head, he scurried along the dock and vaulted lightly over the gunwale onto the stern deck, his cushion-soled sneakers barely making a sound as he landed.

So far, so good.

He placed another two cameras facing backward at the upper corners of the main cabin, to capture any activity (and according to Jimmy Reed, totally illegal dumping) there. He placed a third on the center mounted light as well. That one would be all but impossible to spot.

Last he climbed up into the pilot house and placed three more cameras in what he figured were unobtrusive locations. The place stank of old sweat and seawater.

The smell of fish-murderers, he thought. *I wonder how they would feel if I hauled them in with a huge hook through their cheek, then filleted their guts on the deck here... just for sport! I suspect the taste would not be so sweet!*

He froze as there came a creak from the cabin below him.

Eleven seconds ticked by on his smart watch.

Nothing. It's probably just something shifting below. That's all it is!

He gave it another five then very carefully got off the boat.

Not surprisingly, the girls were still texting. At least Kayla looked up as he rejoined them.

"*What*?" she asked.

"Nothing," he replied. "Just need to get into that barn over there. My guess is that's where the toxic shit is stored, if anyplace."

"Why not here?" Megan asked, pointing to the building they were crouching alongside. She looked as if she'd just woken up midway into a conversation. Which, Jax decided, was pretty much how she *always* looked.

Even Kayla knew the answer to that one. "The *locks*, dummy. The chains and locks on those doors are rusted. No-one's been in this building for a while.

That's my girl, Jax thought, with a little approving nod. It was one of those subtle condescending habits he did constantly, one of many he'd learned from his father. Papa Pierson had a whole catalog of them, doled out liberally between his graduate students in the Fordham University Psychology department and his family.

"How many cameras left?" Kayla asked, handing him back his binoculars.

"Three," Jax replied. "Should be plenty. Come on, let's do this."

He led them along the right side of the dock leading out to the barn where the light was dimmest. The traffic out on the water was still light. Overhead the first stars winked through the clouds, the stiff breeze plucking at their hair and clothes. Jax grinned, feeling a little cocky. He had a vision of himself like one of those underdog Star Wars rebel heroes who no-one suspects will save the day.

The back and front of the barn had two broad sliding doors that could be opened during the day to create a naturally cooled lounging area. Closer to them was an access door. The whole building looked expensively rustic, like something out of a Ralph Lauren ad.

Jax gave the doorknob a cautious turn and was surprised to find it was open.

He almost whispered 'hello?' but checked himself in time.

That's what idiots do in horror movies! he told himself. Ear cocked, he waited a moment and not hearing anything, motioned the girls to follow him in.

Inside the barn was cluttered and musty, the ceiling open to the rafters. Closest to them were stacks of boats and marine equipment while in the center sat a bunch of couches and chairs arranged in a circle on a thick pile area rug. They were lit by metal farmer-style hanging pendant lights. Past that in the shadows were various crates and on a palette a bunch of plastic barrels marked by toxic waste symbols.

What drew the attention of all three, however, was the figure tied spread-eagled to a circular coffee table in the dead center of the seating area: a slim woman with blond hair, face half-covered by it.

She was completely naked.

Jax flicked on the flashlight app on his smartphone and aimed it around the space. The light wasn't that strong and didn't reveal much.

"What the hell?" Megan whispered.

Jax's brow furrowed. He sure as hell didn't expect to find *this*.

He stepped carefully forward, looking left and right. When he got within a couple of yards of the woman, he could see she was bruised, with smears of blood. He felt simultaneously repulsed and aroused. The pubic hair at her crotch was damp and matted.

"Ma'am?" he asked quietly. His voice sounded odd in the muted air. "Are you okay?"

She sat perfectly still. For one terrifying moment he thought she was dead.

Then came a soft groan from under the tangled hair covering her face.

Jax wasn't sure what to do—nothing in his real experience had equipped him for this. Cover her up? Call 9-1-1? Run the hell out of there?

The second response made the most sense. Get someone else to deal with this.

He thumbed off the flashlight app on his phone and had just opened the dialer when he heard a muffled grunt from behind him, followed by a gasp.

"*Boo*," a man's voice spoke. Deep and gravelly.

Jax slowly pivoted around.

A squat, ugly-looking fellow with a busted-looking nose had Kayla by the scruff of the neck. The other hand had a gun to Megan's temple.

Jax was having trouble processing all this. Where had he come from? They must have walked right past him. And how did things go so bad so quickly? Whoever this guy was, he exuded violence and anger like a junkyard pit bull.

Without being asked, Jax put his hands up. His knees shook.

"I'm sorry, we were just looking," he offered, lamely.

The man smiled. His teeth were a rotted set of ivory tombstones.

"Sure, pipsqueak. Do you like what you see?"

Kayla tried to reach back at the hand clutching her with a whine. The man's grasp must have been powerful. He squeezed her neck tighter and shook her like a rag doll. Kayla whimpered and her arms went slack.

"No, I mean, I'm sorry. We came in here by accident!" Jax blabbered.

"Hey, like who the *fuck* do you think you—" Megan started to say, cut off by the blast of the gun.

Megan collapsed like a marionette whose strings were cut, the exit wound spattering blood and brain matter on the side of the kayaks stacked a few feet away.

A stunned silence followed.

Jax stood perfectly still, his stomach feeling like it had plummeted a few stories. For a flickering moment when the man had first appeared, he had a wild hope this might somehow work out, that he still existed in a world where reasonable solutions could still prevail. All that vanished with the gunshot, along with Megan as a living, breathing, functioning human being. For the first time in his life, he fully grasped what a horrifying, brutal, and violent world it was.

Even more interesting, in a detached, terrible kind of way, was how his nervous system simply shut down. Like a switch had been thrown.

Almost.

A warm sensation from his crotch and leg told him his bladder had taken on a mind of its own.

"Aww look at the little baby," the man said. "Did little baby wee-wee his pants?"

Jax wasn't sure he should answer. The gun, now pointed at his head, suggested he might want to reconsider that.

31. YOU AMERICANS HAVE NO TASTE...

By the time Vanek pulled back into the driveway of the Neville House it was nearly 9:30. At the 'Aquarians' House the party was still going, most of it having moved (thankfully) to the in-ground pool out back.

Inside their house, however, Navarre and his friends had gotten into the drink and were singing some naughty French sailor's ditty as Vanek and Dan came through the front door.

"Ahh, *Nous saluons le retour, mon amis*!" Navarre said, raising his beer.

"*Grand laisir de te revoir*," Vanek replied.

"See, he speaks like a civilized man," Navarre said to his friends. "A beer, perhaps? Or whiskey?"

"Whiskey," Vanek said.

"Iced vodka for me," Dan added.

Drinks in hand, Vanek and Dan joined them in the living area, where someone had lit a fire in the fireplace. Food was everywhere. One of the divers, Yves, had been tinkering on the piano.

"We were just discussing how Americans have no taste," Navarre said, in a half-joking taunt. "What do you say to that, William Vanek?"

After a few belts of scotch, Vanek felt his wind was up. "I'd say that's quite a load of bullshit you're serving."

That got a laugh from the Frenchmen.

Philippe nodded toward him with a look that wasn't completely friendly, "Prove it."

Vanek grinned. This was one area where he felt on solid ground.

He walked over to the piano to where Yves sat.

"May I?"

"*Aide-toi*," Yves, said, getting out of the way.

Vanek sat down on the bench, cracked his knuckles and proceeded to plunk out the first few notes of 'Chopsticks'.

The four men broke out in laughter. Dan studied him with a look that might have been disappointment.

Vanek held up his hand for silence, his head bowed as if deep in thought. His little joke had been his way to test the action on the piano, which he found quite good—an Essex, built by Steinway & Sons.

Pausing with his fingertips over the keys for effect, he plunged into the first rolling notes of Gershwin's 'Rhapsody in Blue', building a slow crescendo. Then he was off, breaking out into the first jazzy measures that filled the seaside room with all the exuberant energy of 1920's New York. It was an exciting piece and one Vanek had spent decades mastering.

His fingers flew across the keys.

From the piano, thundering bass chords took off into treble riffs that sparkled like billboards on Broadway.

Vanek played anything from classic to rock-and-roll, but Gershwin was his secret favorite; music he could surrender to and embrace all the ups and downs of life in under fourteen minutes. As far as Vanek was concerned, next to Copland, nothing distilled the musical essence of America in one piece than George Gershwin.

As the final notes echoed out of the piano, Vanek grew aware that no-one was making a sound.

Navarre broke it first, with a steady clap-clap that was quickly joined in by the others.

"Bravo!" someone shouted. Another let out a piercing whistle.

"Encore!" Navarre said. "What else do you have?"

Vanek let out a deprecating laugh. "I don't know."

He saw that Dan was leaning forward watching him intently, her chin propped up by both palms.

"How about something romantic?" she asked.

Vanek thought for a moment. Only one song he knew off the top fit the bill: Irving Berlin's "Always". He preferred the slightly mournful 1926 version by Layton and Johnstone. Although Vanek would never make a career on Broadway, he at least had a passable singing voice:

I'll be loving you, always
With a love that's true, always
When the things you've planned,
need a helping hand,
I will understand... always... always.

The song was a simple but sincere sentimental one that struck a chord with him, particularly the last lines: *Not for just a moment, not for just a day, not for just a year... but for always.*

Again, there came a moment of silence, followed by applause.

"Wow," Dan said, looking away. She finished her vodka and stood up. "I need to take a shower and crash. Night, everyone."

"*Hmm*, that went over well," Vanek joked, after she'd left.

Navarre stood up and walked over to Vanek, sitting down next to him and clapped him on the shoulder while the others went outside to have a smoke. "Ah! So, you are *very* good! There's hope for you Americans after all." He nodded toward the staircase. "She is *très attractive*, no? You should go for a woman like that!"

"Yeah, well, I'm a little too old for this game," Vanek replied.

Navarre leaned toward him and said quietly, "Bullshit."

He stood up. "My friends wanted to go for a nightcap in town. Nothing too crazy. We have a big day tomorrow." Navarre contemplated him for a moment. "Good night. And thank-you."

"Night."

Vanek sat there for a few minutes. It *had* felt good. He hadn't played like that in some time. But he really couldn't accept a woman like Dan would be remotely interested in him. Hell, there were three young, strapping men that made him look like a relic.

He picked up his scotch and made himself comfortable in one of the overstuffed couches, mulling over what his mother had said. The implications weren't reassuring. Not to mention all the new questions about his father. And grandfather.

And what really may have happened at 'Bunker 18'.

He sat there, trying to keep at bay all the terrifying things he'd witnessed in the past two days. The Bunker. The wreck of the *Exeter*. The *worms*.

They flitted and probed at his thoughts.

The logs snapped and crackled in the grate as the fire burned down.

He looked up as Dan returned, now dressed in a bathrobe. She fixed herself a new glass of vodka and to his surprise, wedged herself into the sofa next to him, legs tucked up underneath. Her hair was wrapped up in a towel in that careless way women did that was forever an utter mystery to him. She took a hefty pull of vodka, winced, and took a second one. Her hand sought out his and squeezed it.

Hard.

"Hi," Dan said, interrupting his thoughts. Yet again, he was aware of her closeness, her intense... what? *Woman-ness*? That sounded vaguely ridiculous to him. But the whiff of lavender-scented bath oil wasn't.

"I'd go easy on that. Higher risk of DCS."

He felt her studying him.

Instead of answering him directly, she said, "That was really beautiful music you played. I had no idea."

Vanek made a dismissive gesture. "Nah, strictly amateur stuff. I just used to practice a lot."

"I don't believe that," she said, continuing to study him. He found her scrutiny a little unnerving. "I think that was the real you, showing through just a bit. There's evidence that music has the power to reshape the brain. It's that powerful."

She clinked his glass with hers.

"To music," she added.

"*Salut*," he replied.

He half-turned toward her as he took a pull of his scotch, realizing she was even closer than before. Uncomfortably close. There was an unmistakable sensation of intimacy, so intense it caught him off guard. Her lips were slightly parted. The top of her robe folded open, enough to give him a tantalizing glimpse of one breast.

What the hell are you doing, William Vanek!? Michelle's voice spoke up in his head.

Her lips brushed his, just slightly. It was an incredibly erotic sensation.

He jerked back, almost spilling his drink. Over in the grate, a log popped.

"Look, I…" Vanek stammered.

"—I'm sorry, I'm acting like an idiot!" she interrupted, standing up. She dropped the glass on the coffee table. Turning, she flashed him an odd look and ran out of the room. A moment later came the thud of footsteps and the sound of her bedroom door slamming.

Vanek smacked his forehead. *Dammit! What the hell!? What was up with the woman!? Why on earth would she be even remotely interested in a middle-aged Naval historian? We're not exactly rock-stars!* And on the heels of that, a ridiculously chauvinistic thought: *Why the hell did Gavin have to bring an attractive woman into this!? She should be out chasing some young Marine biologist bucks or a Coast Guard boy or something!*

He sat there blinking, trying to make sense of his emotions, but found he couldn't. The pulse in his temple felt ready to burst.

Nip this in the bud, Vanek! He said to himself, *straighten this out now or everything will turn into a mess.*

With a steady hand, he placed the drink down on the table next to hers.

With that he marched upstairs.

"Dan? We need to talk," Vanek said, quietly.

He knocked on the door a second time, but still there was no answer.

"Hello? Dan? Anybody in there?"

A minute later the door opened.

"Hi."

The towel was gone and her hair messed up, as if she'd run through a wind-tunnel, her expression downcast. He wanted more than anything to scoop her up in his arms and kiss her... yet at the same time couldn't.

Or shouldn't?

Michelle's voice was conspicuously silent this time.

Then the unthinkable happened: without realizing what he was doing he reached over, cupped her chin in both his hands and kissed her full on the lips.

As kisses go, it may not have been an award-winner, but it was a pretty good one - much better than the night before. Dan's eyes went wide. Vanek was aware of the slightly sweet taste of her mouth on his and (again) the hint of lavender in her hair. It may have lasted ten seconds, twenty or even a moment—he was only aware of how supremely wonderful and sensual such an intimate contact could be.

Then all too soon it was over.

He realized what he'd done (not that Dan seemed to be minding) and broke off.

"Oh," she said, as if coming out of a trance.

"Christ," he blurted out. "I had no business doing that!" All at once he was flustered. Unsure what to do with his hands, he opted to rub his temple.

Dan blinked. For a moment she had a girlish vulnerability about her.

"You have an *interesting* way of asking for help."

"Yes, well... um, can we go downstairs and discuss this?"

Her response startled him.

"*No.*"

"*What*?" he was seized by a flash of panic. *Now what? Was she going to call the police?*

"I said... *no*. Kiss me. Again."

"I-I, um."

"If you don't, I'll throw open the window and start screaming bloody murder." To make her point, she took one step over to the hallway window.

Vanek reached and catching her waist, drew her close.

"But the nutty neighbors are all out there!"

"More the reason, then."

This time there was no hesitation. Or holding back. He felt as randy as a sixteen-year-old. How long had it been? Years. Too long.

Still locked in an embrace, she jumped up and wrapped her legs around his hips and hooking thighs with his hands he carried her into her bedroom and onto her bed. The rest was a blur. He pulled her robe open, and she yanked his shirt off over his head. He peeled out of his shorts and underwear and tossed them aside. Grinning, she seized him by the shoulders and rolled him aside, then climbed on top.

There was a delicious moment of anticipation as she straddled him, her hair dangling in his face. He cupped the underside of her breasts, as she leaned down and gave him a teasing kiss, then using her hand she guided him in. Slowly.

The intimacy of it all bordered on painful, of being completely consumed while knowing distantly it was all fleeting.

Still, Vanek lost himself completely for the first time in ages, and the losing felt exquisitely fine.

Vanek looked up at the ceiling, at the shadow play there from the darkening skies and occasional flashes of lightning. From the dresser where'd she set up her iPhone in a dock with speakers came music: a mournful, aching melody that seemed to thread through the room like a desperate request from the airwaves.

It took him a moment to place the song: *Heroes*.

David Bowie.

Dead over three years now.

Never before had he been this acutely aware of the dichotomy between the lunacy and violence existing in the world and the momentary cocoon of safety two people could weave in spite of it.

At least we have that, he thought.

Next to him, Dan stirred and snuggled in tighter, his arm draped over her shoulder so that his fingers rested on the smooth contours of her breast. The sex had been smooth yet hungry, like a particularly smooth brandy you'd forgotten how much you enjoyed, then couldn't get enough of.

He hadn't felt this content in ages. The strange consuming intimacy of the act never failed to surprise him; the way one's entire world suddenly shrunk to dream-like sequences of exploring touches, caresses... sensations, all other concerns blotted out except for nature's base urge to connect. Unite.

Pro-create.

God, he thought, *you didn't even think to use a condom. Are you out of your mind*?

Answer: *yes*.

Both of them, for that matter. But this wasn't an alcohol-induced act. It was fear.

Temporary insanity, Judge, I swear. We just had to wipe out coherent thought and reset, okay? Seeing what we did down there, it has a funny way of fucking with your concept of death and reality.

Dan was half-turned away from him, her breath lightly stirring the hairs on his forearm.

Now what? He had to assume this was all a fluke, brought on by what happened. There was no reason he could think of that Dan Cheung would have any serious interest in him and for that matter, him in her. A momentary lapse of reason, that's all. It happens all the time, right? They were both consenting adults for Chrissakes. But he had to clear the air with her, somehow. Navarre and his friends were due back, and they had a dive to do tomorrow. And what about Gavin? This was all his damn fault anyhow! He was the one who brought her into this.

Dan stirred and to his surprise, put her lips to his arm. She laughed, quietly, then twisted around to face him. With her forefinger she traced the profile of his face, down his throat and chest. He couldn't recall any woman ever doing that to him, not even Michelle.

"What are you thinking?" she asked.

"It's been one hell of a day."

She propped herself up on her elbow, hair dangling over half her face.

"Any thoughts on that?" he added.

She smiled and reached down to his groin.

32. FOR THE LOVE OF MIKE, AND MONEY

Aboard the *Hatshepsut,* the party was on.

Claire Osterberg sat on the u-shaped couch of the upper foredeck, though her mood had grown considerably less buoyant. The combination of too much alcohol and cocaine had left her feeling brittle, yet invincible. She stood by the rail, unsteady, clutching a large vodka and tonic she had no recollection of getting.

From the main cabin below came the throbbing pulse of dance music—Lady Gaga from the sound of it—where the party was still going full tilt at 2:30 a.m. Claire was wide awake, the coke turning the brightly lit world of the surrounding ship sparkly and chrome-edged, a self-contained oasis of energy in a sea of murky blackness.

A fog had drifted in from the deeper Atlantic, obscuring the stars.

Ty was below sandwich dancing with two of her employees from *Asmari*, whom she hoped were smart enough not to put moves on their CEO's fiancé. One wasn't the sharpest pencil, though, the head of marketing who was equal parts pretty and semi-competent.

Claire needed a breather, though, and she tended not to be the jealous type. Still, something troubled her deep down in the hidden compartments where the real Claire's machinery worked. She didn't think it was related (directly at least) to the free-fall black hole that her career had shaped into these days.

This was more about the nightmare she'd had the previous night, with the strange mermaids she used to dream about as a little girl. The animated Disney classic had been a mainstay of her childhood video collection (videos! That wonderful tech anachronism!). Which should have beckoned sweet dreams into her little bed at night, but which inexplicably brought nightmares instead.

The King Triton in these dreams showed up with a terrifying legion of *Mer-monsters* (as she called them), fanged fish-human hybrids with hair like dead seaweed and homicidal faces that might have been people half-transformed into angler fish. Last night the king too had become something hideous. Not the garrulous, bearded white proto-Christian God of the cartoon but a slimy, sunken-cheeked horror with writhing sea-worms for a beard and a mouth full of needlelike, pearlescent teeth.

And the eyes: not just two, but a series of malformed ones set in the skull like glowing silver-blue cysts.

As a rule, Claire wasn't prone to nightmares—at least nothing ever like this—and the lucid power of this one had rattled her to the core. She'd woken up at 3 a.m. not screaming but whimpering in her sleep like a cornered animal about to be eviscerated. When Ty had asked (his smooth hand on her shoulder), she'd dismissed it as a simple anxiety manifestation.

Yet the shadow of it had been flicking in the shadows of her thoughts all day.

Standing here on the bridge of a super-sized yacht that was undeniably the physical embodiment of class, wealth, and success, it seemed even more ridiculous.

But what was all this, really? A temporary manifestation of mankind's vanity against the dark. The unknown.

Those are silly thoughts, she said to herself as she rested her hand on the coaming. *And tomorrow? Everything will work itself out tomorrow! You're here, now. A woman who fought her way to this boat by sheer will, strength, and confidence. And vision. Don't forget about that! About to marry an incredibly successful man. The world is your oyster!*

She smiled and shook her hair in the breeze, relishing the latent sense of power from the vibration of the yacht's twin 1,977hp Caterpillar diesels.

I am...

The yacht gave a sudden lurch to port, causing her drink to slosh out across the rail. She glanced back at the slanted windows of the bridge, where she could just make out the uplit face of the skipper piloting the ship. His fingers danced over the control panel, but then leaned forward and gave her a thumbs up.

She smiled again and tilted her head back.

That was when she became aware that the music below had become something else... it sounded heavier, deeper. *Disturbing*.

Perplexed, she glanced back toward the bridge and was surprised to see no-one there. The yacht continued to slice through the calm Atlantic, unperturbed.

One of Ty's old sayings came to her: "For the love of Mike... and money!"

She never quite understood what it meant, but it seemed funny. He only said it when he was exasperated.

Puzzled, she stood up and started walking (unsteadily) back past the bridge to the aft deck which had a lounge area and bar, to the Minotti dining table with its spread of catered sushi and hors d'oeuvres. She stopped short as she saw the smear of blood on one of the cushions and a clump of long blond hair on the teak decking, as if tossed there.

Sarah, she thought. *That looks just like Sarah Miller's hair. And wow—that must be a piece of scalp attached to it! She must have really pissed-off the wrong person!*

That was ridiculous, of course, who would do such a thing? Pirates? Off Montauk?

She saw that the sliding door was open, but the interior lights of the inside lounge were dimmed. She could hear someone rummaging around in there and a wet, tearing sound.

One eyebrow arched. If that was one of the guests tearing up their towels, she was going to give them hell! They were Egyptian imports and cost a fortune!

There was a heavy *thud* and something came rolling out through the open door, coming to rest sideways.

Her eyes went wide as she saw that it was Ty's head, crudely sliced off with his trachea trailing out from the neck stump. Claire tried to scream but all that came out was a blubbering whimper.

A shape shambled into view, one of the flipper-footed *Mer-monsters* she realized, as if it had crawled out of the previous night's nightmare and onto her yacht. It took a shambling step forward, one flipper foot knocking aside her fiancé's head like so much garbage. Its needle-toothed mouth opened and closed like a fish, the myriad of eyes pulsing.

The yacht of the deck began to tilt as the unattended rudder slewed to one side, but Claire's attention was focused wholly on the apparition before her, and the two more that came around from the other side of the bridge. One clutched a handful of intestines.

Without thinking, Claire threw her drink at the nearest one and jumped off the stern. As she landed on the flat launch deck her right leg snapped and she buckled, her right hand instinctively clutching the chrome support rail.

She turned as there came a wet, heavy footstep behind her.

King Triton stood there, a grotesque apparition from her childhood dreams, his teeth-lined maw widening as the serpent eels of its beard writhed and flopped. From inside the mouth she could see the glint of white worms extending out, undulating, as if tasting her fear.

This time she did scream, as her face blackened and collapsed into itself. It came out shrill and high.

33. THE ROBERT D. BALLARD, OFF MONTAUK

"We've got it on radar, it just surfaced!" came Commander A.J. Hopper's clipped voice from the bridge. She barely managed to keep the tension out of her announcement, making it sound like the spotting of the Deep Sea Remote Operated Vehicle sled known as 'Deep Discovery' or 'D2', was just another routine event.

Down in the room known as 'Mission Control', Ben Reinhardt sat back and ran a shaky hand through his hair. "There is a God," he muttered.

At twenty-seven, stocky, with curly blond hair and his features perpetually set in a deceptively bored expression, Reinhardt's second go in the ROV pilot's chair had all the earmarks of a career-ending disaster for the past hour and a half when the unthinkable had occurred: during their mapping run off the continental shelf, D2 had suffered a catastrophic malfunction and had its tether to its primary ROV, *Seirous* sled, mysteriously cut. Even worse, their sonar systems had shut down, and they'd lost all ability to track its location.

Reinhardt had felt like he was on the verge of a premature coronary when it became clear a six and a half million-dollar piece of NOAA's deep exploration equipment—the only one of its kind—was lost.

On his watch.

In all its voyages of deep-sea exploration, including dives exploring the ocean as deep as twenty-seven thousand feet, nothing like this had ever happened. Equally inexplicable was what the cameras had picked up moments before the incident: a giant, tentacled apparition that reminded him—suspiciously—of the 'Typhon' incident along the Hudson River two years past.

Just past the shipwreck.

Could there have been *two* of those creatures?

There was a terrifying thought.

He couldn't get past the odd feeling, though, that he had just been thinking about it only moments before the disaster struck.

Coincidence?

Possibly. The R-2 had a new electromagnetic field generator set to frequencies meant to draw in ocean life. Perhaps something large had collided with it? A whale?

Reinhardt leaned back in his chair.

A collective sigh went around the control room. Next to him, Alicia Delgado, the co-pilot, rubbed the bridge of her nose with her fingers while on his left the navigator, a recent college grad named Vance Nguyen, toyed idly with the useless navigation joystick on his console. The oversized LED clock overhead read: 21:17:03.

The Mission Control room—located on the main deck facing aft where the sleds were launched off the stern—was the brain center for all the underwater exploration. With its black soundproofed walls and ceiling, banks of monitors and video screens, it looked more like a hi-tech video production suite than a control room designed for managing exploration of the deepest regions on the planet. The oversized HDR monitor to Reinhardt's right was normally the display for the primary camera on the D2 sled. It had been switched over to the *Seirous'* main camera after they'd lost D2, though the sled was now safely back in its harness on the aft deck.

To the far right on the video editing station, the editor was scrubbing through the last captured footage on his smaller, color-calibrated screens, trying to piece together a narrative that made sense.

The second row of monitors behind them—where visiting scientists sat to view the missions—was empty except for one chair, occupied by a weathered-looking man by the name of Nils Hagen. Hagen was an ill-tempered Marine Species specialist from the University of Bergen in Norway, specializing in coastal sea life and habitats.

With the mission scrambled by the loss of D2, Hagen had been reduced to reviewing earlier footage from the morning when he saw something on the video-editor's screen that caught his attention.

"Hey, what is that?" he asked, peering over the top of his own monitor.

"You mean the squid-like thing?"

Hagen squinted, "No. Behind it. In the background... is that a—"

He was interrupted by the ship's bell followed by Commander Hopper's voice: "Bridge to Mission Control, can you come up here, Reinhardt? We're altering course to intercept the ROV."

"Aye-aye commander!" Reinhardt replied. He was confused—he should be on the aft deck overseeing the recovery of the ROV, but orders were orders. The *Ballard* might be a research ship, but it was run as tight as any military vessel.

A few minutes later he was up on the bridge standing next to Commander Hopper. The lights had been reduced to minimal to maximize visibility outside the windows, giving the officers on duty a spectral look, uplit by the monitors and instrument panels.

Hopper was over by the radar station, hands clasped behind her back, standing by the shoulder of the ensign operating it.

"Where is it, sir?" he asked out of habit, though he could see the blip on the HD monitor off their starboard bow.

"A hundred yards off the bow, bearing two-eight-three."

"It doesn't make any sense," he replied.

It most definitely *didn't*. The D2 was designed with positive buoyancy, meaning that should it become separated from the primary *Seirous* sled, it should simply rise to the surface. The *Seirous* sled could be written off in a crisis—D2 was the one loaded with all the million-dollar equipment and parts. But it should have risen more or less *straight* up, within ten minutes max. They had been navigating a widening search pattern for ninety minutes and the rover had surfaced *twenty-miles* away. It didn't seem physically possible.

"Nonetheless, it's there," Hopper said, intruding on his thoughts.

"Yep," Reinhardt agreed. "At least we won't be facing a total shitstorm when the report goes out."

"There's *that*," Hopper replied.

"But that's not why you called me up here, is it?"

Hopper nodded toward the back of the bridge where the chart table and navigation maps were kept. Even with digital technology, navigation was still plotted out on paper charts. Commander Hopper put both hands on the one they'd been using, the latest NOAA Chart of Montauk/Block Island Sound.

She tapped the chart at the location they'd lost D2, now circled in red ink. "This whole situation is, if you'll pardon my French, *fucked-up*. We had a routine dive, in stable conditions at a relatively shallow depth. Given the prevailing tides, if anything, it should have drifted westward, not northward toward the shore at 30 knots. Unless you can tell me different. This is not going to look good on paper. But you're Mr. whiz-kid. You tell me."

Reinhardt grunted. 'Mister Whiz Kid' was an in-joke understatement with them—Reinhardt had been near the top of his class at M.I.T. Though Hopper wasn't exactly a slouch in the brains department either. She favored hands-on tactile experience over textbooks, however.

Still, Reinhardt was scratching his head over how the D2 unity could have traveled so far in that amount of time unless it had been snagged by speedboat. Riptides could only do so much. Some unknown factor was at work, here.

Like a sea monster, pal.

Before what happened on the Hudson River, he would have scoffed at such a concept. Now he knew better. What he'd first witnessed as an anomaly on a side-scan sonar screen had turned into a man-eating leviathan that claimed the lives of hundreds of people.

Make that *two* leviathans: the nightmares from World's End.

Both were dead. There was no question on that account. Still, what they'd seen on the monitor just before the D2 went offline looked very similar. Not exactly, but similar. And yet, some detail was nagging at him.

Think!

The operations officer called from over by the radar station: "Commander?"

"Yes?"

"You might want to have a look at this."

Hopper gave Reinhardt a look that might have said *guess the fun isn't quite over.*

On the port side of the bridge the operations officer—a young man just out of training named Nevill—was staring through the slanted bridge windows with a pair of night vision binoculars.

"Where away?" Hopper asked.

"Dead ahead," Nevill said, handing over his binoculars. "It's D2 all right. But it's taken some major damage."

Hopper looked, made an adjustment, then made a clucking sound out of the side of her mouth. "I'll be damned, Mr. Nevill. This just keeps getting better and better."

Half an hour later they had the D2 back on board. The ROV was smashed out of shape, its tether shredded through as if it had been chewed off, the main unit itself mangled and torn.

Not only was the damage to it severe, it appeared to have been done a long time ago—many of the visible metal parts were rusted and *brittle*. It reminded Reinhardt of an old wreck of a yacht they'd discovered down in Bermuda.

At a glance the unit appeared salvageable, but they wouldn't know the full extent of it until they got it over to the repair facility at Davisville, Rhode Island. In the meantime, the lab technician set to work removing the video back-up drives and data recorder to see what else could be discovered about the final minutes of D2's accident.

After seeing the D2 safely secured in its storage garage, Reinhardt joined Commander Hopper in the modest crew lounge.

"I want the data off those drives pronto," Hopper stated, a hint of irritation creeping into her voice. Reinhardt couldn't blame her. This evening was turning into a shitfest. "We'll set course for Davisville—"

She was cut off as the ship gave a sudden lurch, followed by a sickening slewing motion that had all three of them grabbing for a handhold.

"What the—?" She began, then the ship's alarm went off.

A moment later the lights dimmed and went out.

Reinhardt realized the engines had stopped.

34. SATURDAY MORNING, 6 A.M.

Dawn broke in through foggy tendrils near the furthest reach of Long Island known as 'The End'.

The surf hissed and boomed along the rocks on the seaward side of the Montauk Lighthouse, where decades back, the Army Corps of Engineers had piled them around the base of the cliffs after a particularly tenacious 76-year-old woman by the name of Georgina Reid had single-handedly shown them how to do it.

On this particular morning, a fisherman by the name of Ernie Myers was casting from the narrow beach that ran along the southern edge of the point. Up and behind him, on the rock ledge, his longtime pal and confederate, Jim Parkerson, sat in a folding chair alternately nursing a cigarette and thermos of coffee.

It was too early for the surfers and the weather was on the cool side for August, but that suited the two men just fine.

A trio of errant gulls winged overheard, adding their cries in counterpoint to the crashing surf, while the lighthouse above was wreathed in mist, its red and white banded tower a ghostly sentinel out of another era.

Ernie wore his waders though he kept out of the water—the surf was heavy and after passing fifty he didn't care much anymore for all the hidden boulders and rocks along this stretch. Jim was always content to stay well out of the reach of the water these days, casting his line from the safety of the rock ledge and keeping his cigarettes dry. *Which was a good thing*, as he was always telling Ernie, as the damn things cost a whore's fortune these days and he was *retired.*

Ernie had no clue what a *whore's fortune* was, though it sounded about right, like most things that came out of Jim Parkerson's mouth.

All in all, it had been a decent morning's haul already—five good-sized Porgy's and a striped bass. Ernie had just gotten a hefty tug on his lucky bucktail when he heard a shout from Jim behind him.

"Holy shit!"

Jim, a rail-thin, six-foot-three black man with the bluest eyes Ernie had ever seen, now stood his full height, one gnarled hand touching the tattered brim of his bill-cap.

"What ya carrying on about, goddamnit?" Ernie said, his mouth screwed up as he always did. For a goofy second, he thought Jim had said "Holy ship!"

Jim had apparently run clean out of any more words for the moment, however. Instead, he pointed a finger out toward the ocean. He'd seen it first, on account of his better vantage point.

A ship was headed straight *toward* them.

Ernie's first impression was that it was some haunted ghost ship, like one of those things he sometimes saw on *The Mysterious Sea*, one of his favorite TV programs he watched on weekdays. Only this ship was different.

For starters, it was one of those large, sleek motor yachts seen in Montauk Harbor—the expensive ones, with streamlined, swept-back hulls that suggested a futuristic spaceship. This wasn't just any yacht, though. This was one of the ridiculous Italian jobs—a Baglietto, the same one, if Ernie wasn't mistaken, that belonged to Ty Ekdahl. *Hatshepsut.* He'd seen it many times in its berth at the Montauk Yacht Club, or motoring in and out of the harbor, with Ty at the helm, a cigar clenched in his perfect teeth. Typically, along with Ekdahl's trophy wife and her impossibly beautiful friends enjoying cocktails while sunning themselves on the deck.

Ernie lost count of the times he'd stand on the fishing wharf in the harbor, gazing at them going past with a futile longing, wondering if the crumpled lotto ticket in his wallet might be his magic passport to ascending to their company.

Today however, it looked like Ekdahl—or his ship at least—had taken a wrong turn on its latest cruise and gone to hell and back.

For starters, it was wreathed in half-dried seaweed and kelp, as if it had turned submarine and taken a cruise to the depths of the ocean. There were pronounced scratches and torn out divots on the hull. Several of the tinted black windows were shattered and the radar dome atop the bridge was askew, part of its cover broken off. The whole appearance struck Ernie as somehow *offensive*, as if he'd stumbled across a beautiful swimsuit model (like the ones frequently on his mind) who'd been raped and beaten up.

All that was secondary to the fact that, wherever she'd been, *Hatshepsut* was now about to tear her guts out on the rocks before them.

"Hey! Stop!" Ernie yelled, dropping his pole and waving his arms. Behind him, Carl joined in, putting his two fingers to his lips and letting out his piercing whistle. In a fluke of timing, the sonorous call of the foghorn from the lighthouse joined them.

There didn't seem to be anyone on board to acknowledge them, however, and on it came, fast enough that the bow cut a creamy spray out of the water. From the looks of it, she was attempting to ram straight up onto the beach and right into the tiered boulders protecting the point.

The yacht had a draft of five feet, however, and well before it got to them it hit the largest cluster of submerged boulders. The ship shuddered and canted, the sound of breaking fiberglass and metal filling the air, as if the yacht was screaming in agony. It was hard enough that Ernie felt the ground tremble under his feet.

Carried by its momentum, the yacht plowed ahead a few more yards before grinding to a halt, its bow raised out of the water. The surf pounding and seething against its hull made it appear the ship was in its death throes, which wouldn't be far from the truth if someone didn't get to it.

"Hey!" Ernie yelled again, "Anyone aboard?"

There was no reply, just creaks and groans, accompanied by the surf and sounds of splintering hull.

"Jesus, Carl, what the hell?" He had an urge to wade out and help but knew it would be suicide. With his heavy waders the surf would probably scoop him away or smash him into the rocks.

Carl, who'd seen a wreck or two in his lifetime (but nothing like this since the *Pelican* disaster of '51, and that was from his dad's photos), stared bug-eyed at the wreck. As far as he could tell, there wasn't a living soul aboard, unless they were hiding below decks. For a moment, he had a terrible vision of mutilated, torn apart bodies scattered around the cabins, and something worse: nightmarish Mer-men, their mouths rimmed with needle teeth, gulping chunks of human flesh in manic, rapacious bites.

He realized he already had his cell phone out in one shaking hand, without remembering doing it.

"I'm callin', I'm callin'!" he shouted down to Ernie.

Something about this whole thing was off to him. *A few nautical miles off.*

It took three tries before he was able to punch 9-1-1 on the keypad.

35. A GOOD DAY TO DIVE

"Are you hungry?" Dan asked. The alarm clock had just gone off at seven a.m.

"Starved," Vanek admitted. After two rounds of sex the night before he felt like he'd burned the equivalent calories of a marathon. Maybe two. Hungry or not, he couldn't deny a reluctance to get out of his current position, the silky warmth of Dan's body pressed up to his, her breasts pushing against his bicep.

"How starved?"

"I could eat a horse. Hooves and all."

"Hmmm. That won't win you too many points with the animal rights activists."

"I guess I'll have to eat them too, then."

Dan gave him an amused smile and tweaked his nose playfully. "Let me see what I can drum up. I don't think Arnaud picked up any horses at the IGA, but I'll check."

She sat up and eased out of bed, standing before him without any hint of modesty. Her self-confidence was inspiring. She leaned forward until her nose nearly touched his. The amused smile widened.

"I don't do room service, just so you know."

"I think you already did."

That got him a double pinch to the midsection. He responded by going for her armpits, drawing an ear-splitting shriek. The next thing he knew they were twisting and rolling across the bed, ending half-tangled in the comforter with Dan straddling him. Just as she reached to tickle him again, he rolled her back until he wound up on top. He didn't think a woman could look more beautiful than she did right then, her hair a tangled mess, eyes wide and inviting.

He leaned forward and kissed her slowly, savoring the taste of her lips. She responded by cupping her hand around the base of his head and kissing him back even more erotically. Her body stirred under his.

All at once his vision went dark, then was shredded apart by tears of light—silver, cutting light. A shrieking, chattering sound like sharp knives dinging a rapid-fire staccato against rusted metal. Streaming, bleeding colors: the sensation of incredible speed and the claustrophobic confines of a cabin-like space, oily movement as if parts of his body were amorphic tentacles... a silver-blue orb.

Agonizing pain, as if his nerves were being shredded. The horrifying vastness of space. Sprawling eternities of black like a vacant, never-ending scream. Stretches of time past eons, millions of light years beyond the ability of a human to begin to comprehend. Dead objects, still-born solar systems... the spiraling arms of galaxies in their cosmic dance and roiling radioactive clouds of supernova fanning out, obliterating worlds. Violence of stupendous dimensions vaporizing entire solar systems in the wink of a pulsar. Ions and particles and the unending aura of fear—terror in a yawning vacuum. The beckoning gravitational pull past a sub-frozen, dead planet. A spinning trajectory arcing to a violent, flaming entry point. Heat. Melting layers of an organic exo-skin, adapting, then vapor: billions of water molecules and a plummet to incredible, bone-crushing depth.

Exploding fear. Terror. Death.

And undeath.

Vanek snapped out of it, choking, the scream dying in his throat as he registered icy water all over his face.

Dan was standing over him with an empty glass, staring at him with alarm.

Vanek sputtered and rubbed water out of his eyes and hair.

"Never had someone do *that* to me after sex," he sputtered.

Dan's looked weirded out. "Sorry! I didn't know what else to do. You were having some sort of seizure again. I couldn't shake you out of it!"

"Well, that certainly worked."

She set the glass aside and sat next to him, again unconcerned at her nakedness. In another circumstance, Vanek would have been wowed. Instead he was trying to get his head around what just happened.

Dan put her hand on his knee and squeezed it. It was a motherly gesture, in an odd way, but reassuring.

"What's going on, Will? What's happening to you?"

Vanek tried to focus on the room before him.

The drawing is near he thought, whatever that meant. "Hell, if I know. It's bizarre. It's like having lucid dreaming episodes."

"But this is the third time, in the past two days. And they seem to be getting progressively worse. At this rate, I don't think you should be on the dive this morning."

Vanek had all but forgotten about it. Which struck him as funny. The prospect of going out again on a boat—not to mention thirty miles out to sea—should have filled him with cold, petrifying terror. And he'd completely blanked.

At least he had a valid excuse to get out of it.

Yet... somehow, that didn't give him any sense of relief.

"Well, why don't we wait and see how the day goes, Dan."

She shook her head. "This isn't a tour boat, Will. If something goes wrong out there…"

"I'm *fine*," he said. "A little soaked, perhaps. But fine. It's just some sort of... I just need some rest." He put his hand over hers, "Actually, some food would be good. Unless…?" his hand traveled a little higher on her thigh.

She gave it a playful smack. "I think you already put enough honey in this girl's teapot for the moment. My guess is I won't find any Viagra in your medicine cabinet."

Vanek chuckled. "Not yet at least."

She got up and snagged her bathrobe and gave him a classic over-the-shoulder look. "See you downstairs?"

"Definitely."

As soon as she went out the door, the smile dropped off Vanek's face. The hand on the thigh was a quick misdirection—he was surprised it worked. Part of him had an urge to tell her the truth, but the over-riding part didn't. For one thing, he didn't want to put anything more on what was probably a fluke moment of intimacy. The other was something deeper, stranger: a cold darkness that had probed into his soul.

By the time he made it down to the kitchen, Dan already had the coffee brewing and was scrambling eggs on the stove.

"I just got a text from Arnaud. They already went into town for breakfast—they insisted on getting fresh croissants at the bakery. So much for Hot Pockets. He said to meet them at the dock by 8:30." She looked up at him. "I still don't think you should go."

Vanek poured coffee for both of them and seated himself at the island. Someone had been reading the 'Montauk Project' book and left it near him. He glanced at the cover and shook his head.

Within minutes, Dan had the eggs served, along with a bowl of fresh blueberries and strawberries, sliced apple and toast. It looked like a spread in a high-end B&B.

"Hope you don't mind an informal meal," she said, easing herself onto the stool next to him.

Vanek looked over the food with an admiring eye. The presentation had a certain flair to it. "If your career in marine biology tanks, you could always open a restaurant."

Dan clinked his mug with hers. "God, I hope not. I'll still be paying the student loans off when I'm ninety."

"But this looks like it was done by a pro. Especially the fruit."

"A lot of hours binge-watching cooking shows. People think ocean expeditions are all excitement and adventure. Most of the time the food sucks. Trust me, me I get back on shore I go nuts. Enough talk. Dig in."

***

"Permission to come aboard?" Dan said.

"Granted!" replied Gorecki, raising his coffee. "And here's to swimmin' with bow-legged women!" he added, one of his favorite lines from 'Jaws'.

The morning was one of those bright, hot, Long Island ones that promised plenty of beach time and relief sought in the rolling breakers from the previous day's storm. At the marinas there was plenty of activity amongst the sing-song jangle of yacht-rigging, ship bumpers and seagulls, though most of the hard-core fishermen had been out for hours already.

Vanek was still in a fog from the night before, that peculiar lover's fog that settled in after unexpectedly finding oneself in an intimate situation. One that instantly redefined the contours and shapes of one's view like some kind of mental terraforming.

His world had become imbued with richer color and *thereness*.

So much that it wasn't until he stepped off the dock and onto the trawler that it struck him: *you're going out onto the water, yet again. Back out to sea, buckaroo. That's right! Where God knows what nightmare is waiting for all of you! Did you forget about your worms already? No? And what about that ole yacht that young girl's family went down in? How about a helpful little flashback slideshow!?*

Vanek stopped near the gunwale, fists clenched. He felt his heart hammering in his chest, a random pain shot up his arm. The left side of his head went hot and compressed. He was on the verge of a full-fledge anxiety attack.

"Shit. I blanked," Dan said, touching his forearm. "Will, stay here. You shouldn't *do* this."

Vanek took a slow breath through his nose.

"Don't be ridiculous. I can do this. I *have* to."

"Why?"

That he couldn't explain. Not here in front of everyone at least. Probably not in front of her, either. Part of it was sheer stubbornness. Part of it was anger at himself for being such a weenie about such things. And part of it was the fear that triggered his anger.

Dan gazed up at him, concern written on her features.

He avoided her eyes. At first. Then he forced himself to look directly at her.

"I am *fine*."

"*Final* answer?" Navarre chimed in, half taunting. The other three Frenchmen were sitting in the stern, drinking coffee, eating croissants and looking none the worse for whatever they'd been up to the night before.

Vanek gave Navarre a grim look but pulled up a smile. The effect was ghastly, yet it helped.

"*Final* answer."

"Excellent! It's a good day to dive. We have much work to do! And Davy Jones' locker awaits our visit!"

Vanek wasn't sure if the Frenchman knew of his pun.

A good day to dive. A good day to die!

***

Ten miles away, *Sea Bitch* churned along through a low-rolling surf. Scarpia sat up on the pilot's house, a cigar planted in the side of his mouth. Vanossi sat in the co-pilot's chair, a cigarette in one hand, a thermos of black coffee laced with rum in the other. The radio above the console was playing an old AC/DC tune, something about a highway to hell.

It covered the muffled screams coming from down below.

"Good day to blow this pop stand for good, yeah boss?"

Scarpia grunted. He was feeling better than he had in a long, long time. The session with his masseuse had gone even better than he'd anticipated. Carla had been exceptionally accommodating and brought along a young friend. Scarpia suspected she might be a daughter or niece but figured: *who can tell with these Filipinos—Damn gooks all look the same*! Even so, he'd slipped her an extra fifty. In one hour, he'd be getting a confirmation text via his satellite phone and that fifty would be forgotten pocket change.

A week of sailing and he'd be living high on the hog in Greece under a new identity, with Vanossi and the rest of the nitwits aboard serving as fish-food at the bottom of the Atlantic, along with *Sea Bitch*. 86'ing the crew would have to wait until they were within a stone's throw of the Canary Islands, of course.

Scarpia had carefully planned this out over the past two months. After the last dump (which he intended to do in plain sight as a final *Fuck-you-too* to New York State and its whining libtards) he'd lay a course for the Caribbean, do a short layover in Tobago, then cut across to the other side of the Atlantic to tie up loose ends.

Then... retirement to a small island off the Greek Coast, eating shrimp *saganaki* and drinking *Ouzo* and entertaining the ladies. He might even bring in a couple of those Spanish ones.

Best of all, he'd be free from the weighted noose of his wife and son.

Vanossi stood up, flicking his cigarette over the side.

"Word on the radio is that Ty Ekdahl's yacht beached itself on the Point. Can you believe that?"

Scarpia grunted, "Snot-nosed fucker was probably high on coke."

DiFronzo chuckled. "Yeah, but I wouldn't mind doing that wife of his. I'm going down to check on our crew, make sure everything's A-okay Kosher." He patted the Glock .40 in his waistband. "Need anything?"

"Not a thing," Scarpia replied. And for the moment, at least, that was true.

"For fuck's sake, you do realize how bad this is, Al... yes?" Jimmy Reed said, his voice urgent and low. "You don't actually think Scarpia is going to let either one of us walk off this boat alive, do you?"

Al Stanos wouldn't meet his eye. "He's a little scary sometimes, but he wouldn't do anything that bad. You'll see. He'll pay us and everything will be *fine*."

"*Seriously*? Al, you seemed to have tuned-out the latest news updates. Vanossi fucking raped my girlfriend and they have her tied up right there. Trust me, nothing about this is *fine*." Jimmy glanced at the deck above. The rumble of the trawler's diesels should be plenty loud to drown out their conversation, but Jimmy wasn't sure. Hell, he wasn't sure about anything anymore. Nothing had gone this morning like he'd thought.

For starters, when he arrived at the private dock off East Lake Road, Vanossi had been waiting for him.

With Scarpia.

"Glad you could show up," Vanossi said, grinning. He had a large duffle bag at his feet. Scarpia wasn't smiling at all. Jimmy wasn't sure which one made him more nervous.

"Where's Inga?" Jimmy said, arms crossed.

"She's waiting for you on board," Vanossi said, still grinning.

Jimmy shook his head. "That wasn't the deal."

For a moment no-one said anything. The only sound was the fishing boats motoring out of the harbor and the gulls overhead. Jimmy wondered if he screamed loud enough, one of the boats might hear him. He had a hunch it wouldn't do much good.

Scarpia let out a snort and raised an eyebrow at Vanossi. Vanossi crouched down and unzipped the duffle bag, opening it enough so Jimmy could see what was inside.

It was a woman's head. For a second Jimmy thought it was Inga—the hair was blonde and similar. Part of the skull was missing, plenty of blood and gore. Jimmy's eyes went wide.

Then he caught a glimpse of the eye through the hair and realized it wasn't her. Not that it made anything better—the message couldn't have been clearer. More fundamentally was the immediate shift in their roles, or at least his perception of them: Vanossi was a dangerous lackey but Scarpia was the apex predator here. Under the dead, twin gun barrels of the eyes and cruel mouth of the other man, Jimmy felt his will falter and drain out. He hated Scarpia for it.

Scarpia *knew* it too—he grinned... the ugly, toothy grin of a back-alley rapist who's gotten his victim to acquiesce.

He didn't bother to say anything. He just nodded toward the boat.

After searching him and taking his smartphone off him, they gave Jimmy five minutes with Inge after they cast off. The second shock was finding Jax and his friend tied up and gagged with her. Inge was in shock and non-responsive, her face bruised and puffy. He held her and tried to console her, but she had the thousand-yard stare of a bombing survivor. It crossed his mind he could have ditched all of this and run for it. Instead he was stuck with three people he realized were going to be useless. Probably get him killed. Jax was weeping and his friend—the Asian girl who told him her name was Kayla—looked terrified.

The cabin smelled of dirty socks, ocean mold and failed fishing trips, but was spacious with bunks enough to sleep six. The old paneling and plaid cushions suggested it hadn't been updated since the 1970's and from the aroma, probably not cleaned since then either. Jimmy checked the portholes on either side, but they were rusted shut and too small to crawl through, regardless. A couple of moldy photos of nude women had been tacked to the bulkhead wall, looking tired and wrinkled.

He removed their gags long enough to get the gist of what happened along with the identity of the head in the duffle bag. None of which improved his outlook of the situation. Of the three, he pegged Kayla as the only one who might be remotely capable of helping him get out of this jam. She was the only one whose answers indicated she had most of her cards still in order. Jimmy's instinct was to make a break for it, but that would still leave Inga. Someone had to deal with Vanossi.

That gave him an idea.

"Kayla, if you could get off this boat, what are the chances you could make it to shore? We're maybe a mile out of the harbor."

She gave him a fierce look. "I was the best swimmer in my class—got us to state finals."

Jimmy nodded. "It's clear and the tide should be in your favor. I'll deal with Vanossi, but you'll have to be quick. Get off the boat, dive as deep and stay under as long as you can—I don't think they'll use their guns this close to shore, but who knows. It's a long shot but the only one we got. They're going to kill every one of us. Get to shore, call the Coast Guard, call the Navy, call the Goddamn Marines. Anyone that can help!"

"I'll do it."

No sooner did she speak than Vanossi opened the cabin door.

Jimmy stood up and readied himself, his heart hammering.

"Are you kiddies—"

One thing Jimmy had learned from his father: the best time to hit in a fight was when your opponent was in mid-sentence.

Still, it was a near thing. Vanossi had the door partly open when Jimmy slammed his shoulder into it, his fist connecting with the other man's nose. He heard the satisfying crunch as it broke, then they were tumbling back onto the deck, grappling in an awkward dance. Vanossi grunted, and shoved forward, jamming the pistol in his hand up against Jimmy's ribcage.

Kayla sprinted past and bounding onto the taffrail, dove.

God bless her, Jimmy thought. *She's a pro*.

The retort of the gun going off three times was muffled, but still loud.

To Jimmy it felt like a sledgehammer hit him in the chest. He staggered backward, tried to catch his breath, realized it wasn't happening and dropped to his knees. Gray wool gathered around the edges of his vision.

This ain't so bad, he had time to think as he felt flat onto his face. He dimly registered the cold metal decking against his cheek as he died.

"The girl!" Scarpia shouted from above.

Vanossi ran to the rail but there was nothing, not even a ripple.

"Fuck! Fuck!" he shouted. He had the pistol out and was aiming it at the water, waiting for her to surface.

"Put that away you shit-head!" Scarpia hissed. They were further out than Jimmy had guessed—past a mile and a half actually—but there was an intermittent parade of boats coming out of the harbor and any number of observers from the shore. The last thing they needed was any additional attention. The Coast Guard cutter and Police launch were probably over at the lighthouse just ahead. They could be over here in minutes. Still, they would have to find her.

Al stood by the covered barrels, eyes wide and mouth open like a gob-smacked village idiot.

Scarpia glanced around, weighing options. Still…

"Get that body out of sight!" he snapped. Vanossi had at least holstered his gun but was still scanning the water.

"*Sam…*?" he added, in a tight, murderous tone that finally got through. Vanossi looked up and back at the water again, pointing.

"I didn't... Goddammit she just—"

"Shove it. I'll make a quick circle. If she pops up, grab her. If you can't do that use the harpoon. You can *fucking* handle that, yes!?"

Vanossi shot him a venomous look but nodded.

Scarpia went back to the helm and swung the boat around.

Kayla kicked off her sneakers quickly, then kept swimming as hard as she could. She could hold her breath close to two minutes, but that was without swimming hard in clothes.

Then again, those swim meets didn't involve people hot on blowing people's brains out.

Her mom had died the year before from breast cancer and her father had left her in the care of her grandmother, or rather the other way around.

She absolutely *had* to survive.

Fortunately, her clothes were light and not giving her too much drag. She rose to within a few feet of the surface, guessing she was far enough away to avoid detection. She could hear the rumble of the ship's engines, but it was difficult to tell from which direction. It *seemed* like it was moving away. She kept swimming another twenty yards. Her lungs were now screaming. How long had she been under? Two minutes already? Two and a half? Her strength was good, but bubbles began to leak out of her mouth.

She took a few more strokes, then as carefully as she could, rose to the surface.

Sputtering, she came up and took a huge gulp of air and stifled a scream.

The bow of *Sea Bitch* was almost on top of her.

36. ADRIFT

Aboard the *Robert D Ballard* things had gotten even stranger. The ship was completely without power, even the back-up battery systems were dead. They had two boats on board—the rescue launch and a work boat—but outside of paddling them to shore wouldn't be much help.

Commander Hopper had ordered the distress flares fired while engineering was working on recharging the battery systems with a hand-crank generator. Oddly, the new hand-held lanterns still worked fine.

"How is this possible?" the commander asked Scott Le Blanc, the senior engineer.

"Dunno," Le Blanc replied. "Unless, well, unless somehow whatever shorted out the system affected only our nickel Cadmium or Lithium Ion... wait a sec, the lanterns Reinhardt brought aboard use those new Graphene batteries."

"Is there any way to adapt one of them so we can at least get our radio up and running?"

"I'll go down and ask."

"Commander?" A lean man with close-set eyes stepped up—Lt. Jim Nichols, the operations officer.

"Yes?"

"The ship is starting to drift to the southeast. Doesn't make a shred of sense."

Hopper snorted. "Nothing does right now. But note it in the log. This whole night has been one for the books."

Down in the ROV Garage, Reinhardt tinkered with the D2 unit using one of his lanterns. One of the junior mechanics, a quiet Dominican named Carol Vasquez, was with him. With nothing to do in the Mission Control room he figured he'd make himself useful and see what could be done about the ROV. One of his many talents was his knack for fixing things. At MIT his Mechanical Engineering professor had nicknamed him 'MacGyver'.

"You know, it's not that bad," he said, looking at where the tether cable had been severed. "It's sheared cleanly off. I could splice these suckers. And the rest of the Rover looks beat to hell, but I'm pretty sure it's still usable."

Vasquez shrugged. It was something she excelled at. She glanced at her watch—it was nearly dawn. Then something caught her eye on one of the inside panels she was tinkering with: a dimly blinking light.

"Isn't that one of the battery indicators?" she asked.

Reinhardt craned his head around. "Nah, it's one of the... no shit! That's the video backup drive for one of the auxiliary cameras. That thing still has some juice in it!"

The bulkhead door squeaked and opened as Le Blanc poked his head in.

"Hey, Reinhardt, what on earth are you doing? That thing won't be touched until we have it ashore and fully assessed! And by the way, Captain wants to know if there's any remote way we can tap the batteries on those fancy lights of yours to our portable comm-set to get out a distress call?"

Reinhardt blinked at him several times, as if trying to process this.

"Um, yeah. Sure. Just making myself useful and evaluating the damage for my report. Tell the captain I'll be right up."

He turned to Vasquez, "Never mind him. His asshole is so tight he eats coal and shits diamonds. Humor me and see what you can do to get D2 in some semblance of working order. I have a hunch we're going to need her before this day is through."

Vasquez shot a quick glance at the door Le Blanc had left open, then gave Reinhardt an impish smile, "Aye-aye, sir."

On the bridge, the sun had broken the horizon and sunlight glinted through the windows, casting everything in a golden light. Hopper was sitting in the only chair present, a padded swivel seat reserved exclusively for the captain.

"What do think, Mr. Reinhardt? Can we power up the landsat—"

Before she could complete her sentence, the lights flickered, dimmed, then came on. Somewhere an alarm kicked on. All the lights on the control panels and monitors lit up, throwing the crew into momentary confusion.

"Commander, our systems are back online!" Lt. Nichols said from the Ships Systems console. He reached over and hit the 'engineering alarm' switch, silencing it.

"Get home base on the line. Do we have engines?"

"Yes, sir."

A cheer broke out on the bridge.

"Good," Hopper said, once it had quieted down, taking care not to show her relief. She got out of the seat and stepping over to the bridge consoles, plucked the nearest intercom mic slung from the overhead brass rail. "Attention, attention all hands. This is the captain speaking. The ship has power restored—we'll be getting underway shortly..."

She repeated the announcement and turned to Lt. Nichols. "Run a full diagnostic before we hit the throttles. I don't want to get everyone's hopes up until we're positive we can get this old tub moving."

"Ah, Captain?" Reinhardt chimed in, raising one hand.

"Yes, Mister Reinhardt?"

"I'd like to suggest we head back to where we first lost D2."

She gave him a quizzical look, "You can't be serious?"

"Dead serious."

"Mister Reinhardt, you are aware our last trip to that location is what precipitated this whole mess, that we still have no clue what actually happened and that D2 is severely damaged because of it?"

Reinhardt appeared unfazed. "Correct."

Hopper looked at him like he'd grown two heads. But he could see a glint of curiosity in her eye. The rest of the bridge crew had grown quiet.

"Well?"

"Have you heard about the incident two years ago along the Hudson River, one that began with an unknown species that was first encountered off the Atlantic coast here? A mission which Bob Ballard himself was on?"

"I've heard talk," she acknowledged. Actually, she heard more than that, but wasn't sure she liked where this was going.

Reinhardt looked her straight in the eye. "I was *on* that mission. At least the tail end of it. That was when Mr. Ballard gave me a leg up from Side-Sonar scanning jockey to my current position."

Commander Hopper crossed her arms. Without replying, her eyebrows went up: *and*?

"I don't think this is exactly the same, but something similar. Something far *worse*. The last time some three hundred people died. Tourism season is at its peak all around this area right now. We're the only NOAA vessel in the area. We're way outside Coast Guard jurisdiction. Shouldn't we at least investigate?"

Hopper didn't have to turn her head to see six pairs of eyes glued to her. This was her first mission as the Okeanos' Commander and every action was being measured and gauged.

"In case you forgot, that didn't work out so hot last time. I'm not inclined to put the entire ship at risk."

Reinhardt pulled the solid state drive out of his pocket. "This may change your mind."

37. A PERFECT DAY FOR FISHING

Scarpia cut the engines on *Sea Bitch*, checking their coordinates with the GPS monitor. The morning sun was bright as new dimes on the water, sending shards of light through the cabin windows.

A God-damn perfect day for fishing, he thought. *Though not a bad one for ditching the family and running off to the Mediterranean, either.*

Still, he was starting to sweat. The girl had gotten away, for one thing. Jimmy Reed was dead for another, which meant Vanossi would have to work double duty, like it or not. Mostly it was a hinky feeling that things weren't going right, that the carefully laid ropes connecting all his plans were frayed and about to come apart in ways he couldn't see.

Yet... that wasn't quite the ticket either, was it?

Something ominous hung in the air, like that time he'd walked into a dead-end ally in Queens behind a (equally dead-end) strip club for those wonderful 'ciga-pops' he used to smoke—cigarettes repacked with a tobacco and cocaine mix. He sensed a presence lurking in the shadows at the end of it. A *very bad* presence. The type of bad that had him seriously consider taking the switchblade in his pocket and drawing it across his own throat. He replaced the ciga-pop in its case and quietly backed out of there, feeling whatever it was watching him. The next morning the Daily News ran a page four story of several teenagers found dead—raped and mutilated—at the same location.

This was kind of like that. Which in itself made him uneasy. Antony Scarpia wasn't someone known for his fits of superstition.

Dump the shit and get out of here, quick.

He looked at the barometer and did a double take.

It was falling.

That was odd. They'd just had a storm blow through yesterday and nothing had been forecast on the weather band.

"Hey Tony, why we stopping?"

"Huh?" In a rare instance, Antony Scarpia was *confused*.

Vanossi looked at him funny. "Why we stopping?" he repeated slowly, as if questioning a lost school kid. "We gotta be twenty miles from the drop site!"

Good question.

He checked the GPS again and saw they were way off. *What the hell*? He'd been thinking about that dead alley again. He fought the sudden urge to turn around and hightail it back to port.

"Change of plan. We're dumping early and getting out of here."

A deep line formed between Vanossi's eyebrows. "What ya mea—"

"Shut the fuck up and get down on deck!" Scarpia cut him off.

He'd let the trawler drift with the current while they made their final drop. The hinky feeling was stronger now. Something in the water? Why did he feel like a sitting duck?

While Vanossi clambered down to the aft deck, Scarpia checked the magazine on his Desert Eagle .50, then the Colt assault rifle (with a highly illegal banana clip) in its holder next to the ship's wheel. Adjusting his Greek fishing cap, he stepped over to the rail to oversee the proceedings.

Short and simple was the plan. Once the barrels were hoisted over the side—damn things weighed nearly three hundred pounds—it was a bullet in the head for Al. The kids in the cabin could wait until they were further out to sea. He could have handled the job with just Vanossi, but he was paranoid about those barrels. Even with rubber gloves.

Hell, he wouldn't go near them even with a Hazmat suit.

Jax looked at the smartphone in his hands and tried to ignore Jimmy Reed's body shoved into one corner of the cabin like a sack of potatoes. For all his internet world weariness, he'd never seen a dead person before, let alone one he knew.

Jax's phone had been confiscated before he and Kayla had been forced at gunpoint aboard the trawler. Jimmy's girlfriend, Inga, was still catatonic.

This phone was Jimmy's—a back-up he'd smuggled in his shoe. He'd shoved it in his hands before Kayla had made her break. The problem was they were out of signal range and there weren't any games on it except for the lame *Candy Crush.*

He was sitting there staring blankly when he noticed a blip on the signal bar icon.

Frowning, he thumbed into the system settings.

A few seconds later he realized there was a satellite relay aboard the ship. If he could get the password security key, he could get a text message out to his PlanetJustice friends ashore. Plus, the onboard cameras were linked to the old phone, but also his server back at the house. He could patch them in remotely... if he could get online. Jax tried a variety of passwords, mostly variations on 'Montauk' to no avail. Then he thought about people like Scarpia, who like his parents weren't technically inclined. Utterly afraid of it, actually. Especially for passwords. Pausing, he cleared the entry field and simply hit 'go'.

Five bars appeared in the little connection icon at the upper corner.

The frown became a smile as he began to text.

Vanossi was royally pissed.

Getting Jimmy Reed had been Scarpia's idea, not his. It wasn't *his* fault the asswipe surfer had decided to make a break for it. Now here he was stuck handling the goddamn toxic barrels with dumb-fuck Al, who probably needed to consult a manual just to take a piss in the morning.

If any of that toxic shit affected his erections—or worse—had him shooting mutant glow-in-the-dark jizz, he was going to take his old pal Antony and skin him slowly with his fish knife.

They had the tarp off and already had three of the barrels dumped overboard using the port fishing boom as a crane. The process involved manhandling the barrel onto the hoisting straps and securing them, raising it over the gunwale while one man guided it, then lowering the barrel into the water and dropping it using the safety release. The last had to be done carefully, so the heavy winch latch didn't whip around and knock your brains out.

Vanossi was handling the electric winch control while helping Al maneuver the barrel overboard with his free hand. Even with the heavy-duty rubber gloves, Vanossi was nervous about the process, even more so when PCB-laden sludge began to leak from one of the caps, which wasn't apparent until the barrel was up in the air, horizontal.

The viscous, black substance even *looked* dead, as if it absorbed light.

The leak became worse as the barrel lifted. Al, alarmed, pushed it away from him over the water, causing the hoisting straps to spin and twist.

"Dammit!" Vanossi yelled, losing his grip. "Don't let go of it!"

Al then did something utterly stupid: afraid of getting splashed with the sludge, he snatched up a gaff pole and attempted to prod it away. Instead, the barrel reversed its spin and the pointed end of the gaff hit the cap, knocking it off completely.

Dead-black sludge sprayed out, coating both men and the deck around them.

"Oh fuck!" Al yelled.

Panicked, Vanossi did the only thing he could think of: he thumbed the safety release. Unfortunately, the barrel was already swinging back in toward the boat. Released too quickly, the barrel bounced off the gunwale with a heavy *thud*, spraying more sludge as it catapulted backward into the water. The metal latch arced in like a deadly slingshot, clipping Al's jaw and shattering it. Blood and teeth flew.

"*Aghhh*!" Al screamed, clutching his jaw. He staggered up to Vanossi, trying to clutch at him. "*Lookit whahju dith to me*!"

"Get away, you creep!" Vanossi said, giving him a good shove. Vanossi was only concerned about getting the toxic goop on himself.

Al stumbled against the gunwale, his rubber boots skidding on the sludge.

"*Aya*—" he began, then did an ungainly flip over the rail. A heavy splash followed.

Vanossi wasn't paying attention. He shook off his rubber gloves and wiped at his face furiously, cursing. "Jesus Christ! Goddamn shit is in my eyes!!" It even got into his mouth—foul and metallic tasting.

Something soft and smelly hit him. It took a moment to register it was an old towel.

With the worst of it off he opened his eyes, blinking. Everything bright had a halo around it, as if he'd dunked his head in a pool of over-chlorinated water with his eyes open.

"Great. Just fucking great," Scarpia said. Avoiding the worst of the sludge, he looked up and over the gunwale. There was no sign of Al. That didn't make a lick of sense to Scarpia—the kid must have sunk like a rock.

Which left him with one guy left.

Actually, *two*. The Millennial kid was still in the cabin.

"Clean yourself up and get back to work," Scarpia said. "You've still got two more barrels to go. Get that wet rag of a kid to help you."

"Fuck-you," Vanossi snarled, his temper getting the worst of him. Maybe it was the stinging pain in his eyes, maybe the frustration of dealing with Scarpia too long. Without thinking about it his hand reached back and yanked the magnum out of its holster.

His hand only made it halfway up before the air was split by a resounding bang and the entire top of his head blew apart, sending hair and brains across the gunwale. His eyes crossed, and he crumpled to the deck.

Scarpia stood, glowering, the Desert Eagle in his right hand. He'd recognized murder in Vanossi's face. There was no choice.

"What a fucking mess," he said to himself. He was about to holster the automatic when something slammed into the hull of the boat, knocking him flat on his butt while the sidearm went skittering across the sludge-coated deck. From inside the cabin came a high-pitched scream.

Jax knew something was wrong when he heard Vanossi yelling and something heavy hitting the boat caused it to rock. He tried the cabin door, but it was locked. He'd gotten wrapped up in texting more obsessively than usual, detailing every aspect of his current circumstances down to the smell of the blankets. Then it hit him: what the hell good were his PlanetJustice friends going to be if he was dead?

Inga wasn't any help either.

This bae is so not work, he thought, dismally. *WTF*, he texted, his fingers working on autopilot. *Somethings happening where are u? I need to get FOH now! Check the camera feeds!*

He sat there, feet tapping out a nervous tattoo when he heard the gunshot. Jax's head snapped up. His breath hitched. Just as his fingertips brushed the phone again it was knocked out of his hands as something *huge* rammed into the side of the ship's hull. Hard enough to breach the hull and shatter the wood paneling. Jax tumbled onto the bench opposite Inga, banging his head painfully against the bulkhead.

Water jetted in behind as she sat up again, eyes blinking in confusion as she'd just come out of a dream. The scene was surreal—the dim overhead lights wavered, random water spraying around; in the middle of it, Inga, focusing on Jax as if seeing him for the first time. He had enough time to register how beautiful she truly was, like a Scandinavian mermaid apparition.

Until the ethereal beauty of her features twisted into something awful. Inge screamed, a shrill, high-pitched scream that drilled into his ears.

Jax was petrified. The past twelve hours had been a record for firsts: he'd watched one of his friends get her brains blown out, been kidnapped by a couple of environmental criminals, had another friend shot to death and now this.

Except what exactly *was* this?

The boat gave another lurch as it was rammed again. This time part of the hull gave way and Inge jerked forward. At first Jax couldn't process what he was seeing. Two massive black pincers had broken through the hull and were prying it apart while through a gaping maw in the center a stream of glistening tentacles shot in and fused with Inga's back. As he watched, several burst through her abdomen and one out the side of her neck.

They made Jax think of a homicidal sea anemone fused with a giant black crab. Eerily similar to the creature in "It Came from World's End"—the one that had given him nightmares for days afterward.

And the smell: the ammonia-laden reek of dead fish; of putrescent things disgorged from the unlit deep. It gave off a deep *scissoring* sound, the whispering bass chorus of hungry sea-things.

Inga made gurgling sounds as bright red blood curtained out of her mouth. Another pincer (*how many were there*!?) shot through it and clipped her torso nearly in half, then with a gruesome squishy sound, she doubled over and was yanked backward through the opening.

The ship began to tilt and Jax realized he was sliding toward the thing.

For the first time in his twenty-two odd years on this planet, it finally hit home he could *die*; that the assumed, wide open panorama of his life was about to be hit with an abrupt, brutally painful cancellation ticket.

The boat tipped even further, seawater now filling up the cabin, mixing with the bloody remnants of Inga. The creature surged forward, tentacles flailing wildly; now Jax could see the black carapace of the thing's head and a spray of malformed glowing orbs he took for its eyes.

Jax screamed, clinging to the bench cushion. The ship tilted at a thirty-degree angle, with random items (coffee maker, ropes, fishing gear) falling down and hitting the thing with wet smacks.

Jax spotted the metal grip rail by the cabin door and grabbed it with both hands just as the cushion answered to gravity and dropped down, snatched by one of the pincers. As the tilting of the ship increased, he found himself hanging, pinwheeling his feet to avoid the tentacles. He saw that the impact had pushed the cabin door out of its frame. One tentacle latched onto his shoe, tearing it off. Jax kicked off the cabin wall with his other foot, swung back, then using his momentum, hit the door with both feet.

At first, he didn't think it would work. One of the tentacles lashed at his head, removing a patch of hair and scalp. Then he tumbled through onto the canted back deck, flailing down toward the now submerged starboard gunwale. His ankle hit one of the steel brackets and snapped, then one of the waste barrels bounced past, clipping him on the head and knocking him out.

Scarpia's first reaction when he saw what had rammed his ship was to pull the Desert Eagle and start firing. The .50 caliber bullets had a terrific ability to inflict devastating trauma.

Then he took a second look and reconsidered. Had it been a shark, or even some kind of squid, he would have a remote idea where to fire a lethal shot. With this thing, whatever the hell it was, he hadn't a clue. One thing he *did* process in an instant was that *Sea Bitch* was a goner.

And so was he if he didn't get out of here, quick.

Scarpia was never one for second guessing when the shit hit the fan. He jammed the gun into his holster and clambered up the canting deck, snatching one of the donut live preservers off the side of the ship.

If he had hesitated another minute, he would have seen Jax catapulting out the cabin door. Instead, he climbed atop the port gunwale and did an ungainly leap off the side. The water was ice cold. Coming up sputtering, Scarpia looped his arm and neck through the flotation donut and kicked as hard as he could, hampered by his heavy work boots. The sight of the *Sea Bitch* angling up into a near perpendicular position caused him to redouble his efforts.

His heart pounded in his ears as every cigar and Tequila shot came back to haunt him. Moments later a bolt of pain shot up his chest and into his jaw and he thought: *Fuck, here comes the big one... and here I thought it was a perfect day for fishing.*

38. DEATH BELOW

"I just think you should know what I believe we're dealing with," Vanek said, as they sat gathered in the main cabin of *Catch-22*. Up in the pilot house, Gorecki piloted them to the dive site.

"You think this is some kind of *alien shapeshifter*?" Navarre replied.

"When you put it that way, it sounds pretty loony, but yes, that's the long and short of it."

Dan cut in, "It's almost as if the... *pod*, for lack of a better word, that we discovered yesterday is linked to it. Kind of like a docking bay for an iPhone, to make a ridiculous analogy. This could be an entirely new life form symbiosis we've never witnessed before."

Navarre stared at Vanek, "And how is this tied to what you found in the bunker? And your so-called 'visions'?"

"Maybe you should lay off the funny mushrooms?" Philippe quipped.

Vanek ignored him. "I'm not sure. Look, whatever it is, this thing is tied into what happened at Camp Hero. And best I can tell, it feeds off... no, that's not right... it, it takes the shape of our fear."

"*Ah*, like Salvini's 'Italy First' right-wingers these days!?" Yves offered.

"No, I think what he means is that Donald Trump is waiting for us down there," Michel finally spoke up.

Vanek raised his hands in exasperation but let out a chuckle, "You may not want to go there. But I've been thinking about what happened last time with Dan's speaker. Fortunately, she was able to rig up a second one. Here's how I propose we approach this..."

Catch-22 arrived at the wreck site an hour after *Sea Bitch* would have, if Scarpia's ship were still afloat and not resting on its side on the sea bottom fifteen miles off-shore. Gorecki had taken a course tighter to the Montauk Lighthouse so they could get a first-hand look at Ekdahl's wrecked yacht. As a result, they missed the oil slick and bits of debris (and one floating small-time crook) that marked the death of the trawler.

Gorecki eased off the throttles as they came up on the dive buoy.

Just before they arrived, Navarre had pulled Vanek aside for a private word by the stern rail. Vanek was surprised when he felt something pressed into his hand—a St. Christopher's medal.

"Keep this for me. Just in case. I have an estranged wife and two sons back in Marseilles—Les knows the details. Make sure she gets this. And something else. Before the ONR took everything, I spent time going over the scans of the wreck. If all else fails, I plan to blow up the ship and what's underneath it to hell. Destroy whatever is down there before it takes any more lives. Between the munitions and torpedoes, there is plenty of *'kaboom'*."

"How do you plan to do that?"

Navarre showed him a small compact block of C2 with a digital timer. "Once I plant this, make sure you stay well back, yes? Dan too."

"What about your friends?"

"Don't worry about them. They know the score. Death always swims along with us on every dive, no?"

Shortly after, all of them gathered on the back deck to recheck the dive gear. Navarre had the fresh and invigorated air of someone about to enter their element. Dan by contrast appeared preoccupied and Navarre pointed out two critical things she missed, including a temperamental dive gauge.

He tossed her one of his backups.

"Here. Put it on." Navarre studied her. "Whatever is on your mind, leave it on the boat. Just to remind you we'll be at forty-eight meters again today. This isn't an amateur dive."

"*Got it*," Dan replied, annoyed. She'd gotten another call from Woods Hole this morning. Orca U47 was acting even stranger, having chased off any of his pod approaching the area. Which meant U47 was still *in* the area.

Then had come the private call from Gavin. It hadn't been a pleasant one.

She glanced over at Vanek, standing by the stern and looking out at the water uneasily. She truly liked him, hell, in a strange way she felt a strong surge of affection, which hadn't been part of the deal. Gavin had been clear about that. He'd been such a fussy bookworm when she'd shown up—was it only two days ago?

The man she looked at now was different. Still worried, but there was something else present in his posture, the set of his face. Confidence. Surety. Even a certain hint of mercilessness.

She was pretty sure Gavin had underestimated him.

She had. Even in bed.

Vanek looked over and she gave him a smile, a genuine one, though a stab of guilt accompanied it.

What am I? *You're a shit. A fake and a liar. Am I even—*

"*Ready*?" Navarre, said, so close she started.

"What? Yes, of course," she replied, standing up and zipping her wet suit up. The neoprene head cap followed. At 160 feet the water temperature would be around 40 degrees; conserving every bit of body heat was critical. As was redundancy for any critical equipment. Navarre estimated the dive would take anywhere from half an hour to forty-five minutes including deco stops and there weren't any spare equipment shops where they were going.

"Stay focused," Navarre said. "The nitrogen at 48-meters will mess with your head. If we get separated, remember your dive table."

They all knew this, but it was protocol.

Crouching down, he unsnapped one of the large watertight cases his friends had brought. Inside was an odd-looking weapon that reminded Vanek of the old WWII German StG 44 assault rifles. It had a heavy-duty combat knife fixed at the end of the barrel.

Navarre pulled it out and loaded the unusually wide clip.

"Custom ASM-DT underwater assault rifle," he explained. "Supercavitating 7.62 by51mm armor piercing ammunition. Twenty-six rounds. Fires a *flechette* instead of a bullet. Good up to twenty-five yards underwater."

"Is that even remotely legal?" Vanek asked.

Philippe grinned. "I wouldn't post photos of it on social media, if I were you."

Vanek, who'd handled various firearms but nothing like this, was intrigued. "May I?" he asked.

"Sure. Careful though."

The assault rifle was ungainly for its size and weighed about ten pounds.

"Compressed air?"

Navarre grinned like a kid showing off a new toy. "Yes. Very efficient. Up to 600 rounds per minute. The safety is on the side, like so."

Vanek sighted down the barrel, careful to aim over the side of the ship. The gun felt heavy and dead in his hands. The knife gave it an extra savage appearance. He handed it back with some relief.

"What exactly are you planning on shooting down there?" Dan asked.

"Anything that tries to kill us," he replied, slinging it over his shoulder.

"Turn around," Gorecki said as he helped her into her tanks first. With the dive underway he was all business. He went over her rebreather, regulator and all her gear: two knives, backup lights, Jon Lines, retainers for regulators, dive lights and a pair of lift bags. Navarre's get up was nearly identical—all Navy-grade equipment. Vanek looked him over with an appraising eye—the integrated diving suits had taken a quantum leap in the last decade.

Once all the equipment was checked and rechecked, Navarre stood by the stern and addressed everyone. "I'll take the lead, with Yves, followed by William and Dan. Michel and Philippe will bring up the rear. Again, the goal will be two-fold: to secure a sample from this creature pod, whatever it is, as well as the dumping. Then we get out. Anything down there tries to attack us, *kill* it. Any questions?"

Yves held up his hand, "Where did I leave my socks?"

"Back at the house. Along with your brains, *petit malin*," Navarre shot back.

Vanek stood still, uncomfortable in the heavy gear, trying not to think about what awaited them down there. Would it be worms again this time? Or something more terrifying? He looked up at the sky with its large cumulous clouds scudding overhead. A beautiful summer afternoon. Possibly the last he might ever see. Any of them for that matter. He glanced over at Dan, who gave him a wink and a smile.

It was almost convincing.

She was making final checks on the speaker, which had been jury-rigged to one of the underwater DPV sleds the divers had brought. The sleds were better than the gear the ONR had confiscated. In addition, they had four compact Hammacher Schlemmer mini-scooters to speed up their navigating the wreck—and get them away quickly.

A minute later they went over the side in quick succession, back first. Rising to the surface, they cleared their masks and rebreathers.

"See you in a bit," Navarre said to Gorecki, giving them the thumbs up. A minute later there was nothing to mark their passing but a light ripple on the water.

Then that too was gone.

This time the descent went smoother, all six divers hooked on to the dive line. The water was murkier than the day before, as if trying to conceal the wrecks. The current was stronger. Vanek felt a noticeable pull as they went past the hundred-foot mark.

Even with the cooler water at depth, he still felt himself sweating in his dive suit.

Past 140', Navarre and Philippe switched their lights on, sending their beams probing ahead. Would it be the worms again, he wondered? No. Not likely. He had a grim feeling today it would be much, much worse.

The plan was flimsy, but he was praying it would work.

The wreck of the *Tryton* looked spookier than ever, appearing out of the gloom like the skeleton of an ancient marine dinosaur. Each of them unhooked from the dive line and broke up into their pre-arranged groups: Navarre and Philippe taking the lead with one scooter, Vanek behind them with another, while Dan worked the sled with Yves and Michel tailing her.

When they came upon the *Exeter*, they slowed down. Toward the bow the water seemed darker than usual, as if gathering into itself.

***

The creature was aware of them even before they entered the water. Each had its own peculiar—and enticing—fears. One of them, however, it had an undeniably intimate connection to. A familiarity.

But it was also growing sluggish.

Its hibernation phase was creeping in again, its alien metabolism more focused on stockpiling energy for its next phase. It didn't fear, at least not in the same sense of the victims it fed on, but it was capable of experiencing *disquiet*. Something about these life forms approaching made it more so.

They had fear, yes—it could all but taste the neuro-chemicals firing off in their amygdala the way a dog could sense and savor all the thousand separate smells of a distant beef stew, but it sensed something else too.

Purpose.

These life forms were coming for it specifically.

It found that *interesting*.

Uncomfortable.

Yet... there was no doubt it would devour them too.

***

As they approached the bow of the ship, Navarre signaled to Dan for her group to break off to their position on the upper deck. None of them had any idea exactly how near they had to be to get this thing's attention but gauging from their previous experience, it would have to be quite close.

At the bridge, Dan braced herself against the rail while Yves and Michel stabilized the DPV sled. After activating the speaker box, she flicked on the sled's motor.

Nothing happened.

Inside the turret opening, Vanek and Navarre were close enough to see the pod, and the hideous thing half out of it. The creature was like a cross between a bloated sea-spider and black squid, but something about its appearance and dimensions triggered a powerful loathing, as if it was not meant for human eyes to witness. Particularly the writhing, worm-like appendages connecting it to what they thought of as the 'docking' pod. A bulge at what appeared to be the head had a spray of mis-sized eyes, pulsing silver-blue with a strange bioluminescence from within.

Vanek felt nauseous just looking at it. Watching the slithering connections to the dock made his gorge rise.

Navarre released the safety on his ASM-DT assault rifle, resisting the urge to fire at the thing until the clip was empty and run for it. Instead, he took the C2 out of his dive bag and stuck it on the inside of the hull, right near a stack of collapsed artillery shells. Above him, Philippe had his rifle to his shoulder and was sighting down the barrel, his eyes wide behind his mask.

All three men knew they probably had only seconds before they were detected.

It was *changing.*

Even as it erupted from the pod, its outlines were growing murky, morphing, taking on humanoid shapes. The three men were buffeted by a pressure wave as the thing exploded in size, pushing them back into the ships. Around them the wreck of the *Exeter* let out protesting groans as it shifted.

Up on the bridge deck, the shift was just enough to send Dan sliding backwards while Yves and Michel struggled with the sled. Bubbles erupted from below, followed by a shift in water pressure. Dan felt her ears pop. Then she saw what emerged over the edge of the rail.

Her scream was muffled by her rebreather.

The misshapen head was partly her brothers, with the lower part split by cilia-lined gills that quivered as if in anticipation. A giant crab leg followed, worm-like filaments writhing out from the joints that made Dan think of parasites.

The deep scissoring sound coming from it rose in a crescendo.

Yves fired, the flechettes ripping through the water and into the carapace of the thing's upper body. An inky black cloud burst outward from it. Pinpricks of silver blue light flickered within. It seemed to waver, as if dimming out of existence, then an appendage shot out faster than the eye could follow, neatly slicing Yves in two. For a moment he tried to swim away, his innards tumbling out of his torso, then his arms went limp, bloody bubbles bursting upward around him.

Michel, who was also firing, panicked. He kicked hard and went through the damaged door into the bridge. Terrified, Dan followed him.

Inside their dive lights a single stair leading to the deck below. Michel tapped Dan, indicating she should go first, even as the tentacles shot through smashed windows. Her tank banged off the metal bulkhead as she swam downward. She glanced back to see Michel following her close behind. A second later his head jerked backwards as the top of his skull was sliced off with the neatness of a guillotine. The gun fired wild, sending one of the flechettes right through Dan's left thigh.

She screamed again and tried to kick away with her other leg, seeking shelter in the lower deck. Her heart hammered in her chest, knowing her life was drawing down to mere seconds…

As soon as the thing cleared the pod, Navarre and Philippe shot forward, guns ready. Vanek followed, using his underwater light to look down into it. It was worse than he thought. The pod appeared to be a living entity unto itself, perhaps a more fixed portion of the creature. There were bioluminescent lights inside, but also writhing shapes as if it was lined with worms of some kind. The thick flaps at the top suggested a woman's labia, which struck Vanek as even more bizarre.

Inside it was *pulsing*.

As they approached, it began to change.

Again, there was an obscene, inviting quality to it that triggered both pleasure and fear centers simultaneously, the way in a dream one might find oneself surrendering to a perverse, lascivious act.

In that moment Vanek understood they were way over their heads.

Philippe dropped his rifle and swam right in, arms outstretched. Navarre tried to grab him but missed. Once Philippe came within range, the anchor filaments—as Vanek thought of them—shot out and snatched him in with the speed of a trap-door spider. Blood and bubbles filled the water in inky whorls. Part of an arm floated up out of it.

Vanek went for Philippe's rifle where it landed on the cabin floor. It was like moving in a dream—somehow everything kept going horribly wrong and there didn't seem any way to stop it.

Navarre appeared in front of him, knife in one hand, signaling by pointing it at his dive bag that he was going into the pod to cut out a sample and that Vanek should stay back.

Navarre swam toward the opening, rifle cradled in one arm, knife forward in the other... downward into the opening. His eyes didn't look quite sane.

A dozen or so feet above the pod, Vanek aimed his light down.

The light glinted off something metallic inside, embedded in a blackened area like a tumorous intrusion.

One of the torpedoes.

Navarre cut at the flesh lining of the flap.

Dan looked on in horror as the thing came into the lower deck, its giant pincer forelegs spreading wide, ready to impale her. Her lower gut felt oddly warm and squishy. Below the pincer, a forest of worm-like tentacles grew out of the carapace of its main body. One shot toward her, seizing her foot.

Dan yanked the dive knife out of its sheath as she felt herself get jerked toward it, managing to slice it. Freed, she shot away, clawing over a large dining table—the officers mess—then scrambled to the bulkhead door leading to the main deck.

She had two choices—try to get outside the ship or seek safety deeper within. Her instinct screamed toward the latter: the instinct to hide. But she would be trapped.

Fortunately, the door had been left partly open when the ship sank. Wrenching it open, she burst out and into the open water, legs kicking furiously. Her left thigh was in agony.

Glancing back, she saw a horrifying sight. The thing was erupting out of the bulkhead door, *expanding* it with a scream of metal. Too fast. She knew she wouldn't make it ten yards before it caught her. Even as she thought it, another tentacle struck out and wrapped around her ankle. For a wild second she didn't know if she would attempt to fight—and meet Navarre's horrifying end—or plunge the knife into her throat in a last desperate act of self-control.

Neither happened.

She corkscrewed around, knife in hand, just as something powerful buffeted past her with the force of an underwater locomotive. There was a painful tear in her ankle as the tentacle squeezed, but what had her attention was the black and white whale that shot in for the kill, severing tentacles in one vicious bite.

The one still grasping her ankle fell away in a cloud of blood.

As she kicked away, she saw a dozen more of the tentacles seize the whale in a flash, slicing it to ribbons as the pincers impaled it. It was butchery. Chunks of whale and gore fell every which way in clouds of blood. Dan fought an urge to spit out her rebreather, vomit, and swim straight up to the surface.

Another movement caught her eye—the tow sled, up by the bridge.

As she swam up toward it, several more killer whales shot past her, attacking as a group. She'd never witnessed anything like it before. They sped in at different angles, savagely tearing, slashing, biting. Dan turned away from the butchery, swimming to the sled, remembering the malfunctioning sound cube tethered to her hip.

It was still there! Out of exasperation she resorted to simply banging on the speaker's power button with her fist. Then she turned on the sled.

It *worked.*

The sled wrenched itself out of her grasp and tore off upward at an oblique angle.

In pain and shock, Dan kept swimming until the carnage disappeared into the gloom.

Heart racing, she forced herself to pause and decompress, counting seconds on her dive watch and waiting for the thing to come zooming out of the depths, tentacles flying out to seize her and tear her to ribbons.

Nothing came.

The ankle looked bad. The flechette wound was clean, at least. She pulled a dive bag out of her pouch and wrapped it tight to staunch the worst of the bleeding. Sharks—including the great whites that frequented the area—could sense blood in the water five, six hundred yards away. This area was frequented by them. It would be ironic to escape one nightmare predator only to be eaten by a different one.

None appeared.

Were Navarre and Vanek... and Philippe still alive? She couldn't think straight. The pain was excruciating.

Navarre was so intensely focused that he misjudged the current.

The pod had a sentient quality to it both men had underestimated—it was *waiting*.

Navarre took careful aim... then glanced down as he felt a pressure on his thigh. He had just enough time to register it was a translucent tentacle before the razor-sharp chitinous hooks tore into him.

Navarre screamed, twisting around in agony. The rifle swung backward and cracked Vanek on the side of the head. If it had been above water, the clip would have bashed his skull in. Instead, he blacked out.

When he opened his eyes, he saw something large floating in his light beam: the remains of a decapitated head. Even with the lower jaw gone and most of the left side of the face, he was able to recognize the French aquanaut, the bloodless remaining face fish-white, partial teeth appearing to scream. One eyeball still hung connected by its optical nerve stalk like some kind of gruesome cat's toy.

Vanek gagged in his rebreather.

Dan... where was Dan? And the others?

Do you really think she survived? What in the hell were any of you thinking? Did you figure that mutilated yacht hull was just a joke?

He tried to get his bearings. The pressure of the water was oppressive, the air thick in his rebreather. He felt his pulse racing.

Don't panic!

Followed by: *why in the hell not? You fool, you're going to die down here...*

Something in the beam of his light caught his attention—lying in the sand near the pod.

The ASM-DT assault rifle!

He worked his flippers, increasingly aware how out of shape his legs were. To the right he absently noted a dark area where the hull had been ruptured. As he closed on the rifle, his hand reached out…

... with no warning he felt himself snatched, yanked sideways. His muffled scream filled the rebreather, sending a flurry of bubbles upwards.

Grotesque, rope-like tentacles had seized his legs and were pulling him into the pod, his flailing flashlight revealing a hideous opening. Something snagged his wrist painfully, and he pulled instinctively as he kicked his flippers hard as he could. Bubbles erupted everywhere. Metal thumped hard into his head, causing him to see stars, even as he was pulled through the opening he realized: the gun! He had it by the strap.

He jerked it toward him as he was pulled inside, screaming. As he was drawn down into the strange opening, which went down beneath the hull of the ship and into the space infinitely more terrifying, the gun came with him. He pulled it close, trying to shut out not just the bizarre cocoon-like pod he was entering, but the insidious thoughts probing his mind like

[filaments]

obscene slithering appendages... *lickingslicingclickingcaressingripping…*

Vanek had always had a latent fear of death, a fear of emptiness, a fear of the void, but this was far, far worse. What he was seeing/experiencing inside this alien womb was a corruption, a seething blot staining every atom and cell of his existence.

With it was the sounds: an overall ambient one that sounded like mucus (pus) expanding and contracting, accompanied by mechanical, insectoid clicks and an escaping hiss, as if the space was a hideous robot insect fused with a dying snake.

Sounds that created an awful, resonating response in his nervous system.

He went beyond screaming, slipping into a tortured paralysis.

He was inside a pod/spaceship, but nothing the limits of his mind could translate. It was filled with a kind of amniotic fluid, and (silver-blue) lights, and the part of his mind still processing logic interpreted it as an organic *skin,* that existed not just in this dimension but another. Perhaps several. Even his vision a strange quality to it, like gazing at a dimly lit space through a prism.

The thing that dwelt in it was difficult to articulate; there was a sense of squirming, writhing forms like giant clusters of blue-black maggots/ringworms. He sensed something else: the creature out there was *linked*, connected in some symbiotic fashion the way giant tube worms were connected to their sheathes. Except the creature in this pod could separate for short periods and mutate itself to feed... or *retrieve*... what? He sensed it inside himself: *fear*—or the peculiar flavor electromagnetic activity generated by it. The way certain insects were drawn to or repelled by specific scents or sounds.

Or both.

Perhaps what he was experiencing inside was the scent *and* sound of fear being fed on.

Not exact, but *close enough for government work,* as Vanek's father used to say.

Another thing became evident in his current stasis; it was probing but not consuming him—an exquisitely painful sensation as the filaments invaded through the wetsuit to his skin and muscles... his nerves.

Like floating in a parasitic embryonic state of agony.

He was being *tasted.*

Why?

Because there was something familiar to it inside of him. Connected to him.

He'd sensed that back in the bunker when he'd touched his grandfather's corpse. More than that, though: it was feeding off his fears and anxieties the way a connoisseur would savor the sip of a particularly fine wine or delicacy.

That by itself felt obscene.

Through the odd glimmer of sound and light of the claustrophobic space, his brain registered a dull black cylinder embedded in the wall below him. He shifted himself to get closer, the movement itself causing agony. Despite the prismed quality of everything he was seeing, he was able to read the marking on the side:

U.S. MK 15 Torpedo

He sensed something else too: the creature was approaching. The lights embedded in the organic material of the ship pulsed brighter.

Vanek had an idea. The angle between the torpedo and the shattered hull was almost right. Navarre's C2 was on the bulkhead above it. But he had to get out of this trap. Quickly.

Focus seemed impossible—the horror of what was happening kept pushing him to the brink of insanity.

And yet, a tiny part of his consciousness continued to fight.

Rally!

It was like a million insidious maggots were squirming through his thoughts.

Think!

... the chair!

He seized at it like a lifeline.

The goddamn chair! What about it!??

Not *it*... but a thought. A reaction... a…

Dan, thinking of Dan, sex, death... revulsion... the horror... and then:

he *blinked.*

Not his eyes: his mind.

For a split second his thoughts—his entire nervous system—went blank…

... and became instantly flooded with white light. It acted like a shield, cloaking his mind and deflecting any (fear) trying to penetrate it.

Every invasive connection the pod had with him recoiled. He acted fast: grabbing the handle of the assault rifle, he yanked the release on the emergency float bag with his free hand and shot upwards.

As he did, he flipped the safety and started firing downward. If this worked, he would rocket straight up to the surface and most likely die from the lack of decompression—but it was better than this.

Vanek shot out of the turret ring, his tank ricocheting off the edge with a clang that sent him tumbling... into the remaining tentacles of the mutilated host creature. It seized him instantly in a spinning grab, like a giant spider (or squid) pouncing on its prey.

For a brief instant the creature morphed and reduced itself to an approximation of its natural state: a writhing mass of mangled, wormlike appendages, its tumorous spray of silver-blue eyes flaring, the chitinous ring of teeth pulsing wider in anticipation. The metallic, alien subsonic sounds reaching a fevered pitch.

His existence reduced itself to milliseconds…

The muffled *crump* registered briefly. Most of the shockwave as the forward hull of the destroyer exploded was absorbed by the pulsing body sac of the creature, causing its glittering blue-black blood to erupt outward in streaming tendrils. A series of secondary explosions—from the C2 and possibly from the destroyer's magazine—erupted further back along the hull, tearing it loose from where it was wedged at the top crevasse of the Hyborian Canyon ripping out the remaining parts of the alien ship that had fused with it.

With a groan of metal, the remains of the two vessels slid down the canyon in an undersea avalanche, obscured by roiling sand and debris, muted flashes appearing as secondary armaments detonated.

Vanek realized the thing was trying to free itself of him as they tumbled away in the shockwave. The sonic clicking/scissoring sound had reached a crescendo that threatened to burst his eardrums. Its damaged tentacles writhed frantically, the creature shuddering in its death throes.

Vanek emptied the remainder of the clip, firing wildly. His facemask was sporting several cracks, further obscuring his vision and something seemed to be wrong with his supply—the rebreather hose had torn out, flailing bubbles everywhere. The explosion had compressed all the air out of his lungs and he was fighting to get air when seawater filled his mouth.

Vanek knew he was going to die—the inflated air bag was yanking him and the creature toward the surface. He couldn't reach the air bag... but he saw the thing's row of eyes a few feet away…

With all his remaining strength he rammed the rifle with its attached combat knife at it.

It plunged in, his hand and arm going numb from the electromagnetic current being released: the shock jolted his heart and in an explosion of its death throes, the creature broke loose and shot off into the gloom like a rocket.

Vanek felt his limbs go slack, his heart palpitating as his vision began to dim.

I'm floating, he thought vaguely, *so this is what it's like to die underwater... it's not so bad Michelle... I'm coming…*

39. ESCAPE

The creature was wounded, confused and for lack of a better word, *alarmed.*

In all its existence, nothing like this had ever happened.

Its alien thought processes understood something was considerably wrong with itself and by default, it began cycling rapidly in and out of its nearest dimension to draw energy. This last form it had snatched had something that repulsed it—with shocking strength. Even more confusing was the *other*, emitting signals. It shot up after it, momentarily expanding as it powered up.

There was a clear sense of urgency, a need to find a host.

A need to *transfer*.

Gorecki was sitting in the back of *Catch-22*, reading the latest edition of 'Hamptons Star' when a massive *thud* hit the underside of the boat, jolting him out of his seat and sending his glass of iced tea flying.

"*Skurwysyn*!" he yelled as he landed on the deck. It felt like the yacht had been rammed by a whale. He jumped up to see a ripple in the surface speeding northward.

Toward the shore.

Even worse—he heard the telltale gurgle of water entering below.

40. DITCH PLAINS & A DAY AT THE BEACH

Jerry Logan cut his surfboard at the last minute, deciding the wave wasn't worth it. Still, it was an *epic* surfing day. For Montauk at least. The rollers were good and energetic from the previous day's storm, the sun was bright, he was alive, young, and the world was young with him.

Roughly two dozen surfers were out at Ditch Plains with him including Dave Ducatti, one of the old pros (and Logan's #1 bro). Ducatti was further out, patiently waiting for a really good one while the *groms*—overeager newbies—were jumping at anything.

Logan figured he'd chill and paddle over to Ducatti and get his take on the afternoon forecast. Logan had a BBQ over at Greenport on the North Fork but would blow it off if the surfing stayed good. It'd been a shitty week overall and damned if he would miss a good roll.

Compact and muscled, Logan paddled effortlessly into deeper water with bold, confident strokes, the sunlight glistening off his tanned body.

Twenty yards further and he spotted Ducatti raising his nose like a bloodhound picking up the scent. A moment later he saw it: a wide rolling wave coming in, rising with the powerful swell the really promising ones have. Propping up on his hands, he saw it was better than he'd hoped, a seven to ten-foot *nug*, maybe more.

He grinned.

Awesome!

Following Ducatti's cue, he started paddling himself into position to approach from the left shoulder.

There was something odd about Ducatti's posture, though. For one thing he was shielding his eyes with his hand, as if seeing something truly incredible, his salt-and-pepper hair flailing in the breeze.

The wave gained speed.

Logan paddled another ten yards then came about, glancing left. What he saw was even stranger—Ducatti was paddling furiously *away* from the wave toward the east, and there was a lot of agitation in the water. It made him think of flailing eels.

Big ones.

Damn, dude! he thought. *It's not a shark or anything.*

Something dark and glistening struck out of the water faster than his eye could follow. It was like an optical illusion: one moment Ducatti's lower leg was there, then next, *presto,* the lower two thirds were *gone.*

Subtracted.

If there was any doubt, Ducatti screamed. A shrill, high scream that rattled Logan more than anything. And the blood from his severed femoral artery shot up into the morning sun in a brilliant red fan.

Ducatti rolled on his board and tried to kick with his remaining leg, but the fight was short lived—a sickle-like appendage flicked out of the water and sliced through his left arm and most of his head.

Logan didn't wait to see more. He noted the dark, writhing forms coming toward him with the building crest of the wave and paddled as hard as he could, trying to catch the shoulder of it at an oblique angle where the speed would be the best.

If he couldn't out-swim whatever it was, maybe he could *out-surf* it.

He felt the surge under his board and got up into a crouch, ignoring the fact he was already peeing in his swimming trunks, his heart hammering away in his chest.

Here it comes!

The wave picked him up and he began to cut it with his board, right, left, right, left. He could see the things in the sea green water, writhing, flailing. One thumped the underside of his board, nearly toppling him. Nearby, another surfer caught the wave but was pulled under, his board shooting through the air and doing a spinning tumble, like some oversized fish.

Logan compensated and cut deeper into the pipe, picking up speed. He was terrified and yet undeniably excited.

"Fuck-you!" he screamed as he sped toward the beach. "I'll so out-surf you, motherfucker!"

He believed it, too. A tentacle shot out of the water and he flicked his board behind it, still shouting. Several more thumps but now he was in the sweet spot in the pipe, the board going like a rocket.

"*Kowabunga*!" he screamed, a surfer-warrior cry. There was a cold sting on his ankle and he glanced down in surprise, realizing his foot was half-severed. Even as he lost his balance, another appendage shot out and sliced through most of his abdomen like a razor through butter.

The wave crested over him as he was pulled into it in a spray of blood and gore.

His last thoughts as his head entered the water was of the distant screams coming from the beach.

Then: nothing.

Lana James rolled her eyes and reapplied her lip gloss, the morning sun glinting off her smartphone (set to 'selfie') and causing her to wince. Sixteen, strikingly attractive and skin a hue of rich ebony, she looked more like a young model ready to hit a pricey midtown nightclub with a pool than the open expanse of Montauk's beaches. Her best friend, Stacy Edwards—skin as white as Lana's was black—sat next to her texting her boyfriend (or 'boy-fling', as Lana pegged him) while ignoring her younger brother Scotty, who had been auditioning for *World's Biggest Dweeb* by attempting any irritating antic his fourteen-year-old-mind could concoct to get their attention.

Both girls had spent the better part of an hour-and-a-half getting their make-up on (much to the exasperation of Stacy's mom and dad) before they were ready to put in an appearance on the beach off Surfside Avenue, where the Edwards family had rented a house for two weeks.

It was early, but the Edwards wanted to get in some beach time before heading to Shelter Island for lunch. Lana's parents were coming in from Queens on the evening train—her mother ran a *chichi* Jamaican restaurant there—and Mrs. Edwards had worked out a detailed itinerary before then.

They'd only been there twenty minutes but already the girls were bored. Next to her, Lana had a hardcover copy of Michelle Obama's new book *Becoming* which *was* interesting, but she quickly realized reading at the beach wasn't quite her thing, despite Mrs. Edwards' insistence it was *exactly* what all the Edwards family did.

"Let's go for a walk," Lana said, a smile creeping into the side of her mouth.

"Where?" Stacy asked, not looking up from her texting.

"Up the beach. Ditch Plains is up there. And all those surfer hunks."

"What*ever*."

Lana dropped her phone into her purse and stood up. Her wide-brimmed sun hat snapped in the breeze, "You're such a drip!"

"Nice try, Hunty." She looked up as Lana gave her 'the look'. Hitting *send,* she stood up too. "Oh, all right."

"Where you girls going?" Mrs. Edwards asked from under her umbrella nearby. A thin, dark-eyed woman in her mid-forties, she would have appeared beautiful if it wasn't for the pinched, worry-wort expression that had settled into her face in recent years. Nearly every word out of her mouth was laced with suspicion.

"Just for a walk," Stacey snapped back.

"Don't go too far, stay in sight."

"*Sure* mom." The 'what*ever'* hung unspoken.

"I *mean* it, young ladies. We're heading to lunch in an hour!"

Stacey flashed her an indulgent smile and the two of them sauntered off, heading east toward Ditch Plains.

Mrs. Edwards turned to her husband, who was reading the Wall Street Journal.

"Well?"

"They'll be fine," Mr. Edwards said, keeping his nose buried in the paper.

"You *always* say that. About everything." She made a face and did a bad imitation of him, "*Everything's fine.*"

Scotty leaped up, brandishing his toy light saber. It was the same blue as Finn's, his favorite Star Wars character. He was obsessed with the idea of being a Storm Trooper-turned-hero.

"I'm going to cool my feet!" he announced, not waiting for a response.

"Not past your knees—the surf is too rough! And don't get that saber wet! It cost a fortune!" his mother yelled.

"Promise!" he shouted back.

A half a mile or so up the beach, the girls came to a stop. To their left the bluffs overlooking the ocean were more pronounced, while the sand had given way to well-worn pebbles. Neither of which caused the girls to stop.

There wasn't anyone at the beach.

At least no-one alive.

Body parts, however, were in abundance, scattered near the destroyed surf boards that had washed up.

And something else too: something near them in the water, flailing. Like a thousand tentacles. Spanning roughly ten yards.

The two girls stood frozen, neither able to process this horrifying tableau. From far off—maybe another county or state as far as they were concerned—came the wail of approaching sirens. From the direction they had come, several Southampton Marine Patrol vehicles were racing up the beach, lights flashing.

Lana let out a whimper as the next wave receded, the hissing *glissando* of the water rolling along the rocks counterpointed by the strange scissoring sounds coming from whatever it was lurking in the surf. She watched, horrified, as several body parts—*human* parts—tumbled along with the receding water, one severed hand snatched away by one of the tentacles.

Next to her, Stacey attempted to scream but managed only a strangled cry.

As if in response, the massive thing in the surf surged toward them, more tentacles flailing out of the waves. A particularly large one whipped out in an arc.

"Arghh!" Scotty cried as he leapt in front of the two girls, brandishing his light saber. It was one of the top-of-the-line Spectrum ones his father had gotten him for his birthday. It even had the sound effect to go with it.

Scotty saw himself as Finn fighting Kylo Ren in *The Force Awakens*, part of his fantasy of saving 'Princess' Lana (whom he had a secret crush on). He was so caught in the moment he didn't see the carnage, he simply acted.

Amazingly, he parried the tentacle.

A second one shot out and he parried that one too, twisting his body in one of his many practiced Jedi moves. He didn't see the third one whipping around from the right, about to impale him, though his sister did.

It never struck.

The thing in the ocean—whatever it was—yanked itself back into the surf as if electrified, its receding mass causing the incoming waves to erupt into the air. The suction of air and water displacement nearly pulled all three of them in, though Scotty was able to dig his heels in, saber over his head, both girls grabbing his shoulders reflexively.

Whatever it was, it was gone.

Scotty looked sideways over his shoulder at Lana, who glanced alternately at the water and him in disbelief. He put on his best Han Solo smile, then spotted the severed head rolling on the water a dozen feet away.

The smile vanished as he collapsed in a dead faint.

Despite the intake, it was losing energy too fast. It was always this way before it went into hibernation, but with injuries, the process was accelerating.

Though it had never done this before it sensed this time was different. The pod was gone. It could no longer sense it.

It needed to transfer to a new host. Not here, these specimens weren't *right*... somewhere else.

Now.

41. TO LIVE AND LIVE YET AGAIN

Jax hung on as long as he could, but he'd never been the strongest willed in his family. His mother had always called him the 'runt of the litter' and never failed to remind him that if it wasn't for her protective wing, he would have died after childbirth, like the mewling little cubs on those awful BBC nature shows she watched obsessively. The cub that gets eaten alive by the eagle or hawk or wolf.

Jax was weak, though, inside and out.

After a space, he slid off the board he'd been holding and let himself slide down into the dark. Trembling.

That was when the real fun began.

His slowing heart continued to beat for a minute as he floated down, arms splayed out as he sank.

The last breath seeped out of his mouth in a flurry of bubbles.

He didn't see the amorphous shape speeding toward him from the dark, the thing that once looked squid like but was now little more than a torn shadow, flitting through the ocean at incredible speed.

It hit him like a gossamer blanket, wrapping him in an inky cocoon, encasing the contours of his face as one particular part—an approximation of an egg sac—burst down his mouth and filled him with its writhing alien seed.

A short interval later, his eyes snapped open, glowing iridescent silver-blue.

Vanek was aware of something forcing itself into his mouth. His first response was to fight. Then he felt his shoulder being pinched and opening his eyes, was shocked to see Dan's masked face inches from his own.

He realized she'd pushed his back-up regulator into his mouth and was holding on to him as they floated in the absinthe green ocean. From the light and pressure, it was apparent they were still quite deep.

She tapped her dive watch and held up four fingers in front of his mask, then pointed upwards.

Four minutes.

Vanek nodded.

The mixture coming through his regulator was still thick, but after blacking out, his body apparently defaulted to its own rhythm, the auto-default 'survive' setting kicked-in all by itself.

Funny how it does that.

The pain in his body and limbs seemed distant and numb, like something happening to someone else floating in an isolation tank. Even the horrifying experience of that creature and its pod was already taking on the shadowy outlines of a passing nightmare. The burbling of escaping air, the steady hiss of his breath, the dreamy sounds of the ocean all acted as a balm.

Time had an elastic quality to it. He wondered if he was a suffering from narcosis. When Dan tapped him again, the four minutes had passed: she was making an 'okay' signal and jerked her finger upward several times.

For the first time in what seemed an eternity, Vanek looked up toward the surface over a hundred feet above him, to the sun-shimmering waves.

Catch-22 sat low in the water, but stubbornly refused to sink, due in part to the extra flotation blocks Gorecki had installed during an overhaul the year previous. He perched himself at the rail of the nearly submerged stern deck, life vest on, searching the waves for any sign of survivors. It had been thirty minutes since everyone had dropped over the side, and ten since he'd seen the eruption of bubbles and debris on the surface, neither which he took as a good sign.

Fortunately, the engines were still working, though the pumps were fighting a losing battle.

Gorecki was about to give up. The waves were already becoming choppy, and the squall was moving in fast. The sun dimmed intermittently behind the fast-moving clouds. His best bet he decided, was to motor the damaged boat north until it sank, as that would put him closer to the *Robert D. Ballard*, which the Coast Guard dispatcher informed him was the closest emergency vessel in proximity to respond and was in fact on its way already.

Gorecki had just taken a couple of sloshing steps toward the pilot house ladder when he heard a gasp and cry from behind him. He spun around.

A few yards away, Dan broke the surface, her arm around Vanek in a classic life-saving hold.

"*Jasna cholera*!" he exclaimed: *Holy shit!*

Dan couldn't even find the strength to ask for help. She simply hauled Vanek with her toward the boat, grabbing the gaff hook Gorecki extended out to them.

It was rough work manhandling the two of them on board, with the heavy scuba equipment, but Gorecki did it with the same expediency and strength he hauled fishing nets with.

"What happened!?" he asked, helping them out of the tanks. Vanek looked half-unconscious, his eyes unfocused. "Arnaud? The other divers?"

Dan shook her head. "They didn't make it. What happened to the boat?"

"Something hit us. *Big* something. She's still afloat, but I don't know how long." He helped pull Vanek's head cap off and holding his jaw, looked at him this way and that. "He'll live. Let's get him to the upper deck. Engines are still working. Hull is impacted but salvageable. I'm going to head us back toward shore—Coast Guard said NOAA ship on the way to intercept but we're running out of time. What was that thing? Is it still down there?"

"No," Dan said. "I mean, I'm pretty sure it's dead. But I don't want to wait around either."

"I can agree with that," Gorecki replied. "What's with your leg? You're bleeding."

She looked down and saw with horror the bag she'd tied it off with was dripping blood. She started to undo it and saw how badly the suit and skin had been flailed.

"I'll be fine," she said, her voice growing thick. Her eyes rolled up and she passed out.

Gorecki carried the two of them to the upper deck and got the boat motoring slowly toward north. If there was any uncertainty in his thoughts, it wasn't betrayed by the granite set of his features. He looked like a man determined to do one thing and one thing only: get this ship and its two injured passengers to safety as expediently as possible.

Thirty miles away, Aduba, the 'High Priestess' was standing in the surf, arms outstretched in a 'vee', as if welcoming the coming storm. Behind her on the beach, her odd group of followers mimicked her pose, eyes closed and fluttering as if in ecstasy. Near them someone had set up an iPhone with a Bluetooth sound cube, which blasted 'Age of Aquarius' omnidirectionally.

Aduba's eyes were rolled back so only the whites showed. To her right stood Om, a folded, dull gray pad with odd markings painted on it held aloft in his hands like an offering. The pad was a portable version of the 'BeamX', an electromagnetic energy regulator she borrowed from her massage therapist the year previous and never returned. A head mounted accessory version was centered on her forehead, its circular generator placed where her 'third eye' would be.

She had been babbling in her 'tongues' for quite a few minutes now, long enough that Om was stealing glances at her, wondering where this was all going. She was in a fever pitch. The surf boomed and hissed, sending sheets of foam around her legs, while her chiffon robes rippled in the stiffening breeze. The white paint on her face glistened with drops of water.

"*Hubba kuzza*!" she chanted. "The age is upon us! Enlightenment is here... now! *Ngaarifu ballahuzzah*! To me!!! To meeee!!!!!"

Her voice reached a screaming crescendo, snatched away by the breeze.

Om tried to concentrate, but he was hungry and wondering when they were going to break for lunch.

Then he heard someone behind them gasp.

He opened his eyes and was shocked to see a skinny young black man struggling out of the waves. With glowing, silver-blue eyes. Impossible, yet there it was. Part of him never really believed in Aduba's 'vision', but went along with it mostly out of wishful thinking, but now... this was an honest-to-God otherworldly event, just like she'd prophesied.

Aduba smiled, her eyes still rolled white behind her sunglasses.

"The messenger has come! The goddess has heard!" she said, rushing into the water to help him. "*Brazza*, *brazza*!"

Jax, soaking wet, crawled up to her, his broken leg dangling. As he did, his mouth opened, revealing the black, squirming mass inside. Om sensed something terrible about to happen but was too timid to do anything about it. He always had been.

He stood by like an idiot bystander, sloe-eyed, as Jax put his mouth over Aduba's as if in an erotic kiss. Only Om saw Aduba shudder like she was having a seizure, her arms dropping to her sides and shaking, as Jax conveyed his horrific cargo into this new and ample-sized host.

It was as if all the essence sucked itself out of Jax, while Aduba seemed to expand slightly, as if ingesting a particularly large meal. Jax's body fell away like a fish-white husk, collapsing into the surf. When Aduba turned to her followers, she was grinning and behind the bug-eye sunglasses were two bright points of silver-blue light.

"Follow me," she said, her voice wet and slurry. "Our sacred temple awaits."

Scarpia had no idea how much time had passed when he came to and was more focused on the amazing fact that he was still alive at all. He still hung onto the flotation donut and his teeth were chattering from being in the water too long. Even worse, the waves were choppier and he could see the telltale signs of a squall line moving in.

On the plus side, it felt like whatever attack he'd experienced earlier had passed—his lower body was numb from exposure, but he found he could still kick his legs. Of *Sea Bitch* or anything else there was no sign—just endless water.

Not even a single damn…

The distinct rumble of an approaching boat caught his ear.

Spinning about, he saw a classic fishing boat forty yards away, low in the water and laboring along, but a boat nonetheless!

"Help!" Scarpia shouted and waved his arms.

For a moment he thought they would just motor past, but to his relief he saw the boat veer towards him.

Gorecki threw him a line as he slowed alongside, wondering how many others he'd pull out of the ocean before the day was over. This one looked like a tough customer, one of the fishermen he thought—vaguely familiar.

Probably seen him around the docks, or in town, maybe.

"Lose your boat?" he asked as he helped the man over the stern.

"Yeah," Scarpia said. "Something rammed us a short while ago. My trawler went down with all hands." He looked at the water six inches deep in the stern and nodded. "What happened to you?"

"Rammed too. Must be contagious today." He threw Scarpia a towel. "Lucky for you I saw you! I got two injured passengers. Taking on water, but Coast Guard has a ship coming to meet us. What did you say the name of your boat was?"

Scarpia stood up, running the towel over his head. The friendly smile he'd put on faded. "I didn't." He pulled the .50 out of his waistband and in one fluid motion worked the slide and pointed it at Gorecki's head. "And we're not going anywhere near any fucking Coast Guard vessel."

Gorecki put his hands up. "Whoa, mister! I'm just trying to help!"

"You can help by turning this tub in a different direction."

Gorecki shook his head. "Didn't you hear me? The hull is damaged. I'm taking on water, and I have two injured passengers. There's a squall coming. We'll just sink."

"Too bad for you. Flotation raft on board?"

"Yes, but…"

He was interrupted by the report of the gun. The bullet lodged in the cabin wall behind him.

"I really hate that word '*but'*. Next bullet goes in your head. Where's the fucking raft?"

"Up here," another voice said.

Scarpia glanced up to see Vanek at the back of the pilot's cabin, the ASM-DT assault rifle raised to his shoulder. Pointed down at Scarpia.

Recognition crossed Scarpia's face. "Hah! You're that Navy history pussy. Better put that thing away before you get hurt." He stepped forward, the gun still aimed at Gorecki's head. The eyes staring up at Vanek looked dead and mean.

"*One more step, Mr. Hands, and I'll blow your brains out,*" Vanek said quietly, quoting the classic 'Treasure Island' line. Strangely, he felt utterly calm, cold even. Despite the fact he was holding a loaded weapon at another human being. Not even a quaver in his fingertip.

Scarpia let out a laugh. Then he flicked the Desert Eagle upward and fired.

The retort of the assault rifle out of water was louder than Vanek expected. He fired three times in succession, unaware of the slug that plucked at his shoulder. The three flechettes punched through Scarpia's chest and clean out the other side. Scarpia staggered backward and looked down, brow furrowed, like a man grappling with a particularly complex math equation. He tried to raise the pistol again.

Vanek fired once more.

The flechette went right through his forehead and blew out the back of his skull.

Scarpia staggered backward and did an ungainly backflip off the stern of the boat.

Vanek heard a gasp and saw Dan was standing just behind him, holding herself up by the frame of the cabin. Her eyes, bloodshot with fever, looked at Scarpia's spread-eagled body floating in the choppy waves, back at Vanek, then back to the body.

As they watched, a black fin broke the surface of the water—an orca. A moment later Scarpia's corpse disappeared beneath the waves.

Vanek looked at the gun in his hands as if seeing it for the first time. It felt ugly and heavy in his hands. After a moment contemplating it, he chucked it over the side.

The three of them stood still a minute, then Gorecki clambered up to the pilot house and clapped Vanek on the opposite shoulder where the bullet had nicked him. He stared him in the eye.

"*Thanks*. I remember that man. You did the world a favor."

A *squonk* of an air horn interrupted any further discussion. Bearing down on them was a medium-sized ship painted white. Vanek had no idea how much the other vessel's crew had seen, though with the *Catch-22* facing at them head-on there was a chance it wasn't much.

The ship slowed and veered as it came up on their port bow, revealing the large blue NOAA logo and *R 377* identification letters on the hull.

"Ahoy there!" a voice called from the deck above. "Did someone radio for help?"

"We could use a lift, if you're offering!" Gorecki shouted back.

Vanek sat back on one of the fixed deck stools in the pilot house, feeling exhaustion overtake him. It seemed incredible any of them were still alive, but they were.

Dan sat next to him, inspecting his shoulder.

He looked up as Gorecki put a plastic cup in his hand, and one in Dan's. Vanek caught the strong whiff of brandy. Where'd he'd conjured it up from was a mystery.

"A toast!" he said, raising the silver flask in his hand, answering Vanek's question. "To live... and live again!"

42. CASE CLOSED

Gavin was still sitting in his SUV an hour later when his cell phone rang.

It was an unknown number. Gavin wasn't surprised when he answered it, it was his good friend Dave on the other end.

"Hi Chuck! How's it *hanging*?"

Gavin bristled. The fake cheeriness and wet gravelly voice were too much. "What's up?" he replied, cutting to the chase.

"What, no witty banter this morning? Come on, my good friend. It's an excellent day in Montauk!" When Gavin didn't reply Dave went on, "There's been a change in plans. Meet us over at Camp Hero. 'Bunker 18'. And make absolutely sure William Vanek and Daniel Cheung are with you, understood?"

"But I still don't have the—"

"No need to worry about that. You'll get your final payment. See you in fifteen minutes."

The line went dead.

Gavin frowned. This wasn't part of the plan.

A large vessel coming into the Coast Guard dock caught his attention. He'd sat there listening to his short wave tuned to the Coast Guard channel, trying to puzzle out what the hell had happened out there. No word on Scarpia and his boat, but plenty on *Catch-22* and its three survivors. A recovery was underway for Gorecki's boat which was temporarily abandoned after the NOAA flagship *Robert D. Ballard* had gotten everyone off it. The Coast Guard cutter was circling the wallowing fishing vessel as it was a shipping hazard, waiting for the *Sea Tow* salvage ship to arrive.

There had been another report of a young woman who'd apparently swam ashore—something involving murder and illegal dumping.

What the hell happened out there? Who had survived? And why the sudden change of plans with Dave?

Little red flags were popping up in his mind.

He got the distinct feeling Dave was tying up loose ends and that one Carl Gavin might be near the top of that list. Either way, it wouldn't hurt to have a little padding for insurance. He fired up the Ford and fishtailed out of the parking lot.

His ONR I.D. got him past the security gate at the Coast Guard. When Gavin came strutting up the gangplank, he was shocked to see that of the seven who went out on *Catch-22,* only three remained.

Gorecki had to be all but manhandled off his boat when the *Robert D. Ballard* arrived. Commander Hopper had boated over on the rescue launch to assess it personally and gave him a direct order. She had one person now in need of medical attention and the weather was worsening.

Only when Gorecki saw the Coast Guard cutter approaching did he agree to leave his boat, though he looked as stricken as a father abandoning his child when he finally did.

Hopper assured him every effort would be made to tow his vessel safely back to the harbor.

Down in the medical treatment room their physician, Doctor Healey, did what he could to bandage up Dan's thigh and the wound on her ankle, which to everyone's puzzlement was already radiating the telltale red lines of infection it.

"Doesn't make sense," Dr. Healey muttered. "The seawater should have kept the wound disinfected, at least slowed down any rate of infection."

"What's going on?" Vanek asked. Once aboard with a stiff cup of coffee in hand, he'd shaken off whatever remained of the stupor he'd been in. Still, it felt like everything was still tilting off the rails.

"She's running a mild fever. The wounds appear to be infected already, though. Doesn't make sense. What did this to her, by the way? Did you witness it?"

Vanek considered before answering.

Before Vanek could respond, Dan started mumbling.

The doctor perked up. 'What did she just say? She just said something about 'glowing eyes', didn't she?"

Vanek looked at the doctor. "Honestly, I don't really know. Some kind of mutant sea creature I've never seen before."

That much was true, at least.

Dr. Healey frowned. "Was she symptomatic before the dive? Is it possible she had something already?"

"No," Vanek replied. "And whatever was down there, it's dead or dying. Can't you give her antibiotics?"

"I gave her a shot of doxycycline already. And tetanus. I'd recommend getting her to a hospital and on I.V. antibiotics for three days."

Vanek rubbed his temples. He didn't feel right about any of this.

Reinhardt poked his head in the door. "Commander Hopper's respects. We'll be docking in fifteen minutes. Southampton already has an ambulance waiting."

Five minutes later, Vanek stood on the foredeck. He needed to clear his head, and it was one of the few unmanned areas on the ship.

The lighthouse was coming up on their port bow, while on the horizon to the east, Block Island hovered like a mirage.

"She's a friend of yours?" a voice said at his side.

Vanek turned to see Dr. Healey standing next to him.

"Yes. Sort of. Actually, we just met a few days ago." He took a second look and decided she was quite pretty. Blue-blood features, with fine cheekbones and an aristocratic mouth.

"I overheard them talking downstairs. What is it? What's down there?"

"The boogeyman. The abominable sea-monster. Hell, I don't know.

"Do you think it's dead?"

"I thought so. Now I'm not so sure."

She leaned forward into the rail, her face growing serious. "Well, you better *make* sure. *William*?"

That earned her a third look. "Do I know you?"

She gave him a smile, a sardonic one. "No. I'm nobody. But I've read a couple of your books. Recognized you from the liner notes."

He held out his hand. "You have me at a disadvantage, then."

She took it and gave it a firm shake. "Doctor Susan Healey."

"A pleasure to meet you, Doctor. William Vanek. I'm afraid I'm no Captain Ahab, though. And whatever the hell that thing is, I don't know if it can be killed."

She nodded up at the bridge. "Maybe the commander can help?"

Vanek let out his own laugh. "I don't know. The one guy I thought most capable of doing that got taken apart in seconds."

"I hope I'm not interrupting," said a third voice.

Vanek wheeled about. Dan was standing there, leaning on a crutch. He had an urge to hug her, but the expression on her face was distant... *haunted.*

"I don't understand," he said.

"I don't either. The fever broke. Doctor Healey here did wonders with the bandage. It hurts like hell, but I can get around."

Dr. Healey put her hand on Dan's forehead and checked her pulse. "That is odd," she said. "But she does seem better. Heart rate is elevated. You really should be in bed."

Vanek put his hand on her shoulder. "Are you alright?"

"I don't know, Will. I don't know anymore."

With that she leaned into his arms.

The ship was already veering into the entrance of Montauk Harbor. The usual sprinkling of tourists clambered along the beach and stone jetty, though only a handful of boats were heading out, in spite of the bad weather advisory.

The normality of the situation seemed at such odds to what they'd just been through. Vanek doubted if he would ever view things the same way again.

The operations officer approached. "We have an EMT and ambulance waiting to meet us at the dock," Mr. Neville said.

"I think we'll be fine," Dan said, giving him a polite smile. "I'm sure I can find my way to hospital once we're ashore."

Neville looked uncertain, but he didn't press the issue. He couldn't force a non-crew member to have medical care.

As the ship maneuvered its way to the Star Island dock in front of the Coast Guard Station, Vanek got another surprise: Carl Gavin was waiting for them.

"Come on, I'll give the two of you a lift," he said briskly as they stepped off the gangway. "Something incredible has come up since you've been out there."

Vanek was a little thrown off. "Carl, we've just been through—"

"Never mind that!" Gavin cut him off. Vanek had never seen him behave so rudely.

"I need the two of you, *now*," Gavin said, motioning for them to follow.

Vanek dug his heels in. "Hold on a second. What the hell is going on?"

"Get in the truck and I'll fill you in."

As the four of them piled into Gavin's Ford, Vanek caught the sound of sirens in the distance.

Lots of them.

Once off Star Island, Gavin took off down West Lake Drive at twice the speed limit. When he swerved off onto the Old West Lake Drive, Vanek, riding shotgun, spoke up.

"Chuck, the house is *that* way."

"I *know* where it is, Bill. But it'll wait. We've got more pressing business."

"Where?" Vanek asked, though he had a sinking feeling he knew the answer already.

"'Bunker 18'. You wanted answers? You're going to get them."

Vanek thought about his last visit there with Dan. "I think we've had all the answers we need from there, Chuck. What the hell is going on?"

Gavin pulled out a .357 magnum from a shoulder holster.

"Shut up, Bill. Just shut the hell up."

"Jesus, Chuck, what, are you going to shoot me?"

Gavin didn't answer. He gave Vanek a cold, dead look, and kept driving.

They hooked onto Route 27 in a skid, Gavin nearly creaming a van full of Southeast Asians heading for the lighthouse. They careened off the road onto the shoulder in a cloud of sand, horn blaring. Gavin skidded but corrected the SUV expertly, straightening out and flooring the gas pedal.

Vanek wondered if he should make a move and decided against it. Too many things could go wrong and Dan was in the back seat.

He'd already been to hell and back and the day wasn't over yet.

As they headed east, he glanced in the side view mirror and saw a cluster of emergency vehicle lights. For a brief moment he wondered if they might come to their rescue, then saw them veer off toward Ditch Plains.

They shot up the rise toward the lighthouse, the squall now plucking cats paws off the waves, the thickening clouds taking on an ominous, bruised color.

Vanek's spirits sank even further.

There was another surprise when they arrived at Camp Hero: a roadblock. An unmarked black SUV was parked nearby and outside the guardhouse were two men in black windbreakers, body armor and assault rifles. At first, Vance thought they were Homeland Security but then realized the patches were off.

He wasn't an expert on such things, but they looked fake—like they were glued on, not sewn.

One guard stepped forward, Heckler & Koch automatic rifle at the ready. Gavin rolled down the window.

"I'm expected."

"Carl Gavin," the guard said. It wasn't a question. He leaned in and looked at each of them, his emotionless gaze reminding Vanek of the *Terminator*. His eyes rested on Vanek longer than the rest. Then stepped back. "Follow the guards," he said, nodding them onward.

Gavin glanced out and saw there were a series of armed guards at intervals the whole way in.

This was a major operation.

This time there wasn't any trick to getting to the bunker—the path looked like it had been plowed through by a bulldozer. Armed guards stood around the entrance tube, which had been cleared back a dozen feet. Nearby, an industrial-sized gas generator had been set up with power cables running over the lip.

Overhead the clouds continued to swirl as if Montauk had become the epicenter of a fluke storm system.

Or the center of something much, much worse, Vanek thought, connecting what happened out at the wreck to their last visit to the Bunker. His heart began to pound.

Fright or flight response. In overdrive.

Dan was eyeing the entrance like it was the last place on the planet she wanted to revisit. Vanek took her hand in his and squeezed it.

"They're waiting for you down below, Mr. Gavin," one of the guards said.

"Ladies first," Gavin said to Dan.

Vanek had no idea what they would encounter going back down there, but what he saw shocked him in a different way. All the debris and skeletons had been cleaned out. There was no trace of the things that had come after them earlier and other than the dented steel doors, no indication they had been there at all. The bulkhead had been completely removed and caged work lights strung along both walls, lending the space the depressed feel of a post-Cold War relic.

They were escorted by several guards back to the main chamber. Vanek had difficulty processing the scale of how quickly the bunker had been transformed—the walls and ceiling were covered in a metallic mesh with a rubberized version covering the floor. The chair and corpse of Vanek's grandfather had been removed and a new chair was in its place.

What in the hell is this? Vanek noted with alarm, *it looks like something out of a science fiction movie!*

The control room had been hastily fixed, with fresh armored glass in the oblong view slot. New cables had been run, and the sensors installed on the chair. Several men in lab coats could be seen milling about in there with what appeared to be jury-rigged consoles. The place was a bizarre mishmash of 1940's and modern technology.

On either side of the chair stood armed guards and a man whose peculiar appearance drew Vanek's attention. He might have been anywhere between fifty-five and seventy, with white papery skin and purplish-red lips. The mouth was effeminate and pursed. The eyebrows were non-existent and the eyes—black and empty as gun-barrels—had a fanatical, wide-open gleam. They seemed to be lined with mascara. With the gray suit tailored to the stocky figure and Fedora hat (with a jaunty yellow feather in the brim), the hideous result made Vanek think of his great aunt playing the Master of Ceremonies in *Cabaret* as Sgt. Joe Friday from *Dragnet.*

The man was singularly repulsive. Even more so when he spoke.

"So nice of you and your friends to join us, Carl," the man said in a wet, slurry voice. The lips quivered with each word. "Particularly you, *William.* I've so genuinely looked forward to thissss."

"*Do I know you?*" Vanek's heart trip hammered in his chest. "What in the hell is this about, Carl?" he said, jaw clenched.

"You wouldn't understand, Will, not in a million years," Gavin replied, not meeting his eye. "You live in a quaint make-believe little academia world of books, articles and ship models. The rest of us earn our coin in reality." He turned to the other man. "Well, I delivered as agreed, *Dave.* Now if you don't mind, settle up and I'll be shoving off."

Dave's lips quivered with amusement.

"Delightful as that prospect may be, my good friend, I can't allow that. Loose ends and all that. But not to worry! I also plan to use you—and the lovely lady here—in the name of science!"

"This is your... *umm*, I'm sorry, what 'science' are we talking about here!?" Dan spoke up, stepping forward.

In response, the guards lowered their H&K assault rifles at her.

Dave let out a tittering noise. "Oh, it's a very *unique* science, my dear. We've been developing a new and improved version of the *Neptune's Reckoning* chair for years, but with only limited success. We located an original prototype. But the technology in 1943 was crude—a simplistic analog capture of what we now call at Breckenridge a 'multidimensional fear matrix'. They thought it could be used as a powerful torture tool for interrogations to extract more reliable intel, or if they could find a means to direct it externally, a tool for demoralizing and even causing enemy soldiers to flee in panic. They were clumsy children playing with nitro. When your grandfather stumbled in as a test subject—they only knew he had contact with something odd and had unusual manifestations occurring around him—they inadvertently set off a disaster. The whole program was shut down and sealed, swept under the carpet."

Vanek was struggling to process all this. What kind of man was such a... *weird thing*?

Dave continued, "Made for some pretty good conspiracy stuff, no? There were rumors... but nothing substantial until a colleague of Carl's started snooping about. That's when I was recruited to step in."

Vanek put his fingers to his temple.

"Fear in the brain is like a sandcastle, did you know that? It's really quite amazing! It can materialize into eleven dimensions: 1D rods, 2D planks, 3D cubes, 4D, 5D, and so on, then just as quickly disintegrate. We can capture that now, *digitally*, and re-map it. *Manipulate* it. Do you have any idea of the ramifications of that? What that can be used for? What it means?"

"Yes. It means you're a certified raving lunatic."

Dave ignored him. "This species of creature we've been dealing with—yes, we know a thing or two about it—is an exceedingly powerful amplification device for *fear*. The matrix it generates can warp reality around it. And it literally feeds off the neuro-hormones generated from the... the *what*, William…?"

"*Amygdala*," Vanek replied.

"*Correct*!" Dave responded, his smile revealing a graveyard of yellowed teeth. "A topic you are well acquainted with. So much more than you suspected! Miss. Danielle Cheung, do you have any idea how valuable the ability to physically control levels of mind-numbing fear would be to the right parties in government? How it can be used against one's enemies? Care to wager a guess?"

"*No*," Dan said.

"Please... don't be such a spoilsport! It's... well, it would be *gauche* to talk exact numbers. Let's just put it in the neighborhood of billions plus. But I digress! It's time we got underway with our demon—"

The gunshot was deafening in the confined space.

A second one quickly followed.

43. A FRIGHTENED MAN DOES STUPID THINGS.

By three p.m. the skies over the end of Long Island had grown as dark as night. The Coast Guard had issued a severe weather advisory. Several waterspouts had been reported just offshore and most vacationers (and all but the toughest locals) had holed up indoors. The beaches had emptied out while even the largest craft—including the *Robert D. Ballard*—were secured in port.

The temperature had dropped fifteen degrees since the morning, which made the two people marching out along the Montauk Highway all the stranger.

Walking barefoot, the High Priestess Aduba wore nothing but the bloody tatters of her once-white dress while behind her followed Kellie DeFranco in an equally shredded hospital gown. The charnel-house they'd left behind at the beach property was beyond butchery. It was more like an orgy of violence had exploded there. Quite literally.

Even a glance at these two figures invited terror and lunacy.

Aduba's once puffy features had grown sunken, her skin hanging slack on her skull as if the flesh underneath had melted away, her eyes now all black except for the silver-blue pupils. The upper teeth bared as if she'd put on someone else's dentures. Her luxuriantly-styled black hair now hung like old seaweed.

Kellie's appearance was no less disturbing, the dead eyes with their glowing pupils and too-large-teeth even more hideous on her once pretty features. Any child services counselor would be screaming Code Red... if they had time to say anything coherent before they died.

To the south, several of the guards on the grounds looked up as the SAGE radar array groaned and pivoted on its base.

Which should have been impossible.

From their rooftop hideout at the old barracks building on Daniel Road, several of Jax's 'summer' friends filmed this, though they hadn't been anticipating any of the planned activities until sunset. Jax had set them to be activated by the light-sensitive CdS cells—but with the unnatural darkness, everything had kicked in prematurely.

The Tesla coils fired up, their snaking electrical discharges enhanced by the dramatic skies.

The group at the barracks hi-fived each other.

Time took on an elastic feel.

Vanek tried to process what happened and failed miserably. He looked to his right at Dan, then past her to see Gavin stagger, part of his neck missing. She stepped to his side and tried to help. At least that's what Vanek thought. A second later she straightened up, holding the Glock that Gavin had fired. Gavin collapsed.

Ten feet behind her stood the guard who had shot Gavin, his pistol held in both hands, pointed at her head.

Dan's hands were shaking so much Vanek realized any one of them was at risk of being hit.

"I'm not going to die in here!" Dan said. "I don't know what this sick set-up is about, but Will and I are leaving."

Dave was singularly calm, a ghost of a smile quivering his lips. He seemed delighted about all this. Except for his dead eyes. "A frightened man makes stupid mistakes," he said. "That applies to women too!" He clasped his hands together, the way a teacher might address a dim-witted pupil. "But no need to gild the lily - you *are* going to die here, one way or another. There's no way past that."

"What kind of monster are you!?" Dan asked.

"The best kind," Dave purred.

Vanek saw his eyes flick toward the guard. A third shot rang out.

Dan buckled, hit in the right arm. The gun fell out of her hands to the rubberized floor but didn't go off. Vanek glanced at it but didn't move, icy fingers of panic gripping his gut.

The guard with the pistol closed in, barrel aimed at Vanek's head. The two other guards had their assault rifles shouldered and pointed at Vanek and Dan, positioning themselves to have a clear field of fire.

Despite the paralyzing fear, something occurred to him.

"You won't kill us," he said to Dave, dropping his hands. "I'm betting I'm the key to whatever sick experiment you have planned."

"I would prefer we ran it with you in one piece," Dave concurred. "You see—in its pure form, the creature would blow out the capture device. But in its diluted form—through its contact with you—it's quite usable. Miss. Cheung, however, isn't critical. She can be eliminated."

"*No*!" Vanek interjected. Perhaps it was his own self-delusion or desperation, but he felt an urgent need to stall.

None of this is going to end well, Will, he heard Michelle's voice say. *But what the hell, you might just...*

"Get him in the chair," Dave interrupted. "There's so much more I would have wanted to explain to you, but there simply isn't time. Close the doors."

"This is not a particularly smart idea," Vanek said to him. "In case you didn't notice, the last time this chair was used, things didn't go so well."

Dave chuckled. "Oh, we've tested it several times, to calibrate it. The results weren't pleasant. I tested it myself, briefly. They shut off after a few milliseconds... even so it affected me. But you, my prodigal son, will make history."

"I don't think you really have the slightest idea what you're screwing around with here."

Dave paused as he walked toward the control room. "Oh, but we do."

Vanek didn't go easily. It took three men to strap him in. They took Dan to a chair set up across from him in the rebuilt Faraday cage and were just strapping her down when the handset in one of the guard's belts squawked.

"Say again?" he said, answering it.

The response was a high-pitched scream.

The two guards by the entrance had been briefed on Gavin's arrival and given specific instructions on dealing with any regular visitors, which had become a moot point with the change in weather.

What they were not prepared for were the woman and teenage girl who approached them now.

Tom Hansen—the guard who had spoken with Gavin—was at first convinced they were survivors of a car accident. He upgraded that assessment to escaped mental patients as they got within ten yards.

Unshouldering his H&K he took a ready stance and held one hand up. "Sorry ma'am, the camp is closed until further notice," he said, fulling expecting her to comply. He was disturbed by the fact he could see one breast and the damp mat of pubic hair through the woman's tattered clothes. The girl's nakedness was even more appalling to him—she couldn't be more than thirteen, he guessed.

My daughter's age!

Behind him, his partner Drew Jackson stepped in to block the road, assault rifle also ready.

The woman and girl kept shuffling toward them: two bizarre apparitions on a storm-swept road.

Tom felt the hairs rise on the back of his neck. Something was off—way off—but it took him a moment to register.

The eyes.

And their teeth. Their teeth were all wrong.

Both Tom and Drew had survived two tours in Afghanistan, but this was something they didn't even know how to process—things were coming out of their mouths. Worm-like things. He felt the unreasoning terror of not his first but fifth patrol, where he saw the first of his friends blown to meaty pieces by an RPG. The terror exploded in his brain like tiny nova's as the wormlike filaments entered his face, probing, tasting. His mind—always on a taut string, snapped.

Next to him, Drew stood, lips drawn back in a maniacal grimace, shaking as his knuckles grew white from gripping his gun. As the girl walked up to him, his already dark skin turned pitch black, his features collapsing inward as she entered his mind and drained everything out.

Nearby at the SAGE Tower, electrical currents lanced up and around the metal lattice work, sending showers of sparks below.

The creature—what remained of it inside Aduba—knew it was dying. The transfer had been hasty and imperfect, given the frail anatomy of its new host, and it realized something else that had governed its recent impulses: it was reaching the end of its natural life cycle. The experiment with the girl as a host hadn't succeeded either—she was too undeveloped. Weak. Her mind and body decayed rapidly. The transfer had resulted in a mutation. The sky-zone it found itself in was nowhere near as conducive to molecular manipulation as the sea-zone—it required near direct contact to alter anything and it depleted its reserves.

What had drawn it here wasn't the connection to the bunker, it was *who* and *what* was in it.

The *chair*.

The human with (though it didn't know it as these exact terms) the enlarged amygdala. Now that its defenses were compromised it could see right into it, could see it for the vessel that it was.

It could use this to complete its transformation.

A new hive. To propagate in... and a familiar conduit to draw endless power from.

The wormlike structures now inside Aduba's skull writhed and squirmed.

She shuffled forward.

After closing the Faraday cage and activating it, Dave double-timed into the control room. With its newly installed bulkhead door, armored glass and electromagnetic shielding, it was the safest place in the bunker for the moment.

They should have taken more time—he could see that now—but events had been escalating and it was easier to conduct preliminary field tests in the old 'Bunker 18' before carting everything back to the lab at Breckenridge. If everything went south, the plan was simple: dynamite the bunker and seal it up for good.

He had no intention of doing that, however. The tests on the fear matrix had been successful, if even for a short duration. But the subjects didn't have Vanek's ability. Not even close. Not even himself.

But something else was coming. *That* he hadn't counted on. They would have to hold off testing the modified chair for the moment. Instead, they would use Vanek as bait.

The guards closed the massive bulkhead doors and took up positions on either side.

Vanek sat strapped in the chair, shaking. The headgear was painfully tight and smelled like hell. That was secondary to his circumstances, though: he was trussed and helpless as a sacrificial lamb while whatever was coming—he could sense it in his head like a responder—would be monumentally bad. Somehow the frequency of this device—focused by the crystal—was opening his mind... dissolving his defenses.

He was wide open. Vulnerable.

Muffled screams and sporadic gunfire could be heard beyond the doors. The Faraday cage hummed. Inside the control room, his father and the lab technicians with him waited.

Nothing.

But Vanek could sense it there. Just on the other side. Whatever they thought they'd destroyed down there... was back.

He waited for the door to be blown open.

Instead, it began to *change*.

The steel bulged then *whined*, as if the metal was in agony. Within moments the center area melted and bubbled, as if turning into a primordial *goo*. Several wormlike appendages popped through, forcing an opening in a shape suggesting a woman's vulva, in a kind of obscene birth.

With it came the *scissoring* sounds Vanek recognized.

The physical wrongness of the unfolding scene made him feel physically ill, counterpointed by the thundering of his heart which felt on the verge of bursting.

He didn't register that Dan was desperately trying to hump her chair away from the entrance of the Faraday cage.

The *scissoring* had reached a deep ear-cringing crescendo, infusing every molecule with hungry dread. Rapacious. Angry.

The soldiers on either side of the door were equally bugged-out. One fired off a few tentative rounds, the bullets making dead splat sounds. Then with a tortured groan the doors drooped inward, revealing the monstrosity pushing into the chamber.

It was more gruesome than Vanek had feared.

What remained of Aduba had split down the midsection, revealing a carapace from which jutted an array of jointed, crab-like legs. Deeper in the cavity was an eruption of the worm appendages, writhing with a hunger and intent of their own. At the crown, Aduba's head had collapsed into itself, atop a mound of distorted heads and parts of the all the creatures and animals it had encountered. Some seemed half-alive, others mutating into new ones even as they watched.

Someone kept screaming at the top of their lungs, joined by the staccato *pop-pop-pop* of the automatic rifles, then with the hideous speed of a spider, the thing scurried in and pulverized the soldiers, left then right.

Within moments the soldiers had been reduced to shreds of flesh, severed bones and torn organs.

Then it scrabbled up to the cage, pulsing and quivering as if anxious to commence an obscene copulating.

Vanek caught a glimpse of Dave in the control room shouting while shaking one of the technicians, silenced by the thick glass. It looked like Kellie was in there with them. He still heard screaming and realized it was coming from his own throat. Dan's too—she had maneuvered herself to his side and joined in.

He'd never screamed as loud and continuous in his entire life.

The humming of the cage stopped abruptly, though this was lost under the incessant scissoring the creature was making. And with its proximity came the smell—the revolting miasma of rotting fish, decay, tinged with coppery smell of adrenaline and *fear*.

The cage door melted open.

The creature entered cautiously, its worm-like appendages tasting the air between itself and Vanek. He continued to scream as the filament tentacles pierced his head, neck and open mouth.

The pain was indescribable.

The thing half-mounted the chair, blotting out all light and reason.

44. BEYOND DEATH

The scissoring sound dimmed to a distant background noise, overtaken by a *whooshing* roar like falling through an endless wind tunnel.

This experience was unlike the last one in the pod—Vanek had no frame of reference, he became bodiless, floating in an embryonic void where titanic-sized objects moved inexorably. Entwined with him, like a parasitic spider, was the creature. Or a version of it. None of his usual senses seemed to apply here.

Every aspect seemed to be replaced with terror.

And agony.

The center of his head was a white-hot orb of splitting torment. He could feel the creature in there, writhing, feeding, caressing, intertwining with the center of his thoughts.

The sensation was on the verge of blotting out all sane thought. It went on forever and ever. Torment without end.

The fear was both a paralysis and an erosion, dissolving all other thoughts, desires and memories, turning them into unending, all-consuming terror.

This isn't death, he managed to think over mind-scrambling agony, *this is the nightmare of undeath.*

He yearned for oblivion. He whimpered, pleaded to God for *non-being.*

Stop this! Stopitstopitstopstopit!!!!

The torment continued.

Helpless... he couldn't stop it.

Through the ceaseless agony, some fears were recognizable:

The very first terror of entering the world from his mother's womb, screaming, kicking, wailing. The violence of being torn from embryonic safety into the field of time and existence. The horrifying emptiness of watching their first dog die, hit by a speeding van with "Crimson King Rules!" airbrushed on the side. The first time he was stung by a jellyfish at age nine and convinced he was about to die. The teeth-gnashing accident where he hit black ice near Binghamton and did three full 360's before shooting up Route 17 backwards as a honking tractor trailer slid past, missing him by inches as it jack-knifed and careened off the road, taking out several other cars with it. The muffled scream of metal. Of people dying.

He saw and experienced these things all over again as if his mind was a hyper-real Star Trek Holodeck, playing: "William Vanek's All-time Greatest Terror's Collection!"

All this accompanied by the mind crumbling terror of this creature inside his head, its loathsome writhing: whipworms in brain. Feeding. Expanding.

In this extra-sensory stasis, he picked up on other things, horrible things his mind couldn't have known but were now becoming fused to this conscious state. The girl he got pregnant in college who committed suicide a couple of years later. The blind terror of death and abandonment of the pet rabbit he'd let die one winter in their back yard as a teenager. And not to neglect Michelle: she was there too, whispering how she couldn't bear to live with him any longer, live up to his impossible idea of her, how she became consumed by depression... her fateful whim that forced the accident and caused the shipwreck—she cut the boom loose and kicked the rudder while he and his Dad were on the foredeck desperately trying to take down the foresail—but above all, above all else, the horror of knowing this thing was inside of him, *feeding* on him. Feeding on his fears.

His body decaying, dying... falling apart. Alone.

Vanek had no concept how long this went on, how his mental voice continued shrieking and whimpering.

Past, present. Future terror.

Surely, he must snap! Go stark raving mad!

But he didn't.

Instead, he became aware of something else. A pinprick of light.

Its very emergence was so bizarre in his current state that he had difficulty accepting it was even there.

Yet it *was*.

Light.

Growing light.

He forced himself to ignore the worm-thoughts tearing at his mind like a million tiny ripsaws and focus on this new (old) sensation.

He was aware of

[touch]

Contact. With it a sense he had a *hand*. Of course he did! How else could he sense this?

With that

[touch]

a flood of sensory awareness, the knowledge that it was Dan, or some aspect of her, reaching toward him in this plane of torment.

The touch became a *grasp*.

He could feel her energy, sense her *woman-ness*. The deeper power of her true essence.

He could sense her terrors too: the gulf of sadness at her husband's death, her fears of abandonment, aging... everything. Everything she had been, was, and would be. His peripheral fears blending in—failure. Death. Global Warming. Ebola. Bombs. Entropy. Destruction. Cancer. Meaninglessness of it all. Loneliness. Emptiness.

William.

Her voice! He could hear her voice. Phased, distorted, but distinctly hers.

It became like a tiny lifeline in the eternal blackness.

Beneath all this, the pulsing sound he'd heard on the NASA sound captures—the deep pulse of the universe. *This* universe.

Not so much a pulse, he realized as it became more resolved: a pure note.

He felt something connect: a band of light and sound. Through it he could hear and see everything he had always been, would always be, a transcendent knowledge that every aspect, every moment in his life was in perfect, synchronous harmony.

Nirvana.

Vibration. A beautiful tone.

It repeated a million times, like a *kane* bell echo in the void.

An infinitesimal crack appeared in the black void of fear. The sound was reshaping it—simultaneously deconstructing it.

With it came an absurd random thought: "*Fuck you.*"

One of them—maybe both of them—let out the tiniest laugh. It wasn't even a real laugh, more like a *cluck*, but it was enough. The crack widened. The change accelerated.

He felt the worms hesitate, then redouble its efforts.

Vanek *knew*.

"*Fuck-you and the horse-ship you rode in on*!" his liberated mind-voice said. Then: "God-damn asswipe alien!"

Her grip tightened.

He became aware of yet another new sensation his mind interpreted as *white*. A *white light. The Coming of the White.*

Thewhitelightisright.

It became a mantra.

The creature recoiled, like a lover trying to withdraw before climax.

The fear/thoughts doubled back... rapidly deconstructing the creature.

It screamed. That was new.

Vanek swam back to consciousness, feeling the horrid sensation of the thing's worm/filaments (the special ones it used for feeding off multidimensional fear) rip out of him as it disintegrated (like a sand castle), a weird warbling thinness as if he were simultaneously in two realities at once. The creature was recoiling, its defenses already spent, collapsing into itself.

Consuming into its own fear and terror.

Electrical blue lighting danced all around the cage, as if electromagnetic energy had been cut loose and was scrambling to find somewhere to go.

The creature was shrinking, shriveling, a miasmic cloud enveloping it. It was too painful to look at, to process—like watching a reverse birth inside-out.

With an obscene pop it disappeared, leaving a black, viscous smear.

Vanek realized Dan had toppled him over onto his side, having freed her hand enough to grab his. That had been the link, the deal breaker.

Dan untied him.

The armored glass of the control room was holed through in several places, as if a laser had melted it. There was no sign of the girl, but the open-jawed, emaciated skeleton of Dave stood smashed into the back wall, his chest bloodied by his burst organs.

Vanek tried to stand, stumbled, then straightened as Dan helped him up.

Her face was very close to his.

"Come on sailor, I think you could use a drink."

Outside, the Tesla coils sent up their last fireworks in a fiery—if all too brief—display, then faded as the skies cleared. Vanek and Dan stood at the top of the bunker conduit, holding hands like a disaster-blasted Hansel & Gretel. The broken-up storm clouds made for an incredibly dramatic sunset, the familiar thunder of the distant surf reassuring.

Vanek felt ready to lie down and collapse, though the gory remains of the soldiers nearby recommended otherwise. Yet he was also acutely aware of being alive, breathing, that his heart rate was regular and for the first time in eight years he was willing to bet the bank his blood pressure normal.

Despite the horror of what they'd just been through, he felt preternaturally calm. Relaxed.

Devoid of *fear*.

He figured that would probably come back, later, but for now it was on hold, in orbit perhaps on one of those stars just beginning to wink in the eastern sky.

Perhaps even the one the creature had come from.

Most of all he was intensely aware of the woman standing next to him, that no matter what the future held, she had thrown him a lifeline out of hell.

In the distance he could see the flashing lights of approaching police cars, responding to the erupting fireworks show on the SAGE Radar. They were going to be in for a big surprise when they got here.

He realized Dan was staring at him.

"*Goddamn asswipe alien*!? Jesus Christ! *Seriously!*?" she said.

Vanek shrugged. "It was all I could think of at the moment. Hey, it *worked*."

She smiled. It was a genuine one, more radiant than one from a joke.

"Yeah it did, didn't it?"

"I think so." He really took in that smile. It was better than thinking about all the other things that just happened.

She moved in closer and took his chin in her other hand, avoiding the tiny wounds. Oddly, they were already closing up, as if they didn't belong in this reality.

She kissed him gently on the lips.

"Are you going to be good to me?" she asked. She said it in a kind of girlish way that made him want to hold her forever. Except his arms were practically useless.

"Yes," he replied.

"Promise?"

"*Promise*."

45. ON THE WIRE

"From the City of Angels near the Pacific Ocean God, morning, good evening, wherever you may be, I'm Phil Randi... welcome to *Kirlian Wave* and tonight we have a really special show for you: a live update from Montauk where some very strange events have been unfolding since earlier today…

"The Montauk Project... and folks I mean the *real* Montauk Project... has been hiding there all this time and boy you are going to love this one…"

46. SIX WEEKS LATER

"Here? Really?" Dan asked.

The two of them were standing on the windward side of the Montauk Lighthouse. It was a sun-bleached, late September day carrying the cool edge of winter with the breeze. The briny hint of far oceans came with it.

"Sure. I found out we can rent the grounds. The ceremony can be set up there on the platform on the north edge of the lawn. We'll have the Atlantic Ocean as a backdrop."

"It's kind of romantic," she agreed. "Although 'Dan Vanek' won't get as many surprises as 'Cheung'."

"You can always keep it."

"No, I kind of like it. Edgier."

They stood near the fence, the wind whipping their hair about. Vanek had his hands in the back pockets of his jeans, the collar of his windbreaker turned up against the breeze. Dan was in a sweater with a vest.

She had a certain blush in her cheeks that wasn't there a week ago.

"You sure about buying a house out here?"

"I'm sure. Give me a chance to see my brother more often over the summer."

"Do you think about where that thing came from? What it may have done to us?"

The edge of Vanek's mouth twitched. "No. What's the point?"

Crossing her arms, Dan let out a small *hmpf.*

It was a little lie, and he hated telling it. The MRI and CAT scans hadn't shown anything physiologically altered in either of them, but neither of those instruments could see into their psychology. Vanek felt fine—better than fine, actually—but the odd 'psychic vision' episodes had continued. Not as bad as the earlier ones, but there. The creature had altered him permanently somehow. He hadn't told Dan any of this. She had enough on her plate with the pregnancy.

And he thought about the creature, what it had done to them—to him—and more disturbingly, whether there were any others out there, lurking in hidden parts of the ocean.

He had started putting his feelers out. Just in case.

He tried not to think about what he might be passing on. They were still waiting for her doctor to confirm the test was positive.

"Come on, let's go grab dinner. Then we can have brandies by the fire."

The one thing he liked about the Navy house was the fireplace.

That was why he'd put a bid on it.

Sixty miles offshore aboard the *Robert D. Ballard*, Ben Reinhardt sat absently watching the view screen in Mission Control. They'd just gotten word that the ship would be recommissioned as "*Neptune's Reckoning*" at Ballard's request, after a full refit in port in three weeks and picking up two new passengers. An unknown sponsor in the ONR with deep pockets was footing the bill. From the rumors, it was the Breckenridge Institute, who had a change of heart after certain parties threatened to reveal unsavory activities in recent months.

He was fairly excited—they would have *carte blanche* to seek out and investigate any ocean-related story deemed 'odd or particularly unusual' which Reinhardt read as: 'Anything in the neighborhood of the X-Files.'

Meanwhile, R2 was inspecting the wreck site to see what had happened to the *U.S.S. Exeter*, and they had shifted their scanning to the lower part of the Hyborean Canyon.

His eyes went wide.

He picked up the interphone.

"Holy shit, Commander, you better come down and see this!"

THE END

AFTERWORD & NOTES FOR THE CURIOUS

Once again special thanks to my wife and first critic, Tomiko. Her keen (and wonderfully demented) mind is invaluable in honing my stories and keeping me on track. This particular tale was inspired by our 16-odd years of vacations spent at Montauk and my particular passion for the place, including the fact we were married at the lighthouse one fine September day. It's a pleasure to finally set my imagination to one of the places on Earth I love most.

A few major liberties were taken that will have even a half-sane fisherman in the area shaking his/her head, foremost moving the continental shelf from ninety miles out to thirty, purely in the interest of expediency for the characters and keeping the action more localized.

Research is always the richest part of the process, and of course the people I get to meet along the way. Their contributions are invaluable in shaping the narrative. It's the real pay-off in writing: the sheer amount of things I always learn that only underscores my ignorance.

A big thanks to my beta readers, including Rohan Zhou-Lee and John Parks: as writers we tend to be so self-involved in our little worlds that we often miss the obvious.

Thanks to Paul Gallay, CEO of the Hudson River Keeper for getting back to me with input on toxic waste dumps along the Hudson River—we miss having you as a neighbor. Ed Michels, Harbormaster of the Easthampton Marine Patrol who cut to the chase and called me directly several times to educate me on police maritime procedures and capabilities at Montauk—please thank the two Beach Patrol officers I ran into one chilly April day that gave me further input on the Easthampton Volunteer Rescue Dive Team! Lt. Alaina Fagan of the U.S. Coast Guard for getting back to me on their ships and procedures in and around Montauk. John Murray, dockmaster of the Star Island Yacht Club & Marina and his staff. What a cool place! Nancy Piereth & Lisa Montella and the staff at the Montauk Library for pointing me to all those documents and historic maps on Camp Hero as well as navigating the mysteriously baffling process (to me at least) of creating and emailing .pdf files from their copy machine.

Thanks to Joe St. Amand whose wreck diving advice was invaluable and loved hearing about his work with the amazing Becky Schott—her underwater photography of shipwrecks (at photos.liquidproductions.com) is stunning.

And a huge thank-you to Lt. Rosemary Abbitt, Operations officer of the NOAA flagship Okeanos Explorer, whose unexpected invitation got us a private tour of the ship while it was in port—that was a bucket-list opportunity I will never forget. Lt Abbitt was very generous with her time explaining everything about the ship and its crew—it was quite a hoot to sit in the Mission Control room I had written previously about in "Nightmare from World's End" and watch those entrancing video feeds of recent ocean explorations, not to mention poking around the ROV sled that has visited some of the deepest parts of our planet's oceans—that ship is awesome. It was well worth the drive out to Rhode Island one afternoon to see it. I can't say enough good about the NOAA and its dedicated staff. It's no exaggeration to say they are truly wonderful. I find it inspiring to see and hear people who do something that is just—no other way to put it—cool: spending your life going on exploration missions for the betterment of our oceans, its species and mankind. It was like taking a brief step into a world I only saw on those 'Undersea World of Jacques Cousteau' episodes growing up as a kid. In another life I would have loved to have taken that path.

And finally, thanks to you, dear reader, without whom all this is just a bunch of prattling away in the dark.

-Robert Stava, 2019

Robert Stava is an author living in the Hudson River Valley, not far, apparently, from the village of Wyvern Falls where so many of his horror stories are set. His fourth and fifth novels, “Nightmare from World’s End”, and “Lost World of Kharamu” are published by Severed Press. His short stories have appeared in various anthologies & magazines including the recently released “Cranial Leakage vol II” from Grinning Skull Press. “Neptune’s Reckoning,” from Severed Press, is his ninth novel.

Originally from Cleveland, Ohio, he grew up in the Finger Lakes region of New York State and after pursuing a degree in Fine Arts, wound up making his career in advertising at Y&R and J. Walter Thompson in NYC. He went on to become Creative Director of the 3D Media Group at Arup, an international U.K-based design company before moving to the Hudson Valley and catapulting into the wild world of writing horror fiction in 2010.

In addition to writing, Stava is a trustee on the Ossining Historical Society and is professional member of ITW (International Thriller Writers) and the HWA (Horror Writer’s Association).

CHECK OUT OTHER GREAT DEEP SEA THRILLERS

THRESHER
by Michael Cole

In the aftermath of a hurricane, a series of strange events plague the coastal waters off Florida. People go into the water and never return. Corpses of killer whales drift ashore, ravaged from enormous bite marks. A fishing trawler is found adrift, with a mysterious gash in its hull.

Transferred to the coastal town of Merit, police officer Leonard Riker uncovers the horrible reality of an enormous Thresher shark lurking off the coast. Forty feet in length, it has taken a territorial claim to the waters near the town harbor. Armed with three-inch teeth, a scythe-like caudal fin, and unmatched aggression, the beast seeks to kill anything sharing the waters.

THE GUILLOTINE
by Lucas Pederson

1,000 feet under the surface, Prehistoric Anthropologist, Ash Barrington, and his team are in the midst of a great archeological dig at the bottom of Lake Superior where they find a treasure trove of bones. Bones of dinosaurs that aren't supposed to be in this particular region. In their underwater facility, Infinity Moon, Ash and his team soon discover a series of underground tunnels. Upon exploring, they accidentally open an ice pocket, thawing the prehistoric creature trapped inside. Soon they are being attacked, the facility falling apart around them, by what Ash knows is a dunkleosteus and all those bones were from its prey. Now...Ash and his team are the prey and the creature will stop at nothing to get to them.

facebook.com/severedpress
twitter.com/severedpress

CHECK OUT OTHER GREAT DEEP SEA THRILLERS

THE BREACH
by Edward J. McFadden III

A Category 4 hurricane punched a quarter mile hole in Fire Island, exposing the Great South Bay to the ferocity of the Atlantic Ocean, and the current pulled something terrible through the new breach. A monstrosity of the past mixed with the present has been disturbed and it's found its way into the sheltered waters of Long Island's southern sea.

Nate Tanner lives in Stones Throw, Long Island. A disgraced SCPD detective lieutenant put out to pasture in the marine division because of his Navy background and experience with aquatic crime scenes, Tanner is assigned to hunt the creeper in the bay. But he and his team soon discover they're the ones being hunted.

INFESTATION
by William Meikle

It was supposed to be a simple mission. A suspected Russian spy boat is in trouble in Canadian waters. Investigate and report are the orders.

But when Captain John Banks and his squad arrive, it is to find an empty vessel, and a scene of bloody mayhem.

Soon they are in a fight for their lives, for there are things in the icy seas off Baffin Island, scuttling, hungry things with a taste for human flesh.

They are swarming. And they are growing.

"Scotland's best Horror writer" - Ginger Nuts of Horror

"The premier storyteller of our time." - Famous Monsters of Filmland

CHECK OUT OTHER GREAT DEEP SEA THRILLERS

SHARK: INFESTED WATERS
by P.K. Hawkins

For Simon, the trip was supposed to be a once in a lifetime gift: a journey to the Amazon River Basin, the land that he had dreamed about visiting since he was a child. His enthusiasm for the trip may be tempered by the poor conditions of the boat and their captain leading the tour, but most of the tourists think they can look the other way on it. Except things go wrong quickly. After a horrific accident, Simon and the other tourists find themselves trapped on a tiny island in the middle of the river. It's the rainy season, and the river is rising. The island is surrounded by hungry bull sharks that won't let them swim away. And worst of all, the sharks might not be the only blood-thirsty killers among them. It was supposed to be the trip of a lifetime. Instead, they'll be lucky if they make it out with their lives at all.

DARK WATERS
by Lucas Pederson

Jörmungandr is an ancient Norse sea monster. Thought to be purely a myth until a battleship is torn a part by one.

With his brother on that ship, former Navy Seal and deep-sea diver, Miles Raine, sets out on a personal vendetta against the creature and hopefully save his brother. Bringing with him his old Seal team, the Dagger Points, they embark on a mission that might very well be their last.

But what happens when the hunters become the hunted and the dark waters reveal more than a monster?

Made in the USA
Las Vegas, NV
10 November 2021

34128514R00162